'Ma

Mists of Albion Book 4

A Time Travel Romance Series

By

Joanna Bell

© 2018 Joanna Bell

All Rights Reserved.
This book or any portion thereof may not be reproduced or used in any manner whatsoever without the express permission of the publisher except for the use of brief quotations in a book review. This book is a work of fiction. Any resemblance to persons, living or dead, or places, events or locations is purely coincidental. The characters are all productions of the author's imagination.

Please note that this work is intended only for adults over the age of 18 and all characters represented as 18 or over.

Contents

Chapter 1: Heather 5

Chapter 2: Magnus 12

Chapter 3: Heather 18

Chapter 4: Magnus 35

Chapter 5: Heather 52

Chapter 6: Magnus 62

Chapter 7: Heather 74

Chapter 8: Magnus 90

Chapter 9: Heather 109

Chapter 10: Magnus 129

Chapter 11: Heather 138

Chapter 12: Magnus 181

Chapter 13: Heather 215

Chapter 14: Magnus 229

Chapter 15: Heather 246

Chapter 16: Magnus 264

Chapter 17: Heather 282

Chapter 18: Magnus 296

Chapter 19: Heather 314

Chapter 20: Ora 337

Chapter 21: Heather	349
Chapter 22: Magnus*	363
Chapter 23: Heather	376
Chapter 24: Magnus*	384
Chapter 25: Magnus*	404
Chapter 26: Heather	412
Epilogue: Heather	432
Author Information:	435
The 'Mists of Albion' Series	436
Other Books by Joanna Bell	437

Chapter 1: Heather

My mom almost teared up when it came time to say good-bye. I was conscious, as she enveloped me in what must have been one of the least sincere mother-daughter hugs in history, that to anyone else in the airport we must have looked like a normal family.

"You have a lot of growing up to do, young lady," my mother whispered as she pretended to wipe a tear off one heavily rouged cheek. "I just hope some time in the country will help you see it, too."

I looked up at my dad, standing slightly behind her, refusing to catch my eye. He should have said something. But there were already a thousand times my dad should have said something, and he never did.

"Dad?" I prompted, as the old familiar anger started to rise up in my chest.

"Listen to your mother," he mumbled, stepping forward to offer an awkward hug and then back again immediately so as not to interfere for too long with my mom's dramatic good-bye scene.

Just before I was about to turn away, she suddenly grabbed my face between her hands and let out a wail that caught the attention of everyone within a twenty-foot radius. "Heather!" She sobbed, dabbing at her eyes with a tissue. "Oh Heather! You don't know how hard I've tried to help you! You don't know how difficult this has been for me! You –"

It struck me then, as I noticed a few disapproving looks thrown my way by strangers –who couldn't help but find themselves sympathetic to a pretty blonde woman's tears – that I had my ticket in my hand. For once, I didn't actually have to listen to the woe-is-me lecture my mom was working herself up to right there in the middle of the airport.

I turned, jerking my face out of her claw-like grip, and began to walk away.

"Heather!" She screeched. "Heather, goddamnit, don't you dare walk away from me! Don't you dare!"

I kept walking. My mother doesn't show herself in public. Not the side that isn't pretty and blonde and endlessly suffering at the hands of her useless husband and her wayward disappointment of a daughter – me. She wasn't going to throw a fit right there in front of everyone and I knew it. So I kept walking. I didn't look back. I didn't look at anything. Just straight ahead until I was in my seat on the plane, staring out the window as the sunlight glinted off the silvery wing.

I'd never flown anywhere before, but I wasn't scared. At take-off a wave of exhilaration swept through my whole body at the sudden sensation of flight. I leaned in close to the window, watching as the airport, and then the surrounding fields and the roads and the cars below me got smaller and smaller until the flight leveled off and the middle-aged man next to me peeled his white-knuckled fingers off the armrest and lit a cigarette.

"Can I bum one of those off you?" I asked.

The man, who had a visible sheen of sweat on his forehead, silently handed me one of his cigs and his lighter and then I relaxed back into my seat and took a short drag. I'd never met my aunt Brenda or my uncle Bill, or the disabled younger son I was going to help them care for over the summer. I didn't know anything about River Falls, New York. What I did know is that it was very far away from Los Angeles. As far as I was concerned it could have been Mars – what mattered was the fact that my mother was not going to be there.

As the pale, dry desert gave way to the green patchwork fields of the Midwest, I allowed myself to daydream a little about what River Falls might be like. It was a small town, apparently. And I was from a big city. I had a Sony Walkman and Jordache jeans and a fresh perm, all courtesy of my dad's guilt complex. He wouldn't stand up for me in front of my mom, but he had no problem trying to buy forgiveness for his parental failures. What would the people my age in River Falls think of me? Would they be impressed? Would the boys do double-takes when I walked into the local bar? Would there be one boy in particular, tall and dark and looking not entirely unlike Tom Selleck, who might take an interest in me?

You're not going to River Falls to flirt with boys. You're going to help your aunt and uncle with your cousin.

Yeah, all of those things were true. But none of them meant I couldn't have any fun.

***

A stack of magazines lay on the bed in what was to be 'my' room for the summer, at uncle Bill and aunt Brenda's house in River Falls. My heart sunk a little to see that they were all copies of Seventeen – which I hadn't read since I was twelve. But Bill and Brenda didn't have any daughters, I reminded myself, so they couldn't be expected to know what young women were interested in. On top of the magazines was a small handwritten note. I picked it up, smiling at the kindness of the gesture, the feeling of welcome.

The smile didn't stay on my face for long. The note was a list of rules. 'House Rules.'

1. Absolutely no smoking or drinking.

2. Absolutely no stealing. When you get a job, we will give you an allowance out of your paycheck.

3. Absolutely no backtalk or disrespect.

4. Absolutely no boys allowed in your room.

5. Absolutely no swearing.

6. Absolutely no hitting, punching or violence.

Hot tears of shame stung my eyes – obviously my mother had been in touch with Bill and Brenda. There was no way that list, which was the kind of thing that seemed more appropriate to a juvenile detention facility than a family home, would have found its way onto that stack of magazines if she hadn't.

"Hello, Heather."

I looked up at my aunt Brenda, who had been fairly quiet on the drive back from the airport. Now I recognized her wariness for what it was. Part of me wanted to throw myself at her feet, to beg her to give me a chance, to hold off on judging me until I'd had some time to prove I wasn't the devil in thick, black eyeliner.

But my mom had a way of coming off as the most reasonable person ever, and somehow I could tell from the look on my aunt's face that nothing I could say was going to convince her I wasn't some kind of miscreant.

"Hi," I replied quietly, looking down at the pastel pink carpet.

"Did you see our note?"

I nodded.

"So you understand the rules in our household. We expect you to find a job as soon as possible – Bill can give you a ride if you need one for an interview."

A job. The note had mentioned the same thing. Confused, I smiled up at Brenda, desperate for her to realize I was as interested in avoiding conflict as she was. "I thought I was coming here to look after Brad – is that what you mean by a job?"

Brenda sighed and pursed her lips. "You didn't think you were coming here to stay in our house all summer in exchange for a few hours of babysitting, did you?"

"I –" I started, and then stopped, because in fact that's exactly what I had thought. Because that's exactly what my parents said it was going to be. As far as I knew I was in River Falls to help my aunt and uncle look after their youngest son, Brad. "I'm not trying to be rude – and if you want me to get a job I will – but my mom said I was –"

"Your poor mother!" She cut me off, raising her voice alarmingly. "Don't you think you've put that woman through enough?! You haven't even been here for twenty minutes and you've already broken the rules!"

I closed my eyes tight and drew a slow, deep breath into my lungs, willing myself to stay calm. *You know how persuasive your mother is. It's not Brenda's fault she trusted her. Just get a job and do your best, she'll see the truth soon enough.*

"I'm sorry," I replied. "I – I'm not sure what rule –"

"No backtalk!"

"I'm sorry."

Me and my aunt, little more than strangers, stood facing each other for a few moments, and I could see from the look on her face that she was waiting for me to do something – to yell or scream or blow up or, who knows, run into the kitchen and grab a knife and try to stab them all to death? When I declined to do any yelling or stabbing, she smoothed her hair and told me to be up at six o'clock the next morning to help with Brad. And then she left.

When I was sure she wasn't coming back, I lay down on the bed and stared up at the ceiling, telling myself that whatever I was in for that summer, it couldn't possibly be as bad as being back home in L.A., with my parents.

Chapter 2: Magnus

My leathers were heavy, sticky with blood. Another man's blood, not my own. The deck of the ship was stained dark with it, the oarsmen still spattered with it.

My father – the Jarl – and my older brother, commanded their own ships, sailing close to mine as we closed in on our home village of Apvik, empty-handed.

Empty-handed because we lost? Because we were bested by the disorganized Franks we'd set upon not two nights previously, who had surrendered quickly and then helped to load their grain stories and livestock onto our ships? No. Empty-handed because my dull-witted brother, the next Jarl by rights, had managed to drunkenly spill svass across the sacks of grain, which then went up in flames as soon as a spark from the bonfire happened to alight upon them. I was so angry I couldn't even speak.

"Brother!" Asger shouted from where he stood at the bow of his long-ship – second only in grandness to our father's. "Take that look off your face! Apvik is in the distance, and the village girls await the return of the Jarl's sons!"

I turned away, pretending I hadn't heard over the creaking of the oars and the shouted conversation of the men, and glanced towards my father. He, too, stood at the bow of his Jarl's long-ship, also assiduously pretending had not heard Asger's shouted words.

In truth, it disgusted me. It was not my place as the younger son to question anyone – especially my father the Jarl. And so I didn't question him – not with words, anyway. But anyone looking upon my face would have seen the contempt in which I held my brother, shouting of victory on his long-ship as we returned to Apvik with no spoils, no grain or pigs for the stores. We didn't even have any slaves, because Asger's men were so ill disciplined that they had allowed them to flee during the panic that had ensued when the grain sacks caught fire.

The Franks were nothing to me, strangers in a strange land. But they were men, and it didn't take a gothi to see that they loved their wives and their children as much as we Northern men did. And we had spilled their blood, copious amounts of it, as those same wives and children had looked on, screaming and pleading with us to spare them. And for what? For nothing.

A man of the North kills for necessity, for destiny. He does not revel in bloodshed, as the pigs revel in muck. That is what the gothi said. That is what my father used to say, before the gray began to appear in his beard and the antics of his oldest son made him stop speaking of things like honor.

***

"His head, Mother! You should have seen the way his head came off – so easily it was like a ripe fruit plucked from a late summer branch. Ha! And the wailing of his wife, as if –"

My brother spent our first supper upon our return regaling my mother with tales of the slaughter, and so joyous was his tone you'd think he spoke of Yule revels.

"Enough, son," my father said when he seemed determined to keep going until we had all lost our appetite. "Your mother is just happy to have her boys back, she needn't hear all the details."

Asger quieted down for a moment or two, frowning and taking a great bite of the buttered dark bread I knew my mother had baked because it was his favorite. But he was off again shortly thereafter, with more stories of killed men, killed livestock, burned villages.

Later, when he had left in search of one of the village girls, I helped my mother carry the empty plates and cups to the water's edge, to wash them with the rough sand of the beach.

"You don't have to help me with this, Magnus," she smiled as I followed her down the narrow path to the beach. "It's woman's work, son. You should go with your brother and find yourself a girl. You will marry soon, will you not? I don't think it too much to –"

"Mother," I said gently, kneeling down beside her to wash one of the ornately carved horn cups that only Jarls were allowed to drink out of. "Why do you speak of marriage to me when Asger remains without a wife? Of what importance is it to you if your second son finds a wife if your first –"

"Voss!" She cried suddenly, and my eyes widened at the unfamiliar sound of my mother cursing. "Oh Magnus! Why must you and I always speak in these roundabout ways, as if neither of us can see the truth?!

You do not need to ask me these things, do you? Not really?"

I bowed my head and pretended to be engrossed in the task of scooping wet sand into another of the cups. My mother was right. I did not need to ask her those questions, because I already knew the truth that it seemed only we could see.

"Your brother isn't fit to herd sheep, let alone lead men," she spoke again, her voice very quiet. "It's only the Gods themselves keeping him alive now – and even the Gods' patience runs thin soon enough. Who will take care of your father and I when the gray runs thicker in our hair? Who will take on the name of Jarl when Asger gets himself killed?"

My mother seemed so small beside me. When had I grown so big that my own mother was as tiny as a child next to me? And when had it happened that she felt bold enough to say such things to me, to lay the burden of heirs at the feet of her second son, whose whole life had been an exercise in watching her and my father coddle and fawn over their first?

"You see who it is you've made," I whispered, as my heart pounded in my chest. "All my life you and Father spoke of nothing so much as you spoke of accepting our roles. And now you see what everyone in this village has seen for years and you come to me for –"

Crack!

The sound of palm meeting cheek echoed through the cool night air and I lifted a hand to my face, remembering a time when such a blow would have sent me weeping to my bed.

"How dare you speak to me like that?" My mother spat, but I could hear the wobble in her voice even as she tried to conceal it. "How dare you speak to me as if I'm your father – as if I had some say in this situation! He is the Jarl, Magnus. *The Jarl*. Of all the people, I am perhaps the least well-placed to question him. You have done your duty as a second son – more than your duty, if what your father tells me of rescuing Asger from various scrapes abroad is true – and I have done mine as a wife. I have obeyed my husband, and fed his children at my breast. Look at how big you are, how tall and strong, look at –" she broke off, and buried her face in the crook of her elbow to stifle a sob.

She wasn't wrong. As long as the resentment had been building in my heart at my fate as a younger brother born with all the wit and skill his older brother lacked, is as long as my mother had obeyed my father, refusing to question him when he made bad decisions because it wasn't her place to do so.

"But why must it be?" I asked, softening with pity. "Why must it be this way, Mother? Why must you and I remain silent as Father takes decisions that harm our family – our people – because he cannot see what Asger is?"

My mother turned her face up to me then, no longer angry, and her hazel eyes swam with a faraway look I could not quite decipher. "I don't know, my boy. It is as it is. Not even a Jarl can question the way of things – so who are we? We've done our best, haven't we? And when you look at me with resentment for asking you to take a wife, you must know I ask it for your good as well as mine. You must take a good wife – a smart girl, a girl with wit and fire in her belly. None of these simpering idiots that Asger favors will do for you, Magnus. You must build a life for yourself, a happiness for yourself that does not depend on your father or your brother. You still have a chance to do this."

She left the unspoken part of the sentence, the part where she acknowledged that her own chance was gone, unsaid.

I knew my mother meant well. I knew she spoke from the heart, where she truly wanted the best for me. But still my stomach burned with the rebellion that had been there since I was a child, the part of me that wanted to gather the gothi and my father and the people of the village and proclaim in front of them that I rejected their ideas about duty and rules and things being 'the way they are.' It was not the time to say such things there on the beach with my mother, though.

We walked back to the longhouse together as the evening drew quietly in around us, our hearts full of the things that remained unsaid.

Chapter 3: Heather

Life with my aunt and uncle turned out to be a bit like boot camp. Up at six a.m. every day to help with Brad – their older son, Daniel, had been shipped off to summer camp until late August – and then off to work at the local grocery store where I'd found a job as a checkout girl. Home by five, helping with getting Brad fed and bathed and put into bed and then lights out by nine-thirty.

Two weeks in, and there were no signs of softening on Brenda's part. I was allowed to have Saturday afternoons free, but any enquiries about going out on a Saturday night were shut down at once. She wasn't a kind woman – even her care for her own disabled son tended to the almost military in style, measuring his food out by the ounce and then lecturing him impatiently if he didn't finish it in the allotted time before his bath.

But as rigid as I found Brenda Renner, she wasn't my mother. And that was something.

It was during a break from work one day, as I sat outside the River Falls Grocery King eating a tuna sandwich that I first spotted Judy Decker. She was short and just a little bit pudgy – but the kind of pudgy that actually looked kind of cute on her – and she was wearing a sleeveless Whitesnake concert tee. It was as I was staring at her that she happened to turn and stare right back. Two girls, one in a Whitesnake tee and heavy eyeliner, the other in a Grocery King smock and heavy eyeliner. I think we both knew right away we'd both found a kindred spirit.

"Hey," she said, a little hesitantly.

"Uh, hey."

"You new around here?"

I nodded and swallowed the last of my sandwich. "Yeah. I'm just here for the summer. I'm Heather Renner – Brenda and Bill's niece. I love your shirt. Did it come like that or –"

"Nah. I cut the sleeves off myself. Was gonna cut it down the chest, too, but my mom would go crazy. I'm Judy, by the way. Judy Decker."

We stood chatting in front of the Grocery King for long enough to draw my manager out, scowling, to ask me sarcastically if I had time to take out of my busy social life to come back to work.

"Yeah!" I told him. "I'm sorry – I – just gimme a second. Do you have a pen?"

Jerry – the manager – sighed and pulled a pen out of his breast pocket before handing it to me.

"Give me your hand," I told Judy, quickly writing my number across the back of it when she did so. "Call me, OK? And, uh, try to be polite – my aunt is real uptight."

Judy grinned. "OK. See ya."

***

A couple of days later, the phone rang at Brenda and Bill's house, just as I was helping to clear the dishes off the table after dinner.

"Should I answer it?" I called into the dining room, hoping it was Judy.

"Remember what we told you to say," Brenda called back.

I skipped over to the little 'office' alcove where the phone sat and picked it up.

"Renner residence."

"Hello, this is Judy Decker, I'm calling for Heath –"

It was her! I hadn't been in River Falls for long, but I was already desperately lonely without any friends. "It's me!" I replied, grinning.

We'd barely got the greetings out of the way when Brenda suddenly appeared beside me, her hands on her hips, eying me.

"Hold on a sec," I told Judy, before offering Brenda a polite smile.

"I take it that call is for you?" She demanded, sighing heavily.

"Uh yeah, it is. It's Judy – Judy Decker. I met her at –"

"I don't recall giving you permission to hand out our phone number."

I took a step back, surprised. It hadn't crossed my mind that my aunt and uncle wouldn't allow me to take phone calls from any friends I made. "Oh," I said, glancing down at the floor as I had learned to do during conversations with Brenda. "I'm sorry. I didn't realize you –"

"You have to help me with Brad's bath," my aunt said, taking the phone receiver out of my hand. "And you have to do the dishes. I don't know if you thought you were coming to spend the summer with us so you could spend all your time flirting with boys and –"

"Judy's a girl, aunt Br–"

Without a word to Judy, who was still waiting on the other end of the line, Brenda placed the phone receiver back in the cradle and gave me a sharp look. "And what did we say about backtalk? Your mother told me all about you, Heather, and if you think you're here to have fun this summer all I can say is that you're sorely mistaken. Now hurry up with the dishes so we can get Brad ready for bed."

Speechless at her rudeness but hyper-aware that my aunt was likely to respond badly to almost anything I said, I simply turned and headed back towards the sink, hoping that Judy Decker would see fit to drop by the Grocery King again so I could explain the abrupt end of the call.

***

And luckily for me, that's exactly what she did the next day. I was standing outside again, taking a short smoke break and trying not to think about what I was going to do at the end of the summer when she walked up with a huge grin on her face.

"Are you trying to lose weight?"

I shook my head confused. "No – I mean, my mom always says I need to lose five –"

"No," Judy laughed, pointing at the Diet Coke can sitting on the rickety wooden picnic table that Jerry put in place for his employees to use on their breaks.

"Oh!" I smiled, relieved I wasn't being insulted. "Oh yeah, uh, no. I mean, my mom says I could stand to lose a few pounds and I guess she's –"

"Ugh. You are so totally not fat. Your mom's full of it."

Judy was dressed in an amazing outfit – denim miniskirt, a black cropped mesh tank top over a cropped white t-shirt and a length of ripped black lace tied around one wrist. On her feet were a pair of purple glitter jelly shoes, the kind I was coveting but hadn't been able to find in River Falls.

"About last night," I started, because I had to apologize before I started interrogating her on where she got her shoes. "My aunt wanted me to –"

Judy waved her hand. "It doesn't matter – I heard what she was saying. You weren't kidding about her being uptight were you? What are you, their slave?"

I smiled ruefully and looked out over the parking lot, where a woman in pale yellow short shorts and Dr. Scholl's sandals was clopping across the tarmac and yelling at two little kids who were running literal circles around her. "No. I mean, maybe a little. But believe me, anything's better than being back in L.A. with my mom."

My new maybe-friend slid onto the seat next to me and grabbed my Diet Coke to take a sip. "How old are you?"

"Twenty-two – how about you?"

"Same," Judy replied. "So why don't you just move out then? I mean, if you're twenty-two you don't *have* to be out here in the middle of nowhere, do you?"

I kept my eyes focused on the woman in the parking lot. "No, I don't. I just, uh – something happened back home. I got into some trouble and it..." I trailed off, not knowing how to finish the sentence.

"Some trouble?"

I turned and looked right at Judy Decker. Why not tell her? If she was going to judge me then it was best to get it over with, right? But she didn't really feel like the judging type, and if I needed anything that summer, it was a friend.

"I got pregnant. Last year, when I was in my first year at college. I went back to this boy's room and things got a little out of hand and –"

"Things got a little out of hand? What do you mean?"

A strange vibration seemed to have set up under my skin, one I remembered from the days immediately following the incident in Josh Muller's room. It set my teeth on edge and brought back all those feelings of helplessness and rage and loneliness.

"I mean they got out of hand. I liked him, OK? He was in a frat and he had this great smile and he said it was just so we could listen to records but, uh –"

"He raped you?" Judy asked, very quietly, when I trailed off again.

At once, I lifted my head and looked around, to make sure no one had heard the word being spoken aloud. We were alone. Thank God. My heart hammered in my chest and my mouth suddenly felt dry.

There it was. The word. The one that had stuck in everyone's throat – the one that seemed to be too terrible to speak aloud. Judy must have seen my face turn white because she immediately began apologizing.

"I'm sorry. I have a big mouth – my mom always says so. I didn't mean to – you don't have to talk about –"

"No," I said suddenly – and a little forcefully. Where was Josh Muller? He was probably back on campus, spending the summer partying with his frat brothers. He was nowhere close to River Falls, New York. Neither was my mother. "No, it's alright. No one said he raped me. His parents actually threatened to have *me* kicked out of college if I didn't have an abortion. My mom said I should never have gone back to his room in the first place, and I did, so..."

"But did he? I mean, did he force you?"

It felt surreal to be talking about the incident that, after my parents pulled me out of college and I miscarried before they could try to strong-arm me into a 'procedure,' had literally never been spoken of again. I half-expected a lightning bolt to snake down out of the clear blue sky and strike me down. But there was no lightning bolt. There was just Judy Decker and her kindly, reassuring presence, and a wasp buzzing around the open can of soda on an early summer afternoon.

"Yes, he forced me. I tried to fight back at first but he was pretty strong – a lot stronger than me. He said if I kept fighting he was going to kill me, so I stopped fighting. And no one, uh, no one –" I heard my own voice rising and swallowed, hard, before continuing. "No one believed me. I didn't have any bruises or marks on me, and everyone who was at the party said they saw me leave with Josh."

"So he got away with it? And you had to leave college? And your parents – your mom – believed him? Not you?"

I shrugged. "If you knew my mom, you'd understand. She's never liked me. All she did after it happened was pull me aside and tell me that if I decided to have the baby I shouldn't expect any help from them at all."

"That is so harsh."

"I know. After I left college I just started having these weird episodes where I would feel like I was losing my mind or something. I tried getting a job but it kept happening, and then I started partying a lot more and – here I am, I guess."

We sat quietly for a little while, watching Grocery King customers coming and going in the parking lot. A couple of minutes before I had to go back inside, Judy looked over at me and said:

"I believe you."

I turned to look back at her and she repeated it.

"I believe you, Heather. Same thing happened to someone I know. That must have been so hard without your parents on your side, though."

I had to go back to work. I didn't have time to cry, and I knew Jerry wouldn't be happy if I went back to my till with red eyes and a runny nose.

"Thank you," I whispered to Judy as she gave my hand a squeeze. And then she asked me what I was doing that Sunday.

"Helping my aunt and uncle," I replied, as something in my new friend's eyes sparkled. "Why?"

"Because me and a group of people are going to a concert, and someone dropped out yesterday. I thought you might want to come along?"

Los Angeles – and my life there, which had lately included a lot of concerts and events – seemed a thousand miles away. I didn't know what kind of band would be playing River Falls, New York and I didn't care – a night out was just what I wanted. Maybe if I asked nicely Brenda would let me go? And even if she didn't, talking to Judy had made a few things clear to me – one of which was that there was actually nothing keeping me at my aunt and uncle's house, on their schedule. I didn't want to go home to my parents yet – especially not now that it seemed I might be making some friends – but I was a legal adult. I could help them with Brad and the housework and take a Sunday night off if I wanted to.

"Yeah," I said, nodding. "Yeah I would love to."

"Mad cool! So how about we just meet – um, do you know where the skating rink is?"

"Beside the school, right?"

"That's it. Meet us there at two on Sunday, OK?"

I balked slightly. "Two? As in, two in the afternoon?"

Judy smiled. "Yeah, it's a little early but we gotta drive. Come on, I promise you'll have a good time!"

"OK," I agreed, filled with the double exhilaration of having confessed the incident with Josh and the feeling that Judy and I were on our way to becoming real friends. "OK, yeah, let's do it! Two o'clock, at the skating rink. I'll be there."

I got up to go back inside and Judy grabbed my arm just before I did so.

"I forgot – wear something totally bitchin' on Sunday. And don't forget your hair and make-up!"

I spent the rest of the week doing what I did every day – following the routine. And I never did find the right moment to broach the subject of having Sunday afternoon off with aunt Brenda. So when Sunday actually rolled around and she found me in my room at just past one o'clock in the afternoon with a hot curling iron in one hand and a can of hairspray in the other, her eyebrows immediately flew up. I forced myself to keep calmly attending to achieving the maximum hair volume possible – after all, I didn't have to make excuses to my aunt. Brad was napping and she and Bill could deal with him that evening without me for one night.

"And what do you think you're doing?" She asked finally, when she realized I wasn't going to offer up an explanation without being asked.

"I'm getting ready," I replied. "I'm going out with Judy Decker – remember she called a few days ago?"

Aunt Brenda stood silently for a few moments as her eyes got wider and wider. "You're going where?" She asked, and I could hear from her tone of voice that whatever was coming was not going to be good. "I'm sorry, Heather, but I don't recall giving you permission to –"

"You're right," I cut her off – which I probably shouldn't have done. "You didn't give me permission, because I didn't ask. I'm twenty-two years old and I've done everything you asked since I got here – including handing over most of my paychecks, which I don't actually have to do. It's just one night, I'll be back soon and –"

"You are living in our house!" Brenda barked, her cheeks – already caked in hot pink rouge – getting even pinker. "You are living under our roof! You are eating our food! This isn't some vacation house where you can just come and go as you please – and if you think it is, all it takes is one phone call to your parents and –"

"And what?!" I asked, raising my voice and standing up to face her. "You're going to send me home? After I pay you half my paycheck every two weeks and help you out with Brad for hours every day, on top of my job? Sounds like a bad deal for you, aunt –"

"How dare you!" She spluttered, as I heard uncle Bill calling from downstairs, asking what was going on. "How *dare* you! After we take you into our home! After we –"

I'd had enough. I knelt down and scooped my make-up and hairspray and various hair accessories into my purse and walked out, pushing past my uncle as he made his way towards my bedroom. The last thing I heard before I left was my aunt's aggrieved voice, swearing that she was going to call my parents and send me home on the next flight.

"Yeah right," I said to myself as I headed down through the backyard, boiling with anger.

The walk to the skating rink ended up taking a lot longer than I thought it would. It took so long, in fact, that I didn't even get there before a silver Datsun honked and pulled over to the side of the road just in front of me. Judy's head immediately popped out of the front passenger window.

"Where the hell were you?! We waited and waited and then we decided to come looking for you. Now get in or we're gonna be late!"

There were already five people in the car – three in the backseat and two in the front. After a little maneuvering I found myself half-on, half-off the lap of a man with a big, glorious poof of blonde hair and jeans so tight I hardly dared look at them.

Judy did the introductions. Her boyfriend, Steve, was driving, and in the back with me were Patty, Chad (of the tight jeans) and Christie. Everyone was in a boisterously good mood, and thankfully the windows of the car were all rolled down so I wasn't overcome by hairspray fumes.

It was the first time for weeks that I'd been with a group of people my own age, just talking, hanging out, not worrying about what anyone else was thinking of me. It was only when someone mentioned that it was five-thirty that I thought to ask where we were going. Three and a half hours of driving? Were we going to Canada?

Judy turned around and looked over the passenger seat at me, a huge grin on her face. She looked at Patty, Chad and Christie.

"Should we tell her?"

"Tell me what?" I asked, looking around and seeing now that no one was even trying to hide those 'we know something you don't' expressions on their faces. "Come on, tell me what? Where are we going?"

Christie giggled and shrugged. "Oh, nowhere. There's just this totally obscure British band we heard about, just doing a small show in Buffalo."

"What British band?" I asked, exasperated but happy because the truth was it really didn't matter if we were going to see some band I'd never heard of – I was dressed up, I was with new friends and neither my mom nor my aunt Brenda could do anything about it.

Steve looked at me in the rearview mirror. "You probably haven't heard of them, Heather. I don't think they're famous in California."

"That's fine!" I replied – what did they think I was going to do? Go crazy because the band we were going to see were new to me? "I don't mind. I just wanted to get out of that house for a few hours."

Patty caught my eye, and she had the same secretive smile on her face that Judy did.

"What?!" I asked again. "Oh my God! What is going on with you guys?"

Patty had flame-red hair, teased so high it brushed against the Datsun's roof, and a pink plaid button down shirt on. "It's just some British band," she repeated. "Like Chad said. What was their name again, Judy? Def-something?"

My ears perked up at the exact moment that the tension in the car seemed to crystallize.

"Def?" I asked. "Like – Def Leppard? Are you guys taking me to a –"

I didn't even manage to get the sentence out before Judy screamed "YESSS!" over the seat at me and Christie joined in with:

"Pyromania World Toooooouuuur!"

"No *way*," I exclaimed, refusing to believe it. They were toying with me. They had to be. Def Leppard was my favorite band and I hadn't even managed to see them when they were in Los Angeles.

"Way," Judy giggled.

"Yeah," Patty added. "Way."

"Stop it," I pleaded, holding one of my hands up only to see that it was shaking. "Stop it. Please. I don't know what you're trying to do but please don't pretend we're –"

Judy handed me something. A piece of paper. A ticket. I looked down at it and read the words out loud:

"Brass Ring presents Def Leppard... Buffalo Memorial Auditorium, Sunday June 12th. Twelve dollars and – oh my God. OH MY GOD!"

I put my hands over my face and screamed for joy before grabbing Judy's arm and shaking it, demanding to know why she hadn't told me.

"Because I wasn't sure you were going to be able to come and I didn't want you to feel too bad if you couldn't."

"So this is real? We're *actually* going to see Def Leppard? I tried to go see them in L.A. and the tickets were sold out. I love Def Leppard – I *love* Joe Elliot! Like, I know every single word off Pyromania – that's how much I love them!"

The night was, quite simply, the best of my life up until that point. Because I did know every word of every song, and packed into a venue full of people who also knew them I managed to lose myself in a way I hadn't been able to do since the incident with Josh Muller. I lost myself in the volume, the music, the big hair and smiling faces and banging heads until I was breathless with happiness.

When it was over, and we filtered out into the warm night with the sounds of the music still echoing in our heads and the smell of weed smoke filling the air, I grabbed Judy and pulled her into a tight hug. I didn't need to explain why. Not to her, not to anyone else. Because she already knew.

"Thank you," I whispered as we hung out next to the car, talking to other concert-goers, naming our favorite moments, not yet willing to let the evening go.

"I knew you were gonna love it," she whispered back. "I waited in line for hours for those tickets!"

The drive home to River Falls took a lot longer than it had in the reverse direction. Just getting out of Buffalo took over an hour. By the time Steve dropped me off at the end of Bill and Brenda's driveway, dawn was just beginning to break.

"Don't call me," I said to Judy through the passenger window. "I mean, you can but –"

"Your aunt," she replied, sighing. "I get it. How about I drop by the Grocery King tomorrow? Maybe you can come out with us again next weekend?"

"Yeah?"

"Yeah. We usually just party here in town, though – you might think it's boring."

"Oh no!" I started, before I saw her smile and realized she was joking. "Ha ha, real funny. But I would love to, uh, to hang out next weekend for sure. I'll probably see you tomorrow or sometime this week, then?"

"Yeah, cool. Did you have a good time tonight?"

"Are you kidding?!" I whispered, worried about waking my relatives. "I had so much fun! It was awesome, Judy!"

"Good. Yeah, it was awesome, wasn't it?"

I stood at the side of the road and watched the Datsun's lights fade into the early morning gloom as Steve drove away, and then I turned towards the house.

Chapter 4: Magnus

I made my way down to the bay on the day before we set out on the first summer raid. Most of the ships were out of the water, turned upside down on the pebble beach. Shirtless thralls worked in the sunshine, using rough rags to spread sticky black pitch along the wood. As I approached one turned to me with a respectful nod.

"Don't worry, Magnus, we'll have the fleet ready to sail by the morn."

"I'm not worried," I replied, "as I know you and your men to be skilled and hard-working."

In truth, I didn't much care if the ships were ready the next day or not. My brother had shown no growth or maturing since the previous disastrous raids and my father had shown no new willingness to admit that his oldest son was simply not up to his duties. It was a foregone conclusion that a successful summer of raiding depended almost entirely on our good luck – and I've never liked the feeling of leaving my destiny entirely to luck. So as far as I was concerned, the thralls could set the ships alight if they so chose.

Not that I was about to say such a thing out loud.

I was about to walk away when the thrall said something else under his breath – something I didn't quite catch.

"What was that?" I asked, turning back.

The man would not meet my eye. "It's nothing. Sometimes my tongue seems to wag all on its own. Do not concern yourself with the thoughts of the lower people."

I knew the thrall – Ingvar or Engvald or something like that – and I knew him to be a competent man. I wanted to hear what he had to say. "No," I began, turning to face him fully. "What is it you said?"

Seeing that my interest was real, and understanding – as a man does – that lying would just dishonor him, the thrall spoke the truth.

"I was just noting that if skill and hard work were the measures of a higher man, it would be you sailing the ship to the Jarl's right, and not your brother."

The thrall had smartly kept his voice low, understanding that if others had overheard him disrespecting the next Jarl to that next Jarl's brother, I would have no choice but to whip him. As it was I knew right away that I was expected to feel a great wound had been delivered to me to hear insulting words spoken of my brother. The man in front of me flinched away, expecting violence.

But I did not feel violent. I felt nothing but kinship with the thrall, who through no fault of his own was shirtless on a beach rubbing pitch into the ship's under-boards whilst duller men ate venison at high tables and spoke of the glory that was to be theirs in the coming raids.

"Do not cower," I told him, in soft tones. "As it is not for thralls to disparage a Jarl's son, so it is not for a second son to agree with a thrall. And yet here we are.

Tomorrow the ships sail for the Kingdoms of the Angles – see that their boards are solid, and the pitch applied well."

The man looked up at me then, and a moment passed between us briefly – a simple moment, not of a Jarl's second son looking down on a thrall, but of two men regarding each other, recognizing their sameness even as they went about their different lives.

"Aye, Magnus. I'll see the ships are right for sailing. A Godswind to you in the morning."

***

We sailed at dawn, and the women and children and elderly people saw us off. The Angles knew the people of the North by then, but they were too thinly distributed, and too close to the coast, to do much about us. Their lords tended to stay just slightly further inland, in estates with high wooden palisades and earthen ramparts to protect them. But the peasants and their villages often sat in full view of the open sea, usually defenseless, and it was from them that we took the fullness of our spoils – grain, meat, animals, people.

My mother was especially fraught that morning. So much so that I questioned her as she clung to me and planted kisses all across my cheeks and forehead.

"Have you dreamt the future, Mother?" I asked. "Is there some terrible event you have foreseen? Why do you have that look on your face when it is just the Angles we mean to meet?"

She shook her head quickly. "No, son, I have not dreamt the future. I just worry more and more these days, as it becomes clearer and clearer that..."

That Asger is a fool? I wanted to finish the sentence for her, but did not.

"I'll take care," I replied. "I'll heed Father's orders, and I'll keep a watch for danger. Do not trouble yourself, we'll be home before the moon is full once again."

I kissed my mother's cheek and turned to walk away and then at the last minute she grabbed my wrist and pulled me back so she could whisper in my ear.

"Do not get yourself killed for nothing, my boy! I understand you mean to keep watch for your brother as well as yourself, but I tell you now do not lose your life for his! Please, Magnus!"

I nodded, even as I knew that sacrificing myself in favor of Asger was exactly what my father would expect of me, if a relevant situation were to arise.

It was as if I was being torn in two between understanding my mother's love for me, her desperate wish to keep me safe, and resenting her for asking me, a second son with little power, to take decisions she knew were not mine to take.

If my life is so important, I wanted to say, *why have you said nothing to the person who can really do something about it? Why haven't you spoken to Father?*

But I was no longer a child, and I no longer lived in a world where my parents were without flaw or fault.

So instead of saying anything I simply gave my mother another respectful kiss on the cheek and turned to go to my ship.

The sun that shone brightly as we sailed out of the bay soon hid itself behind a bank of gray cloud, and the sea took on a familiar greenish-gray hue. It stayed that way the next day and the next, until the mist on the third morning thinned and we found ourselves once again blessed with the feeling of warmth on our faces.

The wind had been cooperative and sure enough, we spotted land almost at the high point of the day. The blood quickened in my veins as our ships approached, a reaction that felt as natural as the quickening in other parts of a man upon finding a naked woman in his bed, or meat on his table after days of thin eating.

The usual way was to sail along the coast until we spotted a village – and sometimes to forgo a smaller one on the chances that we would soon happen upon something larger and more bountiful. So when my father's ship took up the lead and we began to sail north, following the contours of the land itself, all seemed to be as it was meant to be.

Asger's ship was just in front of mine, and slightly to the left. He, like myself, stood at the bow, his eyes studying the shoreline for the little huts of the peasants or the tell-tale columns of smoke from their cooking fires rising high into the air.

He spotted the man at the same time I did – I saw his body tighten out of the corner of my eye. It was just one man – no huts, no smoke. Just a man. And he spotted us only a short while after we spotted him, because he stopped whatever it was he was doing and stood up to peer out at the sea, as alert as a deer on the edge of a wolf-infested wood.

"FATHER!" Asger boomed – gesturing to the man on the shore – who turned and fled back into the forest as soon as he realized what – and who – it was he was seeing. "Father!"

Before my father could respond, I waved my arms at Asger and shouted to him across the waves. "Brother, it is but one man! We should wait until –"

"VOSS!" Came the reply, before I had even had time to make my reasoning heard. "It's been three days, Magnus! Why must you constantly buzz in my ear like a fly? We will –"

"Surely we will come soon upon a village!" I yelled back, conscious that Asger could not be made to feel challenged. The moment he felt challenged was always the moment he settled fully into his foolishness.

But it was too late, he was already directing his ship towards the shore. Beyond, my father was watching, and when I saw him make no move to stop Asger from setting ashore at a point where he had but spotted a single man, I set my jaw grimly and turned to my own men, gesturing for them to follow their Jarl.

I hung back on the beach as my brother drew his sword and gave the command to attack, watching my father's face as he tried to remain composed. At once the air filled with the sound of weapons being unsheathed and unbuckled from belts, of arrows being drawn from quivers. And then, a pause. An awkward pause, as the men waited for instructions on what, exactly, it was they were to attack. A moment later, after giving his firstborn a hard look, my father stepped forward.

"Keep your weapons to hand – we will follow the coast until we come upon a –"

"Father!" Came Asger's response. I could feel the discomfort of the warriors as they watched the drama of father and son play out in front of them. "Did you not see the man? He was right here, on the beach – do your eyes grow weak with age? We must give chase!"

My father, the Jarl, saw that Asger was about to order his men down the narrow path in the forest, and simply held his hand up towards us, indicating that we were to stay where we were.

Asger caught my eye, then, and I could see that he did not understand what was happening – or why. I looked away.

"We must give chase!" He repeated, lifting his own sword his over his head and prompting the Jarl, finally, to lose his temper.

"Give chase?" He bellowed, approaching Asger until the tips of their noses were almost touching. "GIVE CHASE?! Am I right in thinking you are about to set a company of Northern warriors on the trail of a *single man?!*"

My brother stepped back, as if a great gust of wind had suddenly blown him full in the face, and shook his head. When he spoke, his voice was smaller and quieter than before.

"But Father – didn't you see –"

"Of course I saw! It seems I see much more than you, my son, despite your jibes about my age. What I saw was – as you said – a single man. Now what is it you think a single man can carry that we would need, that might be worth sending out best warriors in pursuit of?"

I knew the look on my brother's face, then. I recognized it. I had seen that look from the times of my earliest memories. His eyes got wide and his mouth hung open and he looked from side to side, giving the impression of a man who was truly baffled. The worst of it was, I don't think any of it was an act.

"But Father – surely he will lead us to a –"

"What if he's a swineherd? A messenger doing a spot of fishing before he continues on his way? And how long of a start has he got on us now, Asger, as we stand here without horses? Do you think, if there is a village nearby, that this man has not gone straight there to warn of our approach? What did I tell you about the element of surprise? What have I told you A THOUSAND TIMES about the element of surprise!?"

It was only then, after having it laid out in front of him the way one might lay out a simple explanation to a small child, that my brother understood. His lower lip protruded. I could see he was angry, desperate to fight back. The men, embarrassed for him, joined me in looking away.

And then, to spare his son further humiliation, my father declined to order us back to the ships and sent us north, on foot, to look for a village.

Throughout it all, I said nothing. Even as I knew my father understood that even if we found a village, it would be a great trial and inconvenience to carry any goods or prisoners back down the coast to the ships, I said nothing. It was not my place to say anything, and to do so would only have caused more confusion in the ranks. Still, my brother's idiocy, on display before we'd even met any Angles, set my blood near to boiling.

***

The sun was near the horizon when we found what we were looking for. A small group of peasant huts, not large enough to be called a village, set stupidly close to the shore so all we had to do was walk around a headland to be immediately upon it. A woman knelt before a stream, filling a pot with water, and it was she who spotted us first. I watched as the whites of eyes flashed and she opened her mouth to scream, and my father gave the order to attack.

The Angle peasants' luck was bad that day, to be in the way of a band of Northmen whose bloodlust had been kindled and then dashed once already, and whose swords now craved flesh. It would not have taken a quarter of our number to subdue the village, but my father knew the men needed a release. Into the tiny hamlet we poured, hacking and slicing and killing until blood spattered our faces and then, when there were no more people to kill, standing around and looking at each other, not quite sure whether such a victory was worth celebrating or not.

It was in the process of gathering the loose pigs – some of whom I had to exhort Asger's men not to kill, explaining that they were our pigs now, and to kill them would mean taking food out of our own people's mouths – that we found the stone dwelling. At once, I knew what it was. The learned men, the monks, lived in such dwellings. And they often held stores of silver and gold for the local people – sometimes even the local lord. I shouted for the Jarl but time was of the essence – the monk's building was guarded, and I did not want to give anyone the time to flee with the treasure.

I killed the first guard myself, driving my sword through his neck as his eyes bulged wide in his face, and then the second as my men took care of the rest. And then I stormed inside, eyes searching for a chest or a trapdoor or anything that might indicate where the valuables were. On a small table at the other end of a long, narrow room, my eyes came to rest upon something that glinted in the light. Gold?

"Go upstairs!" I shouted to my men. "And down! Turn everything over, take everything of value. Go, now, and we can return home with our heads held high!"

A great clattering followed as my men carried out my orders and I approached the little table, upon which I now saw a smattering of silver items – rings and woven necklaces and a pile of hammered coins. Just as I was about to reach for them, the table itself seemed to shake and I stepped back, lifting the thick cloth and peering underneath.

A boy cowered there, of an age not that much younger than myself, and as soon as he saw me he held up a single hand in submission.

"Please," he begged. "Please, Sir. I am but a poor messenger for the ealdormen – the silver is not mine – the silver is – please, please don't kill me!"

There were no weapons on him, and he was thin and ragged. His fear was real. And at the very moment I was about to let the cloth drop, and to let the boy live, Asger strode up behind me and drew his sword.

"Step aside, brother," he warned. "Why do you hesitate so, over a worthless boy – and an Angle at that? Let me finish what you will not."

But I did not step aside. I had stepped aside before, as was my duty, and I reckoned I would step aside again. But something in the wholly unwarranted arrogance on my brother's face, after I had been forced to march almost a whole afternoon due to his stupidity, kept my feet planted where they were.

"Step aside!" Asger repeated, raising his voice.

"I won't," I replied quietly.

"I'll ask you once more, and not again," my brother spoke, but I could see in his eyes that my defiance troubled him. "Don't make me –"

"He's a boy," I said, gesturing to the trembling figure under the table, who watched us with tears of fear streaming down his cheeks. How many terrified men had I killed before? So many I could not even guess a number. And what was it about that boy that made me almost ashamed to draw my sword? I didn't know. I only knew I would not kill him – nor would I allow Asger to do so. "Look at him, brother. Look at his dressings, look at the way his bones stand out against his flesh. This boy is no monk, he is no warrior. He is no danger to us. Let us take the silver and go now, before Father –"

I don't know why I expected anything resembling thought from Asger. I had barely finished speaking before he was turning to face me, brandishing his sword. And then my blood ran cold – not because I feared him (I did not) but because I had never stood up to him before, and I knew if I was caught doing so it could mean my death.

"How dare you," he sneered, laughing as he looked down at the boy and then back up at me. "You've done it now, Magnus. Do you think I haven't seen you, all my life, watching from the shadows with that look on your face like you could do better if only someone would give you the chance? Do you think I don't know that you believe yourself my better? Well come on then – time to prove it! Lift your sword now if you're so brave!"

I watched, almost frozen with horror, as Asger lifted his sword over his head. And then, when he brought it down, I blocked it with my own blade and had a feeling, as I saw the shock in his eyes, that even if I died it might be worth it to have seen that look.

He screamed with rage at being thwarted in his attempt to kill me, but I was past the point of caring by then. The blow had been blocked, I had officially taken up arms against my own brother – best to see the fight to the end than throw down my weapon and die anyway, for my crimes against familial hierarchy.

Trained by my father's best swordsman since he was half-ten, Asger was not bad with a blade. If you could surprise him, you could beat him – but if you couldn't? You had a fight on your hands. And so I did. Even so, there was an exhilaration lurking underneath the heavy weight of what I was doing, an explosion of what almost felt like joy to finally, finally put actions to the feelings that had been festering so long.

At first, he was getting the best of me. But when I refused to bend my neck to his sword I think the simple fact that he hadn't yet won put a doubt in my brother's heart – and he has never been good with doubt. I was beginning to come back, beginning to play with him a little, when a wail stopped us both cold. The Jarl. He stood at the other end of the room, an expression like one I had never seen before on his face.

And after a brief pause, he began to stride towards us, stopping in front of me first to punch me so hard in the chest I stumbled and fell back onto the cold stone floor.

My father, despite the gray streaks in his beard, was still as strong as an ox. I writhed on the ground, gasping and desperately trying to suck some air back into my lungs as he went for Asger and, at the very last moment before it looked like my brother was about to suffer the same feet as me, he suddenly backed off.

A few of the warriors stood at the other end of the room, and for a few moments there was no sound as everyone, Asger and myself included, waited to see what the Jarl was going to do. He would have been within his rights to kill me right there, and everyone knew it. I scrambled to my feet as soon as I could breathe again, almost paralyzed with fear but, at the same time, determined to face the decider of my fate, whichever outcome he chose.

"Voss," he growled under his breath, and when I looked down at his hands I saw that they were clenched into fists and that he was literally shaking with fury. I had never seen my father so angry in my life.

And it wasn't me his enraged gaze was focused on. No. It was Asger, my brother, who instantly made the mistake of trying to explain himself.

"Father, it was –"

The thin strand of self-control holding the Jarl back snapped at the sound of his son's plaintive voice. He drew one arm back and then delivered an open-handed blow to Asger's left cheek. And then another, and another, until my brother was whimpering with pain.

My father was out of control, everyone could see it. I wanted to stop him, to remind him that some of our men were watching, but I still didn't know if I was going to live or not – and I very much wanted to.

Soon, my brother tired of being battered – for there are few man alive who can submit meekly to such humiliation without at least attempting to fight back. And as soon as he drew himself up to his full height, dodging our father's hand, I saw what was going to happen. Panicked, I turned to the warriors at the door, watching with expressions of disbelief on their faces.

"Out!" I shouted at them, gesturing at the to leave. "OUT! Now! The Jarl has matters to –"

"LET THEM STAY!" My father roared suddenly, not taking his eyes off Asger. "Let them see what a Jarl they have to look forward to when I take my place in the Great Hall! Let them see what a 'man' will lead them into –"

It was the way my father spoke the word 'man' – as if Asger was no man at all – that spurred my brother to brandish his sword and wield it against his Jarl. And, as I stepped back slowly, for the first time in many winters I felt something like pity for my brother. Nothing my father said was wrong – but how long had he known it? How long had everyone known it – my mother, my father, myself and near enough everyone in the village – everyone except Asger himself? And what had anyone done to teach humility and patience to the boy, and then the young man, who seemed not to know such things? What had my parents done but pretended that there were no flaws in their firstborn? Whose fault was it, really, that Asger thought himself faultless when all his life he had been treated as if that is exactly what he was?

But as ever, it was not my place to say anything. Perhaps I should have been grateful that the Jarl's great anger was not directed at me?

So I stood back, as did the warriors near the door and the boy under the table – who had smartly declined to utter so much as a peep – and watched. The Jarl was stronger than his son, more broad with age and experience, but Asger was quicker – and they were not trying to kill each other. Maybe at first, for a short while, they were. But it soon became clear that neither was truly trying to strike any death-blows.

They kept fighting, though, past many points where it seemed to be coming to a natural end and one or the other of them would suddenly call to mind some fresh anger or insult and lift up his sword again.

"Voss," the Jarl panted. "What curse hangs over me that the Gods saw fit to send me you for a son? Why did they –"

"Aye," Asger replied, and for a moment I thought I saw the shadow of a grim smile on his lips. "And why did they see fit to send me you for a father? You who never once saw me for who I truly was? Who never –"

It would have flared up again at that point but both fighters were too exhausted to continue. The Jarl dropped to one knee, his hand clutching the pommel of his sword to hold himself up, and Asger leaned back on the table underneath which the boy still cowered.

"Take the men and find some rabbits, or a deer," my father said to me, seemingly too tired to lift his head to look into my eyes. "We'll make camp here tonight, before returning to the ships and continuing up the coast in the morning."

Heart thudding, I glanced at the ealdorman's boy under the table and nodded my head at him, gesturing that it was safe for him to come out – even though I did not know if it was. It seemed the best chance for him to live at that moment, when my father and brother were both too winded and sick in their hearts with each other to care about a skinny Angle.

When neither chose to relieve the boy of his head, I led him to the door and instructed the men not to kill or take him captive. Before he fled, and with a bravery that surprised me coming from one so young and so clearly not a fighter, he turned and asked me my name. And when I told him, he responded that he was Grinden, and then he thanked me for his life and fled into the woods.

"Why would you let him –" one of the men began but I just turned and looked at him.

"What would we have done with him?" I asked. "Did you see his size? He'll never fight, he wouldn't be any good for working – it cannot be that you wish more blood to be shed?"

The warrior looked away, but not before I could see that even he was not entirely proud of what we had done on that day.

Chapter 5: Heather

I made it almost three more months at my aunt and uncle's house. As punishment for going to the concert, Brenda started taking an even bigger portion of my paychecks, so I barely had enough money to buy myself sandwiches at work, let alone do anything other than window shopping when Judy and I spent a Saturday afternoon at the new mall.

I saved what I could, letting Brenda think I was spending it all on clothes and earrings at the mall, but by the end of July it was only sixty-one dollars and fifty-three cents.

In early August, Judy introduced me to a boy named Mike one afternoon when we were hanging out in her car outside the 7-11, listening to the new Metallica album on her cassette deck. She spotted him getting out of his car and called him over, leaning in before he could hear us and telling me he was newly single – and cute.

And he was – newly single and cute. I can't say that there was some kind of instant, heated attraction there or anything like that, but I'd missed having a crush on someone and, as the memories of what had happened to me back in L.A. were finally beginning to fade, I thought it might be good for me to start spending time with boys again.

Not that I had much time to spend with Mike – or Judy or anyone else. My schedule was as busy as ever, I was doing some babysitting work for a few other couples in River Falls on some evenings after Brad was in bed and my free time was still mostly limited to weekends or the rare times when my aunt or uncle would give me a few hours off. Which on August 24th was exactly what they did in the late afternoon when Bill announced I could have the rest of the day off.

I immediately phoned Judy and made plans to meet at the bowling alley with a few of the other people I was beginning to consider friends – one of whom was Mike. He was there when I arrived and almost at once it was like he had 'claimed' me. Even when Judy and the others got there Mike seemed to be acting like we were there 'together.' When it came time to divide up into teams it was just assumed we were a couple, and then throughout the night Mike himself was solicitous in the way that boys often are when they're dating you – or trying to date you. When he placed a casual hand on my upper thigh when Christie and her boyfriend Doug took their turn, I immediately sprang up and announced I needed to use the ladies room.

"I'll join you," Judy said at once.

As we stood in front of the bathroom mirror she caught my eye in our reflections as I applied a fresh layer of mascara with trembling hands.

"What's up, Heather? Are you OK?"

I shrugged and forced a weak smile onto my face. "Yeah, I'm fine. I'm just, uh – I'm just thinking about, uh –"

"About that boy in L.A.? Josh?"

My stomach turned just to hear his name spoken aloud. "Yeah. I mean, yeah. And Mike is acting a little weird, like we're a couple or something."

Judy pressed her lips together. "Yeah, I noticed that. So you're, like, not into it? You don't like him back?"

I shrugged again. "I don't know. He seems nice – it's not like I *don't* like him, you know? The way he's acting is just wigging me out a little."

"Right," my friend smiled, snapping the cap back on her lipstick and putting in back in her purse. "I'll take care of Mike. Just – gimme a couple of minutes before you join us, alright?"

"Alright," I nodded, relieved and more grateful than I could express for Judy's concern.

***

Later that night, as we all hung out in the parking lot after the bowling alley closed, smoking and listening to the radio in Judy's car, I found myself alone, briefly, after needing to answer the call of nature in the bushes. As I was walking back to the car, still not visible around the corner of the building, Mike suddenly appeared and I almost walked right into him.

"Oh!" I said, smiling and flustered and somehow already alert to some subtle change in his body language. "I'm sorry, I didn't –"

"So you told Judy that I like you, huh?"

I giggled again, nervously, and tried to walk around him. He blocked my way, also smiling.

"No. I mean – I just told Judy I thought you were, uh – well I thought you were acting like we were a couple tonight. And we're not a couple. I just didn't want –"

I didn't even have time to finish my sentence before Mike's tongue was in my mouth and his hands were on my ass, pulling me in against him.

"Mmmph –" I said, trying to turn my head away only to find his hands clamped onto either side of my face, preventing me from doing so. And all at once I was in Josh Muller's dorm room again, my body singing with adrenaline and fear, my mind screaming that he felt a lot stronger than me, that I needed to get the hell away from –

Bright lights suddenly flooded the little area beside the bowling alley. Headlights. Mike and I both looked up, dazzled by their brightness, and I lifted one hand to shield my eyes as a figure opened the driver's side door. Was it the cops? I hoped it was, even if they were just going to yell at us. But it wasn't the cops.

"Heather?"

Uncle Bill. Mike stepped away from me as soon as he realized that the person in the car was male, and that they seemed to know me. And I, more afraid of Mike than of getting into trouble, found myself suddenly very relieved.

My relief didn't last long. My uncle strode towards me, and it was too late to run or protest by the time I saw the angry look on his face.

"Hey!" I said, when he grabbed my upper arm and began to pull me towards the car. "Hey! Stop! Wait a second, I –"

Judy appeared from around the corner and immediately confronted my uncle, demanding that he let go of me. He ignored her, shouting that he and Brenda had been up all night worrying about me.

"It's not even midnight!" Judy responded. "We were just about to drive her –"

"She has a curfew," Bill responded, opening the car door and pushing me into the passenger seat. "She knows she has a curfew. She knows she needs to be home by a certain time, and that if she isn't there will be consequences"

"She's a grown woman! Why are you acting like –"

The car door slamming shut cut off the rest of my friend's protests and I shifted in the uncomfortable plastic seat, my heart pounding. And as angry as I should have been at being dragged away like a wayward teenager, I was actually just grateful that my uncle had shown up when he did – even if there was going to be hell to pay.

***

The next night, after Brad had been tucked into bed, my aunt joined me in the kitchen where I was wiping the counter down and informed me matter-of-factly that she had purchased a return ticket to Los Angeles for me, three days from then.

I looked up as my stomach tightened sourly.

"What?" I asked, blinking. "You –"

"We've purchased a ticket for you to fly back to L.A. on Thursday. This arrangement doesn't seem to be working out."

I looked around the spotless kitchen, and then glanced up the stairs to where Brenda's son was sleeping soundly, bathed and snug in his bed. The kitchen was clean – because I had cleaned it. Brad had been put down with no meltdowns because of me.

"But –" I started, swallowing hard. Back to L.A.? Back to my mother? Back to my life, which had started to seem so dark and hopeless after the incident with Josh Muller? "I – I can't, aunt Brenda. I – why –"

I hated myself for stuttering. I hated myself for being surprised. What right did I have to be surprised? What right did I have, at that point in my life, after being let down by almost every adult I knew, to believe that people were good?

"I'm sorry Heather, but I've discussed it with Bill and we both feel that it is no help to Brad to be around such an unstable young woman."

She might as well have punched me in the stomach. I actually, in the moment, would have preferred that she had. Unstable? What did that mean? I had a pretty good idea what it meant, but aunt Brenda obliged me by spelling it out.

"Bill told me how he found you last night, young lady. He told me he found in the back of the bowling alley, with some man's tongue down your throat and his hands in your shorts –"

"His hands weren't in my shorts!" I cut Brenda off, angry at the bare-faced lie.

"Do you think your parents didn't tell me what you did, Heather?" She continued, ignoring me. "Why do you think they were so eager to get you away from Los Angeles if it wasn't to make sure you didn't fall further into a lifestyle of sex and drugs and God knows what..."

She kept talking, but there was a roaring sound in my ears then, and it grew so loud it drowned out the rest of her words. A lifestyle. That's what it was to my mom. That's what Josh Muller forcing himself on me in his dorm room was. It wasn't something that arrogant frat boy did to me. No. It was a *lifestyle.*

I looked out the kitchen window into the dark backyard, my mind spinning and turning over and over on itself. I wasn't going home.

The thought appeared in my mind and became fact at the same time. I wasn't going home. I was twenty-two. I already had a job and a few friends. Judy shared a small apartment with her older sister – surely she would let me crash on her couch for a few days while I asked Jerry for more hours and looked around for someone who had a spare room and needed a roommate?

The details could wait, though. The important thing was that I definitely wasn't going back to L.A. As I stood in Bill and Brenda Renner's kitchen, looking into my aunt's ungrateful, totally compassionless eyes, something inside me snapped like a twig. Not only wasn't I going home, I wasn't going to spend one more second in that house. Without a word, I strode out of the kitchen and took the stairs that led to my bedroom two at a time.

Brenda followed me, getting right up in my face and whispering sharply so she wouldn't wake Brad. "What do you think you're doing? We still need you to help with Brad in the morning, Heather! We haven't had time to arrange for a replacement to –"

"Fuck you!" I hissed, jerking my arm away when she tried to grab my wrist. That got her attention. She took a step back, he eyes wide with angry surprise, and I just kept throwing my few belongings into the small suitcase I'd traveled to New York with.

Brenda got over her surprise soon enough, and went to grab me again. That time, I shoved her away. Not hard, just enough to let her know I wasn't playing.

My adrenaline was up again, I wasn't thinking about where I was going – I just knew I was going. Not in the morning, but right then, right that moment. I pushed past my aunt just as my uncle started up the stairs, asking what was going on, and then I slid past him, too, and through the kitchen and out the door that led into the backyard.

I ran down across the lawn in the dark, praying I wouldn't trip on anything, and only paused to look back at the house when I'd slipped out through the gate. The outside light came on and I saw the silhouette of my uncle standing in the doorway, peering out into the night. He had a flashlight in his hand, which he aimed in my direction. I ducked.

I could hear them talking – their voices angry, offended – but I could not hear what they were saying. Bill took a few steps into the yard but gave up soon enough, and a few minutes later my eyes had begun to adjust to the darkness.

Now that I was alone, I began to cry quietly, because I understood the break that had just been made. There would be no going back now, no apologies to my aunt and uncle. I'd pushed Brenda, sworn at her. There was no way they would take me back in. And why would I even want them to? They didn't care about me. So it was true – I wasn't going home. And I wasn't going back to the house I'd just fled, either.

Where was I going?

The evening was warm – almost hot – and I knew that beyond the woods lay the road into town, which I could walk down until I got to the gas station with the pay phone I could use to call Judy.

Once more, I glanced back at the house. Not to see if I was being pursued (I wasn't) and not out of sorrow (there was nothing like sorrow in my heart to be leaving that place) but just as a kind of reassurance to myself, a definitive and final goodbye.

And then I turned towards the dark woods and began to carefully make my way down the gentle slope towards them, my suitcase clutched in one hand.

Chapter 6: Magnus

When the camp had been set up for the night, Asger and the Jarl returned, and I could see from their body language as they approached the fire that they had put the acrimony between them to rest. There had never been a fight between them, never weapons drawn – not until that day. And witnessed by some of the men, too. How was that going to be handled? Jarl or not, if a Northman loses the respect of his men – and allowing his firstborn son to take up arms against him is something that could lead to a Jarl losing his warriors' respect – there is little that can be done to regain it.

Those who had been sent to hunt found themselves blessed by Ullr, for they came back with not one but two deer, their sides pierced with arrows and red with blood. It was a good thing for my father, for he knew as well as anyone that men with full bellies are less prone to upset than those who go hungry.

It was just after the meat, roasted on spits over a bed of glowing coals, had been consumed, as the men lolled near the fire, laughing and drowsy, that the Jarl suddenly stood up and called for their attention.

"It won't have gone unnoticed that there was a confrontation earlier today," he said, looking around at the warriors one by one. "Don't bother to look surprised, I know men are as prone to gossip as house-thralls! But I come before you to ask who among you has proven a master at a skill the first time he makes an attempt at it? Who of you hit a target dead-on the first time he picked up a bow? Who didn't find himself stumbling under the weight of his sword the first few times he picked it up?

And why, I ask myself, would I try to pretend that it would be any different for the son of the Jarl?"

I kept my expression serious, because the situation was serious – my father knew he had to make a case for Asger. But I saw at once the false nature of that case – Asger was neither a boy, nor inexperienced in the ways of combat. The men, as my father was telling them, were no doubt recalling their youthful mistakes – indeed I caught a few of them running their fingers over old scars and wounds, their minds cast back to a time when they were not so sure of themselves as they were now.

Surely, I thought, they would see through their Jarl's obvious interest in convincing them that all Asger – a grown man – needed was another chance, further lessons, more experience? Surely they would not miss the truth that stood in front of their eyes – that no matter what words were used to soften the situation, my brother was not up to the task of Jarldom, whether the time should come the next day or not for ten winters.

But they began to nod as my father spoke further, even going to so far as to compare Asger to an older warrior in our village – Waldrun – who was as famous for his skills with a bow as he was for taking years longer than everyone else to learn them.

"What must the people have thought of Waldrun at ten and ten and five?" The Jarl beseeched his warriors. "What laughter must they have held in their chests when another of his arrows sailed straight into the dirt, well short of its target? And what do they think of him now, and the fact that his arrows never miss? Do you see how a man's skill is not fixed? And how an unfixed skill can, as the winters pass, be more of a boon than not?"

My brother did not even have the decency to look ashamed. He sat on a tree stump at my father's right side, his back straight and his demeanor haughty, as if it were his accomplishments our father spoke of, and not those of an old man back in Apvik. It was all so ridiculous. So embarrassing – for all of them. I wanted to leap to my feet, take each of the men by their leathers and shake them.

"How can you believe this?!" I imagined myself yelling. *"When you see the truth of Asger's 'skill' in front of your eyes? He is ten and ten and five – not ten and five – how long must we wait for him to acquire this mysterious skill that somehow we ourselves have managed to acquire at a younger age?!"*

But no one said a thing – including me – and soon enough heavy eyelids were falling, and heads were nodding, and the whole company of us fell asleep, lulled by our Jarl's reassurances and the roasted venison in our bellies.

***

At dawn, we headed south along the coast, taking what goods we had managed to procure from the tiny village and the Angle monks. At the head of the procession – for the path south was narrow, and we had to walk almost in single file – my father and brother walked proudly together, showing no sign of the crossed blades of the previous day. A stinging fire burned in my belly towards Asger, made all the hotter by the fact that it contained my revulsion at the Jarl's acts as well as his own. It is not an easy thing for a son to feel scorn for his own father, and as such I heaped it all onto my brother so as to avoid facing who it was really directed towards.

When the sun was high in the sky, its light pale and diffused through the thin layer of high cloud that was so common in the land of the Angles, a shout came from up ahead. I lifted my head, my senses immediately sharp and focused, my eyes sensitive to any signs of movement.

There seemed to be none. I stepped off the path and began to run past the warriors on my way to the Jarl, to find out what was happening. As I got closer, I could hear voices – angry voices, although held back somehow, not loud enough to carry.

"What is it?" I asked, panting, when I caught up with them.

At once, I saw that the tension was once again between Asger and my father.

"We must return to the ships," my father was whispering angrily, leaning in close to his son so the warriors would not hear the argument. "We've already wasted more than a day on foot, Asger, we cannot –"

"Wasted?!" My brother shot back, not bothering to keep his own voice down. "Wasted, Father? What of the silver I found? What of the –"

"Luck," the Jarl interjected – correctly so. It was luck that brought us to the monk's dwelling – nothing more. I knew it because I had been on many raids by then, and I had learned from experience that raiding tiny hamlets was generally a waste of time and strength – even if the odd one did throw up a treasure or two. "Asger, don't you see it was luck that brought us the silver? And what do you think the odds are of us finding it again now, in another such place?"

    My eye caught something then, to my right. Smoke rising into the air and, when I looked closer, the sight of a couple of straw huts in the woods. Another hamlet. Another place that was not going to be worth our time. And my brother, again insisting that we spend ourselves on his foolish notions. I closed my eyes and took a slow breath, trying to will my anger away.

    "Another village!" Asger suddenly shouted, turning towards the men as my father stood behind him, not quite managing to keep the defeated slope in his shoulders concealed. "We are almost returned to our ships, surely another fight won't finish us off?!"

    He was grinning, waving his sword in the air, completely unaware of the tension in the air.

    The Jarl was not as unaware. The moment he sensed hesitation in the men he made his decision, stepping forward with a scowl on his face and bellowing at them:

    "What did I speak of last night, you dull-wits?! Who among you dares to look away when my son – your future Jarl – speaks? Draw your swords now, before I take them from you and drive them through your cowardly hearts myself!"

It worked. Of course it worked. The men were fighters, not thinkers, trained by many moons of experience never to question their Jarl.

A great feeling of fatigue washed over me like a wave as we entered the area where the huts stood, so unprotected it did not even have a lookout. A small child spotted us coming and, apparently knowing nothing of the fearsome men of the North, smiled happily at my brother. It was at the very same moment that a woman appeared at the child's side, her arms full of vegetable detritus, and showed herself more wary than her offspring. She screamed loudly and it was that scream that started the fight.

If it could be called a fight. My legs, suddenly heavy and weak as if in a dream, almost gave out underneath me and I moved off to the side, stepping into the woods at the edge of the village. I wasn't needed – we outnumbered the peasants three or four to one – and I found, in the moment, that I was less interested in murdering people on Asger's whim than I was in anything else in the world.

It was a new perspective, watching a raid rather than participating in it. I sensed a kind of obligation on the part of the warriors, who surely knew they were in no real danger, and that there were no real spoils to be had. Sure, they bellowed and stomped and dragged people from their homes. They put the torch to a couple of storage huts, and then to a dwelling. But I didn't see anyone killed – not even any of the fighting-age men. What a strange scene.

It got even stranger as I looked up and spotted Asger, still grinning widely, marching down between two huts with his un-bloodied blade held at the ready. And then, behind him, one of the peasants rushing towards him. It wasn't until the very last second that I saw the Angle had an axe in his hand, and that he was raising it over his head. My brother hadn't heard a thing.

"As–" I began to shout, only to realize that it wasn't going to be quick enough. I leapt to my feet and fair flew towards Asger, whose expression, upon seeing his younger sibling coming at him, turned to confusion.

I managed to get my arm in the way of the peasant's arm, blocking the axe – which in all truth was probably far too dull to pierce the Jarl-to-be's skull – and knocking him back against one of the huts where he sat panting and yelling about his grain.

My brother, only working out what had just happened after it was over, flew into a rage. Brandishing his sword, red-faced with fury, he stood over the Angle.

"I am from the North!" He yelled in the man's face. "Do you know what we do in the North when someone tries to kill a Jarl's son? Do you?!"

The peasant, braver than most of his kind, met Asger's eyes even as he trembled. "Aye, I know it. But that's my grain you've taken and without it my children will starve."

I knew the Angle had made a mistake before he did.

"Children?" Asger asked, standing up and looking around at his men, who had surrounded him to see what gruesome fate was going to befall the man with the blunt axe. "What children? Where are they? Men – bring the children to me!"

"Brother," I said quietly, stepping towards him as his men dispersed. "Surely it would be best to see that this man is punished and get back to the sh–"

"Coward!" Asger sneered, looking back at me scornfully. "We have nothing to fear from these people, Magnus, and you urge caution? What will it do to kill this wretch if his bloodline lives on? Do you rid your dwelling of rats by leaving the babies in their nests, is that what you think?"

I held up my hands in submission, not wishing to inflame him further. The peasants – Angle or otherwise – were generally quick to flee, and I hoped that that was what they had done this time. And most of them had. Unfortunately, most is not all. Soon enough there were about seven of them, ranging in age from barely-walking to about ten, all standing in a row in their filthy rags.

"Which of them is yours?" Asger demanded of the peasant, who did what any fair-witted man would do and denied that any of the little ones were his own.

"I'll ask you again," my brother continued, and I could see now in his eyes that he was enjoying the feeling of power he had over the Angle and the children, after the previous day's humiliation. "Which of them are your own?"

The man made a show of glancing up at the dirt-smeared lot in front of him, making sure not to show any flicker of recognition at any of them, although surely he knew them all – even the ones he had not fathered.

"I swear it," he addressed Asger respectfully. "None are mine, sir. Mine have fled into the woods, as I taught them to do when threatened."

Asger roared with anger and reached out, taking a child of about five by the hair and dragging him towards us. I watched as the men behind him exchanged quiet glances. Killing is not a thing that gives men of the North pause, but it tends to happen only in certain circumstances. In the heat of a raid or a battle, when one's blood is up, any living thing within reach is fair game. A man can lose himself in the frenzy. But we were not in the midst of a battle, nor even a raid, as the fight – if it could be called such a thing – was over by then. Asger's men eyed each other because they wondered if he was really about to do what it seemed he was.

"How about this one?" My brother asked the Angle, yanking the child's head to the side, exposing the pale neck and holding his blade close to the skin. "Is this one yours, pig?"

The man set his teeth, but I saw that his lips were wobbling. Still, he held his nerve. "I've never seen him in my life, sir. Please, the boy has nothing to do with –"

I saw it at the same time as the men – and the Angle – saw it. Asger raised his sword quickly, the blade flashing in the weak sunlight, and then brought it down.

The sound of metal screeching against metal filled the small clearing in the woods as I, at the last moment, placed my own sword between my brother's and the child's neck.

"No!" I yelled, not even aware that I was speaking. "Asger! No!"

At once, my brother forgot about the child and the Angle and turned his rage to me. I used my sword to block his, nothing further. I did not attack, I did not try to land any blows. The men stood aside. Well, they stood aside until the Jarl appeared and roared as loud as I had ever heard him roar before.

I dropped my sword. Asger dropped his as well, if a second later and not before 'accidentally' allowing it to slice a shallow leaving present on my right shoulder.

"What are you doing?" My father addressed me, his words sounding like they were coming from a throat so constricted with emotion that they barely made it out. "WHAT ARE YOU DOING, MAGNUS?! Again?! He is your brother! He is your future Jarl, boy! He is –"

"He was about to kill an infant," I said softly, in the pause my father took to suck a great deal of air into his lungs in order to continue his tirade.

"A child," I continued, as eyes widened around me – not least the Jarl's. "Not in battle, Father, but in all calm. He was about to kill an infant not half-ten. I ask you – I ask *all* of you – is that an act of courage? Of necessity? Is that an enemy the needs to be slain, lest he turn around and take your own head off, quick as a wolf?"

Looking down, I saw my father's hand tighten on the pommel of his sword and a feeling of already having gone too, too far came over me. He had spared me the previous day – surely his patience would run out sometime? But instead of bringing calm to my heart the thought brought more defiance, and hotter. What is one more foot of water underneath a drowning man if he is already drowning?

"Look at the men, Father!" I said. "Look at their faces!" At this exhortation, the men all dropped their eyes to the ground, which had suddenly become fascinating to them. "Do you think they do not see what I know you already see? What I know you've seen for years?! Do you think they do not know that Asger is not made to be a Jarl, whether he be your oldest son or –"

A frisson of danger cut through the air like lightning. I had said too much. Everyone knew it. Not only had I said too much, but I'd done so in front of the men. When my father – red-faced and panting in front of me, almost beside himself with rage – regained his abilities to speak and act, I was likely, this time, to be killed. And the warriors, even as I saw in their faces that they sympathized with me, would not disobey their Jarl. I knew that. My father knew it.

The situation was clear, suddenly. The choice was upon me. If I didn't make it, I was going to die at the hands of my own people.

So I did make it. I turned and ran. As Asger and our men stood waiting for their Jarl to command them, I ran.

Into the sun-dappled forest, down a narrow path, over roots and rocks as they stood out of the bare earth, I ran. And soon, I heard that I was being pursued. The sound of weapons slapping against legs, of men's breaths coming hard and heavy, began to bear down on me. If it were not for the twists and turns in the path, I knew they would have spotted me already. And then, at the last second, as I was about to stop and face them with my sword in hand, a hand reached out and pulled me into the undergrowth.

Thinking it was one of my father's men, I began to fight, only to hear, to my great shock, a woman's voice in my ear.

"Stay down! Here – come here, there's a place – behind this tree. Come on!"

Chapter 7: Heather

I got lost in the woods at the bottom of Bill and Brenda's backyard – the very same woods I had walked through multiple times that summer. I thought I was on the path, I could see the odd car passing by on the road in the distance, and then suddenly I felt dizzy and I couldn't quite work out where I was anymore, as I seemed to have stumbled into an area of thicker undergrowth.

After wandering uselessly around in the dark for about an hour, I grew tired and, given it was a warm evening, decided to nap on the soft earth and make my way to the gas station where I could use the pay phone in the morning, when I could better see where I was going.

And then in the morning, the woods on my aunt and uncle's property seemed darker and more impassable than I remembered. They felt different, too, although I couldn't quite put my finger on how. The air was different somehow, softer and quieter. I was also quite thirsty.

Damnit, I muttered, craning my neck to see if I could get my bearings and seeing nothing I recognized. I just needed to pick a direction and follow it – sooner or later I'd find myself somewhere recognizable. Even if it was Bill and Brenda's house, I could just head back through the woods, knowing that time where I was on the path.

I stopped and looked around, trying to decide which way to go. Beside me stood a huge tree, its leaves so thick they almost blocked out the sunlight entirely. I leaned against its trunk and suddenly found myself dizzy again. Not just dizzy – I couldn't breathe. And as soon as

I realized I couldn't breathe, and felt a jagged spike of panic rising up inside me, it was over.

It was over and I was suddenly back where I thought I'd been in the first place – in the middle of the woods on Bill and Brenda Renner's property. Puzzled, I glanced around. I was beside a large tree – but not the same one I had been beside mere seconds before. I reached for one of the thick roots, meaning to use it to help pull myself to my feet again, and fell back into a dark, breathless dizziness.

I shook my head and looked up, blinking. Was I dreaming? What was happening? And then, before I could pinch myself to see if I was actually conscious or not, I heard voices. Male voices. Was it my uncle? Was it the police? Had Brenda called the cops? It wasn't totally beyond the realm of possibility that she would do something like that. I scrambled into some thick bushes – again, thicker than I thought I'd ever seen on the Renner property – and crept forward on my hands and knees.

And what I saw in front of me was enough to have me sighing with relief – I was definitely dreaming. It was the most realistic dream I could remember having, complete with the realistic smell of – well, I didn't know what it was, but it was bad. A few feet in front of me stood a group of people – grown men and children. They were not like any people I had ever seen before in my life. The children were ragged, filthy, their feet bare and their knees scabbed. The men were huge and dressed strangely in leather, their hair worn long and braided. Someone was being yelled at. It was one of the children, slumped down against a – what was that? A hut of some kind? A shed? There were no sheds in the woods, were there?

You're dreaming.

Yes, I was dreaming. One of the least dreamlike dreams of my life, but a dream all the same. What else could it have been?

And then suddenly the child looked up and I saw that it was no child at all but a man – a very small, thin man with a wizened face and straggly gray hair falling about his shoulders. One of the bigger men in leather was questioning him, asking him which was his. Which what was his? The old man was refusing to answer.

And then the angry man yanked one of the kids towards him by the hair, causing the little one to yelp with fear, and held the blade of a sword to his neck.

I wanted to wake up. I wanted to wake up very badly. There was a pit in my stomach, a feeling of dread hanging over the whole scene which was not lessened by the fact that it all seemed so *real.*

Before I could crawl back the way I had come, back into the undergrowth, the man who clutched the tiny child in his hand suddenly raised a sword above his head and I squeezed my eyes shut tight.

They flew open again at the sound of metal clashing with metal. Another man had stepped forward, presumably to save the child, and now the two fought. Well, one of them fought – the angry one, who had fat cheeks and a look in his eyes that I instinctively did not like. The other, if anything slightly larger than his attacker, did nothing more than deflect the blows and dodge out of their way with a deftness I didn't usually associate with someone of his size.

I watched them dance around each other as the blades of the swords clashed again and again. I could hear the heavy breaths of the fighting men, and see the strange apprehension in the eyes of those who stood watching. I'd seen a few fistfights by that point in my life, and I was familiar with the usual air of aggressive excitement that can seize the spectators. There was none of that in the woods that day – some of the watchers, I could tell, wanted nothing more than to look away.

What kind of a dream was this, that felt so similar – and yet also so different – to real life? The thin branches of the bushes pressed against me, the leaves brushed my face, and I did not have time to contemplate dreams versus reality because suddenly another man – older, and dressed in heavier, finer clothing – appeared from behind the hut and the pit of dread in my stomach grew.

The gas station. I had to get to the gas station to call Judy. I had to get away from this odd confrontation in the woods. I had to – if I was sleeping – wake up. The man who had just appeared looked angry. Not at the man who had just threatened to cut a child's throat open, but at the one who had stopped him. There was something in the air now – something ugly. The soldiers – for that is what they looked like, dressed alike in their leather clothes and with the obedient looks of soldiers on their faces – gazed down at the bare earth upon which they stood. A great feeling of foreboding, one I did not know the source of, filled my heart. And along with it came a strong desire to get the hell out of there.

So I did. Slowly, carefully, I braced my hands in the dirt and pushed my body backwards, being very careful not to move too quickly and give my location away. And as soon as I was far enough away to safely stand up, I did so.

The gas station. I had to get there. But to get there, I had to find the road that passed the Renner property on the other side of the fields and the woods from the house. And from where I was standing I couldn't see any fields – I couldn't see anything except more woods. I looked down at my left forearm, running my fingers over it lightly, looking again for signs it was all a dream. And when none came, I dug my fingers into my own flesh, pinching hard enough to make myself whimper. Nothing. What the hell was going on?!

Footsteps. Running footsteps, approaching fast. I jerked my head up quickly as a tingle of fear coursed through my veins. I spotted him through a gap in the trees – the fighting man. Not the man who had held his sword to the child's throat, but the one who had stopped it. He was running. He wasn't just running – he was being chased. And he was almost upon me.

I wasn't conscious of making a decision. All I knew was that just as he reached me he turned and grabbed for his sword to confront his pursuers and I, remembering his bravery in saving the child, suddenly reached up and clutched at his hand, exhorting him to follow me into the undergrowth.

In response, I got a glancing blow to my cheek. The man thought I was his enemy.

"Come here!" I whispered desperately, pulling him from the path and blinking at the stinging pain in my face. My eyes searched for a hiding place as the footsteps of many men bore down on us, and spotted a huge, upturned tree stump. "Behind this tree! Here!"

We dove into the shallow depression behind the tree stump and held our breath. The pursuers hadn't seen us. They ran past – and there must have been a lot of them because it took awhile for the forest to fall quiet again. When it did, the man and I finally turned to look at each other.

He was gorgeous. Seriously. That's the actual first thought that popped into my head. Not 'are we safe?' and not 'why is he dressed like he's in a movie?' No. The very first thing my brain saw fit to take an opinion on was the green-gold depths of his eyes, fringed as they were with long, dark lashes and set, like an action movie hero's, above broad cheekbones.

"Uh – hey," I said, because I couldn't think of anything else. "I'm, uh – I'm Heather."

"Heather," the man with the eyes you could drown in said back to me, as if he'd never heard it before. "Hea-ther. I am Magnus."

Magnus. What a name. It suited him.

I lifted a hand to my cheek, more aware of the pain there now that the danger seemed to have passed, and winced as my fingers brushed against it.

"I hit you," Magnus said, apparently only then recalling that he had. "I – I didn't – I thought you were my brother – or one of his men. I did not intend to –"

"It's OK," I replied, even though I could already see, in the bottom of my field of vision, that the place where the blow had landed was beginning to swell. "I know you thought I was – your brother? Is that who was chasing you?"

"Yes, it was. My brother, and my father, and all the men. Even my own, the ingrates! No matter, Heather, we must find a healing leaf for your face before your eye swells shut."

Before my eye swelled shut? Just how hard had I been hit? "What's a healing leaf?" I asked, surprised to hear such odd talk coming from such a huge man. Because Magnus was not just gorgeous – he was big. Unfeasibly big. Even sitting down, he towered over me, and just the shoulder next to mine seemed almost as broad as the entire width of me. I opened my mouth to ask if he was a bodybuilder and then remembered what he'd just said. "Your brother?" I asked instead. "That was your brother? And your dad? What's going on – why were they chasing you? Is this – are you playing a game or something?"

Magnus shrugged his weighty shoulders. "It's anything but a game. I lifted my sword against my brother – twice in two days – and he is the Jarl-to-be. By rights, either one of them can kill me now. I can never go home."

I did not understand what he was talking about, but it was impossible not to feel compassion at the real sadness in his eyes.

"What?" I asked, smiling tentatively because – surely he was joking? Fighting with your brother meant your father could kill you? And what the hell was a 'Jarl,' anyway? "Your father was trying to – to *kill* you?"

Magnus turned to me, a pained look in his eyes as they slipped down to my swollen cheek. "It is our way in the North. Asger is the firstborn son. After my father, he will be Jarl. It is my duty to obey not just my fath–"

"What's a Jarl?"

"Each part of the North has its own Jarl – it's not like here, where you have one king for one kingdom –"

"A king?" I repeated, chuckling. "We don't have a king!"

The man beside me narrowed his eyes and, for the first time, seemed to take in more of me than my face. His gaze moved down my body – and he made no attempt to disguise it. And I found, where often a man's gaze on my body could feel like a threat, Magnus' did not.

"Are you – foreign?" He asked a few moments later, reaching down to run his fingers along the cuff of my Jordache jeans. "What are these dressings – these are not a woman's dressings. These are not like any dressings I have ever seen before."

To my left, a small bird with jet black feathers alighted on a branch and tilted its head towards us, as if listening intently.

"Look at him," Magnus commented, gesturing towards our feathered companion. "He wonders where you come from, as well."

"I actually come from California," I told him. "I was only supposed to stay for a little while, but now I think – ugh, it's a long story. I need to get to the gas station on the way into town so I can call Ju–"

"The what?"

I felt my brows knitting themselves into an expression of confusion. "The what – what?"

"Where is it you said you were heading? Are you staying at an estate near –"

"The gas station," I told him again. "I need to use the payphone to –"

"The payphone?"

I couldn't help but laugh. Was he deaf? I didn't wonder it in a cruel way, I just wasn't sure what his difficulty was with understanding that I needed to get to the gas station to use the payphone. "Yes," I smiled. "I need to use the payphone at the gas station. So, um –"

Magnus mirrored, on his handsome face, the bafflement that was surely already written across my own. And as we sat beside each other, it occurred to me that nothing that had happened since I'd come across the men shouting at each other in the woods had made any sense. One of them had been holding a sword – a sword! – to a child's neck. And it hadn't been three or four men, either, it had been at least thirty. What were thirty men, dressed in odd leather clothes, doing threatening a bunch of raggedy children in the woods on the Renner's land?

"What is it?" Magnus asked, reaching out suddenly towards my swollen cheek. I flinched away, half from sensing that even the lightest touch would cause pain and half from the growing understanding that something profoundly weird was going on.

"I am sorry about your cheek, girl," he said quietly – and even that was odd. Not 'I'm sorry about your cheek' – like a normal person would say. But 'I'm sorry about your cheek, *girl*' – it was just a strange way to word a sentence. "I did not even realize that I lashed out when you –"

"Where are we?"

Magnus stopped talking when I interrupted him, and then it was his turn to look as if he were suppressing a chuckle. "Where are we? Do you not know?"

But I was not trying to be funny. I was asking because I really needed to know. I looked up at him and asked again: "Where are we?"

"We're in the Kingdom of the East Angles," he replied, seeing that I was serious. "How is it that you don't know where –"

"We're – we're *where?"* I asked, totally uncomprehending now. "The Kingdom of the whats?"

"The Kingdom of the East Angles. For a time you were ruled by Mercia, but your King Aethelstan saw to their defeat not ten winters ago when –"

I knew most of the words Magnus was saying. I hadn't lost the ability to understand language. But none of it meant anything. I'd never once in my life heard any of the names he used – for places or people.

Seeing my complete confusion, Magnus once again asked if I was foreign.

"No!" I snapped, frustrated, before biting my tongue. "I'm sorry, I don't mean to yell at you. I just –"

"How did you come here?" He continued, and there was something tender in his manner that I found I liked. It was easier to calm down with him next to me, his size somehow lending the interaction an air of safety rather than of threat.

I smiled, because surely there was an explanation for all this, and one that would make us both laugh. "I live here," I replied. "With my aunt and uncle – this is their land – their house is –"

"This is Aethelstan's land," Magnus told me. "This is the King's land, girl. Perhaps your aunt and uncle live close-by on one of the estates? If you like, I could help you find their dwelling – Gods know, I will not be returning to the ships with the men. You helped me back then, when I ran for my life. I will see you to safety with your family."

I stared. For a moment, I couldn't think what to say. One of us was crazy. There were two of us having that conversation, and neither, to my mind, were showing obvious signs of psychosis. Still, it was like gazing up at a blue sky next to a man who insisted it was red.

"No," I began slowly, certain of my own sanity. "This is Bill and Brenda Renner's land. Their house is just up the hill behind us, and the gas station is –"

"Show it to me, then."

"The gas station?"

Magnus shook his head, eying me as if I were some exotic species found in an unexpected location, like a tiger at a skating rink. "I do not know what that thing is, Heather. Take me to your aunt and uncle's dwelling, if you say it is close."

So I got up, questioning myself again as to whether or not I might be dreaming, because everything seemed to have the strangeness of a dream even as my five senses seemed to be working perfectly normally. We made our way back to the narrow path and already I could see, as I had seen earlier, before coming across Magnus and his brother fighting, that the woods looked different. Thicker. Darker.

Still, I was confident that once I got my bearings, I would be able to find Bill and Brenda's house. The stand of trees on their property was not even big enough to call a forest, and no matter what side I came out on, I would immediately know where I was. Not wanting to show indecisiveness and make it look like I didn't know exactly where I was going, I turned left and began to follow the path.

I followed it for five minutes, and then ten, and then what felt like more than fifteen. And then, as a sound my ears heard perfectly but my mind refused to take in began to rise through the trees, I suddenly stopped dead still.

"What is it?" Magnus enquired, and when I turned to look at him I saw that he had his sword drawn. He must have seen me eying it. "I am not an Angle, girl. It would be foolish to walk these woods without a weapon to hand."

The sound – a quiet roar, so familiar that just hearing it put me in mind of skipping school and going roller-skating at Venice Beach with Lisa Caldwell – was not going away.

And why did it put me in mind of the beach? Of sand and bikinis and bright blue slurpees? Because it was the sound of the ocean.

The sound of the ocean. In upstate New York, where I knew very well that there was no such geographical feature.

"What is that?" I asked, and for the first time since I had run into Magnus, I could hear the fear in my own voice.

"What is what? Do you hear something, girl? Speak now if you do, for there is only one of me, and one sword –"

"No," I said, nodding my head east, where what I could have sworn was the sound of surf was coming from. "That."

Magnus cocked his head at me, giving me the look I knew I had already given him more than once – the one that said he worried about whether or not I was of completely sound mind. "The sea, girl? Is that what you ask about?"

"The sea?!" I cried, dismayed because I knew that there was no way I was on Bill and Brenda Renner's property anymore – not if what I was hearing was really the ocean. And if I wasn't on Bill and Brenda's Renner's property anymore – then where the hell was I? And how did I get there?

"Yes, the sea. It's right – here, come, it's right here."

The man in leather, so tall the top of my head barely came up to the top of his chest, took my hand, then, and I yanked it away instinctively.

"I – I'm sorry," I babbled, when he turned back to me with a questioning look on his face. "I, uh, I –"

What was I supposed to say? That he was huge and armed and I wasn't even good with small unarmed men touching me? But in the end there was no need to say any of it because there was something about Magnus, perhaps his expression, perhaps something else, that just made it impossible for me to consider him a threat. When he declined to force me to take his hand it was actually I who reached out tentatively, a few moments later, to take his.

Magnus led me the rest of the way down the path, to where it ended. And at the end of it lay what I already knew was there – the sea. The ocean. What ocean? The Atlantic? I didn't know.

Was I losing my mind? I tried to keep my composure but such was my worry and fear that I choked up slightly, and tears of fright filled my eyes.

"You are lost," Magnus said gently, wiping a tear off my non-swollen cheek. "Do not despair, girl, we'll find your way back home. You saved my life there, in the forest. I will see you to your home."

I looked up at him as his image swam in my tear-blurred eyes, and saw that he meant what he was saying. I was so grateful I almost swooned with it when I imagined how scary it would be to be in my predicament alone, with no idea where I was, or how I had come to be there.

"Come," he said, "let us gather the kindling for a fire – it will give you something else to think about. And then we can –"

"I have no idea where I am."

He paused and looked at me. "I know it. But we will need to spend the night in the forest, and for that we need –"

"No," I said, my voice breaking. "You don't understand! I mean I have *no idea* where I am. I don't even know what country I'm in! I don't know anyone who dresses the way you do in New York – or even in America! I don't know how I even got here! I don't –"

I began to hyperventilate. My field of vision, full of an ocean I didn't recognize and a man I didn't know, began to narrow. A feeling of floating came over me, and I turned my head up towards Magnus as the darkness crowded out the light of the day.

My last thought: *Fuck. I'm going to faint.*

Chapter 8: Magnus

I caught the girl's already-limp body in my arms, before she could fall to the ground, and carried her down to the water's edge. And when I knelt at the place where the waves met the sand, and reached down to scoop up a few droplets of cold water to sprinkle on her face, I caught sight of her cheek again.

I had almost broken the skin – in the center of the swollen welt was a dark red spot where her milky cheek had almost opened. And amidst the guilt that crowded my heart at having left such a mark, I tried to work out if she was child or woman. Her height was that of a woman, and her body full where women's bodies are full. But her skin – her face – was like nothing I had ever seen before. Flawless it was – as flawless as that of an infant. And her dressings so odd and masculine – was she one of Aethelstan's daughters, escaped from the royal party as they traveled from one stronghold to another? But how could she be, given her frightened tears at seeming not to recognize where she was?

It was as I pondered her that she stirred, her eyes fluttering open and looking to and fro until they finally settled, focused, on me.

"I'm still here."

"Aye," I nodded, dipping just the tips of my fingers into the water and bringing them to her forehead – something about her invited a gentleness I did not usually feel towards my fellow man – or woman. "You are. Did you hope to wake in another place?"

"I did. I hoped to wake up in River Falls. I need to get to the gas station so I can call Judy. But I'm back here, beside the ocean that shouldn't be there, and I get the feeling it's miles away from River Falls."

She wasn't crying anymore. Her voice was barely higher than a whisper, but the high emotion had passed. Instead there was in her gaze a quiet curiosity tinged with resignation. Wherever she wished to be, her eyes said to me, she was here. And from here we would both find our way, somehow, to the days and places that lay ahead of us.

"You must keep your hands from your cheek," I told her as I helped her to her feet. "If you scratch it, or roll on it in your sleep, the skin will break. And if we can keep it from breaking, we can keep it from festering."

Heather lifted her hand to her swollen face at my words, but pulled it away without touching the welt. And then she looked at me.

She really was beautiful, her face a picture almost of someone who has not gone hungry for long periods of time, or suffered any long illnesses. Her lips were full, her smile wide and generous, and her teeth white and straight and gleaming.

"You said we needed to gather kindling?"

"Uhhh–" I replied, because I had been too caught up in staring at her to hear what she said.

She smiled, then, and asked again if we needed to gather kindling.

"Yes!" I told her, entranced enough by that smile to return it without thinking.

We walked up to the top of the beach and began to wander in the liminal place between the sand and the woods, looking for dried out twigs and sticks to start a fire. When I asked how old she was, she turned to me with a look on her face that said I had just asked something strange – even though I had not.

"What is it?" I said. "Why do you look at me in that way?"

"My mother says a man should never ask a lady her age."

"Is it so?" I questioned, not having heard of such a custom before. "It seems a normal thing to ask, does it not?"

Heather shrugged. "Actually it does. My mom just really likes following rules. Anyway. I'm twenty-two. How about you?"

Twenty-two. I could hear that she spoke numbers, but I did not quite understand them. "I'm ten and ten three," I told her. "And you are – can you say it again? Two and –"

"Ten and ten and what?!" She giggled. "Ten and ten and three? Like – twenty-three, you mean?"

Yes, she was definitely foreign. Even the Angles spoke of ages and amounts in the way we did in the North.

We went back and forth as we gathered wood for the fire, until we came to understand that she was only a single winter younger than me – and she seemed as surprised by the fact as I was. When I told her she appeared to be much younger than ten and ten and two, she responded that it was actually I who appeared older than my age.

Strangers though we were, she was one of those people it's easy to be with. Some people – regardless of their sex – are difficult. The usual small misunderstandings breed confusion rather than amusement, and they seem to insist on making themselves difficult. Heather and I collecting kindling were not like that. I was about to remark upon it when I caught sight of something moving out of the corner of my eye and flung myself to the ground – taking her with me.

"What –" she began to speak, and I put my hand over her mouth.

"Shhh. There's someone there – up the beach."

I lifted my head just above the sea grasses, and squinted my eyes. There was someone there – three someones. They were not my people, though – and they were not armed. One of them carried a basket slung across his arm. Angles. They were gathering oysters from the beach. I took my hand from Heather's mouth and cautioned her to stay low. Unarmed Angles or not, I was in enemy territory – and it seemed increasingly likely that my companion was, too. Remaining hidden was the only thing to do.

"Who is it?"

"Stay down!" I repeated, more forcefully that time. "If they're on the beach there's probably another village nearby, and Jarl's son or not, I don't know how many of them I could take on alone."

Heather lowered herself again and peered at the figures on the beach. And then she peered at me, studying my face as I had done hers when she was in her faint.

I caught her looking at me the same way a few more times as we made our way back into the woods, and each time I expected her to say something – but she did not.

When we found a place off the path, and I thought of the possible proximity not just of the Angles but of my father and brother and our men – their men – it occurred to me that it might not be wise to light a fire.

"The day is warm," I told Heather. "It's probably best we have no fire while the sun shines – I did not think carefully enough about the smoke, nor the fact that I am now alone."

It was true. Even as I walked with the girl – and no other companions – it seemed a part of me still believed I was a member of a company of warriors from the North. A company of warriors from the North is one thing – a powerful thing, able to move at will through an ill-defended land. One warrior from the North, however, in that same foreign land – that is quite another thing. I had to be careful. I had to stop making decisions like I was still one of many, and like there were still five ten's worth of swords at my back.

"What about the smoke?" Heather asked.

"Mmm?" I looked up, lost in thought once more.

"What about the smoke? Won't it just blow away?"

"It will," I told her. "That's exactly why I don't think we should have a fire – the smoke will blow away and give our location to anyone who happens to pass by on the beach – or sail by in the coastal waters."

She was giving me that look again – the one that seemed to suggest she might think me crazy. "And why don't we want anyone to know we're here?"

I chuckled. "You look at me as if I am dull-witted, girl, and you ask question like that? Did you not just see my own brother and father chasing me down? What do you suppose they will do if they find us? Invite us to share their venison?"

Instead of answering, she picked up one of the twigs we had gathered and began to break it into smaller pieces, setting them beside her knee as she went. And then, a short while later, she asked what the people on the beach had been doing.

"The Angles? They were gathering oysters from the rocks for their supper."

I was glad of her presence. I would have been glad of her presence back in Apvik, too, for it's true that a pretty girl rarely finds herself unwelcome. But I was even gladder that afternoon in the Kingdom of the East Angles.

Using one of the small knives I carried with me, strapped to my right ankle, I began to sharpen the point of a stick – which had just the right amount of dryness to be strong and just the right amount of sap still in it to be flexible – into a point. Rabbits were plentiful in the woods and my stomach was beginning to growl.

"What are you doing?"

Something about Heather's eyes made me think her quick-witted. But she had a lot of questions about obvious things, I had to admit.

"I thought I might catch a rabbit or two for supper, unless you prefer to forage for berries?"

"I thought you said the smoke from the fire would give our location away?"

I ran the fat pad of my thumb over the tip of the spear – it was still not sharp enough – and went back to peeling thin layers of it away. "Not after dark, girl. The sun will hang in the sky for a long time tonight, as it does in the summer – but you'll be grateful of something to eat when the darkness comes."

"You talk funny."

I raised my eyes from the spear to see the girl smiling at me. "Do I?" I asked. "I was just thinking that it was you who arranges her words in strange ways."

When the spear was finished, I instructed her to stay where she was and not to move or wander.

"So I should just sit here and wait?" She asked, seeming to be offended. "You don't need any help with the, uh, with the hunting?"

"Do you know how to hunt?" I asked, raising my eyebrows and suspecting I already knew the answer.

"No. I mean – no. But I could help carry something, couldn't I? Or –"

"Rabbits don't weigh very much, girl," I told her. "I see fire in your eyes but I only ask you to stay here for your own sake. If we come across the Angles – or Gods forbid any of my father's men – I can't say I'll be able to fight many of them off before numbers overwhelm me. Do you want to keep your head on your shoulders or not?"

Heather picked up another twig, which she again began to break into small pieces. "I want to keep my head on my shoulders."

"Good. Wait here. Hopefully our bellies will not be empty tonight."

***

As it was I managed to catch three rabbits. The creatures were well-fed and slow in the Kingdom, where the weather was milder all year round, and the wolves not as plentiful as in the North. And when I returned to the place where Heather waited for me, I saw that the pile of broken twig parts beside her had grown considerably.

I lay the rabbits down between us, proud as men often are at their simple offerings, and she reached out tentatively to touch one, snatching her hand away when her fingers came into contact with a small patch of bloodied fur.

"Ugh!"

"What is it?" I asked, alarmed. The rabbit was fresh-killed, surely the maggots had not had time to grow in the flesh yet?

But there were no maggots. There was nothing except fresh blood – indeed it was the blood itself that seemed to give Heather such disturbance. I watched as she wiped her fingers on her dressings, over and over again, and then dragged them through the dirt as if they had touched something especially foul.

"Do you not like rabbit?" I asked.

She turned neatly to the side, as I began to skin one of the animals, and gagged noisily. And then she kept her eyes averted from what I was doing and put her hand over her mouth. "I've never eaten rabbit. Where did you learn how to do that anyway? To just kill rabbits with spears?"

"My father taught me. Well, my uncle taught me how to choose the right stick – not too green, but not too seasoned either – and then how to carve one end into a sharp point. But my father taught me how to hunt with it."

"Why not just use a gun?"

"A what?" I asked, pulling the skin from the third and final rabbit and piercing the length of its body with a thin length of wood.

But Heather was too busy staring, wide-eyed, at my handiwork. And to my disappointment she did not seem impressed so much as she seemed disgusted. If I hadn't been so pre-occupied with other thoughts at the time I might have seen fit to be irritated at her ungratefulness.

There was a lot on her mind as well as my own, that was plain enough to see. We were both lost in our own ways – she in terms of her place on the earth and me in terms of my place with my people. We did not speak of it as the sun dipped low in the sky and the evening stole the light away from us. What was in my heart was too much, at the time, too fresh to speak of just yet – and I suspected it was the same for her. So instead I showed her how to do little things, like how to dig a fire pit in the earth and then how to select stones from the beach in the right shape with which to line the pit.

"Is this right?" She asked, holding up a rock as I kept one eye on our surroundings next to the water.

"Aye, that's right. They only need to be flat on one side."

Back at our little camp, as the first stars began to show themselves over our heads, Heather watched me peel filaments of wood fibers off a piece of sun-dried bark, and then pile it under the crude fire-making contraption I had fashioned from two larger sticks.

"You know how to do a lot of things," she said, clearly impressed, as I coaxed a small ember that had formed where I rubbed the two pieces of wood against each other into the pile of wood floss.

I picked the bundle up, cupping it between my hands, and blew on it until a flame suddenly leapt up, reflecting itself in the shining pools of her eyes as it did so.

"Quickly!" I said, placing the now-burning bundle into the kindling. "Don't let it go out!"

But she still did not seem to know what to do, so I piled the smallest pieces on myself, and then larger ones when the fire had caught, until it was burning hot and full enough to sit back.

We sat silently for a little while, transfixed by the flames, and then I asked her why she didn't know how to do any of the things that I was doing – things that did not seem especially impressive to me.

"A child of the North knows how to light a fire by the time she is six winters old," I said. "Who lights the fires where you come from if not the women? Do they not need the heat to cook?"

Heather tucked a lock of her thick, shiny hair behind one of her ears – and I found myself suddenly more taken by that little seashell of an ear than by the fire. It seemed as if it would be nothing to lean closer and press my lips against her flesh, to taste the salt of the sea air on her skin.

"We cook things in ovens," she replied.

I did not know what an oven was – probably some kind of cooking or heating device, I supposed. But surely it still needed wood – and fire – to work? Before I could question her further she reached up and touched her cheek gently, where the skin has begun to darken into a deep purple bruise.

"I'm sorry," I began, "I –"

"I might have to go to the doctor for this," she cut me off and gave me a rather pointed look. "Or I might have, if you'd hit me any harder. I might have needed stitches. I might have needed to go to the hospital! Do you know if there is a hospital nearby?"

I narrowed my eyes, not quite understanding her tone. "Do you think I do not feel guilty already?" I asked, choosing to assume that was the emotion she was trying to draw from my heart. "I see what I've done to you – and I've had enough injuries to know it must throb with pain. I'm truly sorry, Heather. If I had known it was you trying to help me and not –"

"Oh I know you're sorry," she said, waving her hand through the air in the manner of a Jarl's wife dismissing a thrall. "I just want you to tell me where the closest hospital is."

And just as she did not know how to light a fire, or skin a rabbit, or sharpen a stick into a spear, I did not know what this 'hospital' she spoke of was.

"A healer?" I asked, taking a guess at her meaning. "If there is an Angle village nearby they will probably have a healer. But I do not think it's a good –"

"Not a healer. A *hospital.*"

Was she mocking me? Something in the way she looked at me, almost goading me to answer, made me think she was.

"I do not understand why you try to make a fool of me, girl!" I told her, a little more heatedly than I intended. "I'm sorry for hurting you – indeed, I am truly sorry. But I do not understand why you must poke at me when the rabbits I have killed for us are about to fill your belly and –"

"Magnus."

I looked up at her, and saw at once that I had it wrong – she was not goading me. Thankfully, she laughed.

"Aye, girl, it's hard to read the tones in your voice!" I smiled back at her. But she was not, in fact, finished with me.

"You don't know what a hospital is, do you?"

"No," I told her, because she seemed insistent on extracting the admission from me. "No, I don't know what a hos–, a hosh– "

"Hos-pi-tal," she said quietly, taking care now not to make it seem as if she was laughing at me. "You don't have to be embarrassed. I'm not trying to make fun of –"

"I'm not embarrassed."

Heather's grin got wider then, and it was impossible not chuckle alongside her.

"Perhaps I was a little embarrassed," I admitted.

"Well don't be," she said. "I don't know how to do half the things you do – who cares if you don't know what one word means."

The rabbits, balanced above the embers and turned every little while, were ready. To my great confusion, Heather at first refused to take one, wrinkling her nose once again in disgust. I could not understand it.

"Are you not hungry?" I asked, biting off a chunk of delicious cooked meat.

But she was hungry. Hungry enough that it wasn't long before she was asking to be given a small piece. And then, after chewing it slowly for what seemed like an unnecessarily long time before swallowing, she requested another.

Still she refused to take one of the whole rabbits into her hands, so I was obliged to do it for her, tearing off pieces of the meat and passing it to her as if she were an infant or a very old person. And even then, less than a half day since I had come to know her, I already found it difficult to find her quirks – which in another may have caused irritation – anything other than sweetly charming.

When the rabbits were eaten – in truth, I could have done with more to eat but I didn't want the little foreigner to go without – we sat back, relaxing in the way it is only possible to do with a full belly. I insisted on letting the fire burn low, almost to embers alone, because I was still worried about being found. Heather, too, was still worried. I could see it in her furrowed brow.

"Tomorrow we will find our way," I told her, wanting to provide some reassurance even as I understood it was impossible. "Tomorrow I will –"

"Are you going to find your family?" She asked. "Are you going to talk to them about what happened?"

She did not understand. It must have been different where she came from. "I'm not going to find my family," I replied softly, because it was a truth I myself was still having difficulty with. "I am not going to see them ever again. Not my father, not my brother – and not my mother. Not even Apvik, my home. I will have to find my way back to the North alone, and seek a different place to make my life. It's not as bad as it could be – if I were weak or old, no one would have me. As it is I am still young and strong, so I should be able to find a –"

"Wait." She said, shaking her head slightly as if I had spoken an unbelievable thing. "Wait. *Never?* You can *never* see them again? You can never go home again? Never ever?"

So beautiful was Heather in the firelight, so compelling, that even as she asked me about the things that sent cracks through my heart, I could not help but be taken with the smallest things about her.

"Never ever," I repeated, smiling in spite of myself – and my predicament.

"I mean, I'm just trying to figure out if you mean 'never' as in never-never or –"

"Aye I know what you mean, girl. It is your way of saying it that makes me smile."

Heather sat back, also smiling now. Gods, she was fair. So fair that even as I contemplated the ruination of my life, it seemed all I could think of was her.

"So...?" She prompted, when I forgot we had been in the midst of a conversation.

"Yes," I told her. "I mean never. It is clear you are from a different place, and I assume your customs are different, too. Where I come from – the North – it is forbidden for a second son to take up a weapon against a first son. It is especially forbidden if their father is a Jarl. You saw them chasing me today – if we ever meet again, we will not part without one side or the other losing their life."

"And you said you can, um – you can never go home again, either? Why?"

"Because that's where my father – the Jarl – will be. I will be killed if I go home again."

"Do you have a mother?"

I nodded. "Yes, that is where my mother awaits our return. Her heart will be broken to hear of what's happened. But she will not go against my father, girl. She loves me, but she will not go against him. It – it isn't how it's done, in the North."

As we spoke, I pictured the things I spoke of. I pictured the look on my mother's face, the exact way the tears would spill from her eyes – eyes exactly the same dappled color as my own – when she heard of the fight between Asger and myself. I pictured Apvik, the little village on the coast where I knew every hillock, every path, every stone of the shoreline. I would never see the place again. I would never see my mother again.

I did not weep. It was not in me to weep then, as a young man. But the truth ran through my heart like a knife, causing me to bend forward and put my head in my hands. And when I did, Heather reached for me and closed her soft hand around one of my wrists, wanting to give me comfort.

And comfort she did give me. Comfort and, when I lifted my head to look at her, desire. It happened in an instant – or so it felt. All it took was the meeting of our eyes and I think we both knew it then. Did she see the same thing? Did she see the future in that moment beside the campfire? Perhaps.

I held her with my gaze, reaching down to touch the soft flesh of her arm and running my fingers up to her slender wrists where she touched me. How was it that just the feeling of her arm – her arm! – did such things to me? At once there was the familiar feeling of heaviness against my thigh, desire unfurling through me like a vine as it reaches up for the sunlight.

Heather felt it, too. She did not look away when I reached for her and did not flinch or recoil when I pulled her onto my lap. She hesitated slightly before our first kiss, when her lips trembled so close to mine I could feel her soft breath on my neck.

"What is it?" I asked, aching to taste her. "Do you hear something, girl? Is –"

"No," she whispered. "No. I just – I thought I –"

"Is it too much?" I asked, knowing enough about girls to know that the way their desires worked was not always the same as those of a man. "Is it too hasty?"

It was not too hasty for me. But I was aware that there is no such thing as 'too hasty' for a man of ten and ten and three. She stirred my blood. I felt it from the start. Had she pulled me behind the stump of that tree earlier in the day and slid her hand up under my leathers without so much as telling me her name, it would not have been too soon.

"It's not too much," she said, and her voice was slow and quiet the way the sky is slow and quiet before a summer storm blows in from the sea. "I thought it would be too much – but it isn't."

Her lips opened for me, then, and I felt as if I was drinking from a deep well of lust. She kindled in me a fire, bright and hot and all-consuming, and when I moved to pull her dressings off over her head, she helped me.

"Gods," I breathed, when she sat naked-from-the-belly-up on my lap and I saw that her body matched her face for its perfection. I reached up with one hand, almost overcome with reverence to touch such unmarked flesh as Heather's, and drew my fingers under the bottom curve of one of her breasts. And as the nipple tightened in front of my eyes, without being directly touched, I stiffened under my leathers.

Chapter 9: Heather

I thought I had known desire before that night on the bare, warm earth in the forest with Magnus. I thought I had known the need of a woman for a man. I'd wanted it before, with boys. I'd thrilled to the feeling of being undressed, or kissed hard, or fucked. But whatever it was the man from the North drew out of me, it came from a deeper place than any those who came before him had reached. When he ran his fingers along the underside of my breast – slowly and while looking me right in the eyes – I gasped with what it awoke in my body. Warmth flooded my belly and, when I moved my hips slightly so I could better feel him against me, I felt that my panties were slick.

I looked down, almost in awe, as his fingers slid up, up to my nipple and then over it, his thumb nudging it back and forth until I reached out for his shoulders, pulling him to me, desperate for more.

And the whole time, Josh Muller was further from my mind than he had ever been. I felt none of the old fear. With each touch, Magnus made me hunger for more.

I smiled when he ducked his head and drew my nipple – the one he had teased and played into a state of such oversensitivity it bordered on painful when he withdrew his touch – into his mouth. I didn't smile because anything was funny. I smiled because I couldn't believe what he was doing, and because I loved it so much.

My fingers wove themselves into his dark blond hair and my mouth fell open.

"Oh," I breathed, as his warm, wet mouth sent a bolt of pure lust straight down between my legs. If he didn't stop, he might make me come right there, just like that.

It didn't matter where I was anymore. The fact that an ocean had appeared in upstate New York was no longer my concern. All that mattered was Magnus. And me. And the things he was doing to me.

His hands were big and the skin felt rough against my breasts as he caressed them, squeezing gently, stroking his fingers over each curve until it almost set my teeth on edge to have my pants – and panties – still between us.

We seemed to reach for my fly at the same time, but the jeans were too tight to pull off. It was only with some effort that Magnus' fingers found themselves slipping down, into my panties, between my slippery folds until I was burying my face in his neck and clutching at his shoulders.

He knew what he was doing, too. He didn't spend five minutes rubbing my labia, as one unfortunate boyfriend had seemed to think was the key to unlocking my orgasmic potential. No. Magnus seemed to sense exactly where I needed to be touched, and how. He almost pushed two fingers inside me – and I wanted him inside me so badly I whimpered when he took them out again. But what he did next, using my own wetness to trace light circles around my clit until I was rocking my hips frantically down against him, almost pushed me over the edge. I felt something opening deep in my belly, a door to some essential part of me swinging wide and the orgasm I could feel building in my core – coaxed along on Magnus' expert fingers – rushing through it.

But just as I was about to throw my head back and let the wave of bliss take me, he stopped, taking his hand away and pulling me back in for another kiss.

"No," I panted, beyond the point where I cared about looking desperate. "Magnus, no. Please –"

He stopped kissing me and pulled away, just far enough to see my face.

"I like the way you say my name," he told me, kissing me again, curling his tongue up underneath my own and then stopping again. "I can hear how much you need me in the way you say it, girl."

I tightened my legs, knees bent and wrapped around his hips, around him, grinding my body against his until he exhaled heavily and sank his fingertips into my ass, pulling me down even harder.

"How do I take these off?!" He asked a moment later, when my jeans once again proved almost impossible to remove. I lay back and lifted my ass up off the ground, hooking my fingers into the waistband and pushing them down. Magnus helped, and we yanked and pulled until they finally, finally came off. And along with the jeans went my panties, soaking wet with what he was doing to me.

When I went to sit up again, to pull myself back into the one place on earth I wanted to be – his lap – he stopped me.

"Not yet," he smiled, gently pushing me back down. "I want to see you. Show yourself to me, girl. Show me what's mine."

There was no showy machismo in his tone, no theatre. Magnus wanted me to show him what was 'his' because he knew already that it was. And so did I.

Warm beside the fire, my skin lit with the glow from the flames, I allowed my thighs to fall open. Sensing my vulnerability, loving it, he reached up and took one of my hands in his own as his eyes took me in from neck to breasts to belly and then... lower.

"Gods," he whispered, sitting up and beginning to work frantically at the ties that seemed to hold his leather garment around his waist. I stayed where I was, on my back, knowing what was coming and pleased, in some primal way, to witness the feverishness of his lust, to know that I was the cause of it.

What can I say about the first time I saw Magnus without any clothes on? He was – I didn't have any words for him at the time, because there was no room in my mind for words. All the room available in my body, mind and soul was his, taken up by his broad, muscular torso, the little half-smile that played on his lips as he saw how I looked at him and the full, thick, glistening length of him as he cast his leathers to the side.

I moved to sit up when I saw him in full – and how much he needed me. But he just reached out and put a hand on one of my knees, pushing it to the side just a little, opening me. I looked up at him, realizing even as I spread my legs and welcomed him between my thighs that I had never been so willing, never so ready as I was at that moment.

"You need it," Magnus whispered, settling himself deliciously, torturously between my legs without putting himself inside me, and then chuckling and taking my hand away when I tried to do it for him. "Not yet, girl. Tell me. Tell me how you need it."

"I need it!" I told him at once, wrapping my arms around his neck, pulling him frantically down against me. "I – I need it! Please..."

But he laughed again – a deep laugh that rumbled away through the night air – and sat up so he could look down at my body again with a look of such hunger in his eyes I thought I might be in danger of being devoured.

Not that I would have said no.

I arched my back and opened my legs even wider, until I saw his resolve shake. And when I did, I reached down, pushing my fingertips over the shiny, swollen tip of him until his breath came out in a long sigh.

"Magnus," I said breathlessly as his eyes closed. "Magnus..."

Whatever inner resources he had been using to hold back snapped as I whispered and stroked his own wetness down the length of his cock. He took himself in his hand, leaning down to kiss me as he pushed just the head into me, and then asked me again to tell him that I needed him.

"I need you," I cried softly against his muscled shoulder, my body almost trembling with anticipation of what it was about to receive. "I need you. I need you, please, I –"

And then I got him. Every sweet inch, all at once, until my head was lolling back in the dirt and my mouth was whimpering his name over and over and over.

"Voss," Magnus breathed into my neck – a word I had never heard before. He dragged it out – 'vossssss' – as he pushed himself all the way into me, and then he slid his tongue between my lips and kissed me deeper and dirtier than I had ever been kissed before.

He went slowly at first – I say he because it was his doing, not mine. I wanted more, right from the start. I lifted my hips up to him and put my hands on his ass, trying to get more of him – and faster – but he was the one who held back. It meant that the mountain I was so eager to rush to the top of was scaled more slowly, more carefully. And even as I begged him and bit his earlobes and kissed his thick, muscled neck, I knew he was in charge. I knew I was going to come when *he* wanted me to come. And that drove me almost out of my mind with lust.

"Is it too much?" He asked, when my shaky little cries reached a new pitch. "Am I not giving you what you want, girl? Is that it? Perhaps you are still hungry and it's another rabbit that you want, and not –"

"No! No – I want you – I want –"

"Is this what you want?" He crooned into my ear, just before plunging himself into me again – deeply, completely – and holding himself there for a few seconds.

I couldn't even speak to answer, all the air being pushed out of my lungs with the sheer force of him. And then he did it again, slow and deep, and I felt the first little twitches inside me, the first little ripples of what was to come.

He was close, too, even as he did a much better job of maintaining control than I did. His eyes were closing with each thrust, and when they opened again they were glazed, almost unseeing.

"Magnus!" I squeaked as he thrust his hips down again and then I suddenly found myself close to the airy peak of the mountain. "Magnus! Please!"

That was the end of his control, right there – that moment. He looked down at me once more before placing his forearms on the ground on either side of me, bracing himself. And then he began to fuck me harder, and faster, until very quickly it was all too much and I was suddenly overcome by the hot, sweet bliss that exploded deep inside me and sent its shockwaves out into every part of my body.

"Voss," Magnus said again, his brow shiny with sweat and his jaw set. "Heather, oh, voss, ohhhh..."

And then he was coming, before I'd even finished, as I was still tightening around him, drawing it out of him as he let himself spill into me. His whole body stiffened. His hands – one buried in my hair and one clamped onto my shoulder, pushed my body down so he could thrust deeper and. He opened his mouth against my neck, shouting his pleasure into my flesh.

Afterwards, we lay side by side in the dirt beside the fire, its light revealing the glistening sheen on our naked flesh as we caught our breath. It had never been like that for me before, the build-up never so tense, never so perfectly played. And the orgasm – my God. I was thankful he didn't ask me for anything as we lay together, recovering, because I would definitely have given it to him, whatever it was. My heart. My soul. Anything.

***

I woke at what seemed to be dawn – unusual for me – and immediately sat up in a panic when I remembered where I was – and saw that I was alone.

My clothing lay scattered around and the leather vest-type thing that Magnus had been wearing, as well as the length of leather that he had worn tied around his waist, were wrapped around me.

"The dew fell in the night," a voice came suddenly from behind. He hadn't abandoned me. "You shivered in your sleep, so I covered you with my dressings – your own aren't fit to warm an infant."

I noticed then – and to my great and admittedly somewhat childish amusement, that he was completely naked. He did not seem to be concerned about it, though, as he unwrapped what I saw was my t-shirt and let about eight oysters fall out of it and onto the ground.

"No rabbits," he said apologetically. "I should have woken earlier and –"

"Magnus?"

"What?" He looked up, perplexed as to why I was interrupting. "What is it, girl? Are you not hungry?"

I chuckled. "You're naked."

"I am," he agreed. "Must I comment on your powerful skills of observation, is that it? Do you want to be praised before you eat the breakfast I have found for you?"

I sat up and moved closer to him, nestling my face into his warm shoulder. "Did you just go to the beach and gather oysters naked?"

"What is this concern with my nakedness?!" He replied, taking one of the oysters in his hand and nudging the top of his small knife just underneath the lip of it. "The day is already warm, girl – it's summer. Why would I –"

"But what if somebody saw you?" I giggled. "What if the Angles –"

"It's probably best if they do see me naked, without the dressings of a man of the North. What is this worry for my dressings, anyway? Come on, get up, you should eat something."

But I did not get up. I was still in that place where I had gone the night before, the one where no man had ever even done a little of what Magnus did to me. I smiled to myself as I held tight to his shoulder, feeling safe with him, cared for. It was an unfamiliar state, and all the more intoxicating for it.

Even the way he shucked the oysters seemed to be wonderful, more proof of his superiority over all other men. He moved the knife skillfully, carefully, pushing it for each oyster just under the shell and twisting it sharply when it got to a certain point, leveraging the thick shells open and then setting the two halves down next to each other before moving onto the next.

Which is not to say that the oysters themselves looked appetizing. They looked anything but. Gray, wet, slimy-looking things they were. I was hungry, but looking down at my breakfast I found myself wishing that there was more rabbit.

"What is it you eat in your country?" Magnus asked, laughing, when he saw the look on my face. "Do you have roast pork for every meal, is that it? You shrank from the rabbits – although you enjoyed them in the end, with me to pull the meat from the bones for you – and now you shrink from the oysters?"

I did not tell him what I ate in 'my country,' though, because something had occurred to me – something that would explain the seemingly inexplicable fact of where I was and how I got there. And if that something was true, then I knew Magnus would not recognize most of the things I could tell him I ate, anyway. So instead, driven by the simple feeling of wanting to please him, I picked up one of the half-shells and brought it to my nose, sniffing.

It smelled like the ocean. I looked down. Up close, it looked even slimier. I pressed my lips together so I would not gag, and looked up at him.

"Do you know what we say of oysters in the North, girl?"

"What?"

"We say that eating an oyster is like pleasing a sea-maid with your mouth."

"A sea-maid?"

"A sea-maid, yes. Half fish, half woman. Do you not –"

"Oh! You mean a mermaid."

Magnus looked at me, and there was something in his gaze that made me soften. "A mermaid, is it? Yes, well, as it is – to eat an oyster is to know what it is to be intimate with a mermaid. Perhaps if you eat your oysters I'll please you with my mouth and see if they have infused your flesh with the taste of the waves?"

Until that day, I don't think anyone had ever paid attention to me the way Magnus did. It sounds a ridiculous thing to say, but I don't mean that no one had ever paid any attention to me before. They had, obviously. Boys included. But the attention of Magnus was different – intently focused on me alone, as if his ears had been tuned specifically to the frequency of my voice, and his eyes to the specific colors that made up my lips and my eyes and my hair. It wasn't something he spoke of or told me, it was merely the feeling I got from being with him. It put me in mind of sunshine, and of myself as a plant that has been kept in the shade and suddenly placed outdoors to unfurl its leaves and drink in the golden rays.

I had my suspicions – very strong suspicions by then – about what was going on. If they were true, I wasn't even sure I cared, as long as I kept being allowed to bask in the warmth of Magnus' sweet solicitousness.

So I ate the oyster because he wanted me to eat it and because even then, although it had not been so long at all, I trusted that he wouldn't ask me to do anything that would cause me harm or discomfort. And he watched me gently, encouragingly, smiling with approval when I clamped my lips shut as the first briny taste filled my mouth and I found myself having to resist the strong urge to spit it out immediately.

"You're doing well," he commented as tears of effort and nausea welled up in my eyes, and it was those words that allowed me to close my eyes and swallow and then look up at him, proud of myself.

"And another," he indicated, pointing to the next one. "You need to eat, girl. Who knows how much ground we will need to cover today, and with no horses or ships? You need to keep your strength up."

"What about you?" I asked. "You're bigger than me. You need –"

"I ate half the oysters on the beach before you woke. Come now, at least two more. Do you not like the taste?"

I concentrated on the tastes in my mouth – salty, fishy, oceanic. They were unfamiliar but not exactly unpleasant. It was the texture that bothered me. "It's the feeling of it in my mouth," I said. "It's slimy. It's like – it's like snot."

"It's nothing more than brine," Magnus replied, not dismissing what I'd said but offering another perspective – one he hoped would lead me to eating more oysters. "The wetness is the sea itself, nothing more. Try another one."

So I tried another one – something I knew I never would have done without him there to urge me on. And the second was not as bad as the first. I consciously thought of the juices as seawater, and it made the whole thing easier to swallow. By the third, although I could not yet honestly say I was a fan of oysters, I was beginning to understand why some people liked them so much.

"Good," Magnus said as I swallowed that third one, taking the shell out of my hands and tossing it into the woods. "With luck we'll find some more rabbits – perhaps even a deer – today."

And then he went to stand up and I saw at once that he was – excited.

"Oh!" I said, covering my mouth with one of my hands to muffle a little sighing giggle.

He turned back to me and then followed my gaze down to his own loins. I had never met a man so thoroughly comfortable with his own nakedness before.

"It's your fault," he commented, catching my eye with a grin. "Something about the way you ate those oysters for me. I was just thinking I do not know if I have ever enjoyed anything so much in my life as I just enjoyed watching you eat those oysters, Heather."

A swooning, swooping sensation ran hotly through my belly at his words, and the look in his eyes. I needed him again. At once. I needed to please him as I had the previous night. He knew it, too, because he immediately tossed the sword in his hand to the ground and moved to kneel down in front of me. Only I stopped him before he could do so, looking up from where I sat to take in his full glory.

It was a bold thing for me to do, what I did then. I used to talk about it with friends back in L.A. – giving head. What boys were worthy of this favor, at what point it might be alright to do it for someone else etc. etc. But there was no such weighing or measuring with Magnus. With him, it happened as naturally as the sun rising in the sky over our heads. I put my hands flat on his thick, muscular thighs and pushed my lips gently over the head of him until he leaned his head back and moaned full-throatedly into the warm morning woods.

He was big – even bigger, it seemed, now that he was in my mouth – and I was not the expert I had sometimes pretended to be to my friends back home. But somehow it was OK and I didn't worry about doing something wrong or not being able to please him the 'right' way.

Perhaps it was his obvious, immediate pleasure? The fact that I could feel him growing and stiffening in my mouth as he turned his eyes down to watch? The way his voice became deeper and slower as he whispered my name, stroking my hair off my face and tucking it behind my ears?

Whatever it was, it filled me with the unabashed need to go further. When I felt comfortable with the tip of him in my mouth I opened my lips a little wider, to take more of him in. At once, the salty taste of his excitement flooded the back of my tongue and his fingers tightened on my head.

"Heather," he breathed, drawing himself out of me and then pushing back in again, going a little further that time. "Gods, girl. Gods –"

I popped him out of my mouth and ran the tip of my tongue down his length, and then up again and back down, until I had covered every inch. I took him in my hand and ran the shiny head over my cheek and over my closed lips before opening them and taking it in again. And when I caught his eye that time, he spoke in a ragged voice.

"If you keep looking at me in that way you're going to finish me," he said, stroking my cheek tenderly with his thumb. "You're going to – oh, *voss*, girl – you're going to – finish –"

I loved hearing his voice catching in his throat, feeling the intensity building, knowing what was coming. It spurred me on, driving my lips further down his shaft and my tongue underneath, where I swirled it back and forth in a way that made Magnus' whole body tighten.

"Voss," he breathed, through clenched teeth, and I felt him get exquisitely hard in my mouth. "Voss, Heather. Oh – girl, oh – ohhhh..."

I didn't break eye contact when he came. I gazed up the whole time, telling him with my eyes that I wanted what he was giving me, that there was nothing so sweet as swallowing his warmth as he spilled it on the back of my tongue.

And after he was done, I bit my lower lip and grinned with pride when he stumbled a step back and then sat down, commenting breathlessly that he thought it would be the next day before he could walk again.

***

Magnus was angry when he woke up and saw, as he said, how high the sun was in the sky.

"I should not have slept for so long!" He scolded himself, moving around our little clearing in the woods and gathering various items, wrapping his leathers around his waist before turning to me.

"We cannot stay in the woods forever, Heather – as much as the idea appeals to me now as I look upon your face again. But no, we cannot stay. You must go home, as you say. And I must –"

He paused.

"You must – what?" I asked gently. "Where will you go if you can't go home?"

"Back to the North," he replied, a little brusquely. "I think I might go the long way back – south to Kent and then sail across the channel on a trade-ship to the land of the Franks. Eventually, I'll find my way north again, to a different place, one far from Apvik, where no one will know my name or whose son I am."

"Just like that?" I asked, as we looked around to see if we had left anything and pushed our way through the underbrush to reach the path once more. "You'll just walk south and sail across – what did you say? The channel? With a trader?"

"Yes," he shrugged. "What else is there for me to do? I cannot stay here – this is the Kingdom of the East Angles, and no man of the North is welcome here. And I cannot return to Apvik. What would you have me do, girl?"

I stood looking at him on the path, just before we turned to head towards the sea again, and wondered if I was crazy.

"Will you come with me?" I asked, taking his hand. "It's not far – just to where I saw you fight with your brother – I want to check something."

"You want to what? Girl, must I say it again? This is the land of the Angles, and we already know their dwellings are close to here. Why would you want to seek trouble out? Surely it will find us without our helping it along."

Magnus was clothed again, although not above the waist. His hair was pulled off his face and tied at the nape of his neck with a length of leather. I had never seen anyone with a hair tie like that before. I had never met anyone who thought nothing of walking naked in public. I had never met anyone who did not know what a gas station or a hospital was. And the whole time I had been in the new place, I had not heard a single car, nor spotted a single plane in the sky.

"What is it?" He asked when he saw I was agitated. "I'm sorry for my irritation – it is not your fault. It was easy to lose myself with you last night – and then just now, before I fell into sleep for much longer than I should have. But in truth, worries crowd my thoughts. I do not know if I will live, girl. And knowing you as I do now, even for this brief time – it makes me want to live perhaps more than I ever have."

I had to ask. Either he would answer yes, and we could find our ways home – and maybe even continue to see each other. Or he would answer no, and I would have to go further, ask more questions, dig deeper. I looked up into his eyes, the lashes lit just then with a slender ray of sunlight that had found its way through the heavy canopy of branches.

"Have you ever heard of the United States of America?" I asked.

He had not. Even before he shook his head and told me no, I could see the lack of recognition on his face. "The Unites States of – of what? Of Amri–"

"America."

"America?"

"Yes."

"No."

There it was. I stepped forward and rested my cheek on his chest, afraid because I knew by then that I was not dreaming.

"What is that place?" He asked, sensing my turmoil. "Is it your home?"

I turned my face up to look at him so my chin lay against his chest. "Yes, it is. And can you tell me something else?"

"Just ask it, Heather – anything I can do for you, I will."

"What year is it?"

"What year?" He repeated. "I do not understand what you ask. It's summer, the middle of the year."

"You don't have a number for it?" I continued. "You don't have a way to tell one year from the next?"

Magnus frowned, confused. "An amount? For the year? Only in relation to events, girl. I can say since that since I was born, ten and ten and three winters have passed."

"But you can't say, for example, that it is 1983?"

He could not. I was in a place where they did not have numbers for their years, and they did not have planes or hospitals or sneakers. A place where they had not heard of the USA. And so I knew that I was not just in a place that was far in distance from River Falls, New York, but also one that was far in time. At least that was the working theory, one I had been working on since the previous day. Those dizzy spells in the woods – what if they were more than dizzy spells? What if I was – somehow – passing through time?

"Please," I urged Magnus. "I just need to check one thing. It's close. Will you come with me?"

"I do not seem to be able to say no to you," he mused, more to himself than to me. And then I took his hand and began to lead him back down the path into the woods...

Chapter 10: Magnus

"Don't be afraid."

I smiled indulgently and told her not to worry, that I was not afraid.

And then I was suddenly suspended in darkness blacker than any night, with only her hand in mine to orient myself, and a feeling like I could not quite draw the breath into my lungs. At the moment where I was about to make a liar of myself and my pronunciations of being unafraid, the light suddenly came back and I looked up from where I was lying on the ground, next to Heather.

We were in a wood, but not the one we had just been in. The trees were taller, sparser and –

I leapt to my feet, drawing my sword from its sheath and turning towards the direction where the sound – what was it? A beast? A man? – came from. A roaring filled my ears, of such loudness that it seemed to be all around me, as if it were not even coming from a set place. I whirled around to find Heather, to pull her close to me, and saw that she was relaxed, unworried.

"Come," I urged, taking her wrist. "Do you not hear the beast, girl? Come stand with me, I have my sword."

But Heather just looked around – up into the trees, behind her shoulder, to each side – and she did not seem afraid.

"I was right," she whispered in awed tones. "Oh my God – I was *right*."

And then, before I could even ask her what it was she spoke of, she reached up, took my hand, and tumbled back into the breathless darkness with me. And that time, when the light filled my eyes again, I stepped away from her.

"What was that place?" I asked, looking around to confirm that we were no longer in the other wood. "What have you – where did you take me, girl?"

She must have seen the suspicion on my face because she reached for me again and I snatched my hand away before she could touch it.

"Fine," she said. "I probably shouldn't have done that. I'm sorry. I just – I didn't think it was going to work. I thought that surely it was something else, that I was wrong. But – I'm not wrong. That's where I come from, you know. I can go back there right now if you like, if you cannot trust me now. Just let me know and I'll go. But if not, I'd like to stay here with you. I'd like at least to know that you're on your way home, that you're safe."

"I'm as safe as I'll ever be again," I replied, almost angered by the casual tones with which she spoke of leaving – even though I knew I had no claim on her.

It did not seem possible that she meant me harm. She stood in front of me with such concern in her eyes, such truth behind her words. I reached out and drew my fingers down the side of her face that was not swollen and bruised by my own hand.

"There's nothing there for me," she said quietly, a moment later. "Where I come from, I mean. There's nothing. I have a few friends, but they'll be fine without me. I want to stay with you, Magnus – if that's alright? I don't know how to do anything, you already know that – but I can learn! And –"

Why was it such a boon to my heart to hear her saying she wanted to stay with me? I had a journey south to complete – one that would not be eased, as Heather already seemed to know, by a companion with no fighting or hunting skills. And I had not yet known her two nights – who was she to me?

The answer was that she was something. Already, she was *something* to me. Already I seemed to hang on her words – her opinions and her little thoughts on this or that – more than I hung even on the words of my most trusted warriors.

"You shall come south with me," I told her, as we both smiled with the relief of knowing we were not parting – not just yet. "I will teach you how to find a length of wood, and what type, to turn into a spear. And then I will show you how to form the point so it's not so fine it breaks off in the animal's flesh and not so dull it doesn't piece the hide."

"I don't think I can kill an animal," she replied.

We laced our fingers together and turned to walk back to the sea, before turning south. "You might find your mind changed on that point," I told her, "when you're so hungry your belly aches with it."

***

There was a feeling to that day, coming so soon as it did on the heels of the fight with my brother and the chance encounter with the beautiful girl who walked at my side along the sandy path. It was a feeling almost of being in a strange dream. I kept finding myself thinking of the way my mother would smile when I brought Heather home to meet her, and then remembering that I was not going home. That I was, in all likelihood, never going to see my mother again.

"You're sad," Heather said after we had walked in silence for a little while. She was gentle with me, I could see that part of her already. Her words did not accuse or even question – they simply observed, they cleared a space for me to speak if I wished, or not if I didn't. She made me want to take her in my arms again, lay her back in the sea-grasses and show her my happiness at being at her side. But we were still too close to where I knew my father and brother might be. And even if they had already sailed for home – something I doubted – we still had the Angles to worry about. A raid does not give the lords of the estates time to call in their men, but already I had been in the Kingdom for much longer than the time it takes to launch a raid.

"Aye," I replied, keeping myself alert to our surroundings. "I was just thinking of the smile that would mark my mother's face to meet you, girl. And as soon as I thought it I realized once more – how many times must I realize this? – that I will never see my mother again. It reminds me of almost ten winters ago, when my grandfather died. For many days, indeed for many moons

I thought of him whenever something happened to me, or whenever I had a thing to discuss with someone. Even as I knew he was gone, still my first instinct was always to run to him. When the happening is large enough, enough to shake a whole life like the wind shakes a great old tree in a storm, I see that it takes some time to get used to it, to let it sink in. And so it is still sinking in that I will never see my home or my mother again."

I was glad of the foreigner's hand in mind as I spoke those words and felt my heart swept with bleakness. When I saw her pretty face turned up to mine, and her eyes wet with tears, it was all I could do not to throw myself at her feet and beg her to remain with me for the rest of our days. She had already hinted at her own troubles in life – perhaps she would see fit to speak of them that night, after I built her a fire and killed some more rabbits for her to eat?

For the rest of my life, I remembered that walk down the coast in the land of my enemies. Just as the path upon which my feet fell marked the border between land and sea, it also marked the border between what I came to think of as the two territories of my heart – before Heather, and after Heather. Did I know it at the time? How could I? But it would be a lie to say that I didn't feel a strange momentousness to being with her, to walking south together into a new future.

We stopped not long after beginning our journey. We stopped because she reached for me, and because she was beautiful and I was stupid and young and I did not have it in me to keep refusing my own desires. Even as I knew it was dangerous to take her there, out in the open, neither of us was in mind of any dangers when my hands found their way into her dressings and down to the slippery softness of her sex, so enticing it set my jaw on edge with desire.

"We should move off the path," I said as Heather tilted her head at me, smiling, and ran her hands over her own bare breasts until I forgot we were even on a path, or that there was anything more important than what it was going to feel like to slide my body between her soft thighs.

I clutched her against me, kissing her neck with such hunger as I had never felt, and lay her down on her back. And then, just as I was about to enter her, a sound reached my ears and I froze. And so lust-crazed was I that it didn't immediately register what the sound was, although I must have heard it a thousand times by then.

It was the sound of a sword clanking against another weapon, the way they often do if a man has another knife or dagger strapped to his waist.

"What –" Heather started, and then didn't get to finish because it all came back to me in a rush and I leapt towards the spot where my own sword lay in the grass. Almost too late. A man was in the midst of reaching for it – a moment later and he would have had it, but I knocked him away with the back of my hand and grabbed my blade.

There were four of them, each armed with blades of their own. Angles in their traditional dark-stained leather and summer tunics.

"What's this?" The one I had immediately pegged as the leader asked, cocking an eyebrow at me – and then down at Heather as she lay naked a short distance away. "Couldn't make it into the woods, could you? Can't say that I blame you – look at those tits!"

Quickly, I moved my body between the men and Heather, and held my sword at the ready. Four Angles was more than one, but it was not so many that I did not feel confident in my ability to take them. They were generally badly trained, and these four didn't have the look of full warriors, or King's men.

The one who was goading me seemed oddly confident, though, and that worried me.

"Go on, look at those tits," he commented to his companions. "Not a mark on them! I think I'll fuck her first – but if you bring me two fat rabbits for my supper I'll let you have a go when I've had my fill."

Blind rage. There was no thought, then. Just rage. I stepped forward to take the man by the hair and drive my sword through his neck. And then a small cry came from behind me.

"Magnus."

Heather. Even before I turned I knew from the terror in her voice that we were in trouble. And sure enough, a fifth man had appeared, probably having hidden himself in the woods to effect the ambush – *why* had I allowed myself to let down my guard like that?! – and he had the blade of a small dagger at her throat.

"Drop your sword!" the first man bellowed, as their eyes crawled sickeningly over every bare inch of Heather's body. I looked down at her, silent and wide-eyed with fear, and then back at the men.

"Drop it! I'll cut her throat right now, bastard, if you don't drop it in –"

I dropped my sword. At once, one of the men stepped forward to pick it up.

"This is a fine blade," he commented to his leader, "this is –"

"It's a Northman's blade," came the reply. "A Northman and his wench, alone in the Kingdom? What happened, did you lose your way? Or are you two just off on your own for the afternoon, because you couldn't keep your hands off each other?"

"We should take him back to the estate," the one with the dagger to Heather's throat said. "The lord might want to –"

"Yes, yes, we'll take him back to Lord Eldred. But before that –"

He took a step towards Heather, then, and began to fumble with the leather ties at his waist. I knew what he and his men intended. And I knew I was not going to let it happen.

Luckily, the Angles were even more poorly disciplined than I myself had just been. The man standing over Heather moved to pull his tunic off over his head, immediately revealing the dagger strapped to the back of his waist. I didn't even think. I stepped forward, slipped the weapon out of its leather sheath and leapt in front of him before any of them had time to understand what I was doing.

The man with the knife to Heather's precious neck didn't even realize I had a weapon until I'd plunged it right up to the hilt into his own. He fell back onto the grass, pouring blood from the wound and making an angry gurgling sound in his throat.

I lifted the dagger up, pointing it at the four remaining Angles as I dragged Heather back to me. Four of them, one of me. Four swords, one dagger. One of them bellowed angrily, running at me, and I easily rolled out of the way of his clumsy attack, running the dagger's blade neatly across the back of his ankle, which turned his bellows to howls.

The remaining three men were not so willing to help me best them. Their leader, seeing that my real concern was for Heather and not for myself, did the intelligent thing and snatched her away from me as I defended against another attack. And that time, when I heard her scream, I saw that the threat was no longer rape but death.

I flung the dagger to the ground and showed them my empty hands.

Chapter 11: Heather

It didn't take long, as I found myself dragged naked down a path through the woods in a time that was nothing like my own, to come to the conclusion that I might have made a very big mistake when I decided to stay. The men who took us captive held the tip of a sword against my left breast for the entirety of the time it took to bind Magnus' hands and tie a blindfold around his head. They took no such precautions with me, recognizing as they did that I was absolutely no threat to anyone.

And soon we arrived at what looked to be a small, enclosed village surrounded on all sides by stone walls.

The man who had his hand clamped around my upper arm, and whose putrid breath I had been inhaling for the past twenty minutes, came to a stop in front of a tall, sturdy-looking wooden gate. He leaned in close to me after calling to someone on the other side that it was Hringwyn and his men returning with two prisoners, and promised that he was going to give me a night I would not soon forget. And then he slid one grubby hand down my back and squeezed my ass hard enough to bring tears springing to my eyes.

After what had happened to me back in L.A., I was surprised at how calm I was. But really, what choice did I have? My life was in danger. A man had already been killed, blades had already been held to my neck and my breast. I wanted to survive. To that end, it was as if the calm that lay over me was instinctive, the freeze of a rabbit when a predator appears.

As the gate was opened and Magnus and I dragged through it, I saw that the place was quite crowded. Eyes fell upon my naked body, but with my arms being held I could not cover myself.

"Who is it?" A tall man with a crooked nose and a very large sword asked Hringwyn.

"A Northman. A Northman and a pretty wench – and just as soon as the lord decides what to do with him, I'm going to need some time alone with her."

"A Northman?" The first man asked. "Alone? Are you sure? Why didn't you –"

"Bring the lord," Hringwyn replied heatedly. "I don't have to answer questions from anyone but him."

It wasn't a military encampment. I could see women carrying buckets of water to and fro, and small children in ragged tunics chasing each other around. A few animals – dogs, a large spotted pig – roamed freely. How were we going to get out of this? I had to get a weapon to Magnus. But before that, I had to free him from the ties around his wrists and the blindfold that covered his eyes. And how was I going to do that with two men on either side of me, one of whom had expressed repeated interest in raping me?

So far, I'd been passive. And I would continue to be passive, so long as there was hope of escape. But if it came to what I could see Hringwyn wanted it to come to, I would not be passive any longer.

"Hringwyn!" A voice suddenly boomed as we all turned in the direction from which it came. "What interesting things have you brought from your patrols for me today?"

A man approached, and I knew at once that he must be the lord that everyone was talking about. To my relief, something about him seemed to signal a good nature – he was smiling, almost welcoming in manner. And as soon as he saw that his men had brought human captives – and that one of them was stark naked – he ordered a blanket be found so I could cover myself.

"Thank you," I whispered.

"You're welcome," the lord replied, looking at me and then back at Magnus. "I am Eldred. Why have my men seen fit to take you captive today, do you think?"

I looked around at the men the lord spoke of, but none of them chose to speak in my place.

"I don't know," I replied. "I don't –"

"Come," Eldred smiled. "Do not play games with me, girl. I see that you were naked when you arrived – I hope that Hringwyn here has not –"

"Haven't touched her!" Hringwyn said, leaving out the part where he had definitely tried to touch me, before Magnus stuck a knife into his friend's neck. "Her friend here attacked us and killed Swidhelm, that is why –"

"We didn't attack you!" I cut in, desperate for Lord Eldred to hear the truth. "Hringwyn was going to –"

A bright, sharp pain suddenly radiated outwards from my cheek, the one that was already swollen and sore, and I looked up to see one of Hringwyn's men standing there, having delivered the blow. Seconds later, the sensation of warmth running down my neck told me that he'd broken the skin.

"Don't look at me to save you," Eldred said, raising his eyebrows, surprised, when I glanced towards him to see if he was going to do anything. "If it's true your companion here has killed one of my men, you'll find no mercy in my heart for either of you."

There was blood in my mouth, I could taste it. I'd been hit very hard – hard enough that my ears were still ringing. Not hard enough to shut me up.

"He was going to rape me," I said quietly. "Hringwyn was going to rape me."

Everyone turned to the lord, too see what he would say. He looked at me critically. "And is this man your husband?" He asked, gesturing to Magnus.

"N–"

I didn't even get the word out before Magnus finally spoke, cutting me off. "Yes. Yes, I am her husband. Your men meant to rape her, Lord, surely you –"

"We found them fucking in the middle of the coastal path!" Hringwyn broke in. "Like a pair of dogs! You saw her as well as I did, Lord – you saw her body. Surely you cannot blame a man for being tempted when her husband – if that is what he really is – allows his wife to display herself so brazenly to –"

The sound of Magnus struggling came from behind us, but the men holding me would not allow me to turn and look. A few seconds later there was a loud thud, followed by a groan. They'd hit him.

"Fuck you!" I yelled at Hringwyn, seething with rage at his lies, at his making it seem like Magnus and I were in any way at fault for their attack. "We didn't do anything to you!"

Hringwyn gave me a sneering smile, revealing a set of rotting teeth so foul they almost turned my stomach. "Lord," he said, addressing Eldred. "He's a Northman – what else needs to be said? He's a Northman who killed one of your men. Surely we should hang him tonight, before he has time to plot an escape?"

Lord Eldred looked at me, and then behind me, at Magnus. "As it must be, Hringwyn. Lock her in the captive's hut and hang him before sundown – and then put his head on display at the main gate. If his countrymen come looking for him –"

"No!" I screeched, panicked, my heart beating hard and fast in my chest. Surely Lord Eldred didn't mean it? Just like that? Without even giving Magnus or I a chance to plead our case? "NO! Please! We didn't do anything wrong! We –"

Eldred took a step towards me, shaking his head. "Quiet down, girl – surely you can't be surprised that a captured Northman will be hung? Do you know what they do to us, when they come upon one of us alone in the woods? Do you know what they would do to a girl like yourself, if they found her wandering by herself? Your Northman – for he is not your husband, that I can see – is surely responsible for more defiled girls and murdered boys than any of my men here."

And then he turned, without waiting for or expecting me to respond, and gestured to Hringwyn. "Don't wait until evening – do it now, get it over with."

He began to walk away. I jerked away from the men who were still holding me tight, and twisted my body to kick out at them. "NO!" I screamed again at Lord Eldred's back. "NO! He didn't kill anyone! He SAVED one of you! He saved a child! He's alone because his own people tried to kill him for it! They tried to –"

Another blow glanced off my already-bloodied cheek and my body sagged forwards as I almost lost consciousness.

"No," I mumbled, a few seconds later. "No, please, no, no. He saved a child. A little boy. I saw it. I saw –"

Another blow, hard enough to knock the rest of my words out of my mouth, to be replaced with a low moan of pain. I watched, blinking and disoriented with being hit, as Magnus was dragged past me. His body was limp – they must have hit him on the head and knocked him out – and his leather-clad feet dragged along the ground behind him. I watched, my stomach churning with horror, as someone handed a long rope to Hringwyn and he threw it over the branch of a tree.

"He saved one of you!" I moaned, my words barely understandable by then because my cheek was so swollen. "He saved a child! I saw him –"

And then, as three men struggled to hold Magnus upright enough for Hringwyn to begin looping the rope over his head, a man stepped forward. He was slightly built, and a mass of gray hair hung in his eyes. But he looked at Magnus for a few seconds and then turned to Hringwyn.

"It's true," said. " I see now that it's him – this Northman saved my boy from his own people."

"What!?" Hringwyn shouted, disbelieving. "When – Taber, what do you speak of?! This man, you say? *This* man saved your boy?"

Lord Eldred, hearing the commotion, returned. "What's all this?" He asked. "What did I hear? Does this man defend the Northman?"

Taber bowed his head low, but his voice was clear. "Yes," he replied. "The Northmen took the little hamlet just north of here, where I was visiting my sister to bring her some tallow. One of their party took little Eadward and swung their sword to take off his head – this man stopped it. He blocked the blow with his own blade. I swear it my lord, I saw it with my own eyes. In truth I thought they'd killed him for it – they chased him into the woods after it happened and –"

"And is the boy – Eadward – alright?"

"He's had a fright, Lord, but he's not hurt. This was the man who saved him – I swear it."

Lord Eldred stood looking at Hringwyn and the other men for a few seconds, as they waited for his instructions. I stared at Magnus, willing him to wake up, to speak, to confirm that yes, he had saved the child. He did not wake up.

But Eldred, after a few minutes contemplation, simply nodded his head at Hringwyn. "Untie him. Bring him to the healers to treat the wound to his head. When he is fit to speak I'll talk to him myself. And let the girl go with him."

"But –" Hringwyn started, only to shut up immediately when one of the men at the lord's side gave him a stern shake of the head.

"Do it," Eldred said. "Now. And if I hear that any of you has so much as laid a finger on the girl, it'll be your own heads. Do you understand?"

***

A few minutes later I found myself in one of the little huts inside the village walls with Magnus, still unconscious, lying between myself and an older woman who was missing most of her teeth.

"They've taken his senses," she observed, running her bony fingers over his brow and then parting his hair to look for the source of the blood that ran slowly down his forehead.

"Will he be OK?" I asked, even though it was difficult for me to believe that this wizened old woman in a hut made of straw and mud could have anything truly useful to say on the topic of Magnus' wellbeing. "Will he wake up soon?"

The woman reached for a small wooden pot of a pale green, waxy-looking substance that, when she passed it close to me, seemed to smell herbal. And then she began to dot the substance on the wound that cut about three inches across Magnus' scalp.

"Come here," she gestured, when she was done. "We'll put some on your cheek, too. It's bruised – the two of you look strong enough but your wounds might still fester."

"Oooh," I said, shrinking away when she touched my face and a sharp pain jolted through my head.

"You can do it yourself," she offered, "if that would be easier for you. My name is Wenda, if you would like to know what to call me. And you are –?"

"I am Heather," I replied. "And he is Magnus."

"Eltha?"

"Heather."

She said my name back to me a second time, still mispronouncing it, and I could tell it was unfamiliar to her. And then she handed me the little pot of salve, and I brought it to my nose to smell. It was smelled vegetal, and was stirred through with flecks of green, but there was something else underneath it – something almost meaty. Wenda saw me wrinkle my nose.

"It is tallow mixed with healing herbs and leaves. Do you not have such things where you come from?"

I thought of the antibiotic ointment my mother used to slather on my skinned knees when I was a little girl. "We have something similar," I replied. "But I don't think it's made from – what did you say? Tallow?"

"Tallow, yes – we butchered an old sheep last week, and after the carcass was boiled I was given a –"

"After the carcass was boiled?" I exclaimed, disgusted. What was I putting on myself?

Wenda eyed me the way Magnus had done when I was revolted by the dead rabbits. "Yes, after the carcass was boiled – how else are we to get the fat from it, girl? Surely you know how valuable the fat of an animal is?"

I set the salve down on a rickety wooden table that was strewn with other, similar containers and clay vials, like something out of a children's story about a friendly witch. Then I smiled at Wenda and tried to suppress my disgust over almost having rubbed boiled sheep fat all over my cheek.

"They say your man saved one of our little ones," she said to me, as I glanced worriedly down at Magnus, who still had not stirred. "Is it so?"

I nodded, eager to let as many villagers as I could know of Magnus' good deed. "Yes, he did. And then his own brother and father tried to kill him for it. When your men found us that's what we were doing – running from the Northmen."

Wenda chuckled. "I heard you were doing more than that."

"That's true," I smiled, embarrassed. "But we weren't –"

Before I could finish my sentence, Magnus suddenly groaned and brought one of his hands to his head. At once, I knelt beside him.

"Don't get up," I said, taking his hand in my own. "You're safe. You're with the healer."

I didn't really know if he was safe, but I did know, if he saw fit to get to his feet, that the sight of a Northman stumbling around their village was not likely to be well-received by the Angles.

"Mmm – what, girl? Heather? What are – where –"

And then suddenly his eyes flew open as he seemed to remember what had happened, and he sat up very quickly and looked around for his sword.

"No," I urged, and Wenda came forward to help me prevent him from standing up. "No, Magnus, we're fine here. Someone told the lord about the boy you saved, and he said to take you to the healing hut – which is where you are now – and that he would speak to you later. Just – please, lie down. Your head is bleeding."

Magnus looked at me, and then at Wenda. "Are you hurt?" He asked me, running his eyes over my body, and the tunic the Angles had given me to cover myself. "Did they – are you – your face! Heather, your –"

"I'm fine," I told him, sensing that he was more likely to do something impulsive if he thought I had been injured than over anything that had been done to him alone. "I'm fine. You just need to –"

"Here," Wenda cut in, passing a small clay cup of thick, dark liquid to Magnus. "Drink this, it will help to awaken your senses again."

But before he could take it I grabbed her wrist and took it out of her hand. "Wait," I said, smiling so she hopefully wouldn't think I was being rude or ungrateful. "Just – wait. Sometimes he – uh, sometimes he gets sick from, uh, from – what's in this anyway? What is this?"

"It's pepper-root and milk," Wenda told me. "The root is fresh-ground, girl – it will help him wake up."

I didn't have any idea what pepper-root was, and as it turned out it didn't matter what I thought because Magnus took the cup from my hands and downed it quickly. And then both he and Wenda chuckled at me as I stared at him, waiting to see if anything horrible was going to happen.

"I'm a healer," Wenda told me, shaking her head like she had never met anyone so silly as me. "Why do you look at him as if the waking tonic is going to kill him?"

"She's a foreigner," Magnus told her, pushing himself up to sitting again and exploring his head-wound with his fingertips. "She has some strange ideas."

"Don't touch that!" I squeaked, noticing how dirty his fingers were and, even lacking medical training of any kind, understanding that you didn't want dirt anywhere near an open wound. "I mean – Magnus, please, it's probably best to leave the wound alone."

"She seems to have a bit of the healer's instinct inside her," Wenda commented. "She's right, you should not bother the wound. Let it alone, so it can close up on its own."

Magnus took his hand away from his head. And then he began to run it through the dirt to his left, and then his right. I realized what he was doing before he said anything.

"They took it," I told him. "Your sword – they took it. They say the lord wants to speak to you when you wake up, to ask about the child you saved in the woods."

"Ah the child," Magnus said, nodding. "Is that why I wake in this dwelling and not in the Great Hall of the next life? Have they let me live because of the boy?"

"Yes," I replied, reaching down to caress his cheek. "Yes, the boy's father spoke up for you and the lord said to take you to see the healer."

"I'm surprised the Angles have it in them to be reasonable," he commented. "They're usually no better than beasts when it comes to working out the right –"

"Magnus!" I broke in, eying Wenda. "We aren't alone!"

But Wenda did not look offended. She looked resigned. She gave me a little smile and a shrug. "Men are all the same," she commented in amused tones. "Always so convinced their enemies are beasts and demons. What would they have to do, girl, if they did not fight each other all the time over their imagined differences?"

I looked at Magnus to see how he was taking Wenda's words, but he was fumbling with one of his leather boots, not listening to either of us.

***

We remained in the healer's hut until nightfall, and the Angles placed two guards at the door to make sure we did not try to leave. Magnus was sleepy, but then unable to sleep when he tried – and I was worried he was going to be reckless with the Angle lord when the time came.

And come it did, after the smell of cooking food had filled our nostrils and made our mouths water and our empty bellies rumble. A boy came to the healer's hut and led us to the one building inside the village walls that was made of stone.

"Don't be angry with them," I whispered, before we were led inside. "Magnus, they were going to kill you. When you were passed out – they almost had the rope around your neck! We have to get out of here, OK? Please don't give them another reason to murder you!"

In the lord's hall, a great fire roared at one end of a large, rectangular room, with a table at the other end, placed on an area of the floor that had been raised up a few inches higher than the rest. Behind that table sat Lord Eldred, and on either side stood guards dressed in leather armor and holding swords. More tables were set along either wall in the main, slightly lower section, and a few people – some women but mostly men – sat at them. No one at the lower tables wore armor or carried a weapon – not any I could see. I was thankful of the fire because summer or not I'd already noticed that the evenings tended to cool down quite a bit.

"Ah!" Lord Eldred called from the opposite end of the hall from where we stood. "The Northman who saved an Angle child – come forward."

Magnus and I walked the length of the great room, feeling the gazes of the villagers following us as we did so. And when we were at the part where we needed to step up, and I lifted my foot, I felt a hand suddenly grab my wrist and pull me back.

"You've found yourself a bold woman," the lord addressed Magnus. "Look how she walks at your side, and moves to step in front of me even before you have led her."

Was I not supposed to step up? No one had told me that. I looked at Magnus, and then at the lord.

"Wait there," Lord Eldred instructed me. No further explanation was given – and besides myself, it didn't seem anyone else needed it. All eyes were now on

Magnus, who took his place before the lord in the tunic he had been given to wear, which was too small for him.

"One of my men is almost as big as you, " the lord said. "Hringwyn, have one of Swean's tunics brought for the Northman – what we've given him looks as if it were made for a child."

I watched as Hringwyn, who was standing in the shadows behind Lord Eldred, nodded to another man, who scurried almost silently out of the room upon being given the signal.

Although the Angle lord was treating Magnus with respect – and Magnus himself was standing quietly, not giving anyone reason to fear him – there was a tension in the room, and it was focused on the Northman. The people looked at him the way you might look at a dog who had bitten you once before, but who now seemed calm. There was an air of anticipation, an expectation I could see in the way some of the people at the lower tables were leaning forward with looks of eagerness on their faces.

What did they think was going to happen? Magnus did not have his sword, and the lord's men each had theirs. Did people think he was going to go berserk, running around the room and attacking people with his bare hands?

As it turned out, they did. When the old man with the straggly gray hair was brought in, and encouraged to tell the story of how Magnus had saved his son from the sword of his own brother – a brother who had then tried to hunt him down and kill him for the betrayal – the looks on the faces around me were profoundly skeptical.

"Taber is confused!" A voice finally called out, when the lord began to question him on the details. "Northmen kill our children, Lord Eldred! They don't save them! They tie them to great spits and roast them over the fire for –"

"For supper!" Another voice rang out.

"He can't be trusted!"

"Hang him!"

Lord Eldred let the exhortations to variously hang, burn, behead and drown Magnus continue for longer than I thought appropriate, but he did eventually lift both his hands and gesture to his people to settle down. And then he turned back to Taber.

"Where is he, then? Your boy – where is he?"

"He's with his mother, my lord. Back at our –"

"Bring him to me! I should like to hear the little one's story myself."

Taber balked slightly, even as he tried to hide it. "He's in his bed, my lord. No small thing to his poor mother, who spent the past night soothing him when he awoke screaming, begging for –"

"He's young, Taber," the lord replied, not letting the older man finish. "He'll have forgotten all about it by the time the winter snow melts. Bring him to me now, I wish to hear what he has to say."

Not longer than ten minutes later Taber returned with a small child trailing behind him.

"Come!" Lord Eldred shouted impatiently. "Come, child! Awake! You address your lord now."

Taber leaned down and whispered something into the boy's ear. And then we listened, all of us in the room, as the child told the story of being snatched up by Asger and having a sword held to his neck. When he told the part about Magnus suddenly shoving his sword between Asger's and the boy's own neck, the lord stopped him and asked him to look at Magnus.

"Is this the man who saved you, boy? Look closely – is this his face?"

There was no hesitation. The child nodded quickly, and looked slightly perplexed at being asked to confirm something that to him was obviously true.

"Are you sure of it child?" Eldred asked again. "This man is from the North. And you know what Northmen do to our people, don't you?"

"They kill us," came the small-voiced reply. "They kill us and burn our houses and steal our grain."

"Yes, child, that they do. And worse than that, still! So you must be very careful to tell the truth – you must be *sure* – that this is the man who saved you. For if you get it wrong there's no telling what destruction he will do to our estate – all because you couldn't remember."

Having been informed that he would basically be responsible for Magnus destroying their whole estate if he got it wrong, the boy turned and looked at him one more time and I could feel the other people in the room waiting – hoping, even – that he was going to change his mind.

But he didn't. He simply turned back to the lord and nodded that, yes, Magnus was the man who had saved him.

"Right," Lord Eldred announced, accepting it as truth now. "Take your boy back to his mother, Taber. Mercawb, give him a small sack of grain so the child may eat fresh bread until the new moon."

When Taber and his son had been ushered out of the hall, Lord Eldred adopted a sterner look and turned to Magnus, who suddenly wobbled on his feet and almost stumbled backwards.

"Bring him a chair!" The lord commanded. "His head is not yet healed from the blow, he needs to sit –"

"No," Magnus replied, closing his eyes tightly and then opening them again, shaking his head a little. "No, I can –"

He stumbled again, almost dropping to one knee that time, and Eldred signaled for the chair to be brought. When I took an involuntary step towards him, distressed by seeing his distress, I was stopped again before I could go anywhere.

"Sit," Eldred said, when the chair was in place. "I understand that your people are not allowed to show weakness – indeed, that at the first sign of sickness or injury you are taken into the woods and driven through the heart with a spear – but such barbarity is not our way. We –"

"We do no such thing," Magnus responded, and I could hear a tiredness in his voice that immediately set a low-level of anxiety running through my veins. "When one of us is sick or injured, Lord Eldred, the others –"

Eldred held up a hand to silence him and I felt certain that, were he not injured, Magnus would have continued to make his point – possibly in a way that was less than polite. Perhaps it was not such a bad thing that the blow to his head had laid him low at that point, when the Angles were clearly so jumpy?

"As it is, you have saved the life of one of our children. For this your life will be spared and you – and your woman – will be allowed to stay here within the walls of my estate while you regain your strength – as long as you can give us your word that, should your people arrive to take you back, you –"

"If my people come here," Magnus said, making me wince to see him interrupting Lord Eldred so carelessly, "they will kill me before they kill any of you, I can promise you that. I want to live, Lord Eldred. And because I want to live, I give you my word that I will offer all the help I can in defending your estate against my fellow men of the North. With luck, they are already on their way back across the sea."

"Yes," Eldred nodded. "With luck. And we will need to keep your sword whilst you remain with us – you understand."

Magnus nodded.

"Right, there it is then. The Haesting estate is yours, until your strength has returned. Consider it our thanks for saving the life of Taber's boy."

Magnus nodded again, and then we were led out of the stone hall, into the chilly evening and away to one of the huts that stood very close to one wall of the estate. The man who led us passed me a cloth sack and the larger tunic that had been fetched for Magnus.

"Here," he said, just before leaving. "This can be your shelter, and here is some bread for you to eat. Good-night."

"Good-night," I replied, and then turned to watch him scamper off into the darkness.

Inside the hut, a fire had been lit for us in the small fire-pit. It was a very small space, and looked to have been unused for a long time. Even in the dim light from the fire I could see cobwebs hanging from the straw roof.

"How do you feel?" I asked Magnus, sitting down with him on the floor because there were no chairs to sit on – there was no furniture of any kind except a single table that sat against the curved outer wall.

"Hungry," he replied quietly. "And tired."

I reached into the sack I'd been given and pulled out a piece of rather stale bread, which I handed over.

"You should eat, too," he told me, taking a bite. "It's important that we eat, girl, even if the bread is stale."

"Stale bread?" I grumbled, leaning back against the flimsy hut's outer wall. "You save one of their kids and all they can do is give you stale bread? And say they'll let you sleep on the dirt without killing you? Where I come from, we would do more for –"

"They do a lot," Magnus interrupted me. "They do a lot more than they have to, Heather. Do you not have enemies in United States of America?"

"The," I smiled. "*The* United States of America. And yes, we do have enemies. We just don't – we don't actually run into them very often."

"And if you did, would you give them food and shelter?" He continued, taking another bite of bread. "Even if you were afraid they might turn on you?"

I thought of the Soviet Union and their stockpile of nuclear weapons, the ones I was constantly hearing about on the news. "No," I replied. "I don't think we would. But I don't think they'd be helping us save any of our children, either. I just think it's rude to give you a shitty little hut like this, and stale bread and –"

"Heather!"

"What?"

"Do you not see that they don't have much? You have come from somewhere where food is plentiful – I see it not just in your strong limbs but in the way you looked at those rabbits I killed for you – and the oysters. If you think the Angles – or the people of the North – ever have reason to turn down food, you're wrong. Even stale bread is probably more than they can spare. Did you see the lord give the man Taber a bag of grain, to take with him?"

I nodded. "Yeah."

"It's because he knows they are poor peasants, and that they do not have enough to feed themselves properly. Even these stale crusts you look upon right now with such disdain would be enough to cause most people here to fight over them. I understand if you are not used to such a state of things, girl, but I must ask that you keep that look in your eyes hidden when you deal with the Angles. They're poor but they're proud – and they won't take well to you looking down your nose at their generosity."

"Oh," I said, chastened because I had genuinely not realized that stale bread and a bare floor were a lot for the Angles to give. "Oh. I didn't know that."

"I see that you did not," Magnus replied, smiling sleepily. "I wonder what place it is you are from where you have never had to eat stale bread? In the morning, perhaps you can tell me more about it?"

***

We slept like spoons, Magnus' body curled tightly around mine on the floor to preserve as much heat as possible – we had nothing to warm us but the thin tunics – and in the morning when we woke my body was stiff from the chill. My stomach was also so empty it ached, almost to the paradoxical point of nausea.

"When my strength is back," Magnus said as we sat on the dirt floor looking dejectedly at each other, "I will kill a deer. I'm good with a bow and arrow, even if it is not my usual weapon, and I saw that some of the Angles carried them. If I kill two deer, and give one to them, surely they will not begrudge me borrowing one of their bows?"

I took him out of the dark hut, because the air inside it was too still, and in the morning sun I made the sleepy-headed Northman sit on an old tree stump so I could look at the wound on his head. To my great relief I saw, when I parted his hair, that it already seemed to have scabbed over.

"And how do you feel?" I asked when he stood up, and seemed steady on his feet.

"In truth, girl, I feel fine. The healers in Apvik always say to rest for half a moon after a wound to the head, even if a man doesn't feel he needs it. And right now, I don't feel I need it. What I need now is simply breakfast."

He didn't look like he needed it, either – not standing there in front of me giving every appearance of strength and fitness. Still, I was naturally cautious.

"Perhaps you should take their advice, anyway," I suggested. "The healers, I mean. You –"

"Oh I will," Magnus replied, looking down at the tunic billowing around him in the light breeze and smiling. "It's never done me good to ignore what the wise women say. Look at me in this dressing – I look like a child."

I laughed, because one thing Magnus did not look like was a child. No. Even in silhouette and from a mile away, I knew that it would not be possible to mistake a person of his size and stature for anything other than a man. Even the thought of it stirred something in my belly that I immediately resisted, not wanting to weaken him further with sex when both our stomachs were empty and we'd both fairly comprehensively had the crap beaten out of us the day before.

I looked around. People were everywhere, and all of them looked...busy. No one dawdled, no one chatted amiably, everyone – even most of the children – had the look of determination on their faces that people get when there are things that need doing.

"It's coming up on harvest time," Magnus commented, perhaps seeing that I was curious. "It's the most important time of the year, and the harvest moon is the moon that will determine whether the people eat through the winter or whether they starve. They look preoccupied because they are, hoping for good weather – sun, no rain – and a bountiful harvest."

"Won't Lord Eldred feed them?" I asked, not thinking the question through.

"And what would he feed them with if not the grain they've grown and the fruits they've gathered?"

I looked up at Magnus, with the rising sun behind his head illuminating his golden hair into a blood-stained halo. "Oh. Yeah. I just thought - I thought maybe they could get some grain from, uh – from somewhere else?"

"Yes," he said, perplexed. "But *where?*"

"I don't know," I conceded, thinking to myself that if someone were to suddenly remove all the grocery stores from Los Angeles, the people of 1983 wouldn't know where to get their food, either. They would probably know even less than the Angle peasants, who at least had the experience of knowing how to grow crops for themselves, and raise livestock.

It was into this exchange that a woman, who looked to be about thirty years old, inserted herself.

"Not busy?" She asked me pointedly, grinning a lopsided, gap-toothed grin. "Come and pick peas with me, girl. I'll give you half of what you pick and you can make your Northman a pottage for supper."

I looked up at Magnus, my eyebrows raised at the stranger's presumptuousness, but all he did was shrug. "You might as well – we need to eat. I'll go and see if any of the men will allow me to accompany them outside the walls for rabbits."

"You can't take rabbits!" The woman exclaimed, looking scandalized. "You haven't been taking rabbits, have you?! The beasts of the woods are Lord Eldred's property, and meant only for his table – do ye not know that?"

"Alright," Magnus replied easily. "I'll see if any of them want to gather oysters at the –"

"But gathering oysters is women's work!"

Magnus smiled, amused. "Perhaps I'll spend the day sleeping in the sun, then? And wait for the women to bring me my supper?"

"Go to the lord's hall," the woman replied, not at all intimidated by the Northman towering over her. "You look strong, Lord Eldred will surely find some work for you."

"No!" I cut in, when Magnus looked like he was going to do just as the strange woman had suggested. "Magnus, you're supposed to be resting, remember? The healers in Apvik said –"

"Don't worry, girl," he said, pulling me into his arms and kissing the top of my head. "I'll not do anything too much. But I can't sit here all day, can I?"

It seemed that sitting there all day was exactly what he should have done, but I could see from the look on both of their faces that I was going to be argued down if I disagreed.

And so I went with the woman, who told me her name was Brona and then insisted, as the healer had done before her, on calling me 'Eltha' after I told her my name was Heather. She handed me a straw basket that sat amongst many others of all different sizes against the estate walls by the wooden gate, and then led me out into a cleared area in the woods where a patch of what I assumed were pea plants grew.

And then we began to pick peas. Well, Brona began to pick peas. I knelt down and started to shove the little green pods into my mouth, so hungry was I by then.

"Eltha!"

I kept gobbling, unable to stop myself.

"Eltha!"

That time, a hard slap on the shoulder accompanied my name and I almost toppled over into the pea-plants.

"Hey!" I barked, wrenching my arm out of Brona's grip. "I'm hungry! I haven't eaten a goddamn thing since, like, one mouthful of stale bread last night!"

When I moved to put another peapod into my mouth, Brona – whose grip was much stronger than I would have expected from someone so thin – grabbed my wrist and pried it out of my fingers, staring at me like I'd just keyed her new Camaro.

"Don't do it again, Eltha," she warned, and I saw that she was not joking around. "You smile at me and I don't see what you think is funny. Who do you think planted these peas? You? Who saved the seeds all winter to sow, and then plowed the soil by hand? Was it you? You are a guest here. You would do best to act like it."

I hung my head, chastened and embarrassed and not quite understanding what had come over me. I never would have gone straight to the fridge in a stranger's house and started eating – so why was I doing it with the peas?

Because I was hungry. Not 'I ate a bowl of cereal for breakfast and then skipped lunch' hungry but properly, truly *hungry*, like I didn't recall ever having been before.

"I'm sorry," I whispered. "I – I don't even know why –"

"You were hungry," Brona shrugged, relaxing now that she saw I was no longer a danger to her peas. "I understand how it is – I am hungry, too. But we can't just gobble up all the peas, because then there won't be any for winter, will there? There won't be any to plant when the ground thaws – and what will the old people and the babies and the sick people eat if we –"

"I know," I repeated, very quietly. "I'm sorry. I won't eat anymore."

"I'll slap the smile off your face if you do," came the good-natured reply.

So I picked peas with Brona. I picked peas for a very long time, until the sun on my bare shoulders and the back of my neck began to burn, and my back ached with all the bending down. And when I hobbled into the woods at the edge of the pea-patch to take a short rest in the shade, Brona walked over to me with that look of offense on her face again, and kicked me in the shin.

"Don't!" I pleaded, almost ready to cry from hunger and heat and exhaustion. "Please, Brona – don't kick me –"

She kicked me again. And that time, I did cry. Not from pain – the kick was not very hard – but from self-pity. Brona, hearing my sniffling, sat back on her haunches and started to laugh.

She started to *laugh.*

I looked up – tired, hungry and miserable – and saw that she didn't even have the decency to try to hide the fact that she was laughing at me, that something about the fact that I was suffering amused her to no end. And that suddenly made me very, very angry.

I leapt up and flew at her, intending to deliver a slap like the one she'd given me. "Fuck you!" I yelled. "Fuck! You! I come out here to help you pick peas – *I do you a favor!* – and you laugh at me because I'm hungry?!"

And then, as if it were the easiest thing in the world for her – and maybe it was – Brona blocked my attack and flipped me over onto the ground, pinning me down with one arm across my throat. It knocked the wind right out of me, and I started spluttering and coughing trying to turn my head away as she got right into my face.

"A favor?" She hissed, just as angry as I was by then. "*A favor?* You think *you* have done *me* a favor? What will you eat tonight, you spoiled bint, if not the peas I ALLOWED you to pick alongside me this morn?!"

"Half the peas," I wheezed pedantically, because Brona's arm was still heavy on my throat. "You said I could only keep half!"

"Yes," she replied, her eyes flashing. "Half the peas. How is it you do me a favor again, girl? You do yourself a favor, not me!"

I reached up and tried to free myself from her grip, clawing at her arm uselessly and kicking out with my legs. It didn't work. If anything it just seemed to amuse her further.

"You're surprisingly weak," she commented as I struggled, raising one eyebrow at me as if I were a decidedly curious specimen for her personal study. "You should have seen yourself limping off into the shade after not even a quarter-day of picking peas. I should think you a king's daughter with that skin and that aversion to hard work, but no king's daughter would be accompanying a savage Northman on a journey to –"

And then, suddenly, the entire weight of Brona's body on top of mine eased and I watched, dumbfounded, as she seemed to float away.

But she wasn't floating – she was being lifted. Someone was lifting her. Magnus.

"Get off her," he ordered, taking Brona by the tunic at the back of her neck. "Is this how the Angles treat the wife of the man who saved –"

"She's not your wife!" Brona squeaked, paddling her legs in the air so it was now my turn to smile smugly at her struggles. "Everyone knows it, Northman! Everyone –"

Magnus jerked her back roughly and she smartly decided it was best to stop talking. And then, without letting go of my tormenter, he turned to me.

"What's going on here, then?" He asked, in a tone I did not much care for. "Why do I find you two rolling around in the peas like a couple of children?"

"She kicked me," I replied stiffly. "Not that I have to explain myself to *you*."

Brona's eyes widened and she looked up at Magnus, as if to see what punishment he was about to deliver to me for – for what? And when no punishment came she tried to use my tone to score a point with the Northman.

"See?" She said to him. "Do you see how she is? I kicked her because she went into the shade to rest while I continued to work picking the peas. And then she had the nerve to tell me that she was doing me a favor! As if I forced her to come with me and pick peas for her own supper!"

And to my chagrin, Magnus nodded. "Aye," he said. "She's difficult, to be sure. And lazy."

"Lazy?" I repeated, blinking, unsure I'd heard him correctly. "LAZY?! HOW DO YOU EVEN –"

"Keep your voice down," Magnus admonished. "Or the Angles will come to see what's going on. Is it true you went to the shade to rest while your companion picked peas?"

"Yes!" I spat angrily. "It's hot as hell out here, Magnus! If you'd been out here all morning –"

"I was out all morning," he replied simply. "The lord's men needed some help carrying rocks to repair a section of the wall. You speak as if it was only you working in the sun when in fact it is everyone around you. And only you seem to feel entitled to take rests like some kind of –"

"King's daughter," Brona piped up. "She acts as a king's daughter would. I half think she is one."

Magnus chuckled. "Aye, the thought has crossed my mind too. Now," he looked at me pointedly, and then at Brona. "Am I safe to leave the two of you here, without worrying that you'll spend the rest of the afternoon scrapping and leave the peas unpicked?"

"She was the one who stopped picking –" Brona started, but all it took was a hard look from Magnus to shut her up.

I didn't understand it, her subservience to him when she'd just been such a bitch to me. Was it just because he was a man? When Magnus left us, without my promise that I would behave as he wanted me to behave – because why did I owe him any promises about how I would behave? – I turned to Brona as she picked peas a few feet away.

"Why did you do that?" I asked, letting a handful of waxy peapods slip into my basket and deciding that it was better to be friendly than standoffish after the fight, so there was someone to talk to during the boring pea-picking. "Why did you let him talk to you like that? Like you're a child?"

Brona looked up at me for a few seconds before replying, as if trying to figure me out. "Did you not see he had me by the back of the neck? Did you not see how much bigger he is than either of us? I did not want to be beaten, girl – and if you don't want to be beaten you'll speak to him with more respect."

"He's not going to beat me!" I laughed, but I saw that Brona looked skeptical.

"I barely knew you a morning and you drove me to violent temper," she commented, popping a peapod into her mouth before grinning at me. "And he's a Northman, I reckon he won't be as slow as myself in –"

"Hey!" I cut in, realizing what I'd just seen. "You said we weren't supposed to –"

She handed me a couple of peapods and held her finger conspiratorially to her lips. "Shhhh. Don't tell the lord!"

I ate them quickly, feeling a little better after her small gesture of kindness, and then we got back to picking.

***

We arrived back inside the estate walls just before the sun slipped below the horizon, and my back was so stiff I could barely stand upright. Still, after a whole day of picking peas I had a pretty generous portion for myself and Magnus. Before Brona bid me goodnight, she took me by the wrist and started dragging me somewhere.

"Where are we going?" I asked weakly, desperate to get some food into my belly. "Brona, where –"

"Just come with me!' She urged, pulling me along to an open area beside the lord's stone hall. A large fire pit sat in the center of a cleared space, with two other, smaller fire-pits nearby, each with an iron pot bubbling away over it. The smell of cooking food hanging in the air was so much I actually had to wipe a trail of drool off my chin.

Brona left me to go and talk to one of the women who tended the pots, and then a short while later as I stood transfixed by the smell of meat, she returned with a little cloth sack, which she handed to me.

"Use it for the pottage," she said. "It's not much, but it'll make it taste better."

I opened the sack and looked inside to see a couple of bones, the meat almost entirely scraped off them, along with a couple of things that looked like fat, beige-colored carrots and a bunch of fragrant green herbs I didn't recognize.

"Brona," I whispered, almost emotional at her kind gesture. "You didn't have to –"

"Go on," she smiled, pushing me back in the direction of my hut. "Take these back to your Northman. Perhaps he won't beat you if you feed him something half-decent? I'll come for you in the morning, Eltha."

I didn't bother correcting her. Instead I thanked her one more time and hurried back to the hut, where I found a fire already lit and a little cauldron filled with what looked like oatmeal simmering away over the coals. I also noticed that there was a better table now, and two chairs, and a pile of fresh straw placed against one of the walls. There was no Magnus, though. He arrived a few minutes later, to find me adding the goodies from the sack to the cooking pot.

"Bones?" He asked. "That'll give it some flavor! And potherbs! Where did you get these things, girl?"

"Brona gave them to me."

"Ah," he replied, kneeling down beside me to inspect the stew and leaning in to kiss my neck. "So you two are friends again?"

"I guess," I told him, taking the crudely carved wooden spoon he handed to me and stirring the stew. "What are potherbs?"

"The sneeps – and the greens. Anything that goes into the pot that isn't meat or grain is a potherb."

"Sneeps?" I asked.

"Sneeps, yes – the little pale roots, they'll grow almost anywhere."

The stew took a long time to cook. It took so long that we ate some of it before it was ready, when the oats and the 'sneeps' were not quite soft enough. It was still the best thing I'd ever tasted in my life. We ate until out bellies ached, and then we ate a little more. And when we could not possibly fit another bite of food in, we lay on the straw beside the fire and Magnus ran his fingers through my hair.

"Do you know what?" I asked, as we watched the flames dancing.

"What is it, girl?"

"I don't think I've ever been this tired in my life. Not this kind of tired – like, tired from actual work, you know? Don't laugh at me – I've worked before, I worked at home. But not like it was today, picking peas. At home when I'm working I'm mostly sitting down, and chatting to customers."

"What kind of work is it that can be done sitting down?" Magnus asked. "I'm starting to think it might be true that you come from a high family."

"I promise you I don't," I smiled, leaning against his shoulder. "It's just a different kind of work where I come from."

***

I don't know why I thought the day spent picking peas with Brona was going to be a one-off. Perhaps it was because I was used to work having an end-point. Need to pick all the peas? Serve all the customers? That's a finite task, and when you're done, you can relax – at least for a little while. Right? Wrong. Oh so very wrong. Because on the Haesting estate, as finite as the tasks were, there was always another one to be attended to. After the day spent picking peas, one that made me ache like an old woman, there were plums – small, squishy, sweet plums – to be picked, and then dark berries and then seaweed to be collected from the seashore and carried in sacks back to the small fields that surrounded the estate, where it had to be mixed and turned into the earth with long, rake-like implements that made your arms burn. Errant pigs needed to be found in thick undergrowth and dragged, struggling and squealing, back to their pens. Animals needed to be fed. And on one particularly unpleasant day, rats needed to be killed.

The Angles kept their grain in storehouses, and I was told it was a constant battle to prevent these stores from being eaten by vermin. Brona appeared at the well one morning, as I filled a bucket of water to take back to the hut for the night's pottage, and told me to join her at the grain storehouse when I was done. In her hand she held a curved stick that was thicker at one end than the other. When I met her, she handed one of the sticks to me and told me to stand by the door. So I stood by the door, waiting for the next instruction. But there was no next instruction. Brona went to the crates, made of wood and woven tightly with grasses so no grain spilled out, and began to slap them and lift them up before letting them fall back down to the ground.

"Out!" She yelled. "Out, out!"

And before I could enquire as to what the hell it was she was doing, it suddenly became clear to me in the form of a wave of rats scurrying out from amongst the crates and fleeing towards the door – towards *me*.

I'm not one of those girls who gets squeamish about rodents – even as a child I'd always thought they were kind of cute. But upwards of twenty-five of them running towards me?

"Ahh!" I screeched, clutching at the doorframe and trying to life my feet off the ground. But the storehouse was not built sturdily and one side of it sagged and swayed under my weight and even began to crack before I let go and screamed as the rats began to run over my feet. It probably only took a few seconds – it felt like a lot longer. But when I could no longer feel furry bodies brushing against my ankles I slowly let my eyes open again.

Brona was standing beside the grain-crates, her mouth hanging open and her eyes wide. It had been a few days by then, and I didn't have to ask what her expression meant. I knew what it meant. It meant 'why have I been cursed to babysit this complete moron?'

"What –" she said, still staring at me. "Eltha, what –"

But instead of finishing her sentence she just bent down and rested her forehead on the edge of one of the crates like I was too idiotic to even comment on.

"What was I supposed to do?" I asked, trying not to get heated so I wouldn't get slapped again. "Brona, you didn't even tell me what you wanted me to –"

"You know what those beasts were, though, don't you?" She cut me off, her voice dripping with condescension.

"Rats."

"And you know, Eltha, that rats eat grain – do you not?"

"Uh," I said. "Yeah. Yes. I know rats eat grain."

Brona stood up straight, then, and looked me in the eye. "WELL WHAT DO YOU THINK I WANTED YOU TO DO, THEN?!"

I looked down at the wooden club in my hand and sighed. "Kill them. You wanted me to kill them."

"YES! What's wrong with you, girl? Are you sure you didn't take a knock on the head along with the Northman?! I'd have better luck with one of the children!"

I was already beginning to recognize my daytime companion's moods. She seemed to get frustrated easily – *very* easily – but after she'd vented, yelled at me, smacked me on the back of one hand, she usually cooled down fairly quickly. So I just took her lecture, because truthfully I was almost beginning to understand where it came from. I didn't know what the hell I was doing. Sometimes, when Brona raised her eyebrows at me and gave me that look like she was surprised I hadn't yet managed to drown myself in a puddle, I tried to imagine what it would be like to teach her how to work at the Grocery King in River Falls. I tried to imagine teaching her how the till worked and how to cash out at the end of the day. She'd be just as lost in River Falls as I was in Haesting. Not that that helped me in Haesting. No – in Haesting I was just the dummy she'd been saddled with.

"I wouldn't have known how to kill them anyway," I whispered sheepishly in the grain-house that day under her withering gaze. "I – I wouldn't have been fast enough."

And then, right in front of us, a single rat darted out from under one of the crates and Brona leapt forward, bringing her club down onto the creature and killing it with a single blow.

I turned away at the sound of the death-squeak, and then, when I dared to look back at the tiny, broken body at my feet, I surprised even myself by bursting into sudden, gulping tears.

"Oh my God," I gasped, embarrassed, turning away so Brona couldn't see my face. But the tears kept coming. They kept coming until I was almost doubled over, sobbing at the sight of the poor little dead rat who had, to my soft city heart, only been trying to feed her rat-family.

Thankfully I didn't have to bear Brona's horrified disapproval for too long before she stomped out, disgusted, and left me to my rodent-based grief.

That's where Magnus found me about ten minutes later, perched on one of the grain crates and feeling lower than I had since I'd come to the new place. He took one look at me and I saw his expression change from one that had seemed ready to deliver a stern lecture to one of compassion.

"I don't like it here," I cried, getting emotional again just to see him. "I thought I would – because you were here, I thought I would. But I don't! Brona is horrible, and I never see you during the day – and then at night we're too tired to even talk to each other! And –"

"Shhh," he whispered, kissing the top of my head and wrapping one of his burly arms – arms that seemed so much more suited to that world than my own – around my shoulders. "Shhh, Heather. Come on, girl. Come on, tell me – is it true what Brona says? Do you weep over a dead rat? Must I take you to the healer to have her mix up a cure for madness?"

He was trying to make me laugh. And I did, a little. But there was something more to it, something more than a dead rat. I think he knew it, too.

"We won't stay here for long," he told me, tucking my hair behind one ear – a familiar gesture from him already, and one that made me feel especially cared for. "We're not prisoners. I just need to come up with a real plan for going south – winter will be here soon, you know. You won't have to put up with Brona for that much longer."

Before he left, he kissed my cheeks – both of them, as the one that had been bruised and swollen was healing fast – and promised to see me in the hut, just as soon as he was finished helping some of the other men harvest one of the fields.

He scooped up the dead rat as he left, sensing that I did not want to look at it any longer, and almost made me cry again with his kindness.

Chapter 12: Magnus

I worried about Heather, in those early days on the estate. She was not used to labor, that much was clear – but even in the first half-moon I saw her stamina growing, I watched her go from whining over an hour's work in the woods gathering plums to almost being better at it than the other fruit pickers, who did not have her advantage of robust health.

It was not, however, her stamina that concerned me. It was her heart. She started to become emotional very easily, and prone to fits of tears. It was not that I scorned her tears – if anything her softness just attached me more tightly to her side – but they worried me for the winter ahead, when I knew things would not be any easier than they were during that first sunny autumn.

After the incident with the rats I went to the man who was in charge of the harvest and asked for a small bag of barley, instead of the usual half a loaf of bread and fist-sized chunk of cheese that was my payment for a day's work in the fields. And when I got back to our hut, I gave the bag to Heather and told her it was hers, that we could boil the barley in our pottage and fill our bellies a little fuller for as long as it lasted.

And deliberately, although it hurt me to do so, I did not instruct her on how to store it properly. Sure enough, the next morning there were little holes chewed into the corner of the sack, and some of the barley had been taken.

"Do you think it was rats?" She asked, giving me cause once again to marvel at her naiveté.

"It could be, girl," I told her, although I knew very well it was.

"They only took a little," she observed. "Maybe that's enough for them? I don't mind sharing with them if they only take a little."

And of course, the rats did not take only a little. The next morning, the sack was empty, and Heather's eyes flashed with anger.

"Fuck!" She yelled, slamming her fist down on our table. "Goddamnit, Magnus! It's gone – it's *all* gone! Now we don't have enough to make pottage!"

That day, when Brona took her back to the storehouse to kill rats, she was no longer hesitant to wield the club. And when she returned in the evening with a new bag of barley, she settled into my lap as I sat at the table cracking hazelnuts and kissed my cheek.

"Lesson learned," she whispered in my ear. "Even if I feel a little patronized that you and Brona are devising lessons for me like I'm a child. You could have just told me –"

"Ah," I stopped her before she could finish. "But is it truly so? Would you have listened to myself or Brona if we'd told you? Or does the pain of losing your barley teach the lesson far better than any words could have?"

For a moment, I sensed she was about to argue. But then she just nestled into my chest and laughed. "You're right. I guess I do need to learn things the hard way sometimes. The problem is I only ever realize it *after* I've learned it the hard way."

I slid my hand under her tunic and ran it slowly over her smooth belly. "Such a beautiful girl," I teased, as she squirmed gratifyingly under my touch. "Such a shame you have the character of an ox."

"Magnus!" She scolded, sitting up and moving to smack my shoulder even as she giggled. She wasn't quick enough, though, and I caught her hand before she could land the blow. "I do *not* have the character of an ox!"

"Oh yes you do," I told her, slipping my hand up further, cupping one of her breasts until I saw her eyelids flutter just a little. "Exactly the character of an ox. You're lucky to have met a man so tolerant as myself, girl. Any other would surely have sent you on your way by now."

"Oh really?" She replied. Heather was always asking me that question over the table, with one eyebrow raised and her chin angled haughtily towards me. *Oh really, Magnus? Oh realllly?* It was charming. It was more than charming.

"Yes," I smiled, not wanting to show her just yet what her little sighs and shudders were doing to me. "The other harvestmen laugh at me in the fields, girl, to hear of your disobedience. Some of them say the time will come to teach you a lesson."

"A lesson?" She smiled, reaching down to the hem of her tunic and suddenly pulling it right off over her head so her nakedness was revealed to me all at once.

She'd done it on purpose, to shake my resolve, and she grinned to see her success etched on my face.

"Gods, girl," I whispered, without even intending the words to be spoken aloud.

My cock thickened against my thigh as she leaned back, showing herself to me, and a sweet, slow wave of desire began to tug me away from my senses.

"What was that you were saying?" She asked, still trying to play along as if nothing was having an effect on her, even as I heard the breathlessness creeping into her voice. "You were talking about teaching me a lesson, is that it?"

And before I could answer, she slid one hand down from her breasts, over her belly, and between her pale thighs so I could hear the wetness when she touched herself. She knew already that seeing her give herself pleasure turned me into a little more than a mindless, slavering wolf.

Still, I was not about to concede – not when I could see that she, too, was already close to the end of her patience. I took her wrist in my hand, running my thumb along the inside where her heartbeat pulsed against the skin, and then down, following her own fingers, down further until her breath caught in her throat.

"Yes," I growled, curling my fingers between her slippery lips and dragging them up, and then doing it again and again, all without touching the most sensitive part of her, the part I knew she was aching for me to caress. "A lesson."

"Magnus."

My name spilled out of her lips in a whimper, and I knew I'd won. Heather reached for me, locking her arms around my neck, pulling me close, desperate. Nothing in the world was sweeter than her desperation, nothing so quick to make my balls ache than her need for me. I stood up from my chair and lifted her with me, and then I lay her down on our simple straw bed and watched as she opened her thighs.

"Magnus," she asked for me again, clutching at my shoulders. But I held back, even as I throbbed to be inside her.

"No," I said, pushing her back down. "No. I want to watch you do it to yourself. Now, girl. Show me."

She sighed and complained and reached for me again but when she saw I meant what I said, she could no longer wait to be touched and I found myself transfixed as she ran the tip of her finger over the glistening pink nub at the apex of her sex.

Her body arched up as it did when she was underneath me, and her nipples hardened into points and I had never seen anything so perfect before as that vision of everything that was feminine and lovely right in front of me. It was not long before I pulled my leathers off and wrapped my hand lightly – for anything more than lightly would surely have ended it right then and there – around myself. And when Heather saw what I was doing she begged for me to come inside her.

"Magnus," she whispered, reaching again for me with the hand that was not occupied. "Please – Magnus. Please, I –"

If I had been starved for a moon, and then the Gods had set a feast of roasted venison and buttered bread in front of me and told me not to eat, it would not have been as difficult to heed their command as it was to deny Heather when she begged for me.

"No," I told her again, setting my teeth against the urge to feel her softness enveloping me. "I want you to finish yourself for me. Right now, as I watch. And when you've done as I wish, I'll fill your belly my seed."

Her finger quickened in its secret place, and her head started to loll back on the straw. "Yes," I whispered, as a sharp hunger jolted through me, making it almost impossible to keep away from her. "Yes, girl. Yes, Heather. Show me, girl. Show me –"

Her finger stopped, then. Well, it didn't stop, but it looked almost as if it had. When I looked closely, though, I could see that the movements had just become very small and very, very fast. Heather's hips rolled and bucked under her own touch, her breasts trembling with the pleasure as it burned through her body and her helpless little cries filling our hut.

"Magnus!" She moaned my name even as she pleased herself. "Magnus... Magnus! I – please –"

Sensing that if I waited even a single moment it would be too late, I crawled between her sweat-sheened thighs and buried myself into her with a deep, heavy groan.

"Yes," she breathed, still shuddering and gasping. "Yes, Magnus. I want you to –"

But she didn't even have time to ask, because she was too warm, and too soft, and too perfectly slick and I was spurting into her already. It felt as it if would never end, the pleasure so thick and rich I almost drowned in it, the perfect relief of letting go, of filling her until every drop of tension had been drained out of me.

Afterwards we lay on the straw panting like pursued animals, and listening to each other's breath slowing as we came back to ourselves.

"What have you done to me, girl?" I asked, when I finally had the strength to roll over and look at her in the dim light from the fire's embers. "It's never been like that with anyone else. It's never – it's –"

"Same," she whispered, reaching up to caress my cheek. "I feel like I'm drunk. I think I am drunk – on you."

***

All the next day as I worked in the fields outside the estate wall, swinging my scythe back and forth through the golden wheat, I glowed with whatever it was that was happening between Heather and me.

"The Northman's in love," one of the other harvestmen commented when we took our mid-day meal at the edge of the field where there was some shade. "See how he gazes towards the horizon as if his eyes were blind? It's lovesickness, I've seen it a thousand times."

I got the feeling the Angles were trying to shame me, but I was not shamed. I simply shrugged when they looked at me for a response, and told the man who spoke that I thought he was right.

"And what will ye do with her?" Another – Eadwin, asked. "If ye cannot go back to the North and the winter comes – where will ye take her?"

I bit off another piece of the pale wheat bread that the Angles liked so much, and followed it with a lump of their delicious cheese. "Aye, you find what troubles me," I told him. "I had thought to go south and pay a trader with my labor to take me to the Frankish Kingdom and then eventually back to the North – although not to the part where anyone would know me. Or perhaps even further to the south, who knows? I am strong and young and trained in combat, I would not find it difficult to find someone to pay me for my skills. But now I have her and I tell you, I cannot leave her. It already causes me to wake from my sleep at night."

"You can take her with you, can ye not?" Another man asked.

"She's not fit for travel," offered someone else, whose name I thought was Bradwin. "To hear my Brona tell it the foreign woman is as useless as a blunted scythe. She's –"

"You speak with haste!" I said, cutting him off and sitting up a little straighter so the other harvestmen shrank back from me, just a little. "Useless she is not – inexperienced would be a better way to say it. But even since we have been with you, not even a half-moon, I have watched her learn certain skills so she is even better at it than some of your own women."

"Perhaps you can take her south, then?" Bradwin suggested. "If she learns quickly, you can teach her how to strip a deerskin and sew a heavy cape to keep the wind away?"

"Did you see the berries on the hawthorns?" I asked. "As heavy as I've ever seen them in the North – this winter will be hard. No matter how fast she learns, do you think I can teach her enough to see us through it? If the winds blow cold enough I doubt even if I could make it on my own – but with another? You see why I wake in the night, friends."

It did not feel strange to call the Angles who worked in the fields with me 'friends.' Or if it did, it was only because it didn't. It is impossible to work with people and not come to know them, to hear them speak of their worries and joys, to see them not simply as Angles but as fellow men. That is not to say they saw me the same way, or that anyone had forgotten that my homeland was the North. But as quick as they were to flinch away from any sign of anger in me, I could see they were coming to feel a kinship as well. The young men talked to me of their girls, and asked what the Northern women were like. The older ones spoke of their wives and their children and their worries about seeing them fed and warm through the winter.

That evening, when the sun had dipped low enough to make further harvesting impossible, I returned to the hut with hope in my heart, even as my cares for the winter remained.

"You look happy," Heather said when she first saw me. She was sitting on a large, flat rock I had found and placed next to the fire-pit, and stirring the pottage.

"Aye," I replied, setting the piece of bread I had saved for her from the mid-day meal into her hand. "Today I felt a little less lonely."

She looked up sharply when I said that, her expression curious. "Less lonely? But – Magnus, are you lonely? What about –"

I have seen men become irritated with women for such questions. I have seen them assume a certain forwardness in the woman who asks them, as if she could not countenance that any man might feel lonely with her in his life. But I saw the enquiry for what it was – that careful variety of feminine concern that worries at any dissatisfaction in those she loves. It warmed my heart even further to feel that I was the object of Heather's sweet care.

"I do not know what it was like in your homeland," I said, sitting down beside her and urging her to eat the bread. "But in the North, we are very close to each other. In the village, we know everyone, we speak every day to those who live close to us, we involve ourselves very deeply in each other's lives. Even when a raiding party crosses the sea, I sail with men I have known since I was a baby, men whose families I know almost as my own. You see it is not like that here for us – it can't be, even as the Angles try to show us welcome, because we have no shared history. We did not grow up with these people, we do not know their ways. Do you not feel it, girl? Do you not miss your people?"

Heather surprised me by hesitating, almost as if she had an answer but did not want to give it.

"What is it?" I asked gently. "You do not have to agree with me. If you feel differently, say it."

"It's not that I feel differently," she began, stirring the pottage once again before handing me the spoon to eat what was left on it. "It's just – the way you describe the North, it's not like that where I come from."

"What is it like? Do you not live in a village, with other –"

"I live in a bigger village than anything you've ever seen before," she smiled. It was a smile I recognized by then, one she often gave me when she spoke of things she did not think I would understand. "But we are not as close with the other people as you say you are with your people. I definitely don't know them like my own family, anyway – not the way you describe."

"Do you not work together?" I asked. "Do you not help each other if someone's dwelling burns down, or a particular husband has bad luck hunting – would you not offer meat to his children if they were starving?"

Heather laughed. "People's houses don't burn down very often, and children don't starve. Some of them are hungry, but nobody *starves* to death. Not in the United States."

Once again I found myself exceedingly curious about the place where Heather had come from. "Is it so?" I asked. "No one? *Ever?"*

"Probably at some point people starved in America," she replied. "But not for a long time. Not since the olden days."

We fell quiet as she tended once again to the pottage and I poured some water from the jug for myself. Was she lying? She didn't seem to be – and what would the purpose of such a lie be? To lure me back to her own land? Once again, it did not seem to be something she had any interest in.

"So you don't feel lonely?" I asked, when I had taken my spot at her side again.

She opened her mouth to answer and then closed it again, reconsidering what it was she had been about to tell me. And when she did finally speak, her voice was quiet. "Yes, I feel lonely. It's just – Magnus, I guess I always feel lonely. I mean, not to make it sound like my life is hell or anything, but it's just – yeah, it's not, like, a new thing to me. To feel lonely."

I was shocked by Heather's words. At the anger and hurt that boiled up in my chest on her behalf. And at the same time, I understood that part of me had already known it. Why else would she be so uninterested in finding her way home? Why else did we speak only of traveling south, and then north again eventually, to my own homeland – and not to hers?

"Your people are lucky I do not know how to find them," I told her, feeling a familiar twitch in my right hand as I thought of wielding my sword.

"Why?" She asked, turning her face, which was dotted with sweet little freckles now after days working the sun.

"Do you joke?" I replied, surprised. "Do you not understand the place you have in my heart already, girl? Your people are lucky I do not run my sword through each and every one of them for allowing you to grow up lonely. Are your parents dead? They are not, are they? You speak of them as if they still live. Where were they? Why did they not –"

"You're really angry."

Her words were not accusatory. They sounded, if anything, surprised.

"Of course I'm angry! Would you not be angry if I told you the same? If I told you that I always felt lonely, that it was nothing new to me? Would you not wonder why my mother and father had let loneliness fester in their own child's heart, girl?"

But still, Heather wore that expression of bafflement on her face.

"Why do you look that way?" I asked heatedly. "As if you're surprised?"

"Because I am surprised," she replied slowly. "Because I – I never really thought about it like that before. I never thought to be angry. There are a lot of lonely people in the world, Magnus. Aren't there?"

"Not in the North," I replied. "There is the loneliness that comes with loss, of course – no one can avoid that. But even if a man's wife and children die, the people in the village make sure he is never alone. When a woman loses her baby, the other villagers do not allow her to hide away in her dwelling, not past the mourning period. If a Jarl sees that a parent overlooks a child, causing it harm, he speaks to the parents and shows them their child's sadness. And the child is included in the games with the other children, and loved by the other parents in the village. What happened that your parents were not able to keep your heart full of the things that children's hearts should be full of, girl?"

I had been so busy talking, and so high in emotion that I had not stopped to look at Heather. When I did, I saw that her eyes were shining with tears. It just made me even angrier at those who had let her suffer. And determined that she should not suffer like that anymore.

I was seized with the need to do something, to show that I would not let her feel the things the people before me had. To that end, I leapt up, unsure at first as to what I was actually going to do. And then it came to me.

"Where are you going?" She asked as I grabbed an empty sack from the table. "It's almost dark, Magnus – where are you –"

"Oysters!" I said, because at the time that seemed the thing to do. We had no meat or bones for our pottage that night, and I did not just want to tell Heather I cared – I wanted to show her. In later years the two of us would laugh at the way I suddenly decided, that night, that oysters for the pottage were somehow the solution. I was a young man, then, and eager to prove my heart.

"But the guards," she started, "they won't let you outside the –"

"Yes they will, if I promise to bring some fat oysters back for their own pots."

"Magnus, you can't just –"

"I'll be back before you need to add water to the pottage," I told her, taking her hand and kissing it. "It won't take long at all."

"But –"

"Soon!" I called over my shoulder. "I'll be back soon – and then you can go to sleep with something substantial in your belly."

As it was, my impulsive urge to act, my male need to *do something*, turned out to be an incredibly lucky thing. So lucky I believe it may have saved both our lives.

The sky was the deep blue of twilight when I came out of the woods and onto the beach where the oysters clung to the rocks, and there was only the thinnest band of brilliant orange painted along the horizon. I began to make my way down to the shore when I heard something on the wind. I stopped at once and turned towards it, to see if there was really something there or if the dark was already playing tricks on me.

And then I heard it again, more clearly that time. Voices. Male voices. Quick, gruff – and even if they were too far away to hear, something about the tone made me suspicious. It wasn't like the Angles to be out in the late evening, either – they were a superstitious people, convinced that all manner of demons and outlaws moved into the woods come nightfall. I crouched low and supposed I would need to make my way back into the forest if I was to get close enough to overhear what the men were saying without being seen. But I soon heard, before I could make my way back to the trees, that the voices were getting closer. I ducked behind one of the boulders, slick with seaweed where the high-tide washed over it, and searched the sand with my fingers for a rock, should I need to defend myself.

Soon enough, I could hear that it was only two men who approached, and that they were deep in conversation. I craned my head as far as I could without showing myself.

"Why do we linger?" A voice came out of the darkness. "Does he think we do not know the true reason? Does he think we do not see his wounded pride? No good will come of this, I tell you, no good."

They were very close to me. So close if I had stood up with the rock in my hand, I probably would have been able to bash at least one of their brains out before he even realized he was under attack. But I stayed where I was, to listen further.

"But it is as he said," came the reply. "The Angles cower in their pig-huts."

A frisson ran the length of my spine – 'the Angles' – whoever was speaking was foreign. And I didn't know any foreigners who would be wandering close to the Haesting estate but my fellow Northmen. My heart began to pound as the conversation continued and in his next comment, one of the men confirmed who they were:

"What concern is it of mine what the Angles do?! They know we're here, Sig! The Jarl's pride drives him to put us all in danger – he cannot accept that Magnus has gone."

"What the Jarl cannot accept is that he chose the wrong son. And now he sends us on night raids when we should be sailing for home with our spoils!"

That was it. My father and brother had come for me. And I knew, because I was one of them, that the men of the North do not satisfy themselves with the taking – or killing – of a single man, even if he is the second son of a Jarl. Torches would be brought to the walls of the estate under the cover of darkness, and balls of dry grass coated with the resin of a fir tree would be lit and tossed into the estate. The gates would be easily broken down, and the Angles would be surprised – night raids were not the usual way of the Northmen.

I had to get back to the estate. I had to warn them. But the two men stayed where they were, talking to each other in the dark.

"What is the signal?" One asked, after a brief discussion of the merits of another warrior's younger sister's tits. "An owl hooting?"

"Voss, who saw fit to make you a warrior?" Came the reply. "It is the howl of a wolf – and Asger brings half the men to the estate from the west. We must –"

I did not hear the rest of what was said. It was happening. It wasn't about to happen, it already was happening. My brother already approached the estate from the west, and the two men I overheard waited simply for the signal to bring the rest from the northeast.

Heather was in a hut on that estate, approached in darkness by Northern warriors who would surely show her no mercy. The Angles who I had worked the fields with, and their wives and their children, were on that estate. The lord who had shown me kindness, and decided not to hang me, was on that estate. The boy whose life I had saved, the incident that spurred all of it, was on that estate.

Silently, I stood up, with the rock I had found clutched in one hand. And heavily I brought it down on the head of the man standing closest to me, silhouetted as he was against the last of the day's light. He went down hard – dead or unconscious I did not know – and then I heard the familiar metallic scrape of a sword being unsheathed. I knelt beside the fallen man, drawing his sword, and the remaining warrior who faced me must have assumed I was an Angle, because his first blow was sloppy. Sloppy enough that I had time to bring the blade in my hand up to deflect it, and then to deliver a hard punch to his stomach.

"Voss!" I swore under my breath, and only when the word was out of my mouth did I understand my mistake. The Northern warrior paused very briefly, and in spite of himself, upon hearing a familiar word coming from the Angle he thought he fought with. But it did not take him long to realize who stood before him.

He began to shout at once, turning to the north and calling for reinforcements.

"It's him! It's Magnus! Bring the –"

I put his companion's sword through his neck, and his shouts died away into gurgles as he fell to the ground, soaked with his own blood.

And then I ran. I grabbed a second sword from the dead man's hand and I ran into the woods. As I approached the gate the guards, alerted by the sound of my panting, took their place in front of it.

"The North –"

"Who is it?" One guard asked, because it was too dark to see my face and they were not expecting me to be in such haste when I returned from my oyster picking.

"It's Magnus," I breathed. "The Northmen are here – right now! They come at this very moment from the west and the northeast! Let me in, we must wake the lord and the men – lock the gate behind –"

"What is this?" Came the response. "The Northmen approach at this hour? Is this a trick? Why should we trust you when you are –"

I grabbed the man by the throat and shoved him up against the gate. "This is no trick, my friend. Do as I say or you will die tonight – your village will burn, you children will have swords run through their hearts! Let me in!"

Something in my voice convinced them, and I found the gates opening.

"Bar them!" I shouted. "Bar them shut! Wake the men! Now! Move!"

And then I ran to Lord Eldred's hall as the bellows of the guards began to wake the estate. At the heavy wooden door, another guard stood to stop me and I simply shoved him aside and broke the door open with my shoulder.

"Lord!" I shouted, as I ran, followed by his guard, into the dwelling. "Lord Eldred! The Northmen approach the estate! Wake! Wake the men! Wake the archers and have them take position on the –"

I stopped when Eldred appeared in front of me in his sleeping dressings, demanding to know why I was in his house. I repeated myself and did not have to go far before he understood what was happening. There was a flicker of suspicion in his eyes – just a flicker – but it soon turned to decisiveness. He turned to the guard behind me and bid him to gather the archers. He turned to another man, who had come running at the sound of shouting, to assemble the armed men.

"I will fight," I told him. "Let me warn my girl, and then I will fight with your people. I killed two of them at the beach – here, I have their swords. Just let me –"

"Go!" Eldred nodded. "Go and bring her back here, we have a room underground for the women and children!"

I turned on my heels and left the lord and his men to their preparations, flying across the bare earth of the Haesting estate to the hut that lay next to the wall. The wall that would at any moment see burning clumps of dry grass and resin pitched over it.

"Heather!" I yelled as I approached. "HEATH–"

But she was already standing in the open doorway with a look of confusion on her face.

"What is it?" She asked when I came to her. "Magnus – what's –"

"Come with me," I replied quickly, not waiting for a response before I began to pull her back towards the lord's hall.

"Wait!" She screeched, her eyes suddenly wide with fear as she noticed the commotion going on around us. "Magnus! What are you –"

And then I saw a bright flash in the corner of my eye and turned towards it, already knowing in my heart what it was. The sound of the straw that had been piled next to the wall going up in flames reached my ears almost immediately. And then there was another flash, and another. The third was close enough to Heather and I that she screamed and clutched at my arm.

"Who is it? Magnus! Who –"

"Come with me!" I shouted, over the growing screams and shouts of the Angles as they poured from their little straw dwellings and the flames began to spread. "The lord's house is stone, it will not burn. COME WITH ME!"

And then we ran for our lives – for *her* life – back to Lord Eldred's hall as the sound of ladders clattering against the walls filled my ears. The Northmen – my people – were upon Haesting. In no time at all, the first of them would be over the estate's walls.

"We'll take her," a woman I did not know told me when Heather and I arrived at the door. "Let go of her arm, we'll take her down below with us – she'll be safe, don't worry, I promise –"

But I was not about to trust one of the Angles – not one whose name I did not yet know and had never seemed to set eyes up on before. I did not let go of Heather. I insisted on following the woman as she led us down some stone steps that curled into the earth underneath a trapdoor that was normally obscured with a sheepskin rug. And when I saw that the other women and children huddled there, and more arrived every moment, I kissed Heather quickly and told her to stay there and not to come out until I returned.

I should have anticipated by then, with her seeming ability to misunderstand – or flat-out ignore – even the most basic rules, that she would give me trouble.

"No!" She burst out, clutching at my arm as I went to leave. "Magnus, no! Where are you going?! Don't go back out there! Stay here, with –"

I took her hand off my arm and held her away from me because she was trying to draw me to her. The Angles – even the children – stared at us.

"Look around!" I replied, before she could ask me again. "Girl, look around! Who do you see down here? Do you see any who are not women or children or old men?! This is not the place for the fighting men! Now let me go, at once! I will come for you when it's done."

And then she did look around, as if she hadn't noticed before that there were no men of fighting age down below, as if she was truly surprised to see such a state of affairs.

"Wait!" She begged, when I kissed her once more and turned to leave. "Magnus, wait!"

"I cannot. Stay here. I'll come for you."

I turned to run up the steps, the smell of smoke acrid and sharp in my nose by then, and before I could exit she screamed after me once more:

"Promise! Magnus! Promise me you'll come back!"

In one ear, I could already hear the first clashes of swords. But still I turned at the last moment and caught her frightened eyes in the low torchlight.

"I promise I'll come back."

It was the first time I ever promised a woman I would come back. My mother never asked it of me, although I had sensed the question there on the tip of her tongue a few times, before the raiding parties left when I was younger and more inexperienced. I learned what it was on that night, to feel that last desperate clutch at my dressings, the last hasty kiss planted on my cheek by a woman who loved me – and who was being left behind.

And oddly enough, as I emerged into the smoky, flame-lit estate, it was love that I thought of. It was that note of pure fear in Heather's tone, the cloud of despair that darkened her eyes. She loved me. I did not even know if she knew it – but I knew it then, as I rushed to find Lord Eldred and tell him of the tactics I felt sure my father and brother would use.

I found him, sword in hand, watching one of the Northern warriors mount the wall and jump to the earth below, followed by another, and then another. I caught him just before he was about to rush to where the breach had occurred.

"No!" I shouted, for the sound of the flames and the screaming was very loud by then. "Lord Eldred, it is a distraction! This is not where they will come over the wall – in a moment there will be more – many more – in a different place, and a small party battering the gate. You must –"

The lord and I watched as the Northmen that had surmounted the wall cut down one of the Angles who had bravely gone to meet them, and then another in quick succession. And then he turned and looked at me sharply.

"What is this you say, Magnus? How am I to trust you? Is it not your people coming over those walls? Is it not –"

"Do you see any more coming?!" I asked desperately. "See how it's already working, Lord – your men rush towards that place. Already, the largest number of the Northern warriors will be effecting a larger breach elsewhere. The men won't listen to me – I beg you, call them back! Give me half, I will take them one way around the inside perimeter – you take the other half and go the other way. And keep the gatekeepers in their place. Lord Eldred! Please! We must do this now, before –"

I don't know what it finally was that made the lord of the Haesting estate listen to me, but before I could finish begging him to listen he was calling the men to him, giving them the instructions I had just outlined – and then giving half of them to me.

That night, my heart pumped harder in my chest than it had ever done. I led a group of Angles towards a part of the estate wall that was not well lit, knowing that if I did not succeed, they might think themselves deliberately misled and hang me – not that my greatest concern was for my own life. If I did not succeed there was another life in danger – Heather's. As terror ripped through me at the thought of her coming to harm, another emotion followed in its wake. It was courage. I could not fail. She loved me. Her love gave me strength, it tightened my grip on my sword and made the blows I dealt with it more decisive.

My father always warned Asger and myself of being too certain of victory, and it was not a feeling that I had experienced in battle before. Even that night I would not quite have said it was the certainty of victory. It was more the certainty of giving everything. There was still the possibility of giving everything and coming up short, I knew that. Still, I did not fancy the chances of my weak-hearted brother against my steely determination to get back to the girl who waited for me under the lord's house – the one I had promised to return to.

I led the Angles behind Lord Eldred's hall, where the huts were fewer and pig sties sat side by side, and told them to keep their eyes on the walls for Northmen coming over. There did not seem to be any. There seemed only to be the squealing of the pigs, who could smell the smoke and sense the fright in the air.

We doubled back, and still there was no sign of anyone – there weren't even any of the little resin-soaked fireballs. I almost wanted to laugh – how had my father allowed the attack to happen without even making sure they had their tactics in full order? I knew how. Asger. Asger, and his tendency to let his pride and emotions get ahead of his actual abilities.

"Do you lead us deliberately from the fight?" One of the Angles approached me angrily and tried to take me by the neck of my leather dressings. "Is that what –"

I brought my arm up and batted him away, hard enough to send him flying backwards onto his backside. "No!" I replied, as a few of his fellow warriors turned sharp looks towards me. "I know the tactics of the Northmen – they like to start the assault on an estate with a distraction. That's what those men were, coming over the wall near the huts. Did you not see how few there were of –"

At that moment I was interrupted by a great cracking, splintering sound from the north. It was the front gate, I knew it at once. How stupid was my brother, to concentrate the entire force of his men on such an obvious place? A place the Angles would already be surrounding?

"There!" I shouted to the men. "They breach the gate. I want two of you to stay here and keep an eye on this back wall – the rest of you come with me!"

But there were not going to be any more breaches of the walls that night. I saw at once that Asger had done as I suspected – and as my father must have allowed – and sent the entire force of Northmen through the most obvious place imaginable. The fighting was already heavy when I arrived with the rest of the Angles minutes later. Swords clashed, the bellows and screams of men echoed through the chilly night and the metallic smell of fresh blood filled my nose.

Our numbers seemed to be about equal, but the Angles had the obvious advantage of already surrounding the Northmen, as they poured through the narrow front gate. With one last glance back at Lord Eldred's hall, I gripped my sword tight and leapt into the fray.

There is no thought in a fight, no pondering. And I was glad of that fact as I cut down men I had spent many a raiding party fighting alongside. I was a better swordsman than any of them, and when some of them recognized me and stood for a fleeting moment in a shock of recognition, I took advantage.

"Magnus!" A voice cried at one point. "Magnus fights with the Angles! Traitor! Traitor!"

The fighting seemed to intensify into a frenzy after that, and I was glad of the Angles at my sides as the full force of the North seemed to surround and focus itself on me. At one point a heavy kick to my leg, from behind, almost sent me down to one knee. But one of Lord Eldred's men hauled me up, and I spun around to drive my sword into the chest of the man who had sought to hobble me.

The fight was intense, but not long. When my father's men seemed to sense that they were being bested – which it soon became clear they were – they began, as all men do in those situations, to lose heart. And instead of a warrior Jarl exhorting them to continue, and bellowing tactics, there was no one. It seemed there was no one, anyway.

From the remnants of the Northern warriors who were still standing when the fighting died down, a figure emerged. Asger. When he saw me, he raised his sword and at once two or three Angles jumped to take him on, not knowing who he was. Seeing that my brother was bloodied, and that the arm holding his sword trembled with fatigue, I bid them back down.

"You take up a sword against your own brother?" He addressed me, spitting dramatically at my feet. "You take up a sword against your own father! Surely you are mad, Magnus. There will be no place for you in the Great Hall now. There will be no –"

From all around us came the groans of the dying and wounded. Asger's foot, when he moved to take a step towards me, slipped in a pool of blood. But the living men were silent now, watching the confrontation between the sons of the Jarl.

"You always were better at theatrics than fighting," I chuckled. "Do you forget who truly took up a sword against his own brother? Do you forget –"

"LIAR!" Asger screamed, taking a swing at me that I easily deflected. "Liar! Do you wish to keep your foul secret from your new friends, is that it? Do you wish them to think it was not in fact *you* who first lifted his sword to his own –"

"I lifted my sword in defense of a boy," I replied, drawing myself up to my full height as anger tightened my heart. "You know it as well as I do that my sword was not lifted against anyone, you fool. If you hadn't seen fit to try to murder a child – and not even in the heat of battle! – I would not have seen to block you. And even afterwards, when you came for me, I did no more than defend myself. I did no more than –"

He swung at me again, the whites of his eyes flashing against his bloodied face. The Angles, knowing that the fight was won and that what occurred in front of them then was personal, and not a threat to them, stood back.

"Do that again," I whispered coldly, seeing the hatred twisting my brother's face. "Do that again! SWING AT ME AGAIN, ASGER! Voss, what did our parents do to be cursed with such a –"

My anger was too great, too distracting. When my brother pulled out the jewel-studded dagger that our grandfather had given to me – and that Asger had immediately stolen, to no sanction from our father – and moved to jab me with it, I did not jump out of the way in time. The blade caught my left arm, close to the wrist, and we both looked down to see the blood flowing suddenly from the wound it left there.

Asger was going to die. I adjusted my grip on my sword and brought it up and out, knowing he would at any moment make a stupid move, and that when he did I would finish him.

And then a scream rang out. A woman's scream. Heather.

"Get back!" I shouted at her, not taking my eyes off Asger. "Get back inside, girl! NOW! Get –"

Before she was upon me, one of the Angles snatched her up as she cried and begged me to walk away.

"You're injured!" She shouted. "Magnus! The fighting is done! Come let me take you to the healer to –"

Asger, who had always had a strange ability to see what was in people's hearts – a much better ability than he had with combat – must have seen something in the stance of my body, or heard something in the tone of Heather's voice, for he immediately recognized that he was not seeing a random woman.

"Ah," he commented. "Brother, you have a girl. She's pretty. Have you put your baby in her belly yet? Shall I come back with a larger force and cut it out of her?"

The red veil fell over my eyes, then. I brought my sword down with force, no longer parrying, no longer interested in anything Asger had to say. Even in death he was going as he had lived – with ill-judged words spilling from his lips, and a confidence that did not match his circumstances.

But before the blow landed, another suddenly stopped it, lifting my sword away from Asger's neck with such force that I almost dropped it. It was my father, the Jarl. And when our eyes met I saw his were wet with tears of rage.

"Think what you do," he gasped, shocked to see what had been about to happen. "Magnus! Think what you do – this is your *brother!* This is your future Jarl!"

Lord Eldred, who had appeared at some point during the proceedings, stepped forward to bid my father take his remaining men and leave.

"It is only out of respect to your son that I don't have you killed," he added. "Go now, before I change my mind. GO!"

Asger stumbled towards the gate, but he could not contain himself, even then. He turned around to face me once again, and to issue another threat.

"Keep her close," he said, eying Heather. "Wherever you go, keep her close. Not that it will save her in the end, brother. Not that it will keep me from offering her to my men when I return for you with more Northern warriors. Not that it will keep me from taking her until she bleeds, and then throwing her body in –"

It seemed to happen slowly. In my memory afterwards, it was as if I could remember each moment in isolation. The sound of my blade moving through the air, and the faint glint, from one of the fires that was still not out glimmering along its edge. My father stopping abruptly and the turning, his mouth opening into a scream – although I do not remember the sound of screaming – as Asger fell to his knees, blood spilling out of his mouth and his eyes looking up at me, filled with confusion even then.

I drove my sword in deep, bellowing the whole time, and then put my foot on my brother's chest to withdraw it.

He was dead before he hit the ground.

The Jarl's first son was dead, killed by the second, and the Angles stood poised to kill the Jarl himself, and his few remaining men. I held one arm up to stop them – a final mercy to my mother, so that she would not spend the rest of her years alone.

I knew that my father was finished. He knew it, too. He was as finished as he would have been had the Angles poked him full of holes with their swords. His shoulders slumped as he looked down at Asger's body, and then up at me with that same confused expression that Asger himself had given me just moments before.

"It didn't have to be this way," he said, looking up again, his cheeks shiny with tears and other men's blood. "Magnus, it didn't have –"

"You're right." I proclaimed, as one of the warriors began to drag Asger's body away, to take it back to the ship and then home to Apvik, where it would be burned on a pyre as all the villagers stood around it and pretended that a great man had been lost. "It did not have to be this way, Father!"

We held each other's gaze for a brief moment, I knowing that it would be the last time I would look upon my father, and he knowing that it would be the last time he would look upon his one remaining son.

The emotion gathered in my chest, making me pant with it, as my father and his beaten men left through the gates – but I did not weep. It was not sadness I felt but something else. It was the last words I had spoken to him, the weight of their truth. It did not have to be that way. But it was. Memories from my childhood danced through my mind, spats with Asger, moments where I could see that my father knew the character of each of his sons. And still he chose the one he must have known – he had to have known – would inevitably lead him to the day where he walked, shoulders bent low with grief, through a gate in a foreign land with the body of that very son carried behind.

"Have the woodcutters bring the wood," Lord Eldred said quietly to one of his men, when my father and the warriors carrying Asger's body were out of sight. "And have the builders replace this gate by nightfall tomorrow – and somebody dig a pit outside the walls for the bodies of the Northmen."

The usual boisterousness of victory was nowhere that day, as the light of the dawn began to creep through the trees. The Angles understood what they had just seen, and they wished to show me respect.

"Bring ale from the stores," Eldred added, after placing his hand briefly on my shoulder and looking me in the eyes. "We'll drink to our victory this evening."

And then he was gone, and the rest of the Angles were busied with the tasks he had set them, including the one who was still holding Heather.

She rushed to me when he let go, and I fell to my knees, reaching blindly for her, burying my face in her belly.

"Magnus," she whispered, kneeling in front of me and drawing my face against her neck, holding me tight. "Magnus, oh, Magnus. My love, my love. Magnus."

It was only then that I wept.

Chapter 13: Heather

Something changed in me the day I watched Magnus kill his own brother. Something got harder, older. I became more a woman of the Kingdom of the East Angles and less a girl from Los Angeles, who did not even have it in her, at twenty-two, to stand up to her tyrant mother. Of course the step was one of many on a new path, and not definitive, but for all the rest of my life I remembered the feeling, that day, of having to put my own shock aside, of having to steel myself against the temptation to fall apart.

It was Magnus who made me feel those things. When I took him in my arms in the bloody earth by the front gate, I felt how much he needed me. I knew that it was on me to be his strength in the coming period of his reckoning with what he had just done. I didn't give in because I couldn't. I didn't give in because he needed me not to give in.

Instead, after stroking his hair and kissing him and crooning words of softness and useless comfort into his ears until his heavy breaths began to calm, I led him to the healer and sat beside him, holding his hand and kissing it every now and again as she applied various ointments and herbal potions to the wound on his arm.

It made me feel guilty, the fact that I was almost thankful for the injury – although at the time I did not understand that even a simple cut could often be deadly in my new home. It gave me – it gave *us* – something to focus on, something to look at and comment on and tend to. Something that wasn't Asger's death. Later that morning, as we lay quietly in our hut, he looked up at me.

"I thought I knew," he whispered, running his fingers along the rough hem of my tunic. "I thought I knew I wasn't going home again. But now I think I did not know – not truly. It is final in my heart now, girl. I will never see Apvik again. I will never see my mother again. She will go to her next life hating me."

And I couldn't even argue with him because what use would it have been, trying to convince an intelligent man that his parents would not hate him for killing their firstborn son and heir? We both knew that there was perhaps nothing so effective on earth that a person could do to make you hate them than killing their child – even if the one wielding the blade was also their child.

"I'm not sorry," he added a few moments later, nestling his head into my neck and clinging tightly to me. "I'm not happy, either, do not misunderstand me. But it is a wonder Asger lived as long as he did, and everyone must know that were he not the Jarl's son he probably would not have seen his coming of age day."

"What is a coming of age day?" I asked, because I did not know what to do other than to take my cues from Magnus himself – and he seemed to want to talk.

"It is the day of a man's ten and sixth birthday. It is often sooner for the girls, and on the occasion of their first blood – but for the boys it is always that birthday. We spend the night before it outside the village with the gothi, and drink a tea that induces visions and wisdom. When we return to the village a fight is staged with the boys who came of age before the last winter. No one gets hurt – it is just ritual. But my brother was lucky to make it so far, with how skillfully he courted people's disdain.

Do you know when he was not yet ten winters he stole our father's sword – the Jarl's sword – and tried to take a swing at one of our highest warriors? And for what? For scolding him when he stole a bowl of butter from their table. Fortunately for Lodvig, Asger could barely lift the blade with which he meant to launch his attack. Any other boy in Apvik – including me – who had done such a thing would have been whipped."

"And what happened to Asger?"

"Nothing, girl. Oh, my mother and father made a big show of telling him off in front of Lodvig and his wife, but when they got him home – nothing. He was warned not to do it again. But Asger was never the type to learn a lesson by words alone."

"Sounds like me," I said, thinking of the bag of barley and the rats and intending my comment to be light. But Magnus pushed himself up on his arms and shook his head.

"No!" He replied. "No you are nothing like him, girl. Do not say such things."

We stayed in the hut for a long time, undisturbed by Brona or anyone else who wished us to help with the day's work. It must have been Lord Eldred's doing, to allow Magnus some time alone after the events of the previous night.

Into the afternoon I stroked the Northman's cheek and brushed his hair off his face and tended gently to him. It hadn't even been a month since I'd made the fateful decision to reach out of the undergrowth and pull him into my hiding spot, but already it felt much longer. It would not have been the same, I knew, if I'd met him back in Los Angeles, or River Falls. Back home we would maybe have exchanged phone numbers, met up at the bowling alley for a date or gone to a concert. I smiled as he lay with his head against my thigh, trying to picture Magnus at a bowling alley. He probably would have been good at it – he was good at everything.

"What do you think of?" He asked, seeing that I was lost in thought.

"Luck," I replied softly. "How some people have it, and other people don't."

"And who do you think has luck?"

"I think your parents did not have it," I replied. "The way you describe your brother, and the things I know of you – they must have seen it, right? The must have seen that even though he was older, you were better at everything? Why didn't they decide to make you the next Jarl, after your dad?"

"It doesn't work like that. It is not a Jarl's choice who is the next Jarl. It is not always his oldest son, either – if there is another warrior who stands out in battle and in leadership, the people can refuse the current Jarl's oldest son. But my father was respected – he was a good Jarl, he kept the people well and safe. And so they did not want to oppose him when he wished his eldest son to take over. It was changing recently, some of the people had begun to murmur that the maturing that my father felt so sure would take place in Asger had not come to be. But if it hadn't been him it would not have been me – my father would not have allowed such an obvious condemnation of his firstborn. No, it would have been someone else, someone unrelated."

We fell into a conversation about the society of the North, and then about the gothis Magnus had mentioned – they were religious figures, priests. And then we dozed off in the warm hut, only to be awoken by a voice at the door that afternoon.

Magnus was already awake, his body stiff and alert and only relaxing when he realized it was just one of the Angles.

"There will be a feast –"

"Open the door, boy!" Magnus replied. "No one is going to bite you!"

Slowly, the door opened and a child leaned in. "There will be a feast this evening," he told us, eying Magnus with wary awe. "Lord Eldred sent me to invite you – and the woman. Come to the hall at sundown."

"Aye, at sundown," Magnus replied. "Tell Lord Eldred we'll be there."

After the kid scuttled away I looked up at my Northman – because the quiet hours we had just spent together had solidified his transition, in my mind, from 'the' Northman to 'my' Northman – and smiled.

"'The woman.' Did you hear that? How old was that child – six? And I'm 'the woman?' It makes me sound like livestock. Like property."

"It is the Angles' way," he replied. "They put so much stock in marriage – perhaps I will have to make you my wife so you can get some respect from the Angle children? As it is now, yes, you are my property."

I turned away, grinning because I knew he was trying to provoke a reaction in me. "I'm not your property, Magnus. I think *you* are *my* property!"

"Is it so?" He laughed, pulling me easily across his lap and smacking my ass. "Are you sure?" He spanked me again. "Are you, girl? Why do you let me get away with such things if it is I who is your property?" Another spank.

I giggled and tried to get away, but he held me fast. And then we both seemed to remember the events of the previous night at the same time and Magnus' hand fell still on my rump. I stayed where I was, laying across his thighs on my belly, sensing a sudden change in the air. And then he was pushing my tunic up over my hips, and his hands were no longer playful.

I already knew he was strong. I knew it when he did things like pulling me across his lap with no effort at all, even as I used all my strength to try to struggle away, laughing. I knew it when I saw him carrying heavy logs to our hut to be chopped into firewood – logs I would not be able to move an inch, even if I tried. What I did not know was just how gentle he had been with me when we made love. He had seemed so abandoned, so eager to toss me onto my back or lift me up in the air and wrap my legs around his hips that I hadn't realized how much he'd been holding back.

That afternoon, when he put me on all fours and my knees sank roughly into the dirt floor in our hut, I got my real first taste of the true depth of strength lurking in Magnus' thickly muscled body.

He apologized at once, when he heard me whimper in what was mostly surprise, but I turned and look back over my shoulder, catching his eye. He needed me. All I wanted was to give him what he needed.

"No," I said softly. "No, it's OK. It's –"

My words dissolved into a loud gasp as he tore his leathers from his waist and buried himself inside me. His hands were tight on my hips, his fingers sunk into my flesh, and he was jerking me hard back against him.

I don't remember being conscious of whether or not it hurt to be gripped so hard. I don't really remember being conscious of anything except Magnus and the ragged breaths that were coming from his throat – breaths which I could not truly tell from sobs.

"Heather," he breathed, bending his body, so much bigger than mine, down over me until my shoulders rested on the earth. "Heather, Heather..."

There was nothing and no one who could help him except me. I knew that's what he was telling me, as he took what he needed from my body. And being taken like that – in a way I had once thought I would never be comfortable with – was so sweet and so perfect. The healer, I understood, could apply her unguents. The lord, who invited us to feast with him that night, could apply words of thanks, of respect. And I too could also do those things.

But alongside those human responses, those social instincts, were other, darker, deeper wounds that needed to be tended to. And for those wounds, only I would do. Only my body would heal him.

It happened quickly. And there was something darkly intoxicating about being needed like that, with such urgency. I felt like a paper boat suddenly placed in a rushing river, carried along on the swirling, driving currents of Magnus' lust until my own fingers were curling into the dirt and my own breaths were coming fast and shallow.

"Magnus," I half-whispered, half-gasped as he swept me along and drew me up towards a peak I wanted more than anything. "Magnus!"

"Yes," he breathed into my ear, yanking my hair out of the way so he could kiss my neck. "Yes, girl."

And when he was so close he was already drawing in those deep, long breaths before the moment of release, I came so hard and so suddenly that it almost felt like a shattering, like my whole body exploding into shards of nothing but sensation.

Magnus held me together. His hands gripped my hips even tighter and he pulled me back, holding me there and groaning loudly as I tightened around him over and over. And then he slid one hand up to the back of my neck and pushed me down as he started to come.

It was, when he was finished, almost as if a spell had been broken. He took his hand off my neck and looked at it as if he wasn't quite sure what it had been doing.

"Voss!" He cried, when I rolled over onto my back and we both saw the bright pink marks on my hips where he'd held me. "Voss, girl – look what I've done! Look what –"

"Magnus," I cut him off, taking his face in my hands and looking him in the eyes. "Magnus."

"Heather, I did not mean to hurt you – I did not –"

"Magnus!"

"What?"

I knelt beside him as his warm seed ran down one of my thighs and kissed him. "You didn't hurt me. I'm not hurt. I wanted it like that – I wanted to give you what you needed."

My words sunk in. He looked back at me, his breath still coming heavy, and I saw that he was suddenly struggling with emotion.

"It's OK," I told him, pulling him once again into my arms, overwhelmed with compassion. "It's OK, it's –"

"I killed him. I killed Asger. My brother – I killed my –"

The times would come, in the days and months and years ahead of us, when Magnus would take on my sadness. When he would hold me through the night as I sobbed and raged at the blows life was going to deliver to me. But that time, in the hut within the walls of the Haesting estate, it was my job to take, my job to absorb all of the things and all of the emotions he couldn't deal with alone.

And there was no point in denying what had happened.

"I know," I said, trying and failing to wrap my arms around those impossibly broad shoulders as they shook with grief. "I know, Magnus. I know."

***

That night, at sundown, we walked together into the lord's hall, where the business of the estate took place, and found it set with tables. A trio of musicians sat close to the fire, playing instruments I did not recognize and sending their raucous, buzzing tunes out beyond the stone walls.

Magnus and I were led to one of the tables close to the lord's table, where we could watch other guests entering and being taken to their seats. We were both completely drained, our hearts spent and our bellies empty. If someone had told me, back in my old life, that there were people who saw fit to invite a man to a feast less than a day after watching him kill his own brother, I would not have thought it at all appropriate. But there, in Lord Eldred's hall with our bellies growling and Magnus' heart aching, it felt right.

Roasted meat – venison – was served, along with a stew of sneeps, smoked pork and greens, and cup after cup of ale. The musicians played and the Angles sang songs which they kept stopping in the middle of to teach us the lyrics to, and it was just what we – what *he* – needed.

When we had eaten so much our stomachs ached with it, Lord Eldred stood and held his hands in the air, quieting the hall and casting his eyes over his guests.

"It's not many an estate in the Kingdom that can say they defended against a raiding party of Northmen," he said, after a hush had fallen. "Two winters ago the King's own party was attacked and the King barely escaped with his life. I fear we would be burying more of our own today if it were not for the Northman here, Magnus. He woke me in the night to warn of what was coming, and told us of their tactics. Without him, this would be a funeral feast."

Under the table, I sought Magnus' hand and took it in my own. Beside me, he sat in silence, his eyes focused on the empty wooden bowl on the table in front of him.

Lord Eldred continued. "Do not hang your head, Northman. I witnessed with my own eyes the events of last night. I saw him swing at you three times, I saw him slice open your arm. We all saw these things – and we saw your restraint, too. But what man would think it wrong to kill those who vow to kill our loved ones? What man would see fit to let him go, he who threatened the life of our woman, or our child? No man at all, Magnus. No man at all."

The Angles began to beat their wooden cups against the tables then, just lightly, as Eldred spoke. And when the lord of Haesting told Magnus that he had done them such an act of benevolence that he would be welcome to stay on with them for the winter – and longer – as one of them, the banging of the cups became deafening.

"And the woman, too," Eldred nodded at me. "Wife or not, you may keep her at your side. We make this offer in acknowledgement of the great favor you did us this last night, Northman. Without you, Haesting might have been lost. *I* might have been lost. Stay the winter within my walls."

When Magnus finally lifted his head the banging of cups became frenzied, and some of the Angles who sat close to us reached over to slap him on the back and shout his name. And when it had died down enough, many minutes later, for a speaker to be heard, my Northman turned to Lord Eldred.

"I am grateful for your kind offer, Lord. It has been our privilege to stay in Haesting with you and your people, and to help with the harvest. But I was not made to live under another, although I do not say this with any wish to cause you offense. I –"

"I grant you leave to stay as a freeman," Lord Eldred replied, before Magnus could finish. "You will be given your freedom and not tasked with working to sustain my household or the estate itself. This is my humble gift to you, in return for your acts of loyalty and courage last night. We know what it must have been to face down your own people, and we honor it."

I turned to Magnus, along with everyone else in the hall. And then their mouths all fell slightly open when he responded by turning to me and asking me what I thought of their lord's offer. It was not too often, I suspected, that women were asked their opinions on important matters on the Haesting estate.

"What do you think?" He said, squeezing my hand in his. "In truth, girl, I have been in fear of the winter to come and how we will survive it without –"

"I think we should stay," I smiled. "Lord Eldred has made us – made you – this offer. Your arm needs to heal. In truth I just want to stay with you. You know I don't know very much about living here, or how to do many things – although I'm learning. If you think it's best that we stay here at Haesting, then I think we should, too."

"As it is," Magnus looked back up at Lord Eldred. "We will stay for the winter in Haesting."

A cheer arose, and the cups were banged again as the musicians started once more to play. Little honey-soaked cakes were brought in on trays and set in front of each guest and even Magnus' eyes widened at the sight of them.

"What are they?" I asked, picking mine up and examining it – it was small, and rather hard for a cake. Almost like a half cake, half biscuit hybrid.

"I do not know their name, girl. I only know that honey is almost more precious than gold – Lord Eldred does everyone at these tables a great honor."

The honey-cake was sticky and sweet and delicious when I took a bite, only realizing as I chewed it that I had not tasted a single sweet thing since I came to the Kingdom of the East Angles. And after they were eaten, when I thought things might be about to wind down, more ale was poured, and the music continued to play and soon people were stepping away from the table to dance.

Magnus and I stayed where we were, watching. It was not an occasion for dancing, not for us. And when we went back to our hut, swaying slightly from the ale, I remained awake long after he had dozed off, lying beside him on our straw bed and gently running my fingers down his cheek as he slept.

Chapter 14: Magnus

The next day, before Heather woke, Lord Eldred came to the little hut on the edge of his estate to speak to me. I emerged into the early autumn sunshine with my body and my heart aching, and stood blinking in front of him.

"I do not wish to bring you more trouble in the midst of your grief," the lord started, "but duty compels me to speak to every capable man on the estate. About half of our grain stores burned last night, and the rest of the harvest is now of the utmost –"

"Of course," I replied, understanding immediately. The harvest had been a bountiful one so far, but with half of the stores burned, it was now more important than ever to take the rest of the crops from the fields. Even if it could be managed, the estate still risked starvation. "I will join the men in the field, Lord. If I am to accept your hospitality for the winter, I must also do all I can to ensure that hospitality is well met."

Lord Eldred did not reply right away, and on his face he wore a look of surprise.

"What is it?" I asked.

"I'm sorry," he replied, shaking his head. "Northman – Magnus – I'm sorry. It is just I have spent my whole life being told – and telling others – that the Northmen are savages, barely better than wolves, and completely uncivilized."

I smiled. "It is the same for us. In the North we speak of the Angles living in the mud like pigs, and murdering each other over the merest of slights. You are not a young man, Lord Eldred – and I am not a sheltered man. I have seen enough of the world to know that these stories are just that – stories. In truth we are all the same, all we want is stew for our pots, warm blankets for our children and safety for our people."

The lord of Haesting smiled knowingly, and then seemed to be about to leave before stopping and turning back.

"Oh, and I brought you this. It is the dagger with which your brother cut your arm – he must have dropped it, and his men did not see it in the mud. I thought it should be yours."

At once, Lord Eldred handed me the dagger – the same dagger my grandfather had given me all those many winters ago, after a trip to the busiest trading center in the North. I held it lightly in my hand, running my fingers over the jewels, so carefully inlaid that they sat flush with the gold that held them.

"It's fine work," Eldred commented. "Very fine. One would have to travel a great distance to finds smiths capable of creating such a piece."

"Aye," I nodded. "My grandfather brought it from a trading center as a gift for me. It was my dagger, before Asger stole it from me."

"Then I am glad to return it to the rightful owner."

***

I strapped the dagger to my outer thigh, under my leathers, because it was too precious to leave in the hut, and I did not want its presence to tempt thieves – especially with Heather often there on her own. And then I spent the day in the fields, where the harvest was winding down and the skies had thankfully seen fit to bless us with more sunshine.

To spend the winter within the bosom of the Haesting estate was a better prospect by far than spending it on the move across the frozen landscape with Heather, but it was not enough to put my worries to rest. Half of the grain stores were lost. Come spring, the Angles would be lucky not to have lost any of their own to hunger. How could I justify taking more from the mouths of their children?

I was going to have to find food for us myself. I was going to have to claim my independence as a freeman – that is, a man who is not beholden to a lord on an estate, and one who does not have to give a portion of his crops and meat to that lord. And to do so would mean spending the winter outside the walls of the Haesting estate.

I looked up at the sky as I took a short rest from drawing my scythe back and forth across the stalks of wheat. The weather was still favorable but it was going to be hard work. Hard work that could not be borne by myself alone – I was going to need Heather's help. But it seemed the only thing to do, if I did not want us to spend the cold moons to come beholden to Lord Eldred and his dwindling stocks.

As it was, Heather seemed to be even more enthusiastic about the idea than I was, and after securing the lord's permission to build a small dwelling in the woods close to – but outside – the estate, we set to work.

She knew nothing about building, or weaving the slender trunks of saplings between thicker posts in order to make a fence, or turning the earth over in preparation for planting. But once I explained a task to her, Heather was better than some of the men I had known at working hard. She was strong, for one thing, and her stamina was much improved in just the short time we had been with the Angles.

And the Angles themselves were generous with their help. Even as they had their own tasks to attend to they helped us thatch our roof with straw, and gave us one of their spring pigs just as it was almost fattened for slaughter.

I was almost glad of the work to be done. It left me very little time to spend pondering the sadnesses that had befallen me. Instead, I spent my days with the foreigner, working on our little home. When the winds cooled, it was the two of us together who mixed straw and mud and animal dung together and then spent days working it into the woven branches that made up the walls of our dwelling. It was to me she looked, laughing, when the mud-mix was so cold her fingers lost their nimbleness and I had to sit with her beside the fire until the feeling and dexterity came back to them. And it was to our bed I took her each night, until it felt that I knew each of her cries, each of her squirms and moans and twitches, as well as the back of my own hand.

Without her, a hard winter would have been harder. When the snows blew in after the Yule period and the food dwindled, we had each other. Without her to come home to, I may not have ventured so frequently out into the cold forest to hunt the rabbits Lord Eldred granted me the freedom to take. Without me to watch her back, she may not have spent so long gathering the little hard, red berries that the healer promised would keep our teeth from falling out of our heads until the spring vegetables grew.

It was that time when the hope of the thaw is almost stronger than the reality of it, the last moment of winter's hold on the landscape, when I found myself awoken one night by the sound of whimpering.

"What is it?" I asked, sitting up wide awake when I realized it was Heather. "What is it, girl? Did you dream of –"

"Magnus –"

But she did not dream. She reached down between her legs in the dim light from the fire and brought her hand up between our faces. Her fingers were dark with – what was it? It took me a moment to understand what I was seeing, and when I did, it was as if someone had torn my stomach right out of me. It was blood. Thick and wet and terrifying.

"What –" I stuttered, my mind suddenly unable to process anything beyond panic. "What – Heather, what –"

"I must have been pregnant," she said, in a tone as flat and bleak as I had ever heard her speak with. "Magnus, I must have been pregnant."

I carried her to the healer in the middle of the night, wrapped in our stained bedding, and sat helplessly to the side as the woman confirmed that the bleeding was a lost pregnancy.

"I didn't even know," Heather whispered.

"It's not a rare thing," the healer told her gently. "I'll give you some herbs to boil in water for a tea, to help stop the bleeding. You must go back to bed, and you must stay there until the new moon. This is a time of great weakness for a woman, great vulnerability. You can get sicker if you try to do too much, if you do not take the time to heal."

"But –"

The healer turned to me. "You will stay at her side, Northman? You will make sure she does not leave her bed until the new moon?"

I nodded, but I was in no fit state to take in information. Neither was Heather. When we got back to our dwelling we sat at the table in silence for a period of time, before I remembered that she was supposed to be lying down.

"Who cares?" She asked, her voice suddenly bitter. "Who cares if I lie down or not? I lost the baby, didn't I? What else could happen?"

"The healer said you were to take to bed until the new moon," I told her, reaching for her hand even as I felt I could offer no real help. "She said if you don't rest, you could get weaker. She said –"

Heather looked up at me before I could finish, and the look in her eyes nearly broke my heart.

"I was pregnant?" She whispered plaintively. "Magnus, I was pregnant. With your baby. We were going to have a baby. And now we're not?"

I took her in my arms and brought her to lie beside me in bed when the tears started to spill down her cheeks. "It's as it is," I told her, brushing her hair off her face. "There will be another child, girl."

***

Heather seemed lost after the loss of the child we hadn't even known about. She mourned the baby she had not had time to imagine. And I tended to her, and allowed her the room to do as she needed.

Perhaps she was not the only one who was lost. That spring I felt our impermanence on the earth more deeply than I had ever felt it before. I felt the loss of my family, of my brother and my mother and father and my homeland. I watched the Angles going about their lives, and I watched Heather mourn and it crystallized, like a tree on the horizon as a fog lifts, that she needed something I was not providing.

I needed it, too. We needed to put our roots down. We needed something solid. That night, I left Heather with Brona and went to see Lord Eldred to ask if we might stay on the Haesting estate. Not for another season, or another moon, but for good. I asked if we might become part of their settlement.

"I had thought it already done," Lord Eldred told me as we sat across from each other at the high table. "I think everyone in Haesting thought it already done. Many say the estate would not even be here any longer were it not for you and your help on the night of the raid. It will be good for you – and good for the girl, Heather. How is she?"

I reached down to scratch the ears of a dog who had appeared beside my knee, and sighed. "I don't know. There is so much to do, and she speaks of the child infrequently now. I still see her sometimes, when she does not know I do, staring off at something I cannot see. I know she thinks of the baby then."

"You must give her another baby."

"Aye. But before that I must give her a home. A real home, not somewhere temporary, before we leave for another land. And I must give her the title of wife, so she knows that I will only leave her when death takes me."

A servant brought a flagon of ale and placed it on the table. Lord Eldred poured each of us a cup and we sat quietly for a short while, drinking.

"Yes," he said eventually. "Marry her. Give her a child. If you care for her happiness, you will do these things."

"All I care for is her happiness," I replied. "More than anything else – more than my own."

"You shall take your marriage oaths here, in my hall. Neither of you have any family nearby, and so we will be your family, Magnus. I get ahead of myself, don't I? Before any other plans are made, you must first ask the girl if she wishes to be your wife."

I spent the next few days, as we worked to tend our garden and keep our house, observing Heather. I thought I was being subtle about it, too, until she turned to me one afternoon while she plucked slugs from the mud, before they could get to our peas and greens, and asked if I had a new hobby.

"A what?" I asked, because by that time we were used to each other coming out with words the other had never heard. "A hobby?"

"Yes," she smiled – Gods, what a relief to see her smiling – "a hobby. It's like a pastime, something to do that isn't work. You have seen how Bradwin carves those little animal figurines from wood after dinner? That's a hobby."

"Ah," I replied, still not sure what she was talking about.

"Well do you?" She pressed me. "Have a new hobby? Is watching me your new hobby?"

I closed my eyes and laughed. "I thought you hadn't noticed."

"I notice everything, Magnus."

"That you do."

She came to me across the garden plot, which I had started to enclose with a dry-stone wall, and pulled the brim of her straw hat down over her eyes to block the sun. And then she kissed me on the cheek and grinned.

"So what's going on? Why are you hovering?"

"I have just been thinking," I told her, "of something you said to me before the winter."

"And what was it I said? Come inside with me, I need to get something to drink."

I followed her into our dwelling. "You said you were lonely. You said you had always been lonely."

Heather looked up at me as she held the ladle that we used to scoop ale out of the cask, and I could not read the look in her eyes. "I did say that," she replied, pouring the ale into a cup. "Do you want one?"

I shook my head. "And do you feel it still?" I asked, sitting down at our table and watching her drink the ale with the gusto of a thirsty child.

"Why are you asking me about this?" She responded, looking into her cup and not at me.

I took her hand, then, and clasped it in mine. "Why do you think? Because I don't wish you to be lonely, still. Are you? Do you miss your family? Is it enough to have me, and this little dwelling?"

I could tell from the way she turned her body in the chair that Heather had not expected to have a serious conversation that afternoon. Still, I had to know.

"I don't ask you these things to make you unhappy," I continued, when she did not answer right away. "I only ask them because it has become clear to me over the past season that nothing matters to me as much as you. If you are still lonely, then nothing I've done has been good enough. If you are still lonely, then –"

"I'm not lonely."

I narrowed my eyes, trying to figure out if she was being truthful or just trying to make me stop asking. She must have seen that I was skeptical, because she repeated herself.

"I'm not lonely, Magnus. I'm a little sad, because I lost our baby. I am not as sad as I was, but I am still sad. But I'm not lonely. It's funny, isn't it?"

"What's funny?"

"It's funny that I used to live with so many other people. Not just my parents, but everyone. So many people everywhere, you couldn't get away from them if you tried. All those people and I was lonely. And now, I have one person. I have the Angles, too, but you know what I mean. I have you. And I am not lonely with you, if that's what you're worried about."

The healer had warned that Heather might go through a period of weakness after the baby was lost. She warned that some women never recover from it. But it didn't happen. I looked across the table at her in the warmth of the afternoon, at her hair the color of the chestnuts that fell from the tree behind our dwelling and her eyes the color of the sea on a cloudy day and I saw that she still glowed with health. Even in the winter when the food ran low and we went to bed with our bellies rumbling, she had never lost that sparkle in her eyes.

"Why are you looking at me like that?" She asked. "What's gotten into you?"

"I was just thinking of the place you come from," I told her. "A place where you were never hungry. You have the look about you of a King's daughter, you know – many in Haesting say it. The look of someone who was not deprived of food or warmth as a child. And yet you speak of it as if you don't miss it."

"I don't. Not really. Perhaps I would, if it weren't for you?"

"I spoke to Lord Eldred a few days ago. I told him we would stay. Not for another moon, or two moons, or three, but for good. If you disagree you can tell me why but I was just thinking that there is no longer any reason for me to go anywhere. There's no reason to go across the sea to the Kingdom of the Franks, or back to the North."

Heather hadn't taken her eyes off me. And when I said that there was no longer any reason for me to leave, I saw that they began to glimmer.

"The North isn't my home anymore," I continued. "You are my home. Wherever you are is home. So if you don't want to stay here, then –"

"I do!" She replied, her voice breaking as she got up from the table and came to me, curling herself into my lap and resting her head in the spot under my chin, which seemed to have been made solely for that purpose. "I do want to stay here, Magnus! I want – I want to stay with you. It's like you said – home isn't about a place anymore. Not for me, either. Home is just you now. Home is a person."

I wrapped my arms around her, holding her against me. "And if you'll have me," I said, leaning down to kiss the top of her head. "We'll be married in Lord Eldred's hall."

There was a silence after I said that, one that lasted too long for my comfort. And then she turned her face up to me, as if trying to work out if she'd heard me correctly.

"Did you just propose?" She asked, smiling and wiping a tear off one creamy cheek. "Magnus, did you just casually propose to me as if you were asking me to go picking oysters? Did you just ask me to – to *marry* you?!"

"Yes..." I replied, perplexed. "Is it – is that not how it's done where you come from? In the North my father would have gone to meet your father, and there would have been a negotiation period while our families worked out the terms of the marriage. But as neither of us have any family here, I did not know how to ask. And I notice, Heather, that even as you dance around me like a madwoman, that you have still not given me an –"

"YES!"

"Yes? Is it what you –"

"Yes!" She cried again, her laughter filling my ears. "Yes, Magnus. Yes, yes, yes, yessss!"

I stood up and put my hands on our table, exhaling and more relieved than I thought I would be. Heather noticed at once and came back to me, putting her hand on my back and looking suddenly concerned – although the smile still played at the corners of her mouth.

"What?" She asked. "Did you think I would say no? I only hesitated because I couldn't believe you were really asking. We, uh – that's not how people propose where I come from."

"Isn't it?" I replied. "Have I done it all wrong, girl? How would it be done in the United States of America?"

She smiled. She always smiled when I named her homeland. And then she knelt on one knee at my feet and looked up at me. "Well," she began, "first you would get down on one knee."

"On *one* knee? Not two?"

"No, it has to be one."

"Why?"

"I have no idea," she giggled. "Stop asking questions. OK. So. You get down on one knee. And then you, uh, you offer me a diamond ring. But wait! First you have to give a speech about how much you love me and how wonderful I am."

"Is it so?" I teased. "Only the man must give a speech on the beauty and exceptional character of the woman? What if I want to hear the same said of me? What if I want a jeweled ring, girl?"

Heather reached up and caressed my cheek. "It's not how it's done – but I suppose if you want to hear that you're wonderful and strong and sexy and smart and literally everything I could ever have dreamed of in a man I could say that."

She smiled, but I could see that she spoke the truth, even as her manner was playful. I pulled her up onto my lap and kissed her.

"Do you feel disappointed, girl, that I did not give you a ring? There is sometimes an exchange of rings at the marriage ceremony itself, and there are certain customs that only a married woman can take part in. There is a certain way of braiding the hair, for example, that means a Northwoman is married, and a style of golden arm band that is, again, the mark of a married woman. I suppose we will both find out what the Angles' customs are."

"I'm not disappointed," she whispered. "You are the least disappointing person I have ever met in my life, Magnus. The only thing I'm afraid of is – is –"

It took me a few seconds, in my happiness over Heather's agreeing to marry me, to see that she was crying. I immediately wiped the tears from her cheeks and took her shoulders in my hands, demanding to know what it was she was afraid of.

"I'm afraid of disappointing you," she answered, very quietly. "I'm afraid I won't be able to have any children. The healer said sometimes it happens after a woman loses her baby – she said sometimes she can't have any more. And it's been how long? We – Magnus, we do it all the time! Why am I not pregnant again? Why –"

"Heather!" I spoke loudly and tightened my grip on her, because she had begun to speak with great haste and her words were running into one another. "Heather, girl, look at me!"

She looked at me, and at once I saw in her eyes that what she spoke of was something she had been carrying with her since the baby had been lost. Why had I not thought of it?

"Voss," I swore, balling my hand into a fist and slamming it down on the table. "Voss, girl, I did not see that you carried this burden! I see it now, in your eyes. How could I have missed that? How could I not have know that a woman who loses her child will worry about losing more children? I'm a dull-wit – and I'm sorry. I'm so sorry. It's my task to keep you from your worries – I will work harder at it. Please don't worry – look at yourself, you are healthier than any of the girls on the estate, and you are still young. There will be another child. There will be many children for you – for us."

"Will there?" She asked, her voice shaking slightly.

"Yes," I answered at once.

If only I had known, in my youthful naiveté – for I was still youthful, and naive, when it came to the things I spoke of that day – that one must never make certain pronouncements about matters that are best left to the Gods.

Chapter 15: Heather

Until Magnus proposed, in his sweetly unadorned Northern way, I truly had not even considered that a man – especially a man like him – would one day want to marry me. To marry *me*. Heather Renner, the screw-up. The bad girl. The dummy who wore too much eye make-up and would rather go to concerts than study. Heather Renner, who was so awful even her own mother didn't like her.

Those ways of thinking about myself were fading. Their power, once so great they had almost paralyzed me, began to wane the day I met Magnus the Northman, who didn't seem to think of me as a dummy or a screw-up at all. I respected him. I admired him – more than I had ever respected or admired anyone in my life. And so his obvious love for me finally helped to do away with all of the baggage my mother had spent my life trying to saddle me with. My love for him was as bright and intense as mid-afternoon sunshine. It made me smile to see him walk into a room, and to witness the respect with which the Angles – including Lord Eldred – treated him.

We married in the lord's hall in what I thought might have been early July – neither the Angles nor Magnus called the months by the names I knew. A priest was sent for, although he was like no priest I had ever seen, and the Gods and Goddesses he invoked when he called them to attend our ceremony were not any that I was familiar with.

"You two are almost bound," he intoned in the hall, as we stood in front of him after vowing to always stay true to and support each other, no matter the circumstances of life. "For it to be done, there must be the giving of the swords."

I did not quite know what the 'giving of the swords' was. Brona had explained, and Lord Eldred had sent for a sword to be made especially for me, by the King's own smiths. During the ceremony it was held by a young Angle boy, who waited for the moment to bring it forward. It was Magnus' turn first, though.

He turned to face me and held his blade balanced across his two open hands. "My ancestral sword is yours, Heather. I give it to you to keep, until such time that our sons may keep and use it."

The priest nodded to me, then, and I saw that the Angles were looking at me expectantly. I reached out and took the hilt in my hand, and then both hands as Magnus whispered to me that it was heavy. It *was* heavy. So heavy my almost-husband had to reach out quickly and stop the point from hitting the floor.

And then it was my turn. The Angle child stepped forward, dragging the weapon, which was thankfully held safely in a sheath, to me. And when I could not pick it up, I simply held it by the hilt and faced Magnus to say my words.

A wave of shyness came over me before I began to speak – the hall was crowded with people – and when I started my voice was hoarse. I coughed and looked up into my Northman's eyes, which always served to calm me, and then I started again:

"You have given me your ancestral sword. Now you must have a new blade. With this sword, keep safe our home and family."

When he took the new sword from my hands, lifting it with such ease that I could almost hear the impressed murmur pass among the watching Angles, it was one of the proudest moments of my life. I watched him pull the shining blade from its sheath, and his eyes run over the jewels – red garnets, deep honey-toned amber and, in the very center, a single pearl, which Lord Eldred had told me was an extremely rare and special thing.

"You honor me," Magnus said, his eyes wide at the beauty of the sword and the import of the moment. "There will be nothing greater in my life than to call you wife, Heather."

After the swords, we exchanged rings – simple gold bands – and then an ornately carved wooden key was presented to me by Magnus, as a symbol of my new authority over our household and all the goods within it. We had joked, before the ceremony, that we did not yet have a dwelling grand enough to require keys – and that giving me authority over the food stores was likely to see it all eaten by rats within the next moon. But in Lord Eldred's hall, the moment was not light. It was not somber, either, but there was a seriousness to it, an acknowledgment of the weight of what was happening – two people joining their lives forever.

When the key was safely tied to the thin leather belt that I wore around my waist, over my bride's tunic, the priest bid Magnus and I to kiss each other, to make it official. And when my new husband stepped forward, took my face in his hands and bent to kiss my mouth, a cheer rose up from the Angles – many of whom we now called friends – and two paths, that had been running in parallel for some time, finally merged into one.

***

Before the marriage ceremony, the Angles had split themselves into two halves, roughly based on Brona's blood family on one side and Bradwin's on the other. Each stood in for the families that Magnus and I did not have present, and each made the day an occasion for the entirety of the Haesting estate, rather than just for Magnus and I.

When the ceremony was over, the biggest feast that had been held on the estate since I'd arrived there with a Northman I barely knew took place in Lord Eldred's hall. Huge clay casks of mead were brought up from his personal stores, and the Angle children fought each other over honeycakes while the adults' found their cheeks growing redder with mead and laughter and the warmth of family.

Because the Angles *were* family by then. Not in a forced or ostentatious way – in fact it was not their custom to speak of such things – but simply in the way of it being true in their hearts – and mine. Magnus knew what it was to have family, and community. He knew what it was to be – well, to be *known*. To belong to a group who truly knows and loves you. I, having never known such a thing, reveled in even the smallest pleasures of being close to others. To walk to the estate from our dwelling was to greet – and be greeted by – as many people as you passed on the path. Each smiled warmly at the sight of me, and called me Eltha, and asked after little matters – how was the pea crop doing? did we need help to clear the thickly tangled roots from the field where we intended to plant oats? would we be at the estate that night to drink ale and sing songs?

And so the wedding was not just the making official of my bond to Magnus, it was the making official of our bond to the Haesting estate, and to the Angles themselves. Late on the night, when new levels of boisterousness had been reached, I suddenly sensed a growing tension in the room.

Magnus, who was almost as unfamiliar with the marriage rituals of the Angles as I was, shrugged when I asked him what was going on. And then his friend Eadwin came over to bend down and let us know that the bride-race was about to commence.

"The – the bride what?" Magnus asked, grinning drunkenly because he had had quite a lot of ale.

"I told you of it!" Eadwin laughed, before Bradwin joined him, and I looked around to see that almost everyone had stood up, and was obviously waiting for some kind of signal. "We race to your cottage now, the two parties and the new husband and wife – you must get there before anyone else, Magnus, or you will lose the right to carry your own bride over the –"

It was at that moment that my new husband appeared to remember what it was his friends spoke of, because he suddenly put his cup back down on the table, turned on his heel and ran out of Lord Eldred's hall at great speed. And after him went the Angles – shouting and whooping and racing out into the night as I looked up at Eadwin.

"Well?" He said to me. "Are you coming? It won't do for Magnus to have no bride to carry over the threshold."

And so I ran, too. The path outside of the estate had been set with lit torches, all the way to our home, where I found the Angles crowded around the door trying to wrestle Magnus – who stood fast in the frame – away from it.

"Ah!" A voice arose when I appeared, breathless with running and happiness. "The bride arrives! Magnus has won!"

Our friends burst into song again as I walked carefully up the stone path, that Magnus and I had laid together, to the front door. And when I got there he scooped me into his arms and, to the sound of loud, singing, drunken Angles, carried me over the threshold and inside.

When the door closed behind us, he set me gently on my feet and we looked into each other's eyes, smiling, glowing with joy.

"I wonder, did I do it right?" Magnus asked, chuckling. "Eadwin and the Angles told me how to do it, to wait until you arrived and then take you in my arms through the door – but I do not remember if I was supposed to say some words or not."

I snaked my arms around his waist and put my chin on his chest – one of my favorite things to do – and looked up into his eyes. "Perhaps we will find out tomorrow that we're not married, and we'll have to do it all again?"

"As it is," my new husband bent to kiss my mouth. "I can think of far worse fates than marrying you again, my love. Perhaps we will not get it right the second time, either? Perhaps we will spend the rest of our lives getting married every day?"

Already, I could feel under his leathers what he needed. We had not made love for a half moon before the ceremony – a full moon had been tried for, but neither of us were able to keep away from each other for so long. Still, a half moon was far more than we had gone since meeting, and even with the mead slackening my tongue and fuelling the Angles who still sang and danced outside our cottage, it was not enough to dull the flame that leapt up in my belly at feeling Magnus' arousal.

"Haven't you had too much to drink?" I teased. "I thought I might get some sleep – I'm so tired."

"Oh," he grinned, running his hands down my back and caressing my ass. "You thought you might get some sleep, did you?"

How is it that two weeks can feel so long? When I pushed my fingers around the back of his neck – that smooth, strong neck, the close scent of which was better than any drug for me – and buried them in his hair, it was already enough to have me on fire, my skin tingling with anticipation.

"Mmm," I replied, opening my lips to take his tongue, and to curl my own up into his mouth. "Yeah. I'm tired. We should just go to sleep."

"As it is, wife," he replied, pulling away from me suddenly and collapsing back onto our bed. "Yes, I feel tired, too. Good-night."

Three lit torches illuminated the interior of the cottage. It was enough light to see, from the bulge in Magnus' leathers, that he was in no way interested in sleeping. Still, he did a good job of pretending. He did such a good job that I was forced to crawl on top of him and begin unlacing the ties that held his leathers up. He opened his eyes, then, and looked up at me.

"Take off your tunic. I want to see you."

And so I took off my tunic – slowly, without breaking our intense eye contact. I reached down and took the hem of it in my hands, and then pulled it up over my hips, my belly, my breasts, and finally my head, and tossed it onto the floor. Magnus didn't reach for me right away. He just looked. He drew his eyes like fingers over my torch-lit curves– slow and methodical and torturous.

"Magnus," I whispered, when I could bear the lack of his touch no longer.

"What is it, girl? I thought you were tired? Why do you look at me now as if you need something. What is it you need?"

It was something he specifically liked – me asking him to touch me, to kiss me – to fuck me. He would stop our lovemaking often, to make me beg for him to continue. I loved it as much as he did – perhaps more, because there had never been anything that made me so hot as his raw desire.

"Go on," he urged, reaching up and taking the tip of one of my nipples – just one – between two fingers and rolling it gently, so I could feel the aching, heavy need between my legs growing more intense. "Tell me. Do you not wish to sleep any longer?"

"Magnus –"

He sat up, then, and pulled me against his chest. "What, Heather? Is it more mead you wish for? Shall I ask the Angles to –"

"Magnus!"

He grasped my buttocks in his hands, squeezing, pulling me hard down against him, and nuzzled his head into my breasts. His leathers were half-on, half-off, and all it took from me was a little twist of my hips to feel him there, wet and thick between my bare thighs. A twitch of hunger ran through my sex to feel him so close, and an emptiness that only one thing could fill.

When Magnus reached down between us to take himself in his hands, I was already inhaling, anticipating the sweet sensation of him pushing himself into me. But he didn't do it. He nudged the head between my lips, and ran it up and down, exhaling hard as he passed over my aching opening, but refusing to put it where he knew I needed it.

And then, just when I thought I might go mad from it, he suddenly flipped me over onto my back and put his hands on my thighs, opening me wide.

Outside, the Angles' songs were dying down, but there were still some stragglers hanging on. I didn't care. I didn't care who was out there, or who was going to hear me. When Magnus bent to kiss my mouth, and then moved further down to flick his tongue around each of my nipples, I thought once again that I was going to get what I wanted. But instead of moving back up, he went further, kissing down my belly and then my thighs until they quivered underneath him.

I cried out when his tongue found my clit, and began to circle it slowly, repeatedly, exactly as he knew I liked. But still, I wanted him inside me. Even as he drew me closer and closer to bliss, I ached to be filled.

"Magnus," I begged, as he didn't slow the little movements of his tongue. "Magnus, please. Please."

But he refused. He refused even to use his fingers. When my eyes were starting to flutter shut and I was beginning to lose control, I pushed my fingers down between my legs, intending to push them into myself, but he took my hand away and lowered his whole mouth onto my clit, sucking gently, still working his tongue.

I didn't come all at once. Magnus slowed it down, using his tongue like the expert he was, building my orgasm slowly, brick by brick like a wall of fire, until my whole body arched up off the bed and I screamed his name as white hot bliss bloomed like a firework between my legs.

My husband only stopped when I was completely finished, and I lay panting and temporarily mindless underneath him. And then he rested his cheek on my thigh and looked up at me, his eyes clouded by then almost to the point of unseeing.

When he sat up on his knees, I saw that he was so hard it lay almost against his belly, and that the tip was shiny with pre-cum.

"You don't have to be gentle," I told him, reaching up and stroking his cheek. "Magnus, you don't have to be –"

"Stop," he breathed, before breaking into a grin. "Girl, stop. It's been a half moon. Your words alone will finish me."

His desire for me was an ever-replenishing well, an endless source of joy. To leave him sated gave me a satisfaction I had never known before, one so deep it felt as if it lurked in my very bones – but it never lasted too long. A night spent naked in each other's arms, twisting ourselves into endless configurations of lust, would if anything leave him even hungrier the next day, or the next night, after our work had been done. I had known the shallow, reflexive sexuality of men before. I had even enjoyed it, in the same shallow, reflexive way. But it was Magnus who showed me that there was a whole world of heady delight to explore, a detailed taxonomy of longing – different sighs, fleeting expressions that would pass across his eyes, the specific tightness of his grip on this or that part of my body – that would, if noted down on paper, fill enough pages to write a library's worth of books. We did not have to leave Haesting – we did not even have to leave our bed – to explore this new geography.

And the height of it all for me was always the moment, the silky, fraught seconds, before he came. On the night of our wedding, I wanted to enjoy him as he had just enjoyed me. I wanted to bathe in my husband's pleasure, to draw it out as he had mine. And so when I saw how close he was, and that if he was to enter me at that moment it would all be over very quickly, I agreed to give him some time to cool down.

"You've had a lot of mead," I commented, staring up into his eyes, dark as they were then with desire. "How is it you're so eager with that much mead in your belly?"

"It's been a half-moon," he replied, reaching up to run a hand over one of my breasts, dragging the thumb back and forth over my nipple. "You could pour a whole cask of mead down my throat and I would still be as a boy of ten and six who has just seen his pretty neighbor bathing naked in the sea."

I laughed. "You sound like you're speaking from experience. Were you that boy? Were you spying on your neighbor when you were a teenager?"

As we chatted, Magnus stayed knelt between my legs, and his cock stayed against my thigh, not seeming to lose any of its fervor. "When I was a boy, our longhouse was set back from the others – there was an unfortunate lack of opportunity for spying on pretty girls."

He moved his hand to my other breast, slowly and deliberately, aware that any haste would result in a too-quick conclusion.

"You know this is my favorite thing," I said, reaching down to run my hands over his powerful thighs – as thick and strong as tree-trunks, the cords of muscle visible underneath the skin when he tensed them.

"What's your favorite thing? Giving yourself to me? I already know it, girl. I –"

"No," I replied quietly. "I mean – yes. But I mean this *specifically*. When you're close, when I can see that you're close, when I can hear the way your breath changes. I can see it in you even now, look how tense you are! I think it's my favorite thing in the whole world when you're like this, Magnus."

He blew his breath forcefully out of his mouth and shook his head. "Gods, girl. Gods, *wife*. How am I supposed to last if you speak to me as you do? If you look at me as you do right now?"

"I don't think I want you to wait any longer," I replied, pulling my knees up, opening my legs underneath him.

"Heather –"

His tone was a warning. I ignored it.

"I want it," I whispered, biting my lip and smiling up at him, pushing my body eagerly up off the bed. "Now, Magnus. I don't want you to wait. I don't care if it doesn't last. I just want – OHH."

A heavy sigh pushed the rest of my words out of the way as he suddenly filled me with his entire, rigid length.

"Gods," he breathed, holding himself inside me for a few seconds before pulling out and sinking back in. "Gods, you're so soft, girl. Oh, Gods – Heather –"

"Don't hold back," I urged, caressing his cheek, sensing that he was trying to do so. "I want you to come, Magnus. I want you to come inside me. I want to go to sleep with it all over my thighs, all over my –"

He thrust into me hard, and groaned – quietly at first, but rising to almost a shout as he came – emptying himself deep inside, his whole body stiff.

And I took it. I pulled him down close to me, pressing his face into my neck, tilting my hips up over and over the way he liked me to do.

"Voss," he panted when I felt his body begin to relax, even as his hips still twitched with aftershocks. "Voss, Heather. Gods, I can't move. I don't think I can ever move again."

I kissed his ear, and his neck, and then lifted his head up so I could look him in the eyes.

"I love you," I told him. "I don't just love you when you come like that – or when you make me come like that – I love you all the time, Magnus. I love you like – like I don't even have words to describe."

He smiled one of his adorably dopey, post-sex smiles, and bent to kiss my mouth. "As it is, girl, have I driven the loneliness from your heart? Have I made it so you barely remember what it was to feel such a thing?"

My husband was being serious. I hadn't been expecting it, as he was often quick to an almost drunken state after I'd pleased him – but on our wedding night, I saw at once that what he asked had been on his mind for some time.

"What do you think?" I whispered, kissing him again. "Do I seem lonely to you at all? Do you sense any –"

"Aye, girl, you do not. But I want to hear it."

I kissed his cheek, and then his other cheek, and then his mouth again. "No," I replied. "No I am not lonely anymore, love. Because of you. I'm not lonely because of you. And now that I'm your wife, I'm going to spend the rest of my life showing you how I love you for it – how I love you for everything that you are."

"As it is," he said, rolling onto his back and pulling me in close next to him. "I would be lost without you."

***

And so the Northman from the 9th century and the girl from Los Angeles, USA, were married. I hadn't expected much to change after the ceremony – we'd been living together already for almost a year, first in the little hut on the Haesting estate and then in the cottage just outside the walls. But things did change. Not the actual tasks, not the ways we spent our days. But the feeling between us as we went about these tasks, and as we lived each day. The question of the future was no longer a question but a settled fact. My future was with Magnus, and his was with me. And it had a location now, too. It wasn't going to be somewhere else – somewhere south or north or hundreds of years in the future. It was going to be where we were.

I was surprised, a little, by just how much contentment it brought me. I'd grown up with a mother who lamented her marriage, and her only child, as things that kept her from the life of travel and adventure she dreamed of. And who knows, perhaps my mother truly was destined for a life of travel and adventure before I got in the way? But as I gained a distance of months and then years from her unhappy presence, I became more circumspect about blaming myself for my mom's dissatisfactions.

"It sounds as if she is one of those people who are never happy," Magnus said one night as we ate a stew of sneeps and oysters by candlelight and chatted about my past.

I looked up, surprised at first, and then less so.

"You must have known such a person?" He continued. "My mother's brother was that way. If the sun shone, it was too hot and he complained. If the clouds drew in it was too chilly, and he complained. Weather is a surface thing, but it went deeper with him, too. His wife, who gave him children and a warm hearth, was a source only of annoyance. When she cooked him dinner he complained that the vegetables were hard, rather than being happy that he had a wife to cook him dinner – as not all men have. The way you speak of your mother reminds me of him. It's funny, I always disliked him – my uncle. But now, speaking of this to you, all I feel is pity. Perhaps it is the right way to feel about your mother?"

"You're right," I told him. "At least I think you're right – my mother never really talked to me about how she felt about anything. Not serious things, anyway. But she was definitely one of those people who was never happy – who could always find the one wrong thing in a person or a situation and focus only on that."

"You grow further from her," Magnus said, nodding at the loaf of fresh bread so I would pass it to him. "I see it in you, girl. You hold yourself differently now, to when I first met you. You walk with your shoulders back. Sometimes when I see you I think to myself that I wish she, too, could see you. That she could see you how I see you."

I sometimes caught myself wondering, in the early years of my marriage, if the Northman understood what an earthquake his love was to me. We would sit at our table in the evenings, and talk as we did that night, and I would catch myself looking down at my arms, examining my fingers to see if there was a glow emanating from my skin. He loved me. He did not have to tell me he loved me – although he did, and often – because everything he did showed me it was true. He knew me. He knew me like no one else in my life had ever known me – even my own parents.

"What is it?" He asked that evening, when we spoke of my mother and he saw some of the wonder in my heart flit across my face. "Have you not thought of your mother this way b–"

"It's not that," I replied. "It's – it's you. You notice the way I walk? You notice the way *I hold my shoulders* – and that it's different now, to when we first met?"

"Aye," he replied, narrowing his eyes the way he always did when I said something he thought incredibly dense. "Do you not know that I notice you more than I notice anything else in this world? Do you not know how you hold my attention? This is love, girl – and you know I love you."

"I do know that," I told him. "I just – I know you love me. I do."

"But you remember, still, how it was to grow into yourself with a mother who didn't see you as I see you. You must forget, girl."

"I am forgetting."

He looked up. "I know."

Chapter 16: Magnus

She was happy. And because she was happy, I was happy. And because I was happy, she was happy. It was one of those circumstances like an eddy at the side of a river, feeding itself with the river's flow even as it fed back into the river. The Gods had seen fit to give me the contentment of my life – *she* had seen fit to give me the contentment of my life, and a new fervor took over after we were wed, to see that she was taken care of as she had not been before she came to me.

We were staying in Haesting, and Lord Eldred gave me permission to expand our plot of land, and to make it permanent. The summer after we were wed was long, and the harvest as bountiful as any the Angles could remember. When I began to build a new dwelling, with foundations of stone, my friends from the estate helped to carry the stones and mix the slurry of mud, sand and horsehair that was to hold them together. They helped me fell the large trees that were to make up the frame, and to weave the straw over the roof. And each day we progressed, I felt more and more sure of my ability to take care of Heather, to keep her warm and fed.

Soon we had a small flock of sheep – shaggy beasts with watchful yellow eyes – and another pig to fatten with scraps. Brona taught Heather how to make ale, and how to grind grain into flour with the grinding stones, and which plants and herbs to mix with the bedding-straw to keep the mites away.

The success of the little small-holding I built with my wife gave some of the other Angles itchy feet, whereupon Lord Eldred allowed a few of the more responsible men and their families to do as I had done – to build their homes outside the walls. Eventually a larger stone wall was built, around the new dwellings – and ever farther afield – to keep the wolves from the livestock. And so Haesting grew in those early years when we were lucky to have fair weather and favorable conditions for our crops and animals – not to mention a lull in the raids my own people were known to perpetrate up and down the coast of the Kingdom.

As the estate prospered, so did its fighting men. Lord Eldred often called on me to speak with him of the way the warriors were trained in the North, and then to apply what he had learned to his own people. The Angles had not kept their swordsmen well-trained, preferring instead – at least before I arrived – to count more on luck than skill, and to hope that the estate's position, placed back in the woods and not right on the coast, would help keep them protected. There seemed to be a general belief that should a sustained attacked ever be mounted, and their own warriors bested, that the King would send men to help them. Even after the raid by my own father and brother, some of them chose not to see that there would not be time to call for the King's men when their enemies were at the gates.

Lord Eldred soon saw the folly in this, after the raid. And it was me he tasked, as he had four daughters and no sons, with helping to organize a force of men – less than ten at first but soon encompassing most of the forty or so who were young and strong enough. No longer were these men to spend all of their days helping with the domestic and agricultural tasks, only taking their swords to hand when a threat appeared. Under my instruction they were to train – not just at the sword but some with the bow, some with simple spears – at combat every second day in the morning.

It was not long before Lord Eldred and I could stand watching the men at their training and nod to each other, confident that if another contingent of Northmen, or Mercians, or anyone else appeared out of the woods to demand surrender, Haesting could make a serious go of defending itself.

"I am grateful for your help, Northman," he said one morning as we walked from the training ground back to the hall. The Angles never stopped calling me 'Northman,' – it just changed over time, from a term laced with suspicion to one spoken with affection and fun.

"As it is, Haesting is my home now, Lord. It would not do for me to wish it vulnerable. Part of me is surprised my father has not returned, to punish me for Asger's death. If he ever sees fit to sail back across the sea to this place, we will be ready for him."

"Your father will not return," Eldred replied, stopping to ruffle a child's hair. "He will not face you again, his shame is too great. What a curse the Gods placed upon his head when they made the second son the superior of the first."

I had become almost a son to Eldred by then, or at least a trusted advisor, and he knew of the family history that led to the scene at Haesting's gates, where a son put a sword through his own brother.

"And with this talk of sons, Magnus, I thought it fit to send for one of the King's healers to visit Haesting – I thought she could see to your wife."

Worried, I looked up sharply. "My wife? Lord, is she ill? Is something kept from me about her –"

Eldred lay a hand on my shoulder. "I do not know that your wife is ill. But the time comes for children, does it not? I see the two of you together, and I wonder where is the child that will make you a family?"

"Ah," I replied quietly. Two winters had passed since our wedding ceremony, and Heather's belly did not swell. In truth it was more worrisome for her than for me at that time, and my reply to Lord Eldred was more out of concern for Heather than concern for my own bloodline. "Yes, Lord, it plays on her mind. She tries not to speak of it too often, but I see her looking at the other women with their infants, and..."

"The King's healer comes before the next moon. I will send for your wife when she arrives."

***

And so the King's healer came, and Heather saw her for an entire afternoon, answering questions about her blood cycles and how often we lay together and even what she dreamed of at night.

"She says I am young enough still," my wife reported when she returned that evening. "And that I don't lack enough food to get pregnant. She gave me some herbs to take every day in a tea and a little song to chant every night before I go to bed, to bring dreams that will make my belly more receptive to a baby. Not that I think singing songs is going to help anything."

"Do you not?" I asked, surprised that she would question the importance of our dreams in the events of our waking lives. "Why?"

"Why? Why would they? Whatever the problem is, it's not about dreams, Magnus."

I knew at once that this was one of her beliefs that she still carried with her from home. I was not sure if she even noticed it herself, how dismissive she could be of some of the Angles' beliefs – of some of my beliefs. When the Angle women warned her not to swim in the river that ran out to the sea south of the estate, for the ill health and evil presences that lurked in the depths, Heather laughed and ignored them completely. She did not seem to have the fear of unseen things that the Angles – and my own people – had.

When I asked why she wasn't afraid to swim in the river, after she had returned one day from doing just that, she shrugged, as if the question itself was ridiculous.

"There aren't demons in the water, Magnus," she told me pertly, as a mother will tell a child that sheep cannot fly. "It's just a story they tell to frighten themselves away, because they can't swim. It's useful, but it's not *true.*"

That's how she was with the healer's advice about the songs before bedtime. Completely dismissive.

"But why not try?" I asked, baffled as I had been during the discussion about the river at her certainty. "What if –"

"What if what?!" She responded, her voice suddenly despairing. "What if singing a song before I go to sleep could help me get pregnant? It can't! I wish it could – believe me I wish it could! Do you think I wouldn't do anything? Don't ask me to have hope where there is none! I will take the herbs. But I won't start singing songs to have dreams for my belly or whatever the hell it was the healer said. The last thing I need is false hope."

It was not the time to question my wife on her strange beliefs. Her eyes shone with tears as she looked at me, and I pulled her onto my lap and held her close.

"I love you," I told her. "I love you, girl. Whether we have ten children or none, my love for you will be the same, just as ardent, just as constant. It fair causes me pain to see you this way, and it kills me that there is nothing I can do to change it."

***

A child did not come. When the winters since our marriage were five, Heather seemed to become accepting of the circumstance. My own travels on that unhappy path were different, and I found myself with a feeling of hollowness in my chest sometimes, as I grew older and came to understand more what a family was, and what it was to be a father. Eadwin and Bradwin, my closest friends, each had many children. So many I had trouble recalling all their names.

My friends often complained of their responsibilities, of how they longed for the time before it was on their heads to keep small bellies full. But I, not being responsible for any small bellies, only saw the love they had for their offspring. Bradwin had a little daughter, her eyes as blue as her mother's and her temperament as mischievous as her father's, and she would often find her way to the fields, or wherever it was we were working that day, to walk back to Haesting with us. In truth, it made my heart ache to see them together, although I did not show it.

At night, I began to dream of children. Little girls with braids as dark and glossy as Heather's. Little boys who would reach for me the way Bradwin's girl reached for him. I dreamed of my wife with a babe in her arms, and the look of contentment on her face that I saw sometimes on the faces of the Anglo women, as they held their infants. And always, I woke up to the reality that none of those children were real outside the landscape of my dreams. Their smiles flickered away as wakefulness came upon me, their giggles fading like echoes bouncing down a canyon.

It was into this situation that Lord Eldred came to us one evening, after the work of the day had been done and my wife and I took our supper. When I opened the door to see him a surge of energy ran through my body, and I looked to my side to see that my sword was where it always was.

"We aren't under attack," the lord said, seeing my reaction. "Actually I came to see the two of you with a matter that has been on my mind since the last moon."

We invited him inside and gave him ale and bread, and the lord of Haesting told us that a young peasant girl had died in childbirth, and that the baby, which had also been expected to die, had managed to live a full moon.

"It is fortunate," I replied, as Heather sat uncharacteristically silent beside me.

"Yes," Eldred replied, coughing. "Ceoldor's wife has taken the child to her own breast..."

I sat waiting for the lord to continue, because I did not yet understand why he'd come to tell me of a peasant girl's child, or that it lived even after its mother's death. Children and their mothers were vulnerable, especially in the period close to birth – it was not a rare thing for one or both of them to pass into the next life from the ordeal.

"I hope the babe will live," I offered a few moments later, when it became clear that Eldred was waiting for me to speak. "Ceoldor's wife is strong, she will –"

And then I stopped speaking abruptly when a small cry suddenly came from the direction of the door. It was my wife who leapt to her feet and crossed the cottage in an instant, reaching outside and taking a little woven basket into her hands. When she turned back, and I saw that she was crying, I was even more baffled.

"What is it?" I asked, alarmed. "Heather – why do you –"

"Lord Eldred brings us the child!" She replied, understanding the situation much faster than I did – which was not an unusual circumstance. "Is it true, Lord? What of the father? Is there –"

"The girl did not know who the father was, and none of the men have stepped forward. Ceoldor and his wife say they will keep it if no one else wants it, and I understand that an extra mouth to feed, one not born of your own union, may be an unwelcome thing. Still, I thought you might want to take the child yourselves, as the Gods have not seen fit all these winters to give you one in the usual way."

I opened my mouth to respond, and found that I had no response. A child? A babe, freshly birthed? I did not know the first thing about the creatures – or keeping them alive.

As it happened, none of what I knew or didn't know mattered, because the next thing I saw was my wife reaching into the basket and pulling a tiny bundle – so impossibly tiny – from inside, which she lifted up close to her face, where the tears ran freely down her cheeks.

We kept the child. It was a girl, who we gave the name Eidyth because she smiled a lot and one of the Angle women told Heather that the name meant 'joyous.'

At first, I did not take to her. It was not that I held any special disdain in my heart for the mite – but I certainly did not know what to do with her. Even as I held her in my arms, or tried to feed her goat's milk out of the leather bladder with a tiny hole poked into one corner that Heather had made, she seemed almost otherworldly with her strangely knowing eyes and her smallness that made me afraid I would break her bones.

My wife took to her, though. My wife took to her like I had not seen her take to anything before – except me. She wore the child strapped to her back like the other women, and seemed to know within days what each of her cries meant, and how to soothe them.

For the first time since meeting Heather, after Eidyth came I felt slightly unmoored. I'd seen it before, even as a child myself – a woman's all-encompassing interest in her baby. I'd heard Eadwin and Bradwin complain of it, when their wives had new babies, of how their husbands were forgotten.

Heather did not forget me. Her attentions were elsewhere, at first, and that was a new situation, but I was not like Eadwin and Bradwin. Their children had come quickly, one after the other, and to see their wives with those children was not a noteworthy thing. For me, it was different. To have witnessed Heather's pain – to have felt that pain myself – was to understand what a precious thing it was we had been given. And even if at first I felt apart from the child, I would have had to be blind not to see the look in my wife's eyes as she gazed down at the baby when she slept.

"I love her," Heather said one afternoon, when we sat at the top of the beach watching the sea and she held Eidyth in her arms. "When Lord Eldred brought her to us, I thought maybe I wouldn't. I thought maybe I could only love a baby I gave birth to." She looked up at me, holding up one hand to shield the sun from her eyes. "But I love her. I love her more than I could have imagined it was even possible to love her, Magnus. Sometimes, I –"

She hesitated and looked back out at the sea. I put my arm around her, because I knew why she hesitated. "Do not worry, girl. There is room in your heart for –"

"It doesn't mean I don't love you as much!" She interjected. "Or any less. I've been so worried that you would think I was trading one love for another. But that isn't what –"

I waited for her to look back at me and then held her gaze, so she would know I spoke the truth. "I know it, girl. I know it. It's natural for a woman's focus to switch, when a child is so young. Do you think I resent it? Do you think I resent you – or her? No. I admit that at first I did not quite know what to make of her but as for you, my love? It has been one of the joys of my life to see you with her. Did you not hear me all those times I told you I loved you? Did you not believe me? Your contentment is my own."

And it was. Heather and I were no longer separate people. Even in my thoughts, I would catch myself wondering sometimes if my laughter at an amusing comment was my own, or if I laughed only because I knew exactly how my wife would have done so. We finished each other's sentences, and found that there was often no reason to comment on a small matter, because each of us knew already what the other thought. So as Eidyth grew, and came to recognize me, to reach her fat little arms up for me when I came home after a day of work, it did not need to be explicitly stated that my heart grew new space for her just as Heather's had.

Sometimes I would catch Heather watching us, as I held Eidyth on my lap and she ran her hands over my stubble and screamed with delight when I blew kisses onto her cheeks. In those moments I knew a true peace, a new kind of happiness. It was not even a winter after the little bundle had been brought to our door that it was not possible to distinguish between a family who the Gods had blessed with children of their blood, and my own family. It was just as Heather said – the love, when it came, was all-encompassing, uncomplicated, complete. By the time Eidyth took her first wobbly steps along the flagstones that led to our cottage, my pride was that of any father. In fact it was I who watched her that day, and called excitedly for my wife to come outside and see as our little one put one foot in front of another, and then another and another for the first time.

"The Gods meant us to have her," I whispered one night as we peered into the cradle – a cradle the child was rapidly outgrowing – and watched her sleep. "You're going to ask me to explain, but I cannot. All I can do is feel the truth of it."

"No," Heather replied quietly. "I won't ask you to explain, because I feel it too. Sometimes I think about what would have happened if the woman who gave birth to her had lived – and then I cry. I cry! Over the prospect of a young woman living rather than dying! It scares me sometimes, how much I love Eidyth. The things I would do for her..."

***

It was not too long before I got a glimpse of how much my wife would do for our daughter. It was the second winter after she had made us a family that the girl woke us in the night with a cough that would not loosen its grip. I lifted her out of bed to find that she was wet with vomit, and that her breathing was labored.

The cough lasted into the next day and then the next, and then, at the height of the fits, Eidyth began to slip into unconsciousness and Heather and I found ourselves caught in a flood of terror.

"She's not breathing!" I heard, as I was returning from the estate with a small sack of herbs from the healers, to mix with tallow and rub on the child's chest. "Magnus! SHE'S NOT BREATHING!"

Heather flew out of the cottage, her eyes wide, Eidyth limp in her arms, and we tried to rouse her in any way we could think of. When our daughter's lips began to turn blue and Heather looked at me to do something, it was the most helpless I'd ever felt.

I gasped with relief when she opened her mouth and let out a whimper, and then I sat back on the stones that led to our front door and cried openly, as a child does. Heather did not cry – not right away. She stayed on her feet, her face white, her breathing shallow, and when I reached up to pull her down to me, she shook me off.

"No. No. Magnus – she's dying. Eidyth is dying! I have to – I know where to take her. I know where –"

I only ever saw Heather in that kind of panic a few times. The kind where her words ran into each other and her voice became high and thin and her hands trembled.

"Lord Eldred has sent a messenger to the King's healer," I said. "They will have arrived by now, and by tomorrow –"

"No," she cut me off, shaking her head. "No! These healers aren't helping – they never help! Can't you see that? It's all bullshit! It's all just – it's that thing where you believe something is going to work and so it does work – until it doesn't. I have to go! We – I have to go. I'll take her to a doctor, OK? A real doctor. I need to find that tree in the – Magnus, do you remember where it was that –"

"Heather," I started, getting to my feet and wiping my eyes. "Heather. Heather! Look at me!"

But she didn't look at me. She wasn't even listening. She ran back into the cottage with Eidyth, who was breathing shallowly by then but whose lips had returned to their usual pink hue. And then she started to wrap the leather sandals onto her feet, the ones she only wore when she was going to be walking on the sharp, barnacle-covered rocks at the beach, or if she was going to be traveling a far distance on foot.

"Where are you going?" I asked. "The child needs rest. I'll melt the tallow and we can mix the herbs –"

"I need to find the tree," she repeated. "The tree! Remember the tree in the woods? Remember the day we met, when I took you to my world? I need – I need to find it. There are doctors – healers – there. Real ones. I can get some medicine. Where is the thick linen blanket? It's usually in bed – where is it?! Magnus!"

My wife and I had come to an understanding of where she came from. I remembered the brief, strange journey to what she said was her homeland. She remembered it, too – obviously so, now that she was talking of going back there. But we didn't speak of it. It wasn't a secret, or something we had agreed not to speak of. Heather didn't try to mislead me about the place – quite the opposite, she tended to answer questions candidly when asked. But there were things she wouldn't explain. Or rather, there were things I couldn't understand, even if she did explain. And there was a shared knowledge that the place where Heather came from was not an ordinary place. It was not like the North or the Frankish Kingdom. It was not even like the far east, which I had only heard of from traders who brought colored silks with them when they returned from their journeys. It wasn't a place that could be walked or sailed to.

So when she began to talk, in her panic, of taking Eidyth back to that place, which in my mind I associated only with a brief, long gone moment of fear and confusion, I could not allow it. When she moved to take our daughter out of the cottage only a short time before dusk, I took her arm in my hand and stopped her.

"Let go!" She shrieked, looking back at me as if she was surprised to be touched. "Magnus! Let me – let –"

She tried to shake herself free, but I held her steady. "I cannot let you go," I told her, and my own voice sounded heavy with sadness – it was the first time I touched my wife that way, to bar her, in a serious way, from doing something. "Come back inside, girl. The child breathes again. Put her in her bed and I will warm the –"

"NO! LET GO! Magnus, please! Please let me go!"

She struggled so hard that Eidyth woke fully, and began to cry when she saw her parents shouting and screaming at each other. And still Heather did not relent. Even as the child's cries became hysterical, and she began to cough again, her mother would not stop trying to shake loose my grip.

"Please," I begged. "Heather, you are out of your mind. I do not condemn you for it – I feel it myself, in truth. But look at the sun! It will be dark soon – do you propose to take Eidyth into the woods at night? To look for a tree I feel sure you do not remember the location of? There are wolves nearby, you've heard them howling yourself! I cannot allow you to –"

And then suddenly she broke free, because I had relaxed a little, thinking perhaps she was coming back to herself. At once I leapt after her, catching her arm again before she could escape the little courtyard that surrounded our dwelling. That time, I took Eidyth from her arms as she spun around and momentarily loosened her grip, and then she stood before me, demanding that I give her back.

"Give her to me. Magnus, give her to me! Give her –" she reached out, trying to snatch our daughter, who was screaming with fear and clinging to my neck, from my arms.

"STOP IT!" I shouted, when I could take no more. "Girl, come back inside at once. I'll send for the healer to bring you a calming –"

"Fuck the healer! It *doesn't work*, Magnus! Didn't you hear me?! It's not real! You think those herbs are going to do anything? They're not! She's going to die – she's not getting better, you see it as well as I do. If you want her to live, give her back to me. Now! Give her back so I can –"

I stepped forward to force her back into the cottage, but she caught my eye just as I was about to do so and I think she saw then that I was not going to give Eidyth back to her – and that she did not have the strength to take her from me.

"Fine," she said, breathing deeply, trying to get control of herself. "Fine. I'll go myself. I'll get – I'll bring back some medicine, I'll –"

I moved to grab her again but she jumped out of the way. And then she took off running. Heather was a fast runner – we'd had races on the beach before, which I had only barely won. And now I had a screaming child in my arms.

"It's alright," I lied to Eidyth because I needed it to be true as badly as she did. "It's alright, little one. It's –"

"Magnus?" Bradwin was at the half-height stone wall that surrounded my cottage. "I heard screaming – I – is the child hurt?"

The child wasn't hurt. She was sick. Sick enough that even as I hadn't agreed out loud with Heather's assessment, I feared that it was true – that Eidyth was dying. And still she howled in my arms, although a little less intensely now, and buried her face in my neck. And Heather was out there now, somewhere in the woods as the night began to close in.

"Where is –" Bradwin started, but I ran back into the cottage to get the little woolen bear that Ceoldor's wife had knitted for Eidyth and that she could not sleep without. And then I handed the bear, and my daughter, to my closest friend.

"Heather has lost her mind," I told him, barely managing to keep my own. "She just took off – she just ran off into the woods talking about – talking nonsense. She worries herself to mindlessness over Eidyth. I must go – there are wolves, you must have heard them! I must go and –"

"Go," Bradwin replied, taking the child, who began to scream again and reach for me. "Go now and bring her back, Magnus. We will watch her until you return."

There was no time to express my thanks to Bradwin, but I could see he understood. I darted back into the cottage to grab my sword, and then stopped for only a moment, to kiss Eidyth's cheek and whisper a promise that I would see her soon enough and not to worry, before racing down the path in the direction Heather had gone.

Chapter 17: Heather

I ran faster and further, that evening, than I had ever run before. I ran until my lungs felt like they were going to burst and my knees throbbed from the many tumbles I took in the dim light. I ran until I physically could not run anymore, and all the while I tried to keep one eye on the woods, looking for a tree I thought I remembered clearly. Each time I thought I'd found it I leaned against it, flattening my hands against its bark, only to remain exactly where I was – in a forest in the Kingdom of the East Angles with a daughter at home who was sick enough to put a fear into me the likes of which I'd never known.

When the sun sank fully below the horizon, and it became impossible to see – I had not thought to bring a torch with me – I found my way back out to the coast and collapsed on the beach, sobbing. I wanted to believe that it was all going to be OK, as my husband told me it was. But it didn't take formal medical training to see that whatever it was sending Eidyth into fits of coughing, it was no harmless cold. I could still feel the echo of her limp weight in my arms when she had stopped breathing and lost consciousness – Magnus was right that I was hysterical when I tried to take her with me on my search for the tree, but he was wrong if he thought there was no reason for it.

There was nothing else to do but go back to River Falls. To the 1990s, which it would then be. I wouldn't have any money when I got there, and I would be dressed like a homeless person, but I would be *there*. I would be in a place that had cough medicines and decongestants and antibiotics. Eidyth needed medicine. She wasn't getting better – quite the opposite. Without something more than herbs, she was going to die. And I could not allow that to happen.

I resolved to continue the search for the tree at the first light of dawn. It was north of Haesting, in the woods but close to the coast. I would just have to start methodically taking every path that led inland, seeing where it went, and laying my hands on every tree that looked like it could be the one.

My sleep was fitful. I was tired from the running and the high emotions but the dread in my belly would not let go. I spent the night waking what seemed like every few minutes, confused at first about my whereabouts and then crushed anew every time by the remembrance of Eidyth's sickness.

At dawn, I resumed the search, stiff with discomfort and soreness from the previous night's run. Sleep-deprived and aching, I began to make my way north again, turning west down every path that led into the forest, following it for as long as I thought necessary to spot the tree, which in my memory was not too far from the coast.

As I remembered it, the tree was iconic. It stood apart from other trees – its trunk much thicker, paler than the others, its canopy thicker. But it had been almost ten years then, since I'd last seen it, and all the trees in the woods as I searched began to look the same.

By the time the sun was high in the sky that day, a painful cramp had developed in one of my sides, and my mouth was dry because I wasn't taking enough water. The soles of my feet were bloodied in spite of the leather I'd wrapped them in. I was losing hope.

My husband found me kneeling in the middle of the path, retching and almost delirious with thirst, and immediately held his water-bladder to my lips.

"Oh Heather," he whispered, alternating between holding me against him, stroking my hair, and pulling away to look at me, horrified. "What have you done, girl? What have you done to yourself? Your – your feet! They're like raw pieces of pigflesh! Come, I will –"

"I'm not a 'girl' anymore, Magnus," I replied quietly, my voice hoarse. "You should stop calling me that."

I couldn't have fought him, even if I wanted to. My strength was gone. I began to cry, as the understanding that I was probably not going to be able to find the tree came over me. And I was so dehydrated that there weren't even any tears left to tumble down my face.

"You're always going to be my girl," he replied, holding me tightly to his chest. "When you are nine tens, you are still going to be my girl."

"She's going to die," I rasped, looking up at him imploringly, desperate for him to understand. "If I can find the tree, I can go back to the United States. They have medicines. Not herbs from the healer, but medicines that work. We have treatments to stop coughing, to stop sicknesses. Children don't die of coughs anymore, where I come from. I could go to a pharmacy and get –"

"Heather, you are coming back to Haesting with me now. Even if what you say is true, and your people have more effective potions for illnesses, how long will it take us to find that tree again? Of all the trees in the Kingdom, how will we find that one?"

"It looked different," I replied. "It – it was bigger – wasn't it? Don't you remember? And we don't have to search the whole Kingdom, because we know it was north of Haesting, right? We –"

"It did not look different," he stopped me. "Girl, the tree was as any other. A large one, yes, but it had no mark to set it apart. Come now, I cannot listen to this any longer – you give us both false hope."

"Magnus, no. I –"

But I could not keep speaking. I was too weak. I was too weak even to stand, so my husband carried me back down the coastal path over his shoulder, back to Haesting. And the whole journey there, as I slipped in and out of consciousness, the seed of anger that had been planted at his refusal to take me seriously about the medicines buried itself deep into the soil of my heart.

Eidyth survived that first sickness. But she did not survive it in the way a child from the USA survives a cough – the way I myself had survived numerous childhood colds. She was weakened by the whole episode, so even as she was 'healed' – as the Angles insisted she was – her lungs were weakened. Every time it rained, every time she did not get enough sleep for two or more nights in a row, the cough would come back. She did not lose weight, exactly, because we made sure she always had enough to eat, but where she had previously thrived and grown like I expected children to do, she, after her illness, began to look more and more like the Angle children – pale, not as tall or as solid as I would have liked.

It was not just Eidyth who was different. I was different. My marriage was different. I could not forgive Magnus for bringing me back to Haesting that day, when I had meant to find the tree. Every time I looked at Eidyth and thought her chest a little sunken, or the darkness under her eyes a little too pronounced, rage welled up inside me. Sometimes it felt as if I was barely holding it in, as if at any moment I was on the verge of launching into a screaming tirade, accusing him of being the cause of her weakness, condemning him for forbidding me, like one would forbid a child, to look for the tree.

I did not do a good job of hiding my anger, either. And in his turn, my husband drew himself away from me, becoming more impatient with me when I needed help or did not understand something he spoke of. Eidyth sensed that not all was well with her parents, and herself became more withdrawn. The cottage, which had once echoed with laughter and work and the busy, happy tasks of being a family, became a quieter place – a darker place.

"You must stop punishing him," Brona said to me one day as we – Brona and I, Eidyth, and a few of Brona's younger children – collected oysters at the beach. "It is not the Northman's fault that your daughter got sick. I know the temptation to lay blame, Eltha – believe me, I do. I have never felt rage as I have when my children suffer for no good reason. But it is not his fault. You cannot make him the target of your ire, simply because he is the closest to –"

"You don't know what you're talking about," I replied stiffly, twisting an oyster from one of the seaweed-covered rocks and looking up to see where Eidyth played. "You don't. I don't blame him for her sickness. I blame him for not letting me – I tried to – oh, goddamnit! You're wrong, Brona! OK? I don't think he made her sick – that's so stupid, why would I think that?!"

My friend went back to picking oysters quietly, hearing my strident tone. But that evening, when we walked with the children back to Haesting and stood beside the stone wall to my cottage dividing the oysters between us, she put her arms around me and whispered in my ear:

"I'm not your enemy. I don't give you advice because I think myself above you. I give advice because I have been where you are. Magnus loves the child as much as you do. You must see it. What is more important than her happiness, now? Do you think she cares what hurts her parents carry in their hearts? See how quiet she is, Eltha. See how she wishes her mother smiled again."

It was difficult – it was more than difficult – to hear words like that as anything other than a condemnation. Even as Brona walked away after kissing my cheek, I wanted to shout after her she didn't know anything. That the best thing for Eidyth was to have a mother who would do anything for her – and not a father who stopped her mother from doing those things.

But I did not shout. I just watched, in silence, as she led her brood back down the path to their own cottage. And that evening, I watched my own husband, and my own child, without the veil of anger over my eyes. Magnus looked the same as ever – in his mid thirties by then, he did not, to me, look a day over twenty-five. He was as strong as ever, as upright in his bearing, just as hard-working. But he did not look at me as he used to. In fact he seemed to avoid my eyes altogether.

And Eidyth had the same quality about her – a wariness in her smile, a barely-perceptible hesitation before she spoke or looked at me.

I thought I had been doing a good job. I watched her like a hawk, my chest tightening at the merest hint of a cough, or even a labored breath. At night I knelt beside her as she slept, and wept with fear that she would get sick again. Every day, I made sure she had enough food for every meal, taking my own portion of cream in the springtime and pouring it with her own over her morning porridge, or giving her my portion of meat for her supper. It was not only I who did these things. Magnus gave up his own meat and butter just as often.

But I forced myself, after Brona's words, to watch my husband and my child over the next days. And I forced myself to do it without the always-constant righteous anger lurking in my heart, the feeling that not all that could have been done for Eidyth had been done – and the conviction that it was specifically Magnus' fault. Without that anger, it was easier to see what was in front of my eyes. He did love her as much as I loved her. He loved me, as well. What must he have thought that night, when his wife took off into the dark woods, where wolves had been sighted, and his daughter's chest heaved with sickness?

And the worst of it, the part that even weeks and months later I found it most difficult to let go of – was that he was right about the tree. I wasn't going to find it again. And given that truth, Magnus could not have been said to have done anything wrong in preventing me from killing myself looking for it. Seen in that light, from a different perspective, he had no choice but to bring me home that day. To have done anything else would have been to fail at his job as a husband – protecting his family.

It was news from one of the Angle women, within the walls of the Haesting estate itself, where I went to trade a measure of dried peas for some tallow, that drove me out into the fields later in the afternoon a few days later to find my husband.

Ardith, Ceoldor's wife, was dead. She had developed a fever in the night, and died before the sun had set on the next day. The Angle women spoke of it in tones both somber and unsurprised. How long was it going to take me, I wondered as I headed back to my cottage with a small cask of tallow under one arm, until I knew the kind of place where I was? I mean, I knew where I was. But I still acted as if I didn't. Word of a woman's death was still enough to shock me. Even as my own child had nearly died!

Late that afternoon, after sending Eidyth to spend it with Brona's children, I made my way out to the fields where Magnus worked with the men to plow some freshly cleared land. It did not miss my notice, either, that when he spotted me a certain rigidity took over his body. Still, he jogged down to greet me.

"What is it?" He asked, worried. "Is the child –"

"She's with Brona," I replied. "She's fine. You don't look fine, though. You look worried. Do you remember when I used to come and visit you during the day? When I would bring you some ale and buttered bread to eat?"

"Aye," my husband replied, wiping the sweat from his brow. "I remember. All the other men were so jealous of me, to have a wife like you."

"And they're not jealous anymore?" I asked, although in truth I already knew the answer.

Magnus fell silent for a moment, and then he reached out and took my hand in his. "There are seasons to everything, girl – not just the weather. There are seasons to a marriage."

"And ours is in winter right now. I think I may have made it winter," I replied, looking back up to the field where the men were adjusting the leather collar that bound the oxen. "You must hate me."

"Hate you?!" He replied at once. "Hate? Is that what you think, girl?"

I shrugged. "You're a better person than me, Magnus. I see it now. Maybe I always saw it? I don't know. But even now, after I've treated you coldly for months, you're trying to make me feel better. You –"

"I don't say anything I don't believe to be true," he broke in. "Do you think I don't understand? Do you think I don't see that it is the mother in you that drove you into the woods that night, that made you fight me – and that even now leads you to resent me?"

I almost laughed out loud, but not because anything he said was particularly funny.

"What is it?" He asked, when he saw my expression. "Why do you wear that strange smile on your lips?"

"Because you're so – perfect!" I cried. "I've been a total bitch for months and I came up here to say sorry and to try to see what I could do to make it up to you and you're standing there like some kind of endlessly patient priest, making excuses for –"

"No," he stopped me before I could go any further. "No. It is not excuses I make for you. This is not a petty matter, girl. This is not an argument over whose job it was to close the sheep in the shelter at night. You are Eidyth's mother. As her mother, you would do anything to keep her safe and well – including killing yourself. You had to leave that night, to find the tree. I understand that. It is what any mother would do, if she thought she could do something to heal her sick child. But just as you had to do it, I had to stop you. I had to come for you, and bring you home. Do you think I don't know why you're so angry with me? I do. I accept your anger. But it does not change what my job is as your husband – and as Eidyth's father."

"So," I began, looking up. "You're – you're not angry at me?"

"No. I'm not angry. I see that it could not have been any other way. I admit lately to a sadness in my heart, to see you so unhappy. I wait every day for you to forgive me, and to see that I – like you – only did what I had to do."

Where had he come from? What had I done to deserve him? What strange forces had brought me to the middle of that field, sometime in the deep past, in front of the best man I had ever known?

"I don't deserve you," I said, and he tried to pull me to him, to tell me I was wrong. But I put my hands on his chest and held him away, insisting on my point. "No, Magnus. I'm not just saying it. I literally don't deserve you. Before I met you, I don't even think I knew there were men like you. And now I've spent months treating you like –"

"Shhh," he said. "Girl, I'll not hear any more of this from you. Do not beat yourself in front of me, as if it's a necessary thing – it is not. I said that I understood and I do."

"I'm sorry," I whispered then, finally allowing my husband to pull me against his chest. "I'm so sorry. I –"

"Shhh."

***

And so the season of our marriage and our lives turned again, the darkness that had fallen after Eidyth's illness lifted and we were happy once more, the three of us. It was a different kind of happiness, then, to the untroubled and youthful kind that had characterized our early relationship. I think Magnus himself always knew the things I was required to learn through experience. He grew up in a land that was not too different to the Kingdom of the East Angles, especially when both were compared to Los Angeles in 1983. He already knew, as I did not in my twenties, that poverty and sickness, that *death,* stalked everyone, all the time. He knew that youth and health were guarantees of little, that an abundant harvest one year did not guarantee the same in the next.

I didn't know any of it. Even when I was first in Haesting, and thought that I was getting used to living so close to the cycles of birth and death as seen in the livestock and the people, I was not. Not truly. It took nearly losing Eidyth to learn – and even then, it was not to be my final lesson.

It made the joy of being with them – with my husband and our daughter – that much sweeter, and that much more poignant. I had seen that they could be taken from me.

We had almost seven years together, as a family. Eidyth, after that bout of coughing sickness when she small, never fully recovered. She became, as I said, like the Angle children – prone to all manner of illness and fever. And the spring of my first great loss came too soon – although to say too soon makes it sound as if there were a time when it would not have been too soon. A thousand years would have been too soon.

She came back from the beach one day, our lovely little daughter, with a swelling on her left arm, near the wrist. It was pink and hot to the touch, and she refused to eat dinner. In the night, as Magnus and I hovered over her restless, fevered body, she woke crying, and towards the morning did not quite seem to recognize us anymore.

The healer was sent for, but Eidyth died anyway, later that same day and wrapped in her mother's arms.

That was the day I became old. I don't mean old in the wrinkles and gray hair sense of the term, either. I mean old in the sense of finally and truly, *deeply* understanding that I had absolutely no control over anything. I barely even cried at first. We buried her in the graveyard where the Angles put their dead, and I stood with wide eyes and a feeling like I couldn't breathe throughout the funeral rituals. I maintained that stance – stiff-armed, wide-eyed, shocked – for weeks. She was gone and I knew it. She was not coming back and I knew it.

"I love you," I said to Magnus, two moons after we put our daughter's body in the ground. "I love you but I'm different now. And I'm always going to be different."

He looked up at me, his eyes full of tears, and nodded. "As it is, girl. It is the same for me. Bradwin tells tales of coming home from the fields some days and expecting to see his daughter, the one he lost two winters ago, waiting for him at the gate. I don't know why I do not expect to see our Eidyth, but I don't. It seems all I know is that she's gone."

He broke down and I lifted my body, which was heavy with grief, far enough to take him into my arms so we could cling to each other.

Chapter 18: Magnus

Losing Eidyth was not like losing anyone else. It was not like losing my grandfather, or any of my men. It was not like losing my brother. As I said to Eadwin one day as we sparred with swords, it was sometimes difficult to believe that I had not been dealt a physical blow.

"I feel as if I've fought a bear," I told him, when we paused to catch our breath from the training. "As if a great bear has knocked me down hard enough to steal the breath from my lungs. Sometimes I look down at my body and am surprised that it is not black and blue. You could run me through with that sword right now and it would not leave the mark that her absence has left."

Heather and I stumbled around like those I had seen back in the North, who had spent too many nights with the gothi, and drank too many of the dark teas the gothis brewed. We woke in the mornings, as we always had. We ate our breakfast and went about our daily chores. At night we sat together in the cottage and ate our supper. But we did not do any of these things in the way we used to. We did them almost mindlessly, without thinking. And we would catch each other, sometimes, in moments of strange stasis. One night I returned from the fields and came in the door to find her, having not heard me, standing over the bubbling pottage with her hand holding a spoon, but not moving at all. I hung back, watching, and she stayed there, as still as a standing stone, with no expression on her face for many moments. And when finally I spoke her name she simply turned her head to me, as if she did not even realize what she was doing.

It was the same for me. I would catch myself standing in the woods, leaning on the wooden shepherd's crook I used to herd the unruly pigs back into their sty, and find that the pigs themselves had long disappeared into the undergrowth, searching for chestnuts.

"Will it be like this forever?" My wife asked me one night, almost a full winter after Eidyth died. "Will this – is this just it for us, my love? Will we never see each other smile again?"

"I don't know," I replied. "As it is, we probably need to endure our grief for – for a longer time, perhaps."

"How long? Because I can tell you, I don't feel like I will ever smile again. Even to force my mouth into the shape of a smile seems unnatural. It's like if this goes on for much longer, I'm going to completely forget how to laugh."

At least we did not attack each other after the loss of our daughter. That was something I'd seen happen to other parents – in the North and in the Kingdom – when they lost a child. I don't know why it was different for Heather and me. We were as broken as it was possible to be, but we did not take it out on each other. Maybe we learned our lesson from Eidyth's earlier sickness? Maybe, with no other children, we understood that each of us had only the other?

We had the Angles, too. We had Haesting. It was our home by then, as much as the North and the United States of America had ever been to either of us. But it was only Heather who understood why, for example, I sometimes became despairing in the middle of eating my mid-day meal on a sunny, cold winter's day. It was only she who knew that my despair was because I had suddenly remembered eating a similar meal on a sunny, cold winter's day with our daughter, and that to do so then was to conjure a thought of her so painfully real it was as if I could almost hear her giggle in my ear.

    I think, as the seasons passed, that perhaps neither of us truly wanted to feel better. Our child was gone – how could we smile again? Or laugh, or speak of our hopes for the future? How could we do that when she was in the ground?

    But we did smile again. Heather did not forget how to laugh. Her fears that we would live out the rest of our days in mourning did not come true. Time did not heal, and it did not make us forget, but it forced us to live. And in living, in scything the wheat, and beating the grain from the stalks, in drying the grain and grinding the grain and in feeding the pigs and picking oysters and all the other endless tasks one has to do in order to live, we surfaced, somehow, as if from under a great depth of water. We didn't crawl out of it to sun ourselves on the beach – sunning oneself on the beach, we learned, was an activity for the young, for those who did not yet know what it was to suffer loss. But we brought our heads above the waves, so we could see the beach again, at least.

    At some point we even found ourselves able to speak of Eidyth without weeping or falling into a sadness that would last for days. "She would have liked playing at the beach today," Heather would say as we picked oysters on a sun-blessed summer day. "Do you remember the way she used to laugh at the pigs?" I would ask, as we walked in the woods to the estate and one of the creatures darted out of the bushes in front of us. "Do you remember how she used to scold them? 'Silly pigs! Go back to your sty before the wolves eat you!'"

We remembered her. The Angles remembered her, too, and did not shy away from the mention of her name. A few winters after she was lost, Lord Eldred came to tell us of another orphan born in Haesting, whose aunt and uncle thought we might want to take him as our own.

But we did not.

"I can't do it," Heather said as we spoke of it over pottage that night. "If I lose another like I lost Eidyth, I'll die. I don't say it to be dramatic or to exaggerate, I say it because it's true. In my bones, I know it's true. I'll die, Magnus."

I felt as my wife did, and I told Eldred as much. The orphan baby was sent to live with its aunt and uncle.

***

Four winters after Eidyth was buried, Heather asked me one day if I thought we might find the tree – the one that took her from the United States of America to the Kingdom. She just brought it up in the middle of grinding grain in the courtyard, as I stood at her side and we chatted about the Yule to come, and whether or not it would be an especially cold one.

"Why do you speak of the tree?" I asked. "You haven't mentioned it for many moons now."

She turned the wheel a few more times, and we both watched the rough-ground flour pile up in the middle. "I speak of it because if it weren't for you, I think I would go back."

I turned my head sharply towards my wife. She had never expressed such a sentiment before. Quite the opposite. Ever since I'd first met her, she'd been adamant about *not* going back to her homeland. When she looked up and saw my face, she made a little shrugging gesture.

"What if you die, Magnus? Do you see how the women here live, that don't have husbands? That are old?"

"You're not old, girl."

"That's not the point. The point is if you died, I would eventually be old. An old woman, alone. What would happen to me if –"

"The Angles care for their old people," I cut her off, alarmed by the subject matter. "Do you not see how Lord Eldred sees that the families with old people in them have enough grain to –"

"But what if the Northmen return?! Brona's oldest daughter travels regularly to Caistley now, where she has that boy she will probably marry – in Caistley they speak of raids, even further to the North. They speak of the Angles taken as slaves – what do you think your people would do with an old woman? What do you –"

"Why do we speak of this?!" I demanded. "Girl, we might as well speak of what will happen if the Gods send a sea-wave big enough to wipe out the estate! What is the use in speculating about any of this? All you do is worry yourself."

"I don't know," she said quietly. "I've never heard anyone talk about a wave washing away an estate. But a lot of women lose their husbands. A widow is not a rare thing here. But they usually have their children to help them if –"

"Stop," I replied quietly, reaching down to take her hand off the grinding wheel and hold it in my own. "I have no answers for you, girl. And neither do you know what will happen in the future. Only the Gods know these things."

"I suppose. Do you feel that?"

I brought her hand to my mouth to kiss it. "What?"

"The wind. Do you feel there is just a little warmth left in it now? The frost will be here soon. At least the pig is fat – we will have roast pork for Yule."

I looked over at her as she spoke, trying to imagine her as an old woman. Trying to imagine her dark locks as gray, and her face lined with the passage of time. To me, Heather looked much as she had that first day in the woods, after I challenged Asger. I knew it couldn't be true, and that almost ten and five winters could not have left either of us unchanged, but it was difficult for me to actually pick out the ways. She was leaner, perhaps. Not as full in the cheeks or the limbs as she had been. But still her body responded to me as it always had, and the sight just then of her breasts moving underneath her light tunic as she turned the grinding wheel stirred something in my loins.

"What is it?" She asked, sensing some change in the air between us. "Why do you look at me like –"

Before she could finish, I reached into her tunic and took one breast in my hand. Round, soft, warm, and topped with a nipple that grew stiff against my palm. She laughed gently, and tossed her hair back over her shoulder before turning to look at me with a smile.

"Really? I have almost a whole sack of grain still to grind."

I brought my fingers together over her nipple, pinching it and then rolling it in the way I knew she preferred. "You're right," I replied. "Perhaps you should finish the grain. The pigs need fresh straw, girl. Yes, I'll go and –"

I moved to stand up but she grabbed my wrist and turned her face up to me as I did so, not letting me pull my hand away.

"The pigs can wait for their straw."

"Can they?" I asked, settling down behind her on the stone step and reaching around her body so I could put my other hand in her tunic, too. Her back arched as I took both her breasts in my grip, the way I knew it would, and she leaned her head back for a kiss.

"We should go inside," she breathed, her voice soft. "We – Magnus, anyone could just walk –"

"I don't care," I whispered, pulling her hair out of the way so I could kiss her neck and sliding one of my hands down her belly, under her tunic, until my fingers found her folds, already slick, and the little nub that made her breath catch when I touched it.

Our physical relationship was one thing that never fell off. Even after I'd stopped her from continuing to search for the tree when Eidyth was sick, and she could barely look at me for many moons afterwards, we couldn't keep ourselves from reaching for each other at night. I used to relish watching the fury in her eyes melt away when I was inside her, and the way, when she was close to her peak, she would sometimes smile at me in spite of herself.

It fell off for some people, I knew that. Some of the men who worked the fields with me spoke sadly of their wives diminishing lust, or described the lengths they would go to to persuade their reluctant women. Of course I never made it worse for them by describing how, even at our furthest distance from each other, my wife and I could not seem to dampen our fires. Mostly I just felt sorry for them, and grateful that Heather still tilted her head to the side and sighed when I kissed her, or when I put my hand on her waist and slid it down between her legs.

"Magnus," she whispered, when I slipped two fingers into her wet depths and then pulled them out again and ran them just up beside the spot where she really needed them. Her thighs were open and she was leaned back against my chest, whimpering girlishly as I teased her.

I was rigid against her back, thrusting my hips forward as her little cries made it harder and harder not to just flip her over onto her back and take her right there in the courtyard.

When I did finally begin to touch my wife where she wanted it, I went very, very slowly. I let my fingers dawdle, pausing sometimes for a moment or two after a period of quick movements, just at the point where her breath became shallow and fast.

"No!" She cried, when I brought her almost to the edge and then pulled back before she could tumble over it. "Magnus, no – please – don't stop –"

But there was always a moment when she was too sweet, and too needy, to torture any longer. It came sooner that afternoon, when for some reason I couldn't listen to her begging me for very long before pushing my finger over her sensitive spot again, and then over and over, faster and faster as she moaned and squirmed and then went suddenly stiff against me as the pleasure peaked right where my finger stroked her.

She leaned forward a moment later, panting, laughing, and I saw that I'd left a wet spot on the back of her tunic. My cock throbbed to be inside the slipperiness my fingers had just been enjoying, and my balls ached with their fullness. When I pushed her forward, onto her knees, she knew what to do.

I lifted her tunic up, over her bare thighs, over her rounded ass, and drew myself up between her lips, exhaling heavily at the feeling of her sweet warmth caressing my tip.

"Magnus," she whispered, smiling back over her shoulder at me. "Magnus..."

As I said, I was in no mood to hold back that day. Her coy little smile was enough. I eased myself between her lips, just a little, and then put my hands flat on the ground, burying my face in her neck before pushing the rest of the way in.

Heather braced herself, the heels of her hands digging into the earth as I thrust into her hard, barely pulling out at all because her insides just felt too good – too warm, too slick, too perfect.

"Mmm," I moaned into her shoulder, kissing it, licking my way up to her soft little earlobe. "Mmm, girl. You're going to finish me, I can feel it. You're going to –"

I broke off and thrust into her harder, faster, as the sweetness became acute, and sank my fingers into her hips, pulling her back against me at the moment of letting go so every drop would end up exactly where I wanted it – inside her.

"You'll not go back to your homeland as long as I can give you that," I joked, when I could speak again.

But she looked at me completely seriously as she stood and straightened her tunic, which we hadn't even had time to take off. "You're right. I won't. None of the boys back home could do half of what you can do to me with just a facial expression, or – I don't know, touching my elbow or something."

I never felt more a man than when I'd driven Heather to distraction, or during those moments afterwards when she was pliant and giggly and perfectly open about what I did to her. I sat back on the stone step in our courtyard that afternoon with a wide grin on my face and she bent down to kiss my cheek.

"You're just like one of the roosters," she told me, grinning.

"If I look as pleased with myself as one of the roosters," I replied, pulling her down for another kiss. "It's only because of you, my little hen."

***

The evening darkness began to close in earlier, and the frost fell onto the garden at night after that last sunny afternoon. Heather and I busied ourselves with the autumnal tasks – butchering the spring piglet that had been selected for slaughter, processing and storing the grain, stacking the firewood in the little shack I built to keep it sheltered from the elements and pounding the fruit she gathered with the other women into the tough mixture that would be dried next to the fire and eaten in the depths of the winter, when even the greens in the garden went dormant.

It was close to Yule, which was for the Angles more a purely joyous celebration of life and light than it was a contemplative time – like it had been for my people – when Heather began to complain of sickness. She was three tens and six by then, and we both assumed that she had had some bad water to drink, or some milk that had perhaps sat out a hair too long before being consumed.

But when it lasted for almost a half-moon, and she became at the same time enamored with some foods – the hard cheese we had made that summer – and completely repulsed by others – the smoked pork she had loved for as long as I'd known her – we worriedly called the healer.

The healer left us with some dried herbs, and instructions to brew a tea that would settle my wife's stomach. She seemed, as did we, to assume that something had been eaten and that it was just taking a little longer than usual to lose its hold on Heather's belly.

It was late in the depth of that winter, and I was beginning to wake in the mornings with a pit of dread in my stomach because my wife was still not able to take much food. A sickness that lasts for more than two moons is almost always a bad sign. We lay in our bed on a cold morning, after I refreshed the fire with more logs, and when my hand found its way to her belly, it stopped suddenly, before continuing its journey down to her warmth.

"What is it?" She asked, turning over a little to look at me when she felt my hand still. "Did you forget to close the pigs into the –"

"No," I replied, as my mind tried to come up with explanations for what my hand was feeling that were not dreadful.

"Then what? Why have you gone white?"

"I –" I started. "Heather – your belly."

I drew the blanket off her as she rolled over onto her back, peering down at her body. I joined her in peering.

Did she have a fullness there I had not noticed before? No, surely not – she hadn't been eating!

"Turn towards me," I instructed, convinced it was the angle, or the light – and desperate to believe it was something that innocuous. But there had been that firmness under my hand...

I reached down and passed my palm over her midsection again, and felt it again. It was different. Something was different.

"What are you doing?" She laughed, looking up at me, confused because she'd thought my caresses that morning were going somewhere else.

"Your belly," I repeated. "It's – Heather, feel for yourself."

So then she reached down and ran her hand over her own flesh, pausing halfway through to frown and then doing it again – and again.

"It – what's that?" She asked, sitting up.

And when she sat up, it was even more clear that she was bigger there, fuller than she had been.

In my haste to convince myself that it was not the firm, growing mass under the skin that had taken my mother's sister, I failed to pay too much attention to Heather's expression. I saw that she seemed to be thinking, but that was it. And then, when she suddenly burst into tears, I didn't know what to think.

"No," she whispered, looking down at her belly and running her hands over it again. "No, Magnus. The Gods would not see fit to torture me like this, would they? They wouldn't do this if – they wouldn't do it if – if –"

"If what?!" I replied loudly, wondering if she sensed it was something terrible. "Woman tell me why you weep over this – do you know already that something is wrong?"

And then my wife looked up at me, baffled through her tears. "That something is – wrong? What do – what do you think is wrong? What do you think this is?"

"I have no idea what it is!" I responded. "But you have a look on your face like you do, and you weep, and you speak of being tortured by the Gods. I don't understand what –"

"Am I pregnant again? Is this another baby doomed never to be born?"

The questions were not asked for the sake of asking. Heather gazed at me, her eyes as an animal expecting a blow – and she wanted an answer. Unfortunately I was not able to give her one, not right away, not after the word 'pregnant' had been uttered. Pregnant?

"Pregnant?" I whispered. "Pregnant? But you're, Heather, you're three tens and –"

"I'm thirty-six! Do you think thirty-six is too old to get pregnant? My mom had me when she was thirty-four, Magnus! And two winters ago that Angle woman had a baby when she was forty! It –"

I sat back on our bed, thinking. Three tens and six was, for my people, not an age at which most women were still bearing children. But Heather was right, there had been an Angle woman on the estate who bore a daughter at four tens. I remembered seeing her carrying the child on her chest, with her hair, streaked with some grays, falling over the infant's head.

"Do you speak the truth?" I asked. "Your mother bore you at three tens and four? I remember hearing in the North that if a woman's mother had a child at an older age – or a younger age – then a woman herself was more likely to do so. Do you – Heather – is it possible? Is it possible after all these winters that I have put a baby in your belly?"

She shook her head, weeping freshly. "I don't know! I don't know."

But there was a baby in my wife's belly. As the winter began to soften into early spring, and then into the glorious green abundance of spring itself, her midsection grew. And as it grew, the reason why became more and more obvious. Even the healer confirmed it, eventually, after coming to examine Heather many more times.

Not that our cottage was filled with the kind of unsullied joy that filled the cottages of younger couples, perhaps freshly married and barely ten and ten, when they came to know they would soon be parents. Heather and I had bad memories, we had had lessons in the past, of hopes dashed, of bloodied bed-sheets and, later, a child's funeral. Even the healer and the midwives were circumspect, knowing about the lost baby and the years of coupling with no pregnancies.

"Do not hope for too much," one of the midwives said as she ran her hands over my wife's belly one day. "You know you have had difficulty carrying a child before. It is best not to become too attached to this one before it comes."

I stood back, as I often did when the women tended to Heather, as women tend to each other regarding womanly things, but a sudden urge to take the midwife by the hair and drag her out into the courtyard seized me so strongly that I had to step out of the cottage. A few moments later, the woman who had just given warning to a pregnant woman not to hope for too much joined me.

"You're angry," she observed, seeing my face. "Would you rather I tell your wife that she is assured a healthy, strong baby in a few moons? How much greater will her grief be then if the child is not healthy and strong? You know her history as I do, Northman. Is it not best that we temper our hopes, and save our celebrations for a time when they are truly warranted?"

Nothing the woman said was wrong. The Angles, like the people of the North, were practical. They were practical because they had to be. They warned against false hope because they understood that life did not often reward the falsely hopeful. But I *was* hopeful. And no matter how hard I tried to smother the feeling within my chest, I found that I could not do so. So I shouted at the midwife to take her gloom elsewhere and sent her angrily on her way.

After that, as the child in Heather's belly grew to the point that we could see it moving under the flesh, we both seemed to allow ourselves some small space within which to feel happy.

"Look," she said one night as we sat outside in the courtyard after dark, after supper, and held a candle to the place where a small arm – or was it a leg? – seemed to pass underneath her skin. "He's awake. Now he will keep me awake with his somersaulting all night."

We had both spent much of past few moons speaking of 'the child' or 'the baby,' and wondering whether or not 'it' would come to be born alive and well. But that night Heather used the word 'he.' 'Now *he* will keep me awake...'

"Is it a son?" I asked, reaching out to touch her midsection where the little movements continued. "A boy?"

"I don't know," she replied, smiling with delight as the child seemed to respond to my touch with more vigorous dancing. "It – it feels like maybe it is? I'm probably just imagining it, though. Do you want it to be a boy?"

"In truth I have not allowed myself to hope for one or the other," I replied. "Although in moments of weakness perhaps I catch myself hoping for a girl. Perhaps it is because I remember Eidyth so well, and dream of once again having a little girl who loves her daddy as much as she –"

I stopped speaking abruptly, as emotion suddenly welled up in my chest, and then coughed and forced an odd sounding laugh. "I'm sorry, girl. I don't know what comes over me – they say a woman's emotions are stronger when she carries a child. Perhaps it is the same for –"

"Magnus," Heather whispered, reaching up to caress my cheek in her palm, a gesture that always managed to calm me. "You don't have to be sorry. Of all the people in the world, do you think anyone understands how much you miss Eidyth as clearly as I do?"

I leaned down to rest my head on her belly, and she stroked my hair as the sounds of the small insects and night creatures filled the air.

"If the child is healthy and strong," I said a few moments later, "I don't care what sex it is."

Chapter 19: Heather

I seemed to grow slowly, as a plant grows. You stare at it and do not see it move upwards, or see its leaves unfurling in front of your eyes, but nonetheless it is soon transformed. That's how it was with me. I did not see my belly grow, I only knew that it did. And at a certain point, it became so large I could hardly believe it was real. I would look down on it in Brona's garden – where Magnus insisted I spent my days when he was in the fields or training the men, because he did not want me to be alone at such a time – as if it could not possibly be a part of me.

"I remember that feeling," Brona would say, smiling as her youngest children played around us. "You start to feel like your own body has become separate from you, as if the child has taken over in some way. The last days are hard ones, Heather, but I would advise you to enjoy them while you can. A newborn babe is a trial unlike any other you have experienced."

My movements became awkward and slow as the final moon of my pregnancy passed, and I found myself waddling like a duck rather than walking, and groaning loudly whenever I had to sit down – or get back up. Brona and the other Angle women were warm, and full of well-meant advice. But all seemed to assume that my physical discomfort indicated mental or emotional discomfort. It did not. Most of them were blessed with many children, and their pregnancies, especially after the first one, had mostly been treated as happy inconveniences, the simple time it takes to grow a child before it is ready to come out into the world.

But my swollen ankles, my near-constant need to pee and my enormous belly that made me feel like one of the cows did nothing to dampen the pure joy that grew by the day. Every second of the late pregnancy was like magic to me, as precious and rare as emeralds, an experience I had truly not believed I would ever know. So I laughed along with the Angle women, and nodded and smiled. But I truly had no complaints.

Well. I had no complaints until I woke up in the middle of one of the hottest summer nights I could remember, the heat so oppressive it almost reminded me of California, and felt a dull, clenching pain in the bottom of my belly. I looked down in the darkness, to where the pale moonlight that came through the open door shone on what looked like a different kind of moon. The pain lasted. It was not bad, and it felt almost exactly the same as a menstrual cramp. And then it was gone. I lay back down, but sleep didn't return.

After a few more pains, after dawn began to creep into the cottage, Magnus woke up. And when he saw me lying next to him, alert and staring down at my belly, he sat up at once.

"What is it girl? Do you feel the birth pains? Is that why you have the look on your face? What do you feel? Is it –"

"Magnus."

He took a breath and laughed, so the light fell along his strong jaw-line. "I'm sorry. I – just tell me, girl, so I can stop pouring out questions! Do you feel the birth pains?"

"I think I do," I replied quietly, as he reached for my stomach and placed his big hand flat on top of it. "I feel something. I – ow."

Another cramp came. Was it worse than the one that came before it? I couldn't yet tell. Magnus pressed his hand gently down.

"Shall I bring the midwife? Why do you think the baby does not move, now? Would he not be awake, with the pains beginning to push him out?"

"He's probably asleep," I said. "He seems to sleep when I wake, and wake when I sleep. And – I don't know about the midwife. I don't yet know if –"

"I will bring her now."

***

The first thing Ora – the midwife – did when she arrived at the cottage was bid me open my legs and insert two fingers deep inside me with no warning.

"OW!" I yelled, pushing away her hand, which I knew was not washed because the Angles didn't know anything about germs. "What are you –"

"I need to check to see if I can feel the baby's head," she replied, looking at Magnus before continuing. "Please explain to your wife that it's a necessary thing, to check how far the baby has come. As it is it is going to be some time yet, perhaps more than a day. You must wait for the pains to come quicker, and harder, and call for me again when they do."

When she was gone and another cramp had passed – that one noticeably stronger than any that had come before it, I felt a wave of fear wash over me at the realization that I had just taken the first few steps into a journey I could not control. Magnus seemed to recognize that I needed reassurance because he sat down on the bed, beside me, and took my hand.

"I'm here, girl. I'll not go to the training today – it is with bows and arrows, anyway, and Mercawb is as good as I. Are you thirsty? Shall I bring you ale, or water? There is some bread left from yesterday, perhaps I can –"

I squeezed his hand, distracting him from going on to list each and every item of food and drink in the house, and smiled. "Some water, please. As it is I am not hungry."

And that is how we spent the day, and into the night. The pains came on but it seemed a very slow process, and twice they quickened before slowing again. In the middle of the night, though, as my husband dozed in bed beside me, they seemed to take on a new dimension, so strong that I could no longer smile when they passed.

When Ora returned, more than twenty-four hours after the pain had first started, they were coming fast, and each one put a real fear into me that my belly was about to rip itself in half.

"It won't be long now," Ora said, when the sun way high in the sky once more and both me and the bed were soaked with sweat. "You must endure it, Eltha, and the baby will come."

But the baby didn't come. The sun set and night came around again and I was so tired by then that I began to fall asleep between contractions, waking each time already in the midst of a scream.

When the third dawn of my labor came, the feeling in the cottage became noticeably grim. Magnus no longer wore a smile on his face, and when Ora bid him to leave, and to send her two apprentices, he did so with his shoulders slumped forward and an air of barely concealed panic about him.

"It's not the place for a man," Ora said to me when he was gone. "Now it is only a woman's business what will happen. You must not give up, Eltha. If you give up, your baby will die. You will die."

It was the starkest warning I'd ever been given in my life. And when the two younger midwives arrived and Ora told them each to take one of my arms and hold me down, I felt it in full that it was now life or death. Not just for my child but, as she had said – for me.

Still, it didn't stop. I forgot, in my delirium of pain and exhaustion, about my worry over unwashed hands and allowed the midwives to reach inside me over and over, pulling and prodding and yanking.

When the torture neared its end, and I felt what must have been my child's head exit my body in a fire of pain, Ora suddenly sent her two helpers away. I barely noticed it at the time – it was only later that it struck me what a strange decision it was.

There was no more talking. The only sound in the cottage was the heavy breathing – my own, as I struggled to push out my baby, and Ora's, as she struggled to pull him.

When he was born, she said nothing. She said nothing and I did not even have the strength to lift my head to look at him. But I could still hear. And what I could hear was – nothing. No sound, no crying. There was nothing but the stillness of a tomb as Ora took her knife in her hand and did something between my legs. And then she left. She took something tiny, which had been wrapped in a dirty linen sheet, and she left. And in that moment of confusion, before my mind had the time to assume what had happened, I heard a cry. An infant's cry, just the same as those I had heard from the newborn infants of the Angle women. Just one, and no more.

"Hey!" I shouted into the dark. "Ora! ORA!"

I began screaming her name over and over as I struggled – unsuccessfully – to push myself up to a sitting position. I tried to swing my legs off the bed.

Moments later, after I set up a howling wail and did not stop, the two apprentices returned.

"Where is –" I began, my words slurring into each other as I lay on my bed, which was soaked with blood and sweat and afterbirth. "Where –"

One of the young girls knelt beside my head, and looked up at her friend briefly before taking my hand. "He did not live," she whispered.

"No," I said. "No, girl. I heard him. I heard him! I heard a baby's cry! I –"

"He did not live," she repeated, refusing to meet my eye and glancing up once again at her friend. "It is common for a mother to think she hears a baby's cry when –"

"I don't think I heard it," I insisted, groaning as a wave of dizziness came over me. "I don't – I don't think I heard it. I heard it. Girl, I –"

And then everything went black.

***

When I awoke, it was daytime. The bed I lay in was fresh, with fresh grasses packed into fresh linen. As my eyes adjusted to the bright light, I came to see that my husband was sitting beside me. I tried to say his name but the only sound that came out of my mouth was a weak croak.

When he saw that I was awake, he began to weep.

"Heather!" He exclaimed, blinking as if he could not quite believe what he was seeing. "Heather. My love! Oh, my love – do you wake?"

He was beside himself. I'd never seen him like that, not even when Eidyth died. And I was still confused, weak from blood loss and the physical trauma of birth.

"What's wrong?" I asked, as a strange darkness seemed to come into view in the corner of my eye. I was forgetting something. What was I forgetting?

I looked down at my belly, expecting to place my hand upon it once again, and saw that it was no more. And then the darkness blew over me, a fog of despair, and I began to cry as it all came flooding back.

"No," I said, looking to my husband as he lifted his wet face and looked into my eyes. "No, Magnus. I – I heard him. I heard him cry! When she took him I heard him cry! Why did she take him? Why did she take –"

My husband took me in his arms and held me very tightly. And when he spoke his voice was so thick with emotion it was if he could barely get the words out.

"Ora says it is a normal thing," he said, his eyes bright with tears. "She says it is a normal thing for a woman to think she hears her baby cry, even as he doesn't live."

No. No. I hadn't imagined it. The cry was only one, but it was real. I even remembered how it sounded slightly far away, as Ora took him away out of the courtyard. I looked up at Magnus. "No. It's not – I heard him. I heard him! Why – Magnus, why did she take him? Where is he? Where –"

"He is buried, my love. You have been asleep for five days, and the Angles say a baby who is born without life must be buried at once. They –"

Panic rose up in my chest, and then my throat. Magnus barely managed to roll me onto my side before I vomited onto the floor, and then stayed where I was, leaned half off the bed, retching and disbelieving. He couldn't be dead. I'd felt him moving inside me, he was strong, I knew it. How could he be dead?

I clutched at Magnus' tunic. "Did you see him? Tell me did you see him?"

He shook his head. "Of course I did not see him. What people let a father see his lifeless baby? It was Ola who told me he was a boy."

"So you don't know?" I whispered, through clenched teeth. "You don't know if he's dead! If you didn't see him – and if I heard him cry – how do we know –"

"Heather."

"NO! If you didn't *see* him, with your own eyes – how do we –"

"Heather, Heather."

I did not have the strength to fight. My husband held me close to his chest, and I found that I was out of breath and shaking. Even as I wanted to insist again, and louder, that it didn't make sense for our son to be gone, I didn't have the energy. I fell back into the darkness of slumber, and did not wake again for quite some time.

They say I drifted in and out of consciousness, fighting an infection and the effects of losing a lot of blood during the birth, for almost a half moon. It didn't feel that long. It felt like a single dream, composed of various other dreams. I found myself running through fog-shrouded forests trying to find my baby as his cries echoed around me, not seeming to come from any particular direction. I saw faces from my old life, high school friends, my mother, the second grade teacher who had sighed with annoyance when I accidentally put a staple through my own fingertip. But even when the dreams seemed to be about people or things who weren't my son, they were still, in truth, about my son. Even as I was transformed into an eight year old again, watching the blood bead on my finger before falling, drop by drop, onto the dirty linoleum, there was in the background a terrible anxiety. I searched the landscape of my own mind for days, looking for my baby. I searched through endless dream-forests and countless eerily empty houses filled with doors that simply led to more doors. And all the while the sense that he was close, that he was *right there*, if only I could open the right door, or look under the right fallen tree, tortured me.

When I woke from my sickness, my husband and my friends cared for me. Carefully, and with love, they brought me soups brewed from bones, to restore my strength. Magnus carried me gently out into the courtyard in the afternoons and put me in a special wooden chair that the Angles used for the elderly and invalid. And then he picked flowers as I watched weakly, telling me the name of each one. When he had enough flowers to make a bouquet, he would hand them to me, smiling and telling me that they still weren't as beautiful as I was.

The Angles did not have mirrors. Sometimes, in the still waters of a pond or a puddle, I would catch a quick glimpse of my reflection – but it was never as detailed or finely-grained an image as that I would have seen in a mirror. So I couldn't be sure that my husband lied when he told me the flowers were not more beautiful than I, but I suspected as much.

***

One day in the late summer, when the soft, golden evenings seemed to torment me even more with their beauty, I sat with Magnus out in the courtyard once more.

"It will never be worse than this," I said quietly, as we held hands. "I'm not saying worse things won't happen – because it seems they happen all the time – I'm saying that if they do, it won't hurt this much. Nothing will ever hurt this much again."

"Aye," my husband replied. "I know what you speak of, girl. I thought it could not be worse than losing Eidyth – but we were with her. You held her as she left this world. In truth I cannot think of our son alone, after the midwife took him away, because if I think of it too long, or too often, I will take to my bed and never leave it."

The gentle snorting and snoring of the pigs as they settled in for the night came from the sty behind the house, as well as the sounds, through the trees, of the other families who lived outside Haesting's walls getting ready for bed. The gentle breeze carried Brona's lovingly impatient voice to my ears, as she admonished one of her younger children to put out the candle and go to sleep.

"Why did this happen?" I asked, turning to Magnus in the dusk. "What did we do to deserve this? I keep remembering how happy I was when we met. Right from the very first moment, I was happy with you. How many people can say that? Even at the time it almost worried me, to be so happy, and for so many years. Even then I would catch myself wondering, at night, if there would ever be a price to pay. I wonder is this the price? Our children dead and buried?"

"It is your way," he replied, "to be unhappy with uncertainty. You speak of our early time together – I remember that you were always this way. You always wanted a reason, an explanation, for everything. It was one of the things I first loved about you – that you didn't have this passive response to life, that you didn't just accept the things that displeased you. But I fear there is no explanation for this, girl. The Gods do not concern themselves with our lives on this level, dealing out punishments or rewards, keeping a balance. There is no balance. You seek reasons and patterns because that it who you are, but any that you see are conjured by your own mind. There's no reason we lost Eidyth. There's no reason our son came lifeless into the world. And there's nothing we can do about any of it. Do you not think that I would take on an army of a thousand Northmen if it would buy you a moment's respite from your suffering?"

In the newly fallen night, a hot tear ran down one of my cheeks. I didn't bother to swipe it away. "I know you would do anything," I told him, because I did. My husband had not left my side since I fell into the after-birth fever. We relied at the time on the generosity of Lord Eldred and the Angles to keep us fed and warm, as I was too weak to work and my husband refused to do anything that would take him away from me. And I knew, as surely as I knew the sun would rise the next morning, that he would have done anything I asked of him.

***

The weakness eventually left me. It took a couple of moons, but the day came when I stood up from bed in the morning and felt like a whole, normal person again. Physically, anyway. Magnus said it was because of my childhood. He told me a child is the grown man or woman's foundation, as the stones under our cottage were to the cottage itself. He said that if a child is fed properly, and kept healthy, the woman the child becomes will carry that strength with her until she dies. That she will always benefit from that initial strength.

When I first came to live with the Angles, and with my Northman, who was just as prone to spinning slightly fantastical stories about why this or that person either succumbed or did not to sickness, I thought all their stories were nonsense. Poetic nonsense, but nonsense nonetheless. But I did recover from an illness so severe most of the Angle women would have died from it. And when I recovered, I wasn't weakened. I could see it in the people on the estate, too. Lord Eldred's daughters, who had always had full bellies and warm beds, were noticeably stronger – taller and broader – than the other Angles. And even as I became one of them, my American heart never fully got used to the idea that it was right and good that some should eat better than others simply because they were born to a lord.

"It just doesn't seem fair," I said to Magnus one day as we pulled weeds from our pea field. "And the people don't even seem to mind – even the ones who have lost children to sickness, as we did, seem not to be bothered by the fact that none of the lord's daughters ever succumbed to something like a bad cough."

"Lord Eldred has been lucky," came the reply. "The highers lose their own to sickness all the time, girl. It's not –"

"But they don't lose them as often. You said so yourself, that the only reason I survived after our son was born was my childhood health."

"Aye, it's true. But what would do you expect Lord Eldred to do? Would you take bread from the mouths of your own children to give to others?"

"If I had too much bread I would."

Magnus chuckled. "Well then I suppose the point hinges on what we would consider 'too much' bread, does it not? You understand, by now, that even the highers in the Kingdom do not live as the everyday people in the United States of America, do you not?"

"Yes," I replied. "I understand. I'm just saying, I don't think it's fair."

"It isn't fair, girl. But I don't know whoever told you things were going to be fair."

***

You would think that there are certain things in life that you could never get used to. And you would think that the death of your child was one of those things. You would be right, of course. Losing a child is not a thing a person 'gets used' to. But the wounds of life scab over, and then they slowly grow a thick layer of scar tissue. It is not that we mourned our son any less than we mourned Eidyth. It is not that we felt less pain at his loss than hers. It was that we had already been taught the lesson that his death just reasserted for us – that you can lose anyone, at any time, and your love for them, as great as it is, doesn't make a single bit of difference. Those who are lost to us are lost. Eidyth taught us that. So when we lost our baby boy, it did not take quite so long to accept that he was, in fact, gone. That his only existence would be in his parents' hearts, and in their memories of their hopes for him. We brought flowers to his grave, beside Eidyth's, and lay them in the grass.

The winter after his birth was hard, and Magnus and I could no longer afford the luxury of hiding away in our cottage, grieving. We built a small barn, and spent the first truly cold weeks of the season mixing the mud, straw and dung mixture to slap on the slender willow-weave that made the walls that would keep out first cow warm.

We were not the only ones expanding, either. The Haesting estate continued to spread beyond its walls, and the new stone walls that had been built around the first few homesteads were taken down and rebuilt further out, so there was more room within them. One of the boys from the estate, the son of one of Lord Eldred's men, was sent to one of the King's own estates, to learn smithing. When he returned, Haesting had its own smith, and people from nearby villages and estates began to visit to trade their goods for swords and nails and ploughshares.

The estate continued to prosper, and so did its people. Even the lowest of the Angle peasants were soon moving out of their flimsy huts and into cottages with stone foundations and room to keep a pig out back.

In one way, Magnus and I prospered, too. My husband had the best mind for all things combat and weaponry-related in all of Haesting, including Lord Eldred himself, and he found himself in much demand. Our stocks of grain, dried peas and smoked pork almost overflowed with how many of the Angles needed him to instruct their sons on how to wield a sword.

And myself? I settled, along with my husband, into the knowledge that our lives were what they were. That we were going to live them there, in that place, doing the things we did then, until we either died or some serious catastrophe befell the estate. We had already experienced catastrophe by then – the worst of them all, and twice. It was not that we didn't worry about invaders from the North, or disease – it was that we already knew there was nothing we could do about those threats, so in the meantime there was simply nothing else to do but get on with it.

To that end – getting on with it – I slowly and not entirely deliberately began to take on a healing role in the community. Many of the Angles had thought me benignly mad for quite some time – I swam in the river they shrank from, I freaked out about cleanliness when they saw no need to wash any but the most visible filth off themselves before they ate, or touched an open wound. But when one of the smiths apprentices burned his arm quite badly, I happened to be nearby at the time, and was unable to stop myself from advising against it when one of the Angle women advised rubbing the burn with a mixture of pig dung and tallow.

Before I lost my children, I would not have said anything – I would still have considered myself an outsider on some level, a person whose voice perhaps did not deserve to be heard. But after losing Eidyth and my son, I became much bolder. When the worst has happened, and you're still alive, you can sometimes experience a kind of courage arising from the ashes of your own suffering.

"Do *not* put dung on it!" I warned loudly, when the smith's apprentice stood whimpering and gasping and one of the Angle women had brought a fresh bucket of – well, of pigshit.

The small crowd that had formed around the burned apprentice turned towards me when they heard the strident note in my voice.

"But he's burned," one of the women said. "If we don't put the mix on the burn, it will fester and –"

I stepped forward and grabbed the apprentice higher up on his burned arm, so as not to cause him further pain. And then I told someone to fetch some water that had been boiled, but was now cooled. I was insistent that the water must have been already boiled, too.

It was the injured boy's luck that no one was in too much of a mood to argue with me that day. Most of them wandered away when I seemed to have it in hand, but some of the women stayed to see what I would do, eying me with open skepticism the whole time.

The wound did not fester. Not after I insisted it be cleaned only with boiled, cooled water, and then wrapped in linens that had been left to dry in the bright afternoon sunshine. It wasn't possible in that place to achieve truly sterile bandages, but I knew sunshine was a disinfectant from spending time with my grandmother as a small child, and listening to her talk about how they'd done things when she was a girl.

That incident with the smith's apprentice bought me my first measure of credibility – not as a person, because I already had that with most of the Angles who knew Magnus as a great swordsman and teacher, and knew what we had been through – but as a healer. It gave me, in the minds of the people, a use and wisdom of my own, that wasn't tied to the losses I had suffered or my husband's skills. When the boy's wound, which was deep and nasty, did not fester, and when it had within the week closed up and began to heal, I soon found more people arriving at the low wall that surrounded our courtyard, asking for my help and advice.

I could not explain germ theory to the Angles – I didn't know the ins and outs of it myself. But I did know that cleanliness was important, and filth should be kept away from all wounds, and all vulnerable people. They knew it themselves, in some ways. They knew that milk had to be consumed when it was fresh, and that to drink it after it had sat out for a day would often lead to sickness. They knew to be careful when they butchered their livestock, to keep the contents of the beast's stomach and bowels from spilling over the meat that was to be consumed. They didn't know the precise reason why consuming old milk or unclean meat made them sick, and they didn't really need to, because the important part was knowing it made them sick. I just needed to extend their concern for clean meat and fresh milk to how they treated wounds and injuries.

They knew how to splint bones – better than I did, anyway. But it was I who taught a few of the women not only to use only water that had been boiled for at least the time it took to run to the beach and back – about ten minutes – on any broken skin, but to boil the linen bandages, too, and then to hang them from tree branches in the sunshine until they dried. It was me who taught them to always keep their own hands as clean as possible when handling the bandages or tending to a wound.

As ever with these things, it was just a few of them who listened at first, those who had seen how the apprentice's burn had healed without festering. But then, as those women began to use my techniques, and to see them work with their own families, more wanted to know about them. I soon found myself working hand in hand with the healers in Haesting, and being asked about medical and health issues about which I had no knowledge.

"Ceoldor's son says his wife feels a sensation like beetles crawling across her arms when she lies in bed at night," I told Magnus one evening when he asked me how I'd spent my day. "He wanted to know what he should do about it. But I don't have any idea what it means to feel like beetles are running all over your arms! All I know is that being clean is important when dealing with cuts and wounds – that's it. And now they think I'm some kind of wise doctor!"

My husband scooped a piece of ham from his pottage and ate it. "A wise doctor, is it? You have told me about doctors before, girl. The Angles know only their healers, and their healer's herbs and concoctions. Is it true what you say of your own healers – your doctors – in your homeland? That they can infuse the blood from one man into another, who has suffered an injury and lost most of his own?"

I was never secretive with Magnus about my life in the USA. There was never a reason to be. But I was aware, even more as the years wore on and I came to understand how deeply primitive life for the Angles was, that much of what I could tell him would be so strange as to be almost incomprehensible. The idea of blood transfusions would have seemed like black magic to the Angles. Even to my Northman, after explaining them repeatedly, I could see from the look on his face that part of him couldn't believe that I spoke the truth.

"But how does the man receiving the new blood not simply lose it from the hole used to deliver it?" He asked me once, after I'd tried once more to explain.

"The hole is extremely small," I told him. "It's barely a hole. The needle is so fine the hole it makes looks like the mark left by a bee's sting."

"And how do you have a needle so fine? How do you make a needle that fine, that can still deliver blood?"

Our conversations always foundered on those rocks – when Magnus demanded more and more answers until I found I had none except telling him that the needles just were that thin. I didn't know how they were made, or where, or who made them or the technique they used – I only knew that the needles were that thin.

On the night we spoke of Ceoldor's son's wife, and her itchy arms, Magnus asked me if I wanted to look again for the tree that could take me back to where I came from.

We were in our late thirties by then – or close to it. Magnus said it was actually our late forties but he was wrong – it had not been so many years since the loss of our son. However old we were, we had not spoken of the tree for a long time.

"Why do you ask?" I replied, spreading butter over a piece of bread.

He did not reply right away, but I saw at once that he was worried, even as he tried to hide it.

"What's wrong?" I asked.

"It's probably nothing to worry about," he replied, looking down at his supper. "How many winters has this estate stood now? And how many trained men does she have to defend her walls?"

"It's been a long time," I agreed. "And there are many warriors now, it's true. I heard one of the men living within the walls say that there's a rumor the King himself sees how well-defended Haesting is, and envies us our protections."

"Aye, we are well-defended."

"So why did I see that look on your face, like something bothers you? What is it?"

My husband finished chewing a piece of bread and then once again avoided my gaze. "There's word of new raids by my people – the Northmen, down the coast to the south."

I waited for him to continue, but he did not. "Aren't there often rumors of raids?" I asked, nervous to see that Magnus was truly bothered by whatever it was he wasn't yet telling me.

"Aye, there are. But these – these do not seem to be rumors. A trader from Kent who Lord Eldred says is trustworthy tells of attacks moving up the coast, and increasing in strength. He says even large villages have been burned to the ground, and that the Northmen seem to be renewing their interest in this land once more."

"A trader from Kent? Did you even speak to him yourself?"

"I did. And what I heard was enough to send me to Lord Eldred, who confirmed that he has been hearing the same."

We had been so safe for so long, and lately so secure in our ability to defend ourselves, that I actually found it difficult to imagine a raid – even of Northmen – being successful. Still, the way my husband's mouth was set meant he was taking the news seriously – which meant I took it seriously, knowing that he was more knowledgeable than me when it came to such things.

"Do you think we should move back inside the walls?" I asked.

The walls around the cottages, gardens and fields outside of the main Haesting estate were mostly stone, by that time, but they were meant to keep livestock in, not invaders out. As such they were built no higher than the height of a man's waist.

"I should have put up a palisade with Ceoldor and his sons, as we spoke of," Magnus replied. "Of course we found ourselves busy with other tasks, and now – let me speak with him, and with Eldred again. The Northmen are not upon us yet, but if there is word they approach, yes, we will move back inside the walls of the estate."

Chapter 20: Ora

It had been many a winter since my brief time with the Northman when Eltha's belly swelled with a child. And although I was married to one of my own people by then, and a mother to three boys and one girl, I had not forgotten my time with Asger.

We met when he found me picking oysters on the beach and he drew his sword, threatening to chop off my head if I didn't tell him if I had heard tell of a Northman and an Angle woman, traveling together in the vicinity.

When I told him – truthfully – that I'd heard of no such traveling pair, he let the tip of his sword rest in the wet sand and looked down at me appraisingly.

"Is it so, girl? Perhaps I am only inclined to believe you because you're so pretty."

I remember blushing with pleasure at the compliment, sensing almost right away that the Northman – who was without companions – did not intend to kill me. He seemed more intent on impressing me. After asking me once more if I was sure I had not seen the Northman he sought, or the woman who might be with him, he told me his name was Asger and asked me my own.

"It's Ora," I told him, only to find myself invited into the woods so we could 'talk further.'

As I said, I was innocent. But I was not so innocent that I did not know what it was the Northman wanted. He was better looking than the boys I was used to – taller and stronger, and dressed in fine leathers – and something about his attention made me smile and giggle. I agreed to go into the woods with him to talk further, and we soon found ourselves in a little glade, sitting on a fallen log.

"You distract me," he said, eying my body under my tunic. "I meant to question you about who you have seen passing these parts, but it seems I cannot take my eyes off what I can almost see underneath your dressings."

I giggled again, and bit my lip.

"Perhaps," he suggested, "I would be more able to concentrate if you were to show me what's underneath."

I would have shown him anyway, because I liked the attention he was giving me, but he reached out before I had a chance, and pushed my tunic off one of my shoulders. And then the other, until his eyes grew wide and greedy as the linen fell far enough to reveal my breasts.

"So pretty," he whispered, taking each one in his hands at once, kneading and squeezing, his hands rough and eager. "You're so pretty."

It was only the second time a boy had touched my breasts. It happened once before, only a couple of moons before I met the Northman on the beach. One of the boys from the village found me in the field, looking for a lost pig, and we kissed a little bit. But that boy's breath smelled foul and he was pale and skinny. Asger's skin was smooth and golden with the sun, his shoulders broad and his gaze arrogant. His hands on my breasts produced quite a different feeling than that caused by the village boy.

"Take – take the rest of it off, girl. Hurry, I cannot stay for long!"

I took the rest of my tunic off. There was no ceremony. As soon as Asger saw me naked, he pushed me down onto my back and spread my legs with his hands. It didn't last long. I remember a sharp pain, and then giggling at the look on his face, and then wondering if I should be afraid by how fast he suddenly moved. And then it was over, so soon I thought maybe the deed had not even been done for him – although I remember standing up and feeling the slickness on my thighs that proved it had.

When he began to straighten his leathers out I reached out to take his hand and he brushed it away.

"Asger? Will you come back to –"

"I need to get back to my men!" He snapped. "Girl – why did you accost me so –"

"I did not accost you!" I protested, as my heart sank with disappointment to be treated so dismissively. "You –"

I didn't finish my sentence, because the Northman raised his hand, as if to strike me. "You did! You did, you dirty little wench! Ah, I suppose there are worse ways to be accosted, though, are there not? We will be here until we find the man we look for – my traitor brother – do you live nearby?"

Pleased to hear I might see him again, I told Asger where my village was and which path to take from the beach to find it. And then he left me naked on the ground, sore, and without so much as a kiss.

***

But he came back. He came back that same day, in the evening, and waited in the woods near my father's hut to grab my wrist and yank me unexpectedly into the bushes when I was sent to fetch some sneeps from the garden.

My scream – for I did not yet know who grabbed me – was smothered by a hand over my mouth, and then Asger himself grinning at me.

"Stop yelling, girl! It makes you sound like an old wife – and I do not need to hear such things coming from such a pretty mouth!"

"I'm sorry," I started, smiling to see him again as warmth spread across my belly to know what he had come back for. "I did not expect to –"

Asger began to kiss me. His kisses were like his hands – rough, eager, quick. That time, instead of pushing me down right away – which I would have let him do – he pulled me down next to him so we were both sitting on the ground, and pulled his leathers aside.

"Look what you've done to me," he accused, gesturing down at his cock, which I could only just make out in the fading light. A jolt ran through my belly to see the state he was in, but I wasn't sure what to do. I didn't want to upset him or make him angry again.

"Were you a maid?" He enquired, lifting my tunic off over my head and beginning to roughly handle my breasts again. "This afternoon, in the woods – were you a maid? You made a sound when I was first inside you, as if it hurt, and I was wondering if –"

"Yes," I replied, hearing that my own voice sounded strange because of what Asger was making me feel. "I –"

"Ha!" He chuckled triumphantly. "I don't know whether to call you lucky or unlucky! It isn't many an Angle who can claim a true Northman – the son of the Jarl and the future Jarl himself no less – made her a woman. You have that to boast of to your friends. But it is also true that now you are ruined for life, and will always dream of the things I did to you that men of your own kind cannot."

I didn't quite know what the Northman meant by the things he did to me that other men could not. Everything he had so far done to me seemed that it could have been done by any man. But I didn't say what I thought out loud, because even though I was young and not very knowledgeable about men and their need to feel themselves superior to other men, I sensed that Asger would not react well to questioning.

"Mmm," he breathed heavily when he pushed me back onto the ground and reached down between our bodies to join them. "You're all wet, Ora. Is that because of me? Is that because you thought all day of the things I did to you earlier?"

I smiled and nodded, which only seemed to excite him further.

It was over quickly again. Just as I was beginning to feel a strange, aching need between my legs, Asger suddenly stopped his thrusting and groaned loudly, holding himself inside me as he did.

That's how it went, for a short time. The Northman came to me daily – often more than once daily – to fuck me and then to complain to me of his father's sternness and his own lack of freedom.

"I'm young!" I remember him saying one afternoon, after he had taken me on the beach and then insisted on watching his seed run down my thighs. "Why does my father not understand that?! He expects me to think all day of strategy and tactics and swordsmanship and – ugh, I can't take it. Thankfully I have you to calm me, girl, and your sweet body to give me ease."

In truth, I enjoyed it. I enjoyed the attention, as fleeting as it was. Asger was very attractive, and he had that way about him that some boys have, of never quite giving you enough of themselves to satisfy. I was always attached to boys who gave me that feeling of wanting more.

One night, after he had snuck away from the camp of Northmen, and as he had just finished himself on my breasts, he sat down with a heavy sigh and told me that his father was angry.

"Why?" I asked, because it was my role to ask Asger about himself – as clearly as it was my role to spread my legs for him.

"He worries that my brother is lost, that the rift is not one that can be mended. He rants and raves every evening, sometimes threatening to kill him, other times threatening to take him back and make him the next Jarl instead of me!"

"Is it so?!" I cried, because once again I knew it was expected of me to react with horror. "It can't be, Asger! Why would your father do such a thing?"

"Because he's a foolish old man who does not understand how it is for his firstborn son!" He replied. "He thinks only of himself, only of his 'legacy' – it's all he speaks of. All my life it has been this way, always having to meet his expectations and never quite doing so. I'm sick of it!"

After that night, I did not see Asger again. It was a quarter moon later, as I was walking through the woods one day, that I found myself yanked off the path and assumed it was him, come back to see me once more.

But it was not him. It was a Northman, but it wasn't Asger. It was his father, I knew it right away. There was a similar look to his eyes and mouth, and he was dressed in even finer leathers than his son.

"Lord," I said immediately, bowing my head respectfully as I had been taught to do when dealing with highers.

"I'm the Jarl," Asger's father replied. "Not a lord. And I need to speak with you, girl."

"Is Asger –"

"Asger is dead."

Tears immediately sprang to my eyes, and I covered my mouth with my hands.

"Yes," the Northern Jarl continued. "Dead. Slaughtered by his own brother! I came to your land not a moon ago, with two sons. Now it seems I return to the North with none. Stop your weeping, girl, I did not come to share my misery with you. I come because I need you to promise me something – and I will pay you well for your promise."

I turned my face up, then, my ears pricking at the intimation that I might be well paid. "Yes?" I asked. "What is it you –"

"You say you live near here? It is not within the walls of the estate, is it? The one just south of here?"

"Not within the walls, no. But Lord Eldred owns the land where we grow our crops, and he takes his share of them. It is he who is charged with our safety if –"

"And my son said you are training in the healing arts – is it so?"

I wondered what all the questions were leading to, but Asger's father was a much more serious man than Asger himself, and I was too afraid to do much more than answer him. In the end, it turned out that he wanted me to keep watch for his other son, and his other son's woman. He produced a little gold trinket from one of his leather pouches, and placed it in my hand. It was worked into the shape of a wolf's head, and studded with colored stones all in a circle around the edges.

"Do you know how much this is worth?" He asked. "It is worth more than your whole family will ever own. You can trade this for grain, or livestock, or favor with a different lord, if you ever need to flee. And yet it is not a fraction of the gold I will give you if you do as I ask."

I thought at once of the little hut where I lived with my parents and siblings, and the fact that our bellies often went empty at night. I thought of how we had not been allowed to live inside the walls of the estate because we were too low in station. I thought of how it would be one thing to buy our way in and then, if what Asger's father was saying was true, that it would be quite another to afford walls of our own, and men of our own. To not need to beg favors of those who looked down on us.

"Is it so?" I asked.

"It's as true as anything I have ever said, girl. I must return to the North, but now with no sons, and no legacy, the favor I ask of you is more important to me than you can know. You must swear to me that you will do as I ask. And in return, your family will be rewarded. You will be rich beyond what you can imagine. But only if you do as I say."

"I'll do it," I promised, not yet sure what 'it' was but too entranced by the promise of more gold to imagine there was anything I wouldn't do. "Just tell me what you need me to do, Jarl."

What Asger's father needed me to do was kidnap a baby. What he instructed me to do before that was keep watch on his other son – Magnus – and the woman he was with. He did not think it likely they would stay in Haesting, but if they did, I was to observe the son, and any woman he seemed to be with, and wait for signs of pregnancy. In the event of a baby being born I was to see to it that I was there at the birth, and then to take the child away – to pretend illness or perhaps even death to the parents.

The Jarl said he would send a small ship twice a year, with a small crew of two or three men to meet me in the early spring and the late autumn on the beach where I had met Asger, and that I was to report all I had learned to the men who would be on the ship. He also said, because he knew what his son and I had been doing together, that if I had a baby in my own belly he would bring me and my entire family back to the North with him if I wished, to live as highers.

I didn't quite believe him about the last part, because as avaricious and stupid as I was at that age, even I could see that the Jarl's interest was in any grandchildren he might get his hands on, to carry on his legacy. It was not in Angle peasant girls. If I had Asger's baby, the Jarl had no reason to look after me or my family once he had his hands on the child.

Not that I had a baby in my own belly, which became clear soon after the Jarl left and my blood returned.

What I did have was a gold wolf's head for a trinket, and the promise of much more gold where that came from. I began to travel to the Haesting estate with my aunt Wenda when she would visit to tend to the sick or deliver a baby. It was not suspicious, because it was known that I was probably to be the healer after her.

The Northman Magnus married the foreigner, and they lost a pregnancy. I reported that to the Northmen who came in a small ship to the bay, as the Jarl had said they would, always in the early spring, often before the thaw had even started, and then again late in the autumn. I also reported that the couple had taken on another woman's baby as their own, but the Jarl was interested only in his own blood.

As the winters passed, the ship started to come once a year, rather than twice. And then there was one year when it did not come at all, in any season. But the year that Eltha's belly began to grow, and I came to realize that it was indeed, after all those years, another pregnancy, they turned up on time and I gave them the news. Within two moons they were back, with a gold ring for me to keep hidden and renewed promises of more.

So I did as the Jarl had asked, so many winters before. I took the baby, who was born alive – but barely – and whisked him away to the beach, where a small contingent of Northmen waited near the camp they had made in the woods. And when I handed the little bundle over, I was given a heavy sack in return, filled with gold as promised.

The child will not live, I told myself as I walked back to the estate to prepare an empty grave for its parents to visit. *It does matter that you gave him to the Northmen, the only difference is in which grave will contain him. His parent's hearts would be broken if you had done what you did, or not.*

After the deed was done and a moon or two had passed, I truly did not think too much of it anymore. And when I did it was only to remind myself that it wasn't often that a mother labored that long and lived – and it was almost unheard of that both the mother and the child lived. Besides, Magnus the Northman had killed his own brother. It was right that he should lose his son for such a crime. That is what I told myself.

I used some of the gold to pay masons to build a cottage with stone foundations, and a stone courtyard like that of the Northman and his wife. When that was done, I paid a man to travel south, to Colchester, and purchase a gown of blue colored silk for me. And then my husband and I took on two men, trained with swords and bows, to be in our service and to provide us with protections now that we had become people who owned things that were worth protecting.

I did not think I would have reason again to think of the Northern Jarl, or the baby that came so many years later and the gold he was willing to trade for it.

But as it happened, there was something inside me, some instinct or goodness, that I had not anticipated. And when news came that Magnus was gravely wounded, and soon to die, I found myself seized by a sudden urge to find him and confess my crime.

Chapter 21: Heather

The final disaster, in the trilogy of disasters that marked my life, came when the Northmen extended their raids further north than they had for years. I woke in the night to find myself alone in bed and the sound of horses hooves in the distance.

"Mag–"

"Shhhh!"

He did not need to shush me again. We knew each other as well as ourselves by then, and I had heard something in his tone that told me he was serious.

"The Northmen," he whispered a second later. "They come in the night, Heather."

At once, I remembered that we had plans to move within the walls of Haesting the next day – only hours away – and then found myself distracted by the sound of a woman's scream, and then men shouting, and the metallic sound of swords clashing.

"They attack Ceoldor and his family!" Magnus whispered, turning to me. "Heather! You must go – out the back, through the pig gate. Go to western gate. I will join you in –"

Another scream ran out, closer then, and I was almost sure it was Ceoldor.

"No!" I whispered back, as my heart pounded in my chest. "Magnus – come with me – why would you –"

"Go now! Girl, I will meet you there. There are many of them, and I need to help –"

"Please come with me," I begged, because something about that night felt foreboding. "Magnus, please –"

And then I found myself hauled out of bed and shoved towards back door to the cottage. "GO! NOW!"

I went. As the sounds of hooves approached the courtyard, and my husband drew his sword, I went. I ran out past the pigsty and, as he had told me to do, around the back of the estate to the smaller western gate, rather than the main northern one.

Within the walls, the men were already preparing to defend Haesting. I found myself ushered into the same small underground room as I had been all those years ago, when Magnus' father and brother attacked. All around me the women and children and old men of the estate crowded anxiously together, asking each other if they had seen the attackers, and how many in number they had been.

The battle lasted many hours, and when we were allowed out the day was almost past. I emerged into daylight, and a scene of bloody chaos. Bodies lay everywhere, Northmen and Angles, and the air stank of death. It was Lord Eldred himself, his fine leathers soaked with blood, who approached me first.

"Eltha. You must –"

"Lord Eldred!" I exclaimed, horrified to see the lord of Haesting himself in such a terrible condition. "Lord – have you seen Magnus? Where is –"

"He is in the hall, tended by the healers. You must go to him, Eltha. You –"

I did not hear what else it was that Lord Eldred said, because I was running towards the hall, trying to reassure myself in a panic that at least he was alive. 'He is in the hall, tended by the healers.' Healers do not tend to dead men. So my husband was alive. But wounded, perhaps? It couldn't be badly. He was the best swordsman in Haesting, so it was not possible that he could be badly wounded. It was not possible.

When I saw him, I also saw at once that I was wrong. It was possible for Magnus to be badly wounded, and that he was. A gash ran almost the full way from his shoulder to his elbow, so deep I could see the white flash of bone in its depths. I fell to my knees at his side, screaming at one of the young healer's apprentices to being the clean bandages from my cottage before touching my husband.

"Heather?"

"Yes," I replied, unable to control the emotion rising in my throat. "Yes, my love. Do you – do you not see me? I am right here. Right here beside you!"

Magnus turned his head, his eyes open, towards me. But he did not see. It was bad. It did not take a healer to see how bad it was. His gums, when I lifted his lips, were pale with blood loss, and the straw underneath him was soaked red.

"I love you," I cried, because I thought he was going to die right that moment, in front of me. "I love you! Magnus – why didn't you come with me when –"

"Because they were upon us," he whispered, his breathing labored. "And because it is my job to keep you alive. I held them back long enough for you to get within the walls, did I not? Are you hurt?"

"No," I replied, as warm tears streamed down my cheeks. "No I'm not hurt. But what worth is my life if I am without you, Magnus? What –" I broke down again.

"What worth," he repeated weakly. "What worth? Girl, your life is worth a thousand of my own. And a thousand times I would give mine for yours."

When it became clear that Magnus was not going to die right that minute, I asked Ora, who was in attendance with all the younger healers, because the hall was filled with wounded men, if I might have time to return to my cottage and fetch the bottle of strong alcohol I had brewed from sneeps, to use as a disinfectant.

The cottage was destroyed – all the cottages outside the walls were destroyed. The parts that could be burned were burned, and the stone walls had been smashed to pieces. The pigs lay dead in their sties. But the sneep alcohol was intact, still snug at the bottom of a wooden chest that sat in the corner of what had once been my home. I grabbed it, along with a pile of clean bandages, and ran back to the estate, even as part of my mind was accepting, by then, that no amount of alcohol or bandages were going to be enough to keep a wound so deep from festering.

And as it was, there was no time for it to fester. I found Ora bent over my husband, whispering something in his ear, and then I watched as his eyes rolled back in his head.

"Come," Ora said, laying a hand on my shoulder. "There are men we can still save, Eltha. Your husband is lost. Come and help –"

"Get away from me!" I screeched, slapping her hand away and desperately pressing my fingers to Magnus' neck, feeling for a pulse. And there it was, so weak it was almost imperceptible. I crouched over him, resting my head on his chest, weeping.

"Please don't leave me," I whispered. "Please, Magnus. I don't know how to live without you. I don't - I don't know what to do without you. Please, please."

It went on like that for hours, a woman whose hair was streaked with gray and whose hands had lost the suppleness of youth bent over her dying husband, imploring him not to leave her alone in the world, her heart as panicked and lost as that of a rabbit before the hunter deals the final blow.

And then he woke, just before sunset, and I felt his hand tighten around mine.

"Magnus!" I whispered, looking up, smiling even as I knew it was goodbye.

"You smile," he whispered, his voice so low I could barely hear it. "Such a beautiful smile, my love. That smile has been the light of my life, do you know it?"

"Yes," I nodded, choking with emotion. "Yes, yes."

"It is right that you smile. It is not many who have a love like ours. Even when you put me in the ground, you will still have our love. Until the day I see you again, you will have it."

A cold electricity seized my limbs, a certain knowledge that the moment was upon us, the moment I suppose I had always known would come, but had hoped it would not be so soon.

"Magnus," I wept. "Magnus, please don't –"

"Listen. Listen, my love. Our son – our son –"

He broke off, and a horrible choking sound came from his throat.

"Our son will be there, too," I told him. "And Eidyth. We will all be –"

"Our son –"

He was trying to say something, but the words would not come. All of my attention was on him, and being with him, and making sure he knew, as he went to the next world, that he was loved.

"The healer – Ora –"

"Shhh," I said, stroking his hair off his still-handsome face, so I could kiss his cheeks. "Shhh, my love. I'm here. I'm –"

"He lives. Our son lives. The healer took him. That night, that night –"

I drew back, far enough to look into Magnus' eyes. "What?" I asked, unsure if I'd heard him correctly. "What did you say? Our son lives? No, my love. He does not live, not in this world. He –"

"Heather!"

The last word my husband spoke was my name. His eyes widened as he spoke it, and his grip tightened, and then, suddenly, he was gone. He was gone and the world changed in an instant from a place of love and familiarity, of places and events I cared about, to one of distance, as if death had placed me on an island, and all who I could see and hear were on a far shore.

I did not think of much, including his last words, for three moons or more. Haesting was in disarray, and the broken down estate, with its stores looted and burned, resembled nothing so much as my own heart. I dreamed of Magnus almost every night, horrible dreams where I suddenly walked in on him as a young man, sitting around a table with a wife and a family I didn't recognize, or found him at an estate just a little further up the coast, with a look on his face when he saw me like I was a stranger to him. I always woke from those dreams with the thought that perhaps he wasn't dead, perhaps he was just somewhere else, another estate or village. And then, after having that thought for a few minutes, it would dissipate and once again I would come to know that he gone.

Sometimes I tried to comfort myself with the knowledge that nothing mattered anymore. It didn't matter that our cottage was torn down and its straw roof burned, or our pigs killed and our cows set loose. It didn't matter that I had nothing except my husband's dagger, because the Northmen stole his sword and I buried him with the one he had given me at our wedding. I wore the gold dagger strapped to my thigh and wrapped in rags so no one would know what it was and think to steal it. Nothing mattered without Magnus. All I was doing after he left me was waiting to die. So if the Northmen returned and took me, or the Mercians thought to do the same, and make me a slave, it was of no consequence.

I did ask Ora, the healer, what she thought of Magnus' pronouncement that our son had somehow lived. I still remembered that cry on the night of his birth, the one everyone was adamant my mind had conjured from nothing. She would not meet my eyes when she answered that my husband had been near death, that his thoughts were a mess, that he did not know what he said.

"The other things he said made sense, though," I replied, as the healer fussed with a small tub of herbed tallow, opening and closing it over and over.

"What would you have me say?" She asked finally. "How many years ago did the child come into the world? He did not live, Eltha – it should be obvious to you by now. And even if it's not, what does it matter?"

She was right about the last part. Even if my husband's last words were true – and how could they be? – what did it matter? Even if somehow our son lived, it seemed certain that he lived somewhere else, with other people he thought were his parents.

No, it was not possible. He was gone, as Magnus was gone, as Eidyth was gone. And it was in my heart I carried their memories, until the day would come when I, too, would pass into the next life.

***

I did not weep so much after Magnus' death as I had after Eidyth's, or our son's. It was not because I loved him any less. Indeed, I loved him so much that when he went, a part of my heart went with him, so I knew – or I thought I knew – that I would never again love anyone as I had my husband or my lost children. Or perhaps it was the part that produced tears? Perhaps my lack of lachrymosity was that I had been given a finite amount of tears in life, and by then they had all been spent on my heartbreaks? All I knew is that when my husband left the world, I no longer had anything to hold onto. I was adrift.

When the Northmen returned, not a year after the first new raid on Haesting, they succeeded in taking the estate. Lord Eldred fled with his daughters and their families, and a few swordsmen, and I never saw him again. Many were killed. I was almost killed, until one of the Angles saved me by telling the Northmen of my healing skills.

For a time, I traveled with them. At first it was with their raiding party, which was all men. Later, perhaps a year, perhaps two, more of them arrived from the North, and with them came women and children and men who were not warriors. I then became attached to the latter group, an older Angle woman with no husband or children, but enough skills with tending to wounds to make me worth more than the effort to swing a sword and take off my head.

Instead of lords, the Northmen had Jarls – what Magnus' brother would have been had Magnus not killed him. The first Jarl I traveled with was cruel, and took great joy in killing and destruction. The second, who brought with him the women and children from his homeland, was not as bad. I say 'not as bad' – but I was little more than a slave. They did not give me, or those like me, enough to eat, or thick enough blankets to keep warm at night. And without adequate food, I found myself weak and sick, always coughing, always shivering in the night. Often I would find myself sleeping with the hounds, because the animals at least offered some warmth.

It was with the second Jarl – Tor – that I expected to die. I became so enmeshed with his people that he brought me back to the North with him when they returned, and I lived in a little village next to the sea and acted as the healer for the people. It was a strange thing, at first, to be among Magnus' people, and in his homeland, but after asking a few of the villagers if they knew of him, or his father, and receiving only blank stares in return, I gave up. Wherever Magnus had come from, it was not the same part of the North that I went with Jarl Tor.

It seemed a year, perhaps two or three, when we returned to the Kingdom of the East Angles. I had lost track of time by then, so the summers all blurred into one summer, and the winters all into one winter. I would not even describe myself as unhappy, because unhappy seems to indicate the presence of emotion. After Magnus died, and after it had sunk in that he was not coming back no matter how fervently I wished for it, I seemed to just stop feeling. Even if my stomach ached with hunger, I could take bread if it was offered, or go without, and feel the same about either outcome. If some of the other low people tried to befriend me, or ask me about my life, I would answer them with brief, flat answers that let them know I was not interested in a connection.

Perhaps I felt a little something when I saw the coast of the Kingdom of the East Angles come into view, from the ship I sailed on, smaller than the rest and filled with the thralls, as the Northerners called those who were little better than slaves. But whatever I felt, it was fleeting, and gone as soon as my heart remembered that the place no longer contained the people who had made it special to me.

As it happened, we made camp near to where Haesting had been – I was not permitted to wander freely but I recognized the coastline as being just north of the old estate. Sometimes, when I was sent to gather berries with some of the other thralls, I would keep one eye half open for the tree. Not that I was searching for it to return to the United States – not at all. The place, if it was even still there and not yet destroyed by nuclear war, would be as alien to me then as the deep past was when I first came through the tree. I was just aware that I was in the general vicinity of where it would be, and curious to see if it even still existed.

And then one day I found myself traveling south, with another Jarl who had arrived to help with the conquering and settlement of the Kingdom by his Northern brethren. Ragnar was his name, and I was sent at the back of a group of his warriors, and the warriors of a second Jarl, as they moved south to confront the King of the East Angles himself. I listened to the battle with little interest, awaiting the arrival of the wounded and dying. And then a girl appeared – a woman, really – and casually mentioned that she would need to get to a hospital to have her wound treated.

A hospital. The word struck my brain like a sledgehammer and I remember stumbling slightly, barely remaining on my feet. Further questioning revealed that she was from where I was from – the United States, and *when* I was from – the future. She did not seem to understand, right away, where she was. She came to understand, though, as she ignored my warnings to return to the tree and return home as soon as possible, or risk losing herself forever in the past. She came to understand almost before it was too late, and we both discovered that there were two more from our time – two more women, one who already had a Jarl's child, and another in her belly. Paige and Emma, Jarl's wives, they knew where they were and they did not wish to return. Sophie, who had a child back in the United States, and who was slightly older than the other two, did.

And on the night that she left, after the Angles had briefly taken us captive and the Northmen had rescued us, I faced, for the first time since I had come to the Kingdom, the possibility of going home. The girls had already advised me to return, questioning why I would stay in the past where I had no one, and no status. They were young, and they did not understand that even if I were to return, I would still have no one, and no status.

But I liked Sophie. She was warm and smart and I wanted to see her safely south, back to the tree.

We left in the night, so her Jarl Ivar would not realize she was missing until dawn, and started south on the Great Road, which I had heard talk of in Haesting, but never traveled on. We were far from the coast at the time, and I knew the Jarl would have tracking men – and hounds.

To that end, I persuaded Sophie to walk in streams when we could find them, even if it left our feet wet and cold. Hounds couldn't follow trails in streams – nor could men.

It was a difficult journey, and more than once I sensed I was holding her back. But Sophie refused to leave me behind and when we got further south and I recognized where we were – or thought I did – I showed her an alternate route, so if the Jarl was following, he might not find us.

The tree itself, when Sophie found it, did not look as it did in my memories. It was bigger than I remembered it, its roots and branches more numerous, thicker, it's trunk taller.

"We should go," Sophie urged nervously as we stood gazing at it. "We shouldn't waste time – the Jarl's men could be right behind us. You are coming, right?"

Chapter 22: Magnus*

All my life, from the time of my first hazy memories, I lived with the feeling of being somehow apart. I often caught the villagers in Apvik looking at me out of the corners of their eyes, sometimes whispering as they did so, and thinking I hadn't seen them. Their interest always seemed slightly pitying, rather than malicious, and it happened so frequently I soon let it pass without thought. It wasn't as if I didn't have an explanation for their pity – I was the son of the man who would have been the Jarl, grandson of the actual Jarl, raised by my grandparents because my own mother and father were dead. I was a figure of sadness, a motherless – and fatherless – boy, no less worthy of compassion because of my upbringing in a Jarl's high household.

That is, at least, what I thought when I was young. My grandparents, the Jarl and his wife, were always reluctant to speak of their son. I understood it to be painful for them and tried not to ask too many questions of an elderly couple who had lost their firstborn.

There were a few taunts from other children, when we played in the fields. One girl in particular, the daughter of another high person in Apvik, seemed to take great delight in telling me repeatedly that I was not a Jarl's son at all. But when I lost my patience and pushed her up against one of the barn walls one afternoon when we were not yet ten winters, she dissolved into tears and refused to say what she meant.

My grandmother was prone to strange fits of melancholy, too. Every now and again I would catch her staring wistfully at me as I played in the longhouse on a rainy day, or when I returned from a day training with child's swords.

"What is it?" I would ask sometimes, when I caught her doing it. "Why do you look at me like that, grandmother?"

Usually, she would shake her head and put a smile on her face and tell me she had forgotten where she put her knife, or that she was thinking of a conversation she had that morning with one of the village women. But every now and again she would approach and take my face in her hands and stare down at me.

"You look just like him," she would say sometimes, as her eyes welled with tears. "Just like him!"

Of course I assumed by 'him' she meant my father Asger, the Jarl-to-be who had died heroically in battle in the Kingdom of the East Angles.

When I was ten and five, my grandfather – the Jarl – died. He fell into a ravine whilst hunting a stag, and dashed his head on some rocks. And when he died, my grandmother began to slip away. At first her grief seemed expected, as grief is when one loses one's husband. But instead of returning to her routines after three moons, as was the way of mourning in Apvik, she began to spend more and more time in bed, staring out the door she would ask me to keep open, so she could see the waves in the distance.

I was to be Jarl, but at ten and five was not considered ready yet. Another man, one of my grandfather's most trusted friends, took on the role in the interim. It was this man – Kiarr – who became responsible for my training and education, and it was he who came to find me at the beach one day to tell me my grandmother called for me urgently.

Back in the longhouse, I found her in her usual place in bed, reaching one of her tiny, gnarled hands towards me.

"Grandmother," I said, taking her hand in mine. "Kiarr says you wanted –"

"Sit, boy. Sit, Asger. I have something to tell you. Go and get a chair, this won't be quick."

I brought one of the heavy wooden chairs from the table and placed it at her bedside.

"Look how strong you are already," she rasped. "Ten and five and already as strong as a grown man. If what Kiarr says about your training with the sword is true, you will be Jarl before you are ten and ten and one, my love."

But my grandmother had not called me back from my day's activities to praise my strength in carrying chairs. I sat down beside her, still holding her hand in mine, and asked what it was she needed to speak to me about.

"I will be with your grandfather soon," she told me. "Do you see how I fade away? I will not go like he did, all at once. No. I will go gradually, bit by bit. Already I am more in the next life than this one. But before I go, there is something you must know. I was told never to tell you the things I am about to tell you, Asger. But now I see the young man you are becoming and I cannot keep my son's son from knowing the truth of his father – and himself."

My head dropped to my chest as my grandmother spoke matter-of-factly about her death, which I had known was coming but had not quite been faced with so starkly until she put words to it. I had no parents, and as such my grandparents were my parents, and my grief at their deaths the grief of any child who faces being orphaned.

But my grandmother didn't have time to watch me wipe my eyes and weep at her side.

"The first thing you must know, is that your name is not Asger. You are Magnus, boy. Your name is Magnus, as was your father's. It is not just your name that is his – I look at you and it is as if the years have spun backwards and it is Magnus himself who stands before me, with that look in his eyes that I see in yours sometimes, of unspoken impatience. He –"

"My name is not Asger?" I asked, thinking my grandmother was beginning to lose her mind. "Why do you say –"

"Because your father is not Asger! The Jarl and I had two sons. Asger and Magnus. Asger was the Jarl-to-be. But all that you heard of him from your grandfather the Jarl – about his bravery, his talent, his skill with a sword and the warmth he carried in his heart for those who were beneath him – those things are true only of Magnus."

My grandmother did not seem to be lost in madness. I looked down at her and in truth she looked more alert than I had seen her for a moon or more.

"I see how you look at me," she continued. "And if you hate me, and you hate the Jarl for our lies, I will understand it. He could not live with Asger's shameful death in the Kingdom of the East Angles, and so –"

"So my father died a shameful death?" I asked, horrified. "Is that why the people in Apvik have been staring at me all my life, as if –"

"No! Listen to me, boy. He was not your father. Asger was not your father. It was Magnus who brought you forth, and it was, it was..."

She trailed off and we sat in silence for some time, as I let the news take hold in my mind. I was not the son of the Jarl-to-be, Asger? I was the son of Magnus, the second son? And if it was all true, why had they spun such a story? If my real father was the brave and good son, why had they pretended otherwise? When I asked my grandmother these questions, a single tear slid down one of her cheeks and she gripped my hand a little tighter.

"If I tell you the answers," she whispered. "You are going to hate me."

"I'm not," I told her. "There's nothing you could do to make me hate you, grandmother. If the truth has been kept from me, or twisted around to resemble something it isn't, I know it was not on your prompting. I know you had to listen to your husband."

My grandmother sobbed quietly when I said that, and wiped more tears from her cheeks. "You even have your father's understanding," she said. "He was often angry with me, for obeying a man he came to think unreasonable, or defending a son he came to think unworthy of defense. But he always understood that I had no choice – as he himself did not, being born second to Asger. As it is, child, I must tell you before I lose my courage. I do not know that your parents are even dead."

I heard the words. There was no sudden gust of wind to carry them out of the longhouse before they found my ears. I heard them, but I did not quite understand them, not right away.

"What is it you say? You do not – you do not –"

"I do not even know that your parents are dead! There was a fight, my precious boy. A fight in the Kingdom of the East Angles, between Asger and Magnus. You know as well as I do the penalty for a second son to take up arms against his elder brother! But it was Asger who died, at Magnus' hands, and the Jarl who returned to tell me that one son was dead, and the other lost to us forever."

"But," I said, shaking my head as if to clear it and feeling my heart hammering away in my throat. "But – how –"

"He stayed in the Kingdom. Magnus stayed in the Kingdom when his father and his brother came to kill him, and instead he killed his brother. He took a wife, and made a life for himself there, and all the while the Jarl – your grandfather – took updates from a local peasant girl on any children that might be born of the union. It was so long, boy. It was so long we thought the marriage would be childless, until one day many winters later word came that Magnus' wife was pregnant. The Jarl sent a ship, and gold for the peasant girl, and a few of his best men to wait for the birth. And when the child – when you – were born, the –"

"The peasant girl who grandfather paid in gold stole me away?" I asked, my voice as flat as my heart was stirred near to a frenzy. "Is that what you tell me? The Jarl took me away from my mother and father?! HE STOLE MY MOTHER AND FATHER'S ONLY CHILD AWAY FROM THEM?!"

I put my face in my hands as my heart broke for the parents I had thought long dead, and the torment they must have suffered.

"What were they told?" I cried. "What were my parents told?"

"I assume they were told you were dead, I do not know for sure. I tried to warn the Jarl against it. I tried to tell him that you would one day learn the truth – it is not as if there are not many here in Apvik who know it. And after all this time, still all I can think of in the early morning when I wake and cannot find sleep again, is of Magnus in that other land, thinking his only child dead. Thinking –"

My grandmother's voice broke then, and she wept with me. There was rage in my heart, and it came close to alighting on her. But it was as she said – she could not have stopped the Jarl. I knew my grandfather, I knew his stubbornness. He was not a cruel husband, but he was also not one to be persuaded by a wife, or a child, if his mind was made up.

"So you have spent my whole life with this secret," I said. "With knowing that your son thought me dead. And I have spent my whole life with it too, without knowing it."

I had so many questions. I stayed with my grandmother after nightfall, raining them upon her head – most of which she could not answer. She knew only the barest details, as my grandfather the Jarl, in his shame at what his first son had been and his inability to admit it to himself, had not spoken of it often.

"What of the people?" I asked, after the sun had long set. "If the men saw Magnus kill Asger, why did they go along with calling me Asger, and allowing me to –"

"Your grandfather was the Jarl, Magnus. I will call you Magnus tonight, boy, as it is your true name and it feels right to do it even at this late time. As it is, your grandfather was the Jarl. He spun a story about an Angle girl falling pregnant with Asger's child, and then in those years that passed between Asger's death and the appearance of the baby – of you – here in Apvik, of that child growing old enough to have a child of their own, and of you being that child. Of course no one believed it – perhaps they would have, if you had not been so obviously your father's son, so similar to Magnus in look and manner that no one could deny you were his. But what were the people to do? They feared your father – but they loved him, too. They were bound to obey their

Jarl. And many understood the torment he had been put through by having the bad luck to father a son like Asger. You were the Jarl's blood. The Jarl's sons were gone – dead or elsewhere, and you were the link to the Jarl. That was what mattered."

***

Less than two days after she told me of my origins, my grandmother died. I, as the sole remaining direct descendant of the late Jarl's bloodline in Apvik, carried the torch that lit her funeral pyre. And when her ashes had blown away on the wind, I continued my training and learning with Kiarr and some of the other warriors. I did not speak to anyone of what had been revealed to me.

But when I was ten and seven, and the first opportunity presented itself to sail to the Kingdom of the East Angles with the warriors, I insisted on taking it. Kiarr tried to talk me out of my determination, thinking me too young, but I ignored him. It was battle he thought I wanted – but I couldn't have cared less for battle. What I wanted was to find my parents. And if they were dead, I wanted to find someone – anyone – who could speak to me of them, and tell me what and who they had been.

As it was, Kiarr kept a close eye on me, understanding as he did that if I died, his old friend the Jarl's bloodline died. Still, I had opportunities, in various small hamlets, to make enquiries after a man from the North with the name Magnus, and his Angle wife.

Nobody had heard of such a man. Or perhaps some had and were too frightened to tell me as I stood over them with my sword in my hand? As it was, I returned to Apvik with no new knowledge of my parents or where they might be or if they were even alive. The next raiding party, one winter later, brought similar results.

And then when I was ten and nine, I went on my third trip across the sea to the Kingdom of my birth, and it was not one for raiding that time. The people of the North were then intent on conquering and settlement more than they were on taking pigs and gold. I sailed for the first time with my own ships, although I was not yet Jarl and would not be, according to Kiarr, until I had reached ten and ten.

When we came ashore we found our people already there in abundance, with large camps built along the coast and the King of the East Angles having already surrendered. That night, as I sat with the high warriors from some of the coastal camps, they spoke of a party of Jarls and men who had already moved inland, the first force to do so, and were probably just then in the midst of taking Thetford for the people of the North.

"When Thetford falls, the Kingdom of the East Angles will be ours in full," one man said, "as their King has already pledged his fealty."

I asked them if they had, in their conquering of the coastal villages, come across a man by the name of Magnus, who was of the North but living with the Angles and his wife. They had not.

When I rode inland, following the Great Road, I did not ride to find my mother and father, because I still had no idea of their whereabouts. I went inland to find the Jarls who took Thetford, because such was my restlessness that I found I could not stay in one place. There was as much chance of finding my parents in one place in the Kingdom as in any other. The way my grandmother told it, it sounded as if perhaps they had lived close to the sea, but in truth she did not mention how far the peasant girl had traveled with her little bundle – me – before handing it over to the Jarl's men. Perhaps it was a journey no longer than my own to the beach in Apvik – perhaps it was a day or more?

I found Thetford in the hands of a band of Northern Jarls and their men. It was almost winter, and the place was busy with that half-panicked energy that always takes over during the autumn season, when the people worry about whether or not they have enough to see them through the cold to come.

Just inside the gates, a great Jarl on a horse rode through behind me, with a deer carcass slung over the horse behind him and large retinue of men.

"A visitor," he said when he saw me standing there beside my own horse, clearly without any idea of where to go or who to speak to. "A Northern visitor, if I interpret that style of leathers correctly. Who are you?"

"I am Magnus," I replied, even though after four years the name still felt strange in my mouth, because I had chosen to stick with Asger whilst I still lived in Apvik, so as not to confuse people. "I – I am from Apvik, in the North. I will be Jarl come the next winter, but as it is I am too young."

"A Jarl-to-be," the Jarl replied, smiling. "Have you come with a message? Is there word of further movement on the coasts? Do more men come behind us down the Great Road?"

"I, uh," I started. "Yes, I think so. Not that I have been sent to tell you – it is just what I heard in the camp. They said you had come to take Thetford, and that after the winter, more would follow in your path."

"But you were not sent to bring this news?"

I shook my head. "No."

"Then why are you here?"

The Jarl was not being unfriendly. If anything he was being far kinder than he needed to be to a stranger who had just showed up at the gates of a freshly-conquered town. I could have been anyone. I could have been an Angle in disguise.

"I – I am here – I am here because I look for someone," I replied, flustered. "And because I was bored on the coast. It is not my greatest amusement to burn the huts of peasants, Jarl."

Something about that made the Jarl smile. "Aye," he said. "Nor is it mine. I am Eirik. You will surely understand that I cannot just leave you to wander the streets of Thetford on your own, not being sure of who you are yet – but I invite you to join us for supper. We will eat the stag I've killed, you can meet the other Jarls, and perhaps you can give a clearer description of your purpose in Thetford when you have a full belly?"

Chapter 23: Heather

How can I describe what it is to come home after thirty-five years? What words can there be to tell what it is to find the place with two faces – one so familiar it makes you pinch yourself and wonder if you were ever truly away, and another so alien it makes you shake with how badly you want to flee back to the place where you spent those thirty-five years?

Everything seemed big and loud and brightly colored in River Falls. From the first moment I emerged from the tree with Sophie, I could not keep my attention on one thing for more than a few seconds before another thing stole it away. The woods were the woods, as they had been. River Falls was River Falls, as it had been. On the very surface, things seemed not so different. The roads were full of cars – more cars, and strangely shaped, but cars, with wheels, and drivers who would honk and gesture impatiently at anyone they deemed to be taking a fraction of a second too long in making a turn. At the cabin in the woods where Sophie brought me, I found a refrigerator and an oven, and a bed to sleep on – all familiar things, things I remembered.

But below the surface, River Falls was in truth so different I would not have been able to function were it not for Sophie – and her little daughter Ashley – who showed me the ways of the future. Yes, the cars still had four wheels and they still ran on the roads. But they spoke to you now, just like KITT in Knight Rider. And no one seemed to think it was worth commenting on! There were a lot of buttons in the future, a lot of beeps and chirps and trills, and a lot of flat, glossy surfaces. There was a button for everything. You didn't put a key into the lock to open a car door, you pressed a button. You didn't turn a knob to heat up the oven, you pressed a button. You didn't pay with cash or fill out a check when you paid for groceries, you pressed a series of soft plastic buttons and the money transferred itself, as if by magic, from a customer's bank account to the grocery store's. And as these buttons needed constant pressing, they also provided a strange, beeping soundtrack to life. I was surrounded by beeps, constantly whirling around at the sound of one, and then turning back at the sound of another.

"You'll get used to it," Ashley reassured me. And she was right, in a way. I did start to get used to it. But only after months of tagging along behind Sophie like an invalid, having to learn how to live and function in the world almost as a small child has to.

The Jarl Sophie had been with during her brief time in the past came through the tree after her, and I wasn't surprised. They were in love, and I knew – better than she did at the time – what love could make a man do. She was pre-occupied with her love, and her child, and I was just grateful to be included in her life, and introduced to the people in it.

When Magnus' gold dagger sold at auction for an amount of money I found myself almost wholly unable to process, I understood that the final chapter of my life was written. It hadn't yet been lived, but I knew what it was to be. I thought I knew it, anyway. A house in River Falls, where I could be near Sophie's children – who became to me as important as the grandchildren I didn't have – and her mother, and her friends, and Sophie herself. Another house, in the woods, set on many private acres where I could retreat when all the flashing lights and chirps and distractions became too much – which was about once a week.

Life is strange. If I had been asked, at twenty, who my closest friend would be at almost sixty, I would not have said a Viking Jarl. But Sophie's husband and I could not help but become close, as we were perhaps the only two people in existence who understood how truly bewildering the future was. Ivar would visit my acreage often, mostly when he, too, found himself overwhelmed, and we would forage for mushrooms together, or chop wood for the fire, or spend hours trying to recreate the pottages and stews we remembered from our past lives.

A great Jarl and a second son's widow – an unlikely friendship. We would joke about it sometimes when we ate – often only by the light of candles, as we were in agreement, even after some time spent in its midst, that the future was far too brightly lit.

"Served supper by a Jarl," I would chuckle when he placed a bowl of steaming chicken stew in front of me. "It's a wonder your hand knows the movements."

"Shut up, woman," he would rib me affectionately. "It is not I who wrote the rules of this place."

"And what do you think of them?" I asked one evening, as we sat out on the covered porch of my house, listening to the sounds of night falling over the woods. "I was no one after my husband died and your people took Haesting – I was little more than a slave. But you – you were a great man, Ivar. Everyone had to listen to you – the Jarl of Jarls. Do you not miss it?"

The Northman thought for a few moments. "Do I miss it? I don't know if 'miss' is the right word. Are there times when I wish I could order people to do things and see them done? Yes. But the way things are here seems to work for them does it not? Do these Americans lack food, or safety? It seems to me I have never seen a more comfortable populace – they fear neither invaders nor hunger. They do not need strong men with swords because they have moved beyond that life. Back in our time, strong men with swords were still the rulers of the world. But if my daughters having full bellies, and hospitals to care for them if they sicken means me losing my place, as one of those strong men with swords? I'll take it. I'm a father now, a husband. There is nothing so important to me as my family."

I liked Ivar. Even had he not been the only person I could talk to of the past, I would have liked him. He was wise, and he didn't live for his own ego.

"And what of you?" He asked. "If the Gods would return your husband to you, would you go back?"

"I would," I replied, without hesitation. "And don't think that means I do not care for my life here or the people in it. I have come to love your daughters as if they were my own grandchildren, Jarl. I would miss them. I would miss you and Sophie and everyone else. But you know what it is to love, and so you know my answer could only be that I would go to wherever my husband was, if the Gods saw fit to return him to me."

"Aye, I know it."

***

I was not lonely in River Falls. Not in the way most people think of loneliness, not in the way I was when I was young and living in Los Angeles. Most think loneliness is about people, and that if you have people around you, you cannot be lonely. In River Falls, I had people. People I loved, and who loved me. But I had no one who knew me when I wasn't yet an old woman, and that is another kind of loneliness. Sometimes, in the midst of one of the feasts I would throw at my home in the country, I would find myself standing in the kitchen, waiting for this or that dish to finish cooking and a paradoxical feeling of aloneness would steal over my heart at the sounds of laughter and conversation coming from the dining room. Sophie – and her family and friends – took me in. They didn't take me in as a favor or to make me some kind of mascot, they took me into their family and their hearts. And still those quiet moments would catch me unguarded sometimes and I would almost fall to my knees, crying for the husband who I had lost so many years before, wanting nothing more than to speak to him one last time, to tell him of my new life.

"You will see him again."

It was Ivar, who always moved surprisingly quietly for such a large man. And he'd found me lost in one of my 'moments' in the kitchen, aching for Magnus.

"Do you not believe it? Do you not believe you will see him again? I know many here in this place do not believe such things."

"I don't know," I replied, closing my eyes briefly. "I don't know."

"You will. It will not be in this life, or any life like it, but you will be with him again. I can tell from the way you speak of him, that your love was strong. Death does not break a bond like that. It only changes its nature."

I blinked away a tear and turned back to the stove, where a cheese sauce – Sophie and Ivar's daughters liked nothing so much as macaroni and cheese – thickened. "I hope you're right," I replied. "I don't even truly know what you mean, but I hope you're right."

"I am. There are many things I've questioned since coming here, but this is not one of them. How can it be? The one thing that remains the same, between our old world and this world, is love. They drive cars and fly in airplanes and pay for their food with pieces of plastic, but love is unchanged, is it not? Do you see any difference?"

I lowered a whisk into the thick cheese sauce. "No. Not in love."

"As it is, Heather. You will see him again. And until that day comes, you have all of us to drive you out of your mind and show up at your house every week demanding to be fed!"

***

So that was my life. Not unhappy at all, not lonely or without meaning. But shot through with a melancholy that could sometimes feel quite acute.

I took to gardening with some fervor. All the money in the world – which indeed, seemed to be in my possession – was not necessary. As long as I had a trowel, some seeds and a watering can, my days passed in contentment. I soon bought some chickens, and two cows, who I cleared and fenced a portion of my land for, and settled into my life as a 'rich lady farmer' as Sophie teasingly called me.

It was a fall afternoon when I got the phone call. One of those perfect autumnal afternoons where the sky is a deep blue and the sun still brings enough warmth to make a jacket unnecessary – even as the trees have begun to don their bright red and yellow attire.

"Heather?"

It was Sophie. And she sounded strange.

"Yes, it's me. What is it? Is something wrong?"

She paused. "No. Nothing's wrong. I was just – I was wondering if you were home this evening."

"Of course. Where else would I be? Are you sure nothing's wrong, girl? You sound as if –"

"Heather! Nothing is wrong, I promise you!"

"Alright. Were you thinking of bringing the girls to visit? I can show Ashley the pumpkins if she wants, they're –"

"No," Sophie interrupted again. It wasn't like her to interrupt. It wasn't like her to sound so stilted and odd.

"No, I mean – perhaps this weekend? I'm sure Ash would love to check on the progress of the pumpkins."

I furrowed my brow. "If you're not stopping by, then why are you calling to see if I'm home this evening?"

There was another pause. "Heather?"

"Yes?" I replied, thoroughly confused.

"Just make sure you're home this evening, OK?"

Chapter 24: Magnus*

Not all the Angles had fled Thetford. Many chose to remain, and pledge fealty to the Northern Jarls who were now in charge. It was some of those Angles that I approached over the next few days, asking after a man named Magnus and his wife. Magnus was not a common name for the people of the Kingdom, which made my task somewhat easier.

None in Thetford, however, had heard of him – or even anyone who sounded like it could be him, with a different name. And I did not know my own mother's name, so I couldn't ask if anyone knew of her.

Jarl Eirik saw something in me, it seemed, because he took me into his household for the duration of my short stay, and invited me on most days to eat with him and his men. On a night shortly before I left to return to the coast, I found myself brought to a different longhouse than the usual one, where Eirik's men would drink dark ale with me deep into the evening.

Inside, instead of warriors, I found Eirik's wife and children, and a few others. I bowed my head respectfully as I entered, aware that it was a privilege to be invited to eat with a Jarl's family and close friends.

"I'm Paige," a woman who wore the golden armband of a Jarl's wife told me. "And this is Emma, wife of Jarl Ragnar. The rascal who hides under the table is Eirik, our first son."

I greeted everyone as they were introduced, and saw that Paige held another child to her breast.

"What brings you to Thetford alone?" Emma asked, when the venison stew had been served and Paige reassured me that Jarl Eirik would not mind if we began our feasting before he arrived.

"I seek a man," I told her. "And a woman. But it is only the man's name I know."

"You seek a man?" She replied, eying me. "What man? A Northerner? Has someone done you wrong?"

"Magnus seeks his father," a booming voice came from behind, as Jarl Eirik entered the longhouse. "His father also carries the name Magnus. He seeks his mother, too, although for her he does not have even a name."

"And how is it you came to be in the Kingdom of the East Angles," Paige joined in, "looking for your mother and father? You are from the North, are you not? Why do you seek your parents here, in the Kingdom?"

And so I was obliged once again to tell the tale of how I had come to the land of the Angles to look for my parents. Paige and Emma followed closely, asking clarifying questions I did not have the answers to, and expressing their sympathy at my plight. It was after we had taken enough stew to fair burst our bellies that Emma sat up and looked at me.

"Magnus, right? You said your father's name is Magnus, like your own?"

I nodded, watching as she turned to Paige and addressed the next question to her. "Didn't that old woman – Heather – say her husband was called Magnus? In fact didn't she even say he was a Northerner? Am I remembering it right?"

At once, the attention of everyone in the room fell on Paige as we waited to hear if her memory matched Emma's. She narrowed her eyes, thinking.

"Yes – I – yes, she did mention a husband named Magnus, didn't she? Yes – she did! I remember her speaking of him when we bathed in the river. I – oh my God – I think she even mentioned that she lost a child. Were you there when she spoke of it? She said she had lost one in the womb and one at birth – did she not?"

I forced myself to remain seated, and to keep the calm expression on my face even as the weak little flame of hope that has been burning in my chest since my grandmother told me of my origins burst into a fire at the conversation taking place in front of me.

"Is it so?" I asked, as the women looked at each other, trying to figure out if their memories were well-recalled or not. "Is it – you said – her husband's name was Magnus?"

"Her husband was long dead," came the reply, and with it the feeling of having been struck with something large and heavy. "Oh – Magnus, I'm sorry. I didn't think to – I'm sorry! What is the likelihood of it being your father, anyway? What are the odds of –"

"I'd say the odds aren't bad," Jarl Eirik broke in. "You say the old woman spoke of a Northern husband, whose name was Magnus? And she was herself not a

Northerner? How many marriages between Angles and Northmen can there have been so many winters ago? And how many that produced only a single child, dead at birth? Dead – or stolen? You said your grandmother told you that you were taken at birth, did she not, Magnus?"

"Yes," I breathed in response, as a feeling of dizziness came over me. "Yes, I – yes, she said I was taken at birth, by the peasant girl who my father paid in gold."

"So they will have told your mother and father you died," Eirik continued. "There was no other excuse they could have offered, was there?"

A hush fell over the room. Paige and Emma looked at each other, wide-eyed with the possibility that the woman they spoke of could be my mother, and Eirik kept an almost fatherly eye on me, waiting to see how I would react to the possible news.

"So," I started, a short time later, and when I found myself able to speak once more. "This woman, this – Heather, is that her name? Where is – is she here in Thetford?"

Paige and Emma once again threw meaningful looks, which I did not understand, at each other. It was Paige who responded.

"No," she said gently. "She isn't in Thetford. She isn't – Magnus, she isn't anywhere, uh, anywhere near –"

"Is she dead?!" I cut in, sitting up straighter in my chair, my stomach seized with a sudden fear. How cruelly perfect would it be to learn that my mother was dead just as I learned that there were people in Thetford who knew her?

"No," Paige replied slowly. "She's not dead. Not that I know of, anyway. But she – Magnus, she isn't *here.*"

"Yes, you already said that," I replied hurriedly, only to sit back and apologize a moment later when I noticed Eirik's stern glare. He was a kind man, and reasonable, but he was not about to let me snap at his wife – or his fellow Jarl's wife.

"I'm sorry," I continued in a softer tone. "My impatience gets the better of me – I was five and ten when my grandmother first told me of my parents, you understand. It has been such a long time since then. But if you could tell me where she is – I have come all this way inland on my own, I can surely find my way to another village or estate in the Kingdom."

Once again, the two women eyed each other. What secret was it they knew of that I did not?

It was Paige who bid me to meet them the next morning at the stocks in the center of Thetford, if I wanted to know more about where my mother was. I didn't understand why they couldn't just tell me that night, but as they were high people, I agreed to the meeting.

***

That night, I barely slept. I kept repeating the name they had given to the woman they spoke of – Heather – over and over in my mind. Was this 'Heather' my mother? How many days ride would it take me to get to where she lived? What would I say at the moment of meeting, how would I tell her who I was? And would she even believe me? Would she see something of herself in me, even if she thought I was crazy?

All night I asked myself those questions, over and over, until the dawn light came over Thetford and I made my way, bleary-eyed and badly slept, to the stocks.

And then, when the sun was almost at its highest point, both women appeared, and once again exchanged their secretive, almost worried looks, when they saw me.

"What did you think?" I asked, smiling. "That I would not be here? Finding my parents – or just my mother, if my father is already gone to the next world – is all there is for me. It is my only task."

"It's a beautiful day," Paige said, gesturing for me to stand. "Do you feel like walking? Let's walk to the gardens and pick some kale and sneeps for the stewpot."

And so we walked the narrow streets of Thetford, where the people, still in their autumn rush, went to and fro all around us.

"Why do you seem so reluctant to speak of my m– of Heather?" I asked, when we had been walking for a short time and neither woman had seen fit to mention the matter at hand. "You said you did not believe her dead?"

"No," Emma replied, again with that careful slowness that was starting to make me feel short-tempered. "No, we don't think she's dead."

"Has she done something terrible?" I followed up, wracking my brain for some reason the two Jarl's wives could have for behaving so strangely. "Is she – is she sick?"

"No," Paige told me, and there was kindness in her voice. "No she hasn't done anything terrible and I don't think she's sick – she wasn't sick when we last saw her, anyway."

Again a lull fell over the conversation. We had almost made it to the Thetford garden fields when I couldn't contain myself any longer.

"Why do you torture me?" I asked impatiently, causing both women to turn and look at me. "Do you think I don't see the way you look at each other?! What is it? You say she is not dead, she has not committed a terrible crime, she is not sick – that you know of. So what is it? Why won't you tell me where she is when it seems such a simple thing?"

"Ah," Emma replied at once. "But it is not actually such a simple thing as you think."

"I am trained with a sword," I told them. "And a good rider – I do not overwork my horse. Wherever Heather is, I promise you I can ride there. Even if she has left the Kingdoms of this land – if she's traveled south across the water to the Frankish Kingdom, I can find my way to –"

"But you can't," Paige said. "You can't ride to where Heather is."

I stood on the spot, shaking my head slightly. What did she mean? Was she teasing me? The expression on her face said she was not. "If you mean she has sailed across –"

"I don't mean she sailed anywhere. She didn't."

"Then what?!" I burst out, almost at my wit's end. "Then why do you say I cannot ride to find her? Why don't you –"

"We talked about this," Emma said, cutting off my plaintive questions. "Here, shall we sit here in the gardens? There is much to talk about – perhaps we should sit?"

So we sat on the edge of the gardens, and Emma continued.

"As I said, we spoke of this – Paige and I – before coming here to meet you. Is it true what you say, that this is your only task? Do you not have people to return to? If you find your mother, what do you intend to do?"

The Jarl's wives could not have been more than five winters older than me, and yet the way they spoke to me, in motherly tones, seemed to both annoy and please me. "I am ten and nine," I reminded them with a respectful smile. "Not ten. Are there those who expect me to become their Jarl, when my training is complete? Yes, there are. My grandfather's people, back in the North – in Apvik. But my grandfather is dead, and so is my grandmother. My whole childhood, I thought my mother and father were dead, too. Do you know what it is, to be a small child without a mother or a father?

To my surprise, Jarl Eirik's wife nodded. "I do. My mother died when I was five, and my father – who is now happy here with the Northern people – took to his bed until I was grown. I understand what it is to be alone in that way – to some extent, as it is."

"And so you understand what it is in my heart, then?" I continued. "You understand that I do not seek to find my mother so I can introduce myself and kiss her cheek and then go back to my life in the North? If my mother lives, I will take her with me, so I can care for her for the rest of her days. If she lives, we must be together. It is as it is, a mother must be with her child."

"And what if she doesn't want to come back to the North with you?" Paige asked. "What if, when you find her, she is content where she is?"

I sat back a little on the soft earth of the garden, pausing because I had not thought what I would do if my mother refused to come back to the North with me.

"Heather isn't a Northwoman," Emma told me. "She's not even, in truth, an Angle."

"What is she, then?"

Emma smiled. "She's from the same place that Paige and I are from."

It made sense, when Emma said that she and Eirik's wife were neither of the North nor were they

Angles. Although no one had told me, I had sensed, even in our brief time together, something foreign about the two of them, even if I could not quite name what it was. They had a boldness about them that, even in Jarl's wives, I found slightly surprising. "And where is it you and Paige –"

"That is why we ask you these questions," Paige cut me off. "Because the place we are from – the place Heather is from, and the place she is right now, if all went well with her plans – is not like other places. It is not like 'the North' or 'Mercia' or 'the Frankish Kingdom.'"

I met her gaze, and then that of Emma, waiting for the explanation to continue. When it did not, I threw my hands up and chuckled.

"Is it a riddle?" I asked. "I'm sorry, but I have no thought as to what it is you tell me. I do not know what you mean when you say that it is 'not like other places.'"

Emma leaned in then, as if she were about to share a secret, and told me in a whisper that it was not a riddle.

"And not a trick, either. Where we are from is not another place, Magnus. Well, it is, but not a place you can ride your horse to, or sail to, or walk to. It is another world. I don't say 'another world' to confuse you further, but because that is the simple truth. It is *another world.*"

Another world. I closed my eyes. *Another world.* I had only one understanding of other worlds. "So... she *is* dead?" I asked hesitantly. "My mother is –"

"Are we dead?" Paige responded with a smile.

"You, uh – no," I replied. "No, clearly neither of you are dead. But, I – what is another world but death? How does one travel to another world – one that cannot be reached by horse or boat or foot – if not death?"

I was confused. I was more confused than I had ever been in my life. I kept looking up, from Paige to Emma and back again, waiting for the moment when they would burst into laughter and admit they played a trick on me. But the conversation had gone on too long then to be a trick – and if it was still somehow a game to them, it was an exceptionally cruel one.

"I'm sorry," I said quietly, a moment later. "I – I have no understanding of what it is you tell me. I don't see it – all I want is to find my mother. If she is in another world, as you say, and you know how to get there, then please tell me the way. Is it even necessary that I understand the circumstances if you can tell me how to get there?"

"I understand your impatience," Paige replied. "I understand it because I would feel it in your place. And you're right, in a sense – it is not truly necessary that you understand the whereabouts of Heather, as long as you can get there – which you can. We don't speak with you like this to torment you or for our own amusement. We do it because we know the place you will be going, and we know that when you get there, however ready you think you are for it, you will not be. Did you know that where Heather is, you will not be allowed to carry a sword? We only speak to you as we do because we see how ready you are to go. But if we send you off with no idea of your destination, you are liable to get yourself into quite a lot of trouble before you find your mother."

"You think me too young and impetuous," I addressed the two women, seeing in their eyes that they did. "And I do not deny being either of those things. But I will say it again – the most important thing to me is to find my mother. If there are things you can tell me that will make finding her easier, then I am willing to listen. I am not a Jarl yet, but do you think I have not already learned the lesson that charging into any new situation with my sword drawn is not always the right way to go through life? If you say I must leave my sword then I will leave my sword, even if it will be a reluctant parting."

"Yes," Emma said. "You must leave your sword. And you must prepare yourself to see and hear and experience things you have never dreamed of. You must prepare yourself to be very careful, and very watchful, and not to take fright at –"

"I do not take fright easily," I boasted, because it happened to be true. "I do not –"

"You might," Paige commented, "if you knew what you were talking about."

We fell quiet for a time, then, in the garden. If I was reading the Jarl's wives right, they had agreed to tell me how to get to where Heather – the woman who might be my mother – was. They had at least not said they would not tell me. I could feel the tension between them, the nervousness at what they, too, sensed they were going to do.

"We cannot keep a son from his mother," Paige said eventually. "We will show you how to find Heather. But you must swear, Magnus – you must *swear* – not to speak of this to anyone."

"I swear it," I replied. "I'll not speak a –"

"And we cannot show you until the thaw."

The thaw? The winter winds had not yet blown into Thetford as we sat in the garden. "But I travel alone!" I replied. "Even in winter, I can travel well enough with just my horse and a bow to hunt rabbits. You don't have to wait until the thaw to –"

"But we do," Emma told me. "We do, because you won't be traveling alone. You're not going to somewhere obvious, Magnus. You're not going to a certain town or a certain estate. You're going to a – well, you're going to a tree. And we cannot give you accurate enough directions to find this tree, as nondescript as it is, without coming with –"

"A tree?"

Paige smiled. "Yes, a tree. Did you hear what we said about other worlds, and strange things, and not being about to ride to where Heather is – or didn't you?"

"But –"

"You cannot go south alone. We will ride with you when the thaw comes. And you'd be careful to mind that we don't owe you anything, Northman. It is a kindness we do you, because we like you and we see that you are sincere in your wish to find your mother. You are welcome to spend the winter here in Thetford, if you wish. Eirik and Ragnar have already agreed to allow it."

***

I sent word to Kiarr on the coast, that I would overwinter in Thetford, and Jarl Eirik found me quarters with his retinue. I ran into Paige and Emma often that winter, sometimes at supper, sometimes just in the streets of Thetford, and would try to extract information from them on where it was I was going, come the thaw. But they were quiet, and stingy with details.

They were right that a kindness had been done, though. They did not have to tell me anything about Heather, or where she was, or even that she might be my mother. And in respect of this kindness I did my best to contribute to the smooth running of Thetford when the cold came. I patrolled the city walls with Eirik's men, and accompanied the hunters when they rode out for deer. I did my duty at the various gates to the town, watching for attackers, questioning any arrivals. In turn, the Northern warriors took me as a friend, and brought me with them on their revels at the end of each winter moon.

When the days began to lengthen once more, after the Yule time, it was Jarl Ragnar who commented that he would be sad to see me go, and that I had proven myself a loyal and hard worker, even as I knew I would one day be a Jarl like him.

"It is not many men, who know they will one day be Jarl, who are content with guard duty at the city gates," he said one afternoon, as I carried a barrel of ale to his quarters. "Or carrying ale!"

"If what your wife says is true, and the place I go to find my mother has no Jarls – and no use for Jarls – perhaps it's just as well," I replied.

I had not intended my reply to be anything other than a show of humility, but Jarl Ragnar had clearly been talking to his wife about my upcoming journey.

"Is it so?" He asked, looking me straight in the eye. "Do you think you could let go of the role you had always hoped –"

"I hoped for nothing so much as I hoped for a mother and a father!" I replied, somewhat heatedly, before immediately apologizing. "I'm sorry, Jarl, I – this subject is one that –"

"It's nothing, boy. I can only imagine what it must have been for you to grow up without a mother and father. All I meant was that it's possible for men to get attached to an idea of themselves, a picture of themselves that they carry only in their minds. Do you understand? See that you do not spend your life trying to live up to an image only you have seen, Magnus."

I set the barrel of ale down on a heavy wooden table carved with likenesses and scenes from Northern myths and stories. "In truth, Jarl, the image was never my own. It was my grandfather's. He lost his sons, and it was I who was to compensate for that loss. But if you think I myself ever took any great interest in being a Jarl, in truth I did not. A child knows only what those around him know, and so when I was young I can say perhaps I looked forward to wearing fine furs and having the people defer to me, or bow their heads respectfully. But ever since learning the truth of my birth, I have found that if anything being Jarl is a future burden I half-wish I did not bear. If Kiarr and the people of Apvik wanted to hand the honor to someone else –"

"Find this woman you think might be your mother first," Ragnar broke in before I could finish. "You are young, yet. Find Heather and then ask yourself if being Jarl is your life's task."

***

When the time came to ride southeast, I was surprised to see both how small the traveling party was, and how full of high people. Both Paige and Emma rode with me – and so did their Jarls.

"Is it so?" I asked, when we met at the gates just before dawn broke on a cloudy day not long into the thaw. "The Jarls travel with us? Both of them?"

"Thetford is peaceful," Emma replied. "And Jarl Styrr will remain. It will not be a long journey, but it cannot be one that is known amongst the men. We must keep our reasons to travel southeast within this tight group, Magnus – did you not understand when I told you as much, before the winter came?"

"Aye, I understood," I told her. "I just did not realize you intended to share those reasons with quite so few."

And so we rode southeast, first down the Great Road and then off it, towards the coast. Our progress was swift, as neither Jarl Eirik nor Jarl Ragnar wished to spend more time than necessary exposed to the dangers of the road, and away from Thetford. On the day after our fifth night spent sleeping in the woods, we came to the sea, and then began to make our way back into the woods, down a path Paige and Emma seemed to agree was the one. My stomach began to churn with nerves, as I sensed we were close.

But no village appeared – as the women had said it would not. No castle, no estate came out of the woods. When we came to a stop, and I looked around, in truth I could see nothing of note. We were simply in the middle of the forest, on a narrow path, with no landmarks of note in any direction.

And then Emma and Paige instructed the Jarls – for those two women seemed sometimes to be in the habit of instructing their husbands, as surprising as it was to me – to keep watch in both directions on the path.

I found myself led into the undergrowth, then, and once again waiting for the laughter, the announcement that it was all a rather long-winded game. But neither of the women looked like they were joking.

"We're here," Paige said suddenly, when we were not far off the trail. "We're – this is it. This is the tree."

I looked around. We were surrounded by trees. One in particular seemed bigger than the others, but still no different to any others of its kind and proportions. I reached out to touch it, to ask if this was the tree she spoke of, and Emma blocked my hand with her arm. And then, to my utter shock, she disappeared.

Emma disappeared. She did not fall to the side or hide in some bushes. She simply *disappeared*. Right in front of my eyes.

"What –" I said, turning to Paige to see if she had just seen her friend *cease to be* right in front of her. And then, before I even had time to note the total lack of surprise on Paige's face, Emma reappeared. Right where she had been not a moment before. When she saw what must have been a look of great shock on my face, she smiled.

"I thought you said you were ready to go to another world, in order to find the woman who might be your mother?"

"I –" I said, stuttering, near-stupefied with what I'd just seen. "I – I am. I –"

"That is how you get to it," Paige added gently, seeing how confused I was. "We told you it was a tree, didn't we? It is the tree that will take you to where she might be. Are you sure you're ready? Because if you are, we have some things to tell you before you go."

"I'm ready," I said again, and my voice sounded much surer than my heart felt, at that moment. I'd never heard anyone speak of a tree that took you to other worlds. No gothi ever spoke of such a thing that I heard. And yet I'd just seen a Jarl's wife disappear and reappear in front of my eyes.

Both women then joined in giving me advice on what to do when I arrived in the new place. They told me that instead of asking for Heather, I should ask anyone I encountered to bring me to 'Sophie Foster' – that this 'Sophie Foster' had been in our world, and would know how to find Heather. They also told me not to imagine I could fight my way out of any difficult situations I might find myself in – in fact they advised me not to fight at all, which sounded extremely risky, but which they were both insistent on.

"It's just as real as here," Emma said, "where you're going. You're going to think it's not – it's what we both thought, when we came here. It took us both a long time to accept that this place was real, but you must accept it at once, if you are to find Heather. You must follow our advice, and you must trust that the things you see and hear that might frighten you or seem impossible are not impossible, or magical, or anything like that."

"Give us your sword," Paige added, when the moment came and my heart pounded in my chest with the unknown future I was about to step into. "We will lay it here, in the bushes, off the path. If you return, it will be waiting for you."

I handed over my sword and then stood in front of the tree, still not quite convinced it hadn't all been a trick, and feeling strangely naked without my blade in my hand.

"If you return," she continued, "and you cannot find your people, find us. We will be in Thetford for a few more moons at least, but the Jarls intend to continue moving inland. Find us, and you will always have a place at our table, Magnus."

And then she kissed me on the cheek, as did Emma, and I did as they had told me to do and lay both of my hands flat against the trunk of the tree.

Chapter 25: Magnus*

I fell forward, as if off a cliff, and felt myself tumbling through the air even as I had seen the solid earth and the woods and the tree in front of me not a moment before. When I turned to look for Paige and Emma, there was nothing but darkness, and it was suddenly hard to draw breath, as if smoke from an unseen fire filled my chest. I reached up to clutch at my throat, gasping, and then suddenly the world blinked back into existence. The earth was once again underneath my feet, the sun once again shining on my head.

"What is –" I started, and then realized that I was alone. I turned around, looking for the Jarl's wives, and then around again. They were nowhere to be seen. The woods themselves looked different, the trees taller and set further apart, the thick undergrowth gone.

Another world.

That's what the women said. More than once – many times. Did I think them liars? No. It was the difference between hearing that there is another world and suddenly finding yourself in it. My heart beat fast in my chest, knocking against my ribs so hard I imagined anyone standing nearby could hear it.

A sound unlike any I'd ever heard filled my ears, then, drowning out that of my own heartbeat, and as the instinct to fight or run kicked in I forced myself to stay where I was, to remember what Paige and Emma had said.

You're going to hear things – and see things – you've never seen or heard before. They're going to be loud. Don't be afraid, they're not wild animals. It's just how the people in that world travel.

I lifted my head in the direction of the roar and saw, just as I had been warned, a sight that made me close my eyes and then open them again. Something bright red, as bright as a summer poppy – brighter – traveling at a speed my eyes could not even keep up with. It was from this beast the roar was coming. And then, as soon as it was past, another one came after it, silver and glinting in the sunlight.

Don't be afraid. They're not wild animals.

Whatever they were, they didn't seem interested in me. They sailed past at a distance, across a field. Again I spun around, searching the woods with my gaze. There was no-one to be seen. I had to find someone to talk to, to ask where Sophie Foster was. I was in another world for a reason, and it wasn't to stand around staring at trees. To that end, I took a deep breath and began to walk out of the woods, and across the field.

Very soon, I came to a road. Its surface was smooth, alien, unlike anything I'd ever seen. There was no mud, no marks of horses hooves. There was just this hard smoothness, that did not spring back when I tried to push my foot into it.

Emma and Paige were right – the brightly colored, roaring beasts were transport of some kind, as they stayed entirely within the confines of the road. Most of them appeared headed in one direction, and so that is the direction in which I walked, too. It did not take long, after I started walking, for a loud, blaring note to sound, so loud it drove me into the bushes at the side of the road.

And then someone was shouting at me.

"Get off the fucking road, idiot! What are you doing?!"

I looked up, bewildered. A man, inside one of the traveling contraptions, was shouting. At me. Why was he shouting at me?

"Well?!" He yelled, when I didn't respond. "What are you, high? You're gonna get run over, asshole! Stay off the road!"

And then a roar filled my ears and he was gone. Moments later, it happened again. That time it was a woman. And instead of continuing to yell at me when she saw how confused I was, she pulled over a little ahead of me and leaned out towards me.

"Hey," she said, and something about the way the word sounded in her mouth reminded me of the way the Jarl's wives spoke. "Are you OK?"

I ran up to where she also sat in one of the roaring creatures, looking out at me with concern.

"I'm looking for Sophie Foster," I told her. "Can you – can you tell me where she lives?"

The woman, whose age I could not quite discern from looking at her, smiled. "Who? Sophie who? I'm sorry I don't know who that is. Why are you wandering around in the middle of the road?"

"I'm trying to – I'm looking for Sophie Foster. I need to find her. I –"

"OK, I got that. But why are you walking down the middle of the road? Are you drunk?"

I smiled back, then, and shook my head because I was about as far from drunk as I had ever been. "No, I'm not drunk. And I – am I – I'm not allowed on the road?"

The woman seemed pretty adamant that walking on the road was some kind of affront. And Paige and Emma had warned me not to cause any affront in their world.

"No," came the slow response, as if she thought she might be talking to a dull-wit. "You're not allowed to be walking in the middle of the road. The road is for cars. You're going to get run over."

As if to make her point, another of the roaring beasts – cars? – suddenly appeared behind the woman and filled the air with that same blaring sound I remembered from a few moments ago. And then it swung out and moved around us, as the man inside shouted angrily.

"Listen," the woman said. "You have to get off the road, OK? Like, right now. You're going to get yourself killed. Are you going into River Falls? I can –"

River Falls. Yes. I knew that name. That's where Paige and Emma said Sophie Foster would be. "Yes!" I replied. "River Falls – that's where I'm going!"

"I can give you a ride if you want. Not that I should be picking up strange men on the road, but you remind me of my son. Michael Packer, graduated from River Falls High in 2016 – do you know him?"

I did not know Michael Packer, and I told his mother as much. I didn't tell her anything else, though, because as soon as I was inside her car, the world began to pass by at such a rate that it became a blur. I became dizzy with it almost immediately.

"Urgh," I groaned, as the dizziness became nausea. "Urgh, I –"

We stopped suddenly and the woman – Angela, she said her name was – leapt out and only just made it around to my side to yank open my door in time before I vomited all over the ground.

"Are you sure you haven't been drinking?" She asked disapprovingly as I retched. "Jesus, you almost puked all over my car. If that's going to happen again, warn me, OK?"

"I'm sorry," I rasped, wiping my mouth. "I didn't – I didn't –"

Twice more we had to stop so I could vomit in the ditch at the side of the road.

"How do you see?" I asked Angela after the second time, when we were moving again and I was pretty sure I had nothing left in my belly to bring up. "How do you see anything? It's all going by so – fast."

She turned in her seat to look at me, one eyebrow raised skeptically. "You might not have been drinking, young man, but you're as high as a kite, aren't you? I should take you straight to the police station, is what I should do."

I didn't know what the police station was, but from the way Angela was threatening to take me there, it didn't sound like somewhere I wanted to go. "No," I said, looking down at my feet so I wouldn't have to watch the world speeding by anymore. "No, I – please, I just need to find Sophie Foster. It's really important. She's the only person who might know where my mother is."

"Your mother?" Angela asked, visibly softening the way women often do over lost children – even the fully grown kind. "You're looking for your mom? Is she in River Falls?"

"I don't know. I don't know where she is. All I know is that Sophie Foster might know."

"Sophie Foster, huh? I can't say I know the name, but – OK, hold on."

Angela moved the car off the road and reached into her pocket to take out a smooth, flat shiny object that she immediately began brushing her fingertips over.

"I'll Google her. She's in River Falls, right?"

But I didn't answer right away because I was too busy staring at the object in her hands.

"River Falls," she repeated. "You said Sophie Foster is in River Falls? And what's your name?"

I kept my eyes on the object in Angela's hands, as different colors and lights flashed across it like in a gothi's vision. "It's, uh," I said. "It's – Magnus. My name is Magnus."

"OK Magnus, let's see if we can find this Sophie Foster. Ah – here we go, here's her Facebook page. It looks old. But – is this her?"

She held the device out towards me and I shrank away, worried that it might burn me if I touched it. Things that bright were often hot, in my experience. But Angela was holding it just fine, so I took a quick peek. The image of a woman's face loomed on the flat surface. Not a likeness carved in wood or leather, but an exact image, no different from real life.

"Well?" Angela asked gently. "Do you recognize her? Is that –"

"I've never seen her before," I replied quickly, my voice thick with panic. "I don't know what she looks like. I don't know what –"

It was then that my companion noticed just how baffled I was and reached out suddenly to rub my shoulder. "It's OK," she reassured me, assuming my worried reaction was about finding my mother, and not about the magical device she held in her hand. "We'll find her. Don't worry. I'll just, uh – oh, look! It says she's a police officer with the River Falls PD – well that's handy, isn't it? I just give them a call then, if that's alright?"

I had absolutely no idea what Angela was talking about. But she seemed to think she was close to finding

Sophie Foster so I just nodded quickly in response to her question.

A moment later, she spoke again:

"Hi – I'm looking for a Sophie Foster. Can you tell me if she still –"

"What?" I replied, rubbing my head. "No, *I'm* looking for Sophie Fos–"

Angela held her hand up to stop me talking and then continued talking to – whoever it was she was talking to, which did not appear to be me. Was it herself? Was I in the hands of a madwoman?

She turned to me a short time later, smiling and having just said goodbye to an unseen person. "They can't give me her number – obviously – but they're going to call Sophie and give her my number, and hopefully she'll call back and you can talk to her. How about that? Why do you look so scared, this is good news!"

Chapter 26: Heather

I had an enormous and wildly expensive range installed in my house in the country, when the windfall from my husband's dagger came in. Imported from France and built from cast iron and steel, almost certain to stand longer than the house around it, it was one of the few things in the future that seemed almost unchanged from the deep past. Of course it was not the same as a series of roaring fire-pits, or the stone ovens the Angles used to bake their bread, but it was still basically fire in service of cooking food. I loved it. The day that a person could come to my house and not find a huge pot of stew or a boiling vat of jam bubbling away on top of it was indeed a rare one.

It was in front of that range, stirring one of those vats of jam – blackberry – that I was standing when the buzzer from my security gate went off.

Who's that? I wondered, throwing the kitchen towel over one shoulder and making my way to the front door so I could look at the CCTV screen.

Sophie had specifically said she wasn't coming by. Although she had been oddly insistent that I be home that evening. Were they planning something? It wasn't my birthday.

I got to the security panel and peered at the screen. Someone was there. A man. A man who looked like –

No. Heather, no. Stop it.

Even after I came back to the United States, and the future, even years after the love of my life was lost, I would still, every now and again, seem to catch sight of him. Sometimes it was in an aisle at the grocery store, other times on the beach at the lake where Sophie bought a house. It seemed to happen almost everywhere, and each time it did, even as my brain knew it couldn't be him, my heart broke a little for that fleeting second of hope.

So it wasn't Magnus at my gate that night, because it couldn't be. It was simply someone who looked a little like him. A lot like him, actually, although I did not quite trust myself to be able to make such judgments. I took a long, shaky breath and swallowed, and then pressed the button to talk.

"Who is it?"

I almost laughed out loud, then, as whoever it was at my gate jumped about three feet into the air and looked around comically, as if God himself had just spoken.

I pressed the button again. "Hello?"

Once again, the man looked around. And that time, my heart nearly skipped another beat because there was – what was it? There was something about him, something about the particular cant of his shoulders as he turned – that almost made me burst into tears for how much it made me think of my husband. I pressed the back of my hand to my lips and blinked away a tear. And still, there was no reply.

"I'm in the middle of making blackberry jam," I said a moment later, not bothering to keep a slight note of annoyance out of my voice when the man continued to respond with silence. "So if you don't mind stating your business, I'd like to get –"

"Heather?"

I barely heard him speak my name, because he was looking back towards the road and not facing the security camera, but I managed.

"Yes?"

"Heather?"

"Yes, I'm Heather! You're talking to me right now! And if –"

"I'm looking for Heather."

I sighed. Who was this man? And why was he directing his questions into the early evening, and not the camera right in front of him?

I wasn't worried or scared. Maybe I should have been, with all that money from the dagger. But I just – wasn't. River Falls wasn't that kind of place.

"You're going to make me come down there?" I asked. "Aren't you? Didn't you hear me when I said I was in the middle of –"

And then he climbed the gate. A nine foot cast iron security gate with stone walls of equal height on either side, and the man just climbed it like it was nothing.

And even then, I wasn't scared. I was quite a bit more annoyed than I had been, though.

"Damnit!" I yelled, throwing the kitchen towel down and turning the gas off before marching out the door to confront the impatient idiot who'd just scaled my gate.

It was evening, then, but there was still enough light to see the figure approaching me up the gravel driveway. There was still enough light to make me do a gasping double-take when I saw him coming towards me, not squashed into the confines of the little CCTV security screen as he had been.

When I stumbled and fell to my knees, he started running towards me and even his run – Jesus, even his run was like Magnus' run. That same smooth, catlike gait, that same almost childlike bounce that had never left, even as the grays became numerous in his hair...

"Oh my God," I cried, wiping my eyes as the man approached. "I – I'm sorry. It's just that you – you look – I'm sorry! I'm so –"

"Heather?"

He crouched down and I looked up, still on my knees in the gravel, still shaking. And when I looked up, I swear it seemed to be my husband. The way the last of the light picked out the jaw-line, and the ears...

"No," I said to myself, out loud. "No. No. No."

"Heather? Are you Heather? I am –"

"Come here," I barked, taking his hand and pulling myself to my feet. "Come – come here."

And then I fair dragged the poor young man – because he was young, I could see it by then – down the driveway, towards the light where I could get a better look at him.

When I thought there was enough light to see properly, I dared to look at him once more. My eyes held his gaze for a second, maybe two before I had to look away, because I was sobbing.

"A ghost," I cried, bringing my hands up to my face because it was too painful to look again at a person who I knew was not who he seemed to be. "A ghost before me, as if the years had not passed, and death not taken him from –"

"Who do you speak of?"

I didn't hear the question. My head was too full of grief, freshened by seeing a face so like the one I had known all those years ago. I could barely stand up, but I couldn't sit down, either. I didn't know what I was doing.

"Why have you come?" I cried, when I could get the words to come out of my throat again. "Why – who are you – why have you come here?"

"Who do you speak of? Who is it you say I resemble?"

That time, I heard the questions. The man before me was young – very young, in his late teens or early twenties, and when I looked again at his face, squinting because it was almost like looking at the sun, I saw that he was in some distress too.

"You look," I began, still out of breath with emotion, "like someone I once knew. You look like a man –"

"Like who?! Who do I look like?"

"Like my husband!" I cried. "You look just like Magnus! You look so much like him I half-believe I'm dreaming right now, to see you in front of me. Look at your –" I reached out without thinking and touched the young man's cheek – "face. Look at your face! It is just like his – even your expression is his. Oh, who are you? If this is a dream, let me wake now before I lose myself in grief once more. Let me –"

"I am Magnus."

My legs gave way underneath me and I would have fallen to the ground if two strong arms hadn't caught me. I don't remember seeing or hearing or really being aware of anything as I found myself helped to a carved wooden bench next to the door. And once I was there, it was a long time, many minutes, before I could speak again.

"Who sent you?" I asked quietly, as the little moths began to flutter around the light, now the sun had set fully. "Who sent you to torture me? Who sent you, with your face so familiar it's as if he stands in front of me at this very moment?"

"I came by my own will," came the response, and I could hear a wobble in the man's voice, as if he himself was near tears. "I came from the Kingdom of the East Angles, because my grandmother told me, in the winter that she died, that my parents were in that place, and that my father's name was Magnus."

I looked up again, and forced myself not to turn away from the face that tore at my heart. He seemed to mean what he was saying. But it couldn't be. It couldn't.

"In the Kingdom I found Jarl Eirik, and Jarl Ragnar in Thetford, and their wives Paige and Emma. When I told them of my quest to find my parents, and asked if they knew of a Northman with the name Magnus, and his wife –"

"Emma?" I asked, dazed. "Paige and Emma? And Jarl Eirik – and – you're a Northman?"

"Yes, Heather," the young man replied, taking one of my hands in both of his. "I'm a Northman. So was my father. He had a wife in the Kingdom, and they had a baby – just one, and many years ago. The peasant girl who helped at the birth told them the baby died but he – I – didn't die. They stole me. They took me away to the North to be raised by my grandfather, the Jarl –"

Maybe it should have been easy for me to see the truth. It was, after all, literally staring me in the face. He was the spitting image of Magnus, so alike him it was uncanny, and nothing he said violated any boundaries of possibility. But still, I could not believe it. Not right away. My heart rose in my chest with hope, and my mind almost shut down with how fervently I wanted it to be true. But still, I could not believe it. What if I *was* dreaming? What if I'd fallen in the kitchen, and bashed my head against that expensive range, and the young man in front of me was just a vision of my unconscious mind as I lay knocked-out on the kitchen floor? Even the tiniest possibility that it wasn't real was too much. To hear that my son – that *our* son – might have lived, to believe it, and then to wake to the cold reality where his tiny bones still lay in the thousand year old ground of the Kingdom would surely kill me.

"Is it you?" He asked, as I sat silent and shocked beside him, my whole body shaking. "Did you have a husband named Magnus – a Northman? And did you have but the one baby, a son they told you died at birth? Please say something. Please, speak. I have thought of finding you – if it is you – every day since I was five and ten. I have – I have waited. I have hoped. And now, you say nothing. You leave me to wonder if my quest is over or if –"

"Five and ten," I whispered, smiling to hear the way the it was spoken in that other place, where I had lived most of my life. "Five and ten. Is it you, my love? I don't speak because I don't dare. Is it you? How can it be you? I didn't even – I didn't even hold you! They took you from me before I was even allowed to lay eyes on you! They –"

"It's me," he said, and then he did begin to cry. "It's me, Mother. It's me."

We fell into each other's arms, and held each other tight as we cried for happiness. And when we parted, just briefly and many minutes later, I took his face – his beautiful face – in my hands.

"Gods," I breathed. "Gods, look at you. You are just like him. You –"

And then I remembered something. I remembered the day I lost my husband, and coming into the hall to find Ora bent over him.

"He knew," I continued, astonished. "He – he knew! She told him! She must have told him, before he went. He was –"

"Who? Who told –"

"Your father," I replied quickly. "On the day he died I found the healer speaking to him in low tones – the same healer who delivered our son – who delivered *you.* And just before he went he said that you lived. I thought it the ravings of a man near death but now I understand that she told him the truth before he went. Oh, thank the Gods!"

I reached out and grabbed the young man – my son – by the shoulders. "Do you understand what I'm telling you? He died knowing you lived! Oh, thank the Gods he knew."

"So it's true? He's gone?"

I nodded, seeing a flame of hope flicker out in my boy's hazel eyes. "Yes, many years – many winters ago.

He died saving my life, protecting me. He was the best man I ever knew."

***

That night, I woke many times. And each time, I had once again to go through the ritual of getting out of bed, and creeping down the hallway to one of the guest bedrooms, to peek in the door and make sure the young man, Magnus, my son, still slept there.

I was almost sixty years old by then, and comfortable – even happy – with the idea that my days of love and adventures were over. When I looked back on my life, it was with clear eyes. Yes, I had suffered. But I was wise enough by then to understand that my suffering was never a punishment, that it was just the way things turned out for me. But I hadn't *just* suffered. I loved, too. And I was loved. And it was a great love, one of those loves that not even most of us get to experience. When I lay my head on the pillow at night, it was truly without regret or grievance in my heart.

So when the young man who looked so heart-breakingly like my husband showed up, and said he was my son, it didn't seem to fit into the story I told myself about my own life.

Wait, I wanted to say. *This doesn't happen to me. I'm not the person this happens to. I had my great love, and I was mother to a beautiful little girl and a lost son. And now this? The son I had thought dead returns, handsome and grown? Surely it's too good to be true. Surely I don't deserve such joy.*

But it wasn't too good to be true. The next morning, we sat at my huge kitchen table, the one I had bought specially so it could fit all of my friends around it, and glanced shyly at each other as we ate oatmeal.

We spoke at first of details. How had he found the tree? How did he find Sophie? And slowly the details became more intimate, so Magnus was asking me about his father, and Haesting, and how we had come to meet on that day so many years ago.

And all the while I could not take my eyes off him. I could not stop telling him how much he reminded me of the older Magnus. He was pleased to hear it, too, even as he was slightly embarrassed at my constant repetition.

What I did not do was ask if he meant to stay. He was grown, albeit very young still, and I knew that in the Kingdom – and in the North – people take on the responsibilities of adulthood sooner than they did in modern times.

"You are wealthy," he said at one point, as I took him on a tour of my property, showing him the chickens, the cows, the horses and the neatly laid out planting beds. "Sophie told me as much. She said that my father had something to do with it – that he left you something?"

"Yes," I smiled, slipping my arm through my son's – he was as tall as my husband had been – perhaps even slightly taller. "His dagger. I don't know how much Paige and Emma explained to you, but you understand that this place isn't just a different location, don't you? It's a different time. Over a thousand years separates the

Kingdom of the East Angles, and the North, from this place. So if you can imagine, your father's golden dagger, which was already worth quite a lot in the old time, was worth so much more here."

"The Jarl's wives told me that men no longer fight with swords – or daggers. If there is no use for it, then why –"

"Its use is as an object," I replied. "A treasure. There were no intact Viking daggers left in this world – all had been lost to time, or to being broken down and melted for their gold and jewels hundreds of years ago. And then there was suddenly one intact Viking dagger. Can you understand how much something like that would be worth – the only thing of its kind in existence?"

I could tell that Magnus still did not quite understand what I meant, because his mindset was still that of a Northman from the 9th century. A dagger was a tool to him, a weapon. It was to be used, not looked at. It was alright. He would, if he stayed, have much to learn about where his mother lived.

"And now you are wealthier than a king?"

"I don't know about that," I replied, leaning my head against his arm briefly – it was still difficult to believe he was actually at my side. "How wealthy is a king? I don't know any kings – we don't have them here."

I showed my son my house, and my land. I showed him my livestock, and told him what seeds had been planted in the garden. I wanted him to know the type of person I was, and to understand that even though I no longer lived in the Kingdom of the East Angles, that it was still part of me.

There was just so much to say. A literal lifetime to catch up on. We talked into the night on that first day, and then again on the second and the third and so on until it seemed there would never not be something to talk about.

When he had stayed with me for a week, and we sat at the dining table eating a stew thickened with peas – my best approximation, as I told my son, of what his father and I used to eat almost every night – he asked me if I was happy he had come back.

I looked up from my bowl, surprised. "What?" I replied. "Am I *happy?* Magnus, do I seem happy to you? Do you see how I have not stopped smiling since you arrived? Can you imagine what it is to lose your only son and then to – no, I suppose you can't imagine. You're too young."

He nodded, and returned my smile. "Yes, I see your smile, Mother. But I know this is a complex meeting, is it not? That I am a fully-formed man and not a sweet little infant. I worry that you – that we – see each other almost as novelties. That –"

I reached out, and took his hand in mine, holding it tight. "Novelties, is it? I do not know how you see me, Magnus – and it is not for me to say, either. But as to you? It is not complex at all. It is not something that needs to be pondered, or explained at length. You are my son. And when I say you're the spitting image of your father, I mean it. But I see other things in you now that you have been here for a few days. Your eyes are the same color as his, but the shape is like mine, is it not? It is true I still have difficulty sometimes, looking at you and connecting the man in front of me with the infant I was not even allowed to set eyes on all those years ago. It is not a difficulty in loving you, it is a difficulty in believing I would be so lucky, that fate would give me a second chance like that."

"So you love me?"

At first I thought I was mistaken, only imagining I heard a crack in his voice, when he asked me that question. But then I saw that his eyes swam with tears – and so, immediately, did mine.

"Do I love you?" I asked. "Magnus, there hasn't been a single second that I did not love you, not since the day the healers confirmed you were in my belly! Do you understand? Do you think love ends when death comes? It doesn't. I have loved you every day, every moment since then!"

I made him laugh, then, because the dining table was so big it actually took me some time to get up from my chair and run all the way around to where he sat on the opposite side, and then to put my arms around him.

"Next time just ask me to come across the table," he said, laughing through his tears.

"Will do."

A few minutes passed quietly as I held my boy – who was so big I could barely get my arms around him. And then he spoke again.

"I used to think about you," he said. "When I was young. I didn't talk about it very much, because I didn't want to hurt my grandparents – and because, perhaps, I sensed even then that there was some part of the story I had not been told. But I thought about you all the time. They told me Asger was my father, and that he was a great man. I thought I had some idea, then, of who he was. But you? You were a mystery. I used to watch my friends when they hurt themselves, and how their mothers would bend over them and whisper comfort in their ears and tend to the their wounds. Sometimes I wouldn't be able to bear it and I would run away to the woods to cry for you – to cry that I didn't have you to do the same for me."

"Oh my God," I whispered, as my heart fair broke in two to think of my boy when he was small, crying for his mother. "Oh my God. Magnus, I'm sorry. I –"

"It's not your fault, Mother. I know it –"

"I don't mean it like that. I just mean that to think of you as you just described almost feels like it will kill me. I want you to know, my love, that if you stay in this world, I will spend every single day of the rest of my life making certain that you never feel that way again. Do you hear me? There is nothing so important to me as you. Please don't ask me to explain – you are like me in that way, you know. Your father was always getting annoyed with me for needing an explanation for everything! As it is, it is just the truth of my heart I tell you now."

He stayed. He stayed into the summer, and we would sit out on the back porch of an evening, sipping lemonade and commenting on how the light did not last as long into the night as it did in the North.

He met the people in my life, too. Sophie and Ivar and their children, Maria, Sophie's mother and all of the extended social group. Only Sophie and Ivar knew his full story, and it was Ivar who took him under his wing.

"He's got a strong heart," Ivar said one night as we stood outside after a light summer meal, and Ashley chased Freya around our legs. "He is like his father, as you say? He says if he had stayed, he would be the Jarl by now and I can only believe that he would have been a great one. He has all the qualities of a Jarl, including a quick mind – and he still has his youth."

Ivar must have then seen the anxiety on my face because he asked at once what was wrong.

"You say he would be a great Jarl," I replied. "Do you think it best for him if he returns to fulfill that destiny? He will not be a Jarl here, as you know. It is the reason I have not asked him if he means to stay for good. I worry that he would not live the life here that he always envisaged for himself."

I half-expected Ivar to talk once again of the medical advances in the future, and the prosperity and the safety of even the lower people – as he often did. But he turned to me, with his brow furrowed, and gave me a real answer.

"I have daughters," he said. "Perhaps one day I will have a son, but as it is my children are girls. And they are growing up here, in a world without Jarls and Kings and warriors making up a large proportion of the people. I am free not to worry about whether they will compare their lives here to what they might have been in the past – because in truth there is no real argument, given the fact of their being girls, that here is the preferable time and place for them. But for a boy? For a young man, as Magnus is – as strong and smart and vital as he is?"

"Exactly!" I replied. "What will he do here? If he stays, will he wake up one day when he's forty and regret that he didn't take his place as a Jarl, in the past? Will he believe that he wasted his youth on –"

"Why don't the two of you just ask me these things, if they concern you so?" Magnus' voice joined us suddenly, making me jump. He'd snuck up behind us, unheard – as he was in the habit of doing.

Ivar turned to him, smiling. "We can't ask you these things. You are too young yet to know the answers. We only speak of it because who you are is so obvious, and your mother worries that you will not find fulfillment in this life, where there is little of the glory available to young men as there is in the North."

"Is it so?" My son responded, as pride in his self-possession welled up in my chest. He was not rude to us, or snappy, he just assumed he had as much right to speak, and to an opinion, as we did. "There is little glory here available to young men? They have warriors here. In fact it would seem to me that they have many more kinds of men – and women – here than we have in the North, Ivar. Do you know that Sophie's daughter is teaching me to read? Already I can read some of the books she gives me, even if I am slow. And when I can read, I can go to college. Or I can –"

"College?" I asked, shaking my head at the idea of a Northern would-be Jarl sitting in a college classroom. "I – what? Magnus, you think of college?"

"College," he replied, shrugging. "Or the military – if it is what I think. Or perhaps I will marry next week and father twenty children. Or spend my time gardening, or building, or traveling. In the North I will be Jarl. I won't be anything else but a Jarl, because there is nothing else for me to be but a Jarl. In this place, I can do with my life what my heart leads me to do. Is it not exactly as you said, Mother? Both of you stand here before me, do you not? In this place? Have you not made your choices?"

"We have," I said. "We have. I just – Magnus, I worry that you're too young. I worry that you'll regret it if you don't take up your role as the Jarl –"

"My role? My *role* as the Jarl? I'm not even the son of the Jarl, Mother. The only thing that will make me Jarl if I return to the North will be the lies of a dead man. I could go on right now, listing what I might make of my life if I stay here but there is only one reason I truly need."

"And what is that?" I asked, as Ivar bowed his head slightly, seeming to know already what my son was going to say.

"It's you, Mother. Sometimes I hear you speak of my life as if it's this – this separate thing. As if the threads of our lives had not begun to weave themselves together even when I was in your belly! You brought me into this world – you and my father – you *gave* me this life you speak of almost as if you believe yourself to be a weight around my neck. What son would I be, what kind of man would I be, if I left my own mother alone, after seeing how many winters she had already spent alone?"

"No," I started, because I wanted to give Magnus every chance without the worry of disappointing me hanging over his head. "No, I don't want this to be about me. This has to be –"

"But it is about you!" He cried, cupping my face in his hands and kissing my cheeks, one after the other. "What kind of place is this that family is not the most important thing there is in life, and the first thing to which a man owes his duty? I want to be with you, Mother. I want to be here, with you. As I have heard you say – I am not a dull-wit. I am strong, and I am not easily afraid. Do you think I cannot make a good life for myself here, with you? Do you think one of those pretty girls at the grocery store will not have me as her husband?"

I laughed, and then kept smiling even as my laughter turned to tears for all that had gone before that moment – and all that would come after it.

"Do you know that I used to work at that grocery store?" I asked, as my son wiped a tear off my cheek.

"Yes," he replied softly. "Yes, I know."

Epilogue: Heather

And so the child I had given birth to more than twenty years before came back to me. He came back with his father's crooked smile on his lips and his father's courageous heart. And he came back with my stubbornness, and my refusal to accept anything just because someone told me it was 'as it was.' Within six months of his arrival in River Falls he was reading well, and studying the history of the place where his father and I had lived together – the Kingdom of the East Angles.

He missed his home, of course. Ivar helped with that, as did I. But whenever I fretted – which was often – Magnus would come to me with his that big grin on his face and give me a huge bear-hug and reassure me that his home was wherever I was.

There were girls, too. Oh, so many girls. Tall girls, short girls, giggly blonde girls and a particular fiery redhead, American girls, a Mexican girl, a French girl, shy girls, all kinds of girls. Not that I could blame them – Magnus was as handsome and good-hearted as his father – and if anything even more gregarious.

Almost three years after he showed up at the end of my driveway, we hosted a dinner at my country house. The occasion was my son's acceptance into a graduate history program at an Ivy League university. He started at the local adult education college, but it had soon become clear that his talent for history was rare and special, and that's when the offers had started to pour in from prestigious institutions with very famous names. We had a party when he settled on one in particular, and invited everyone we knew.

A Northern feast – or as close as we could manage to replicate one – was prepared. Ivar, a keen hunter, brought the venison, and Ashley and Freya picked root vegetables from my garden to make a stew. Just before the meal was served, Sophie found me in the kitchen, standing in the doorway and gazing happily out over the table where everyone was seated.

"You must be so proud," she said, putting her arm around my shoulders. "Look at him – he's such a star. And humble with it, too, so no one can hate him for being handsome and smart and good at everything."

I nodded, unable to respond right away because the emotions – pride, happiness, contentment – were thick in my throat.

Everyone came to that party. Sophie, Ivar, Ashley, Freya, Sophie's mother, Maria, Maria's handsome new boyfriend, Maria's grandmother and various other people who had been included in our group over the years. Not everyone knew why we were eating venison, or why some of the people at the table were catching each other's eyes and giving each other little looks of recognition and remembering, but everyone knew they were loved, and that we were all a family.

It was much later that night that I found myself in the doorway once more, having just carried a stack of dishes away to make room for more wine and coffee. Magnus was surrounded by a rapt audience – as he often was, wherever he went. I couldn't even hear what he was saying, but I could see the laughing faces around him as he joked and told tales of faraway lands and times.

It was in that moment that he looked up, just momentarily, and caught my eye. And when he did, I saw that he was happy. The son of my love was happy, and so I was happy, and so proud. We held each others' gaze for a few seconds, not needing words, not needing anything except to see the joy on each other's faces. Magnus' father's presence was all around us, built into the walls of the house that his golden dagger bought, etched into the angles of his son's face and forever written into the book of my heart.

And then Ashley tugged at his sleeve and Magnus turned back to her, to continue telling his story.

***

Author Information:

To sign-up for the Joanna Bell Reader's Group and be the first to know about new releases and our exclusive-to-readers monthly giveaways click here:

http://eepurl.com/c2jWP1

To 'Follow' Joanna on Amazon:

https://www.amazon.com/Joanna-Bell/e/B0768K811G

(click the yellow 'Follow' button on the left!)

To contact Joanna please e-mail her at:
authorjoannabell@gmail.com

The 'Mists of Albion' Series

Eirik: Mists of Albion Book 1:

https://www.amazon.com/dp/B077GLX3TZ

Ragnar: Mists of Albion Book 2:

https://www.amazon.com/dp/B0799YYWYT

Ivar: Mists of Albion Book 3:

https://www.amazon.com/dp/B0799B28KR

Other Books by Joanna Bell

How To Catch A Cowboy: A Small Town Montana Romance

https://www.amazon.com/dp/B075FF65S3

Manufactured by Amazon.ca
Bolton, ON